"Grea   arrington
Bayle   ∨ empha-
sise th   ry Gee is
thoughtful, funny, original. And pretty thoroughly
mind-expanding in the tradition of Wells, David Lind-
say, Stapledon and Clarke. In fact everything you
yearn to find in a good contemporary SF novel. Really
enjoyed it!"
  —SFWA Grandmaster **Michael Moorcock**

"[Gee is] a visionary space voyager of the first order... The Sigil is in the grand tradition of Stapledo-
nian space opera, and provides not only an explanation for why this universe is the way it is, but gives us
the many vivid wild adventures on the part of some
(very appealing) conscious characters acting to make
it that way. Awesome stuff, and a true pleasure to read
page by page."
  —Kim Stanley Robinson, award-winning author of
Red Mars

"One of the very best books I've ever read."
  —Critique.org

"Fast-moving, insanely inventive science fiction in the
grand manner—;seldom has the fate of the galaxy
been handled on such a large scale. Gee draws on
archeology, geology, physics, and biology to create a
rich tapestry with surprises woven into every thread."
  —Nancy Kress

RAGE OF STARS

Book Three of
THE SIGIL TRILOGY

RAGE OF STARS

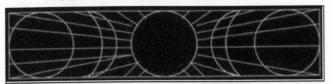

Book Three of
THE SIGIL TRILOGY

Henry Gee

ReAnimus Press

Breathing Life into Great Books

ReAnimus Press
1100 Johnson Road #16-143
Golden, CO 80402
www.ReAnimus.com

Cover art by Clay Hagebusch

ISBN-13: 978-0615706368

First print edition: September, 2012

10 9 8 7 6 5 4 3 2 1

For Karl, who gave his name to a small, destructive and (mercifully) fictional asteroid.

Acknowledgments

The germ of this story—or, rather, two germs—can be found in two SF vignettes I wrote in *Nature*, one pseudonymously. One, called *Et in articulo mortis* (*Nature* **405**, 21; 2000) describes Post-Embryonic Petrosis as an evolutionary response to star-hungry dragons. The other, *Are We Not Men?* (*Nature* **435**, 1286; 2005) reported the emergence of many hitherto-mythical hominids onto the world stage, including Sand Druids and Jive Monkeys. Perhaps ill-advisedly, I thought I'd put the two ideas together in a box and see what came out. The result is as you see.

I offer my thanks to Karl Ziemelis, Andrew Burt, Vonda McIntyre, Ian Watson, Jack Cohen, Brian Clegg, Bruce Goatly, John Gilbey, Richard P. Grant, Heather Corbett Etchevers, Jennifer Rohn, Chris Surridge, Peter Watts and all the residents of the LabLit community forums, and the many others who read various drafts of this book, for their continuing encouragement and comments. David Doughan and Adam Rutherford helped me with my Latin, and Tony Kerstein with my Hebrew.

Chapter 1. Caveman.

Omo River Valley, East Africa, Earth, *c.* 4,000,000 years ago.

Perhaps in this neglected spot is laid
Some heart once pregnant with celestial fire;
Hands, that the rod of empire might have sway'd,
Or waked to ecstasy the living lyre.
Thomas Gray — *Elegy written in a Country Churchyard*

Old Kra looks out of his cave. The land below is his beauty, his glory, everything he knows. Flowing gray, brown and blue, far, far below is the River Omo, mother of life, flowing her milk into Lake Turkana, where live Brother Fish, Brother Turtle and Big Papa Croc. But the land round the Omo is brown now and dry where before it was green, all green, and leaping with Brother Pig and Brother Gazelle. It is now scorched and dead. Brother Pig and Brother Gazelle left this land long ago.

His tribe tells him he's a crazy man.

He tells them no: the land is like this because you have turned your backs on the Goddess. Our Goddess once had five-and-five big fat dugs but her dugs have all dried up, because you kill our Little Brother Pithek, and you mustn't kill him any more.

Old Kra is the Big Man of his tribe. Many sun-rounds since, in the time they now call the Time Of Long Grass, he wrestled Brother Leopard, breaking his jaw; he brought home Brother Pig and Brother Gazelle, he pronged many wives in the long grass and made many blind kits. Old Kra is the Big Man for many sun-rounds. So the bad men of the tribe say nothing.

They say yes, Big Man; they say No, Big Man.

They do what Big Man says.

But many sun-rounds fly by in flash of rainy seasons, a flash of dry seasons, and now Old Kra is a graymuzzle. His back legs don't work right any more. But still they call him Big Man, they do what Big Man says, and many wives keep him warm at night though his prong doesn't work so good any more because he is not a Big Man any more, but Old Man.

But then Old Kra sees rainy seasons hotter than he remembers when he was a young blood hunting Brother Pig and Brother Gazelle and Little Brother Pithek. And rainy seasons are rainy no more, just big clouds riding high and moving on so grass grows long no more and Brother Pig and Brother Gazelle are far away. Only Little Brother Pithek, he likes the dry. Little Brother Pithek makes knives with stones and bones from the dry water.

And Old Kra sees dry seasons colder than he remembers: the wind has teeth that bite at night. Old Kra says all this to his tribe, and says Goddess says do this, do that, but do not kill Little Brother Pithek. This is strange to the tribe because soon there'll be nothing to hunt *except* Little Brother Pithek, that'll be all there'll be, because Brother Pig and Brother Gazelle are now far away.

First they just make jokes behind his back. They wave their prongs after him in village so he can't see, and they laugh. They bide their time. They do nothing until Big Wife Number One dies and goes to Big Sky Water. Then the bad men of the tribe tell Old Kra, you're no good any more, You're not Big Man, but crazy man.

I am no crazy man, says Old Kra, I am with Goddess. I listen to the Goddess.

Who's this Goddess, they say. No Goddess has been round here lately. What does Goddess say to you, Old Kra Crazy Man, eh?

Old Kra now thinks they're listening but it's just a trick to beat him all the more. He sees that now. So Old Kra starts explaining again like he explained before how the Goddess tells him in dreams and visions in the night that the tribe must stop killing Little Brother Pithek and eating him. 'We must look after Little Brother Pithek,' says the Goddess: 'they are Holy People, chosen, as Holy as our tribe'. That's why he's called Little Brother, not Big Brother, like Brother Pig and Brother Gazelle. He now thinks he's making sense because the tribe is listening. So Old Kra says more, saying that the tribe must leave this old land and go where Brother Pig and Brother Gazelle have gone. The tribe must find new land. So the Goddess says.

But they say—dreams and visions, we see no dreams and visions. You're just a crazy old man, you're just missing Big Wife Number One with warm arms and big dugs five-and-five, no harm in it, but no wife want you now because your prong works no more. You are crazy and you can make no kits. So you go now, Old Man. We need a Young Man hunting Little Brother Pithek.

Then the tribe drives Old Kra from the village. They beat him with sticks, they beat him with bones, they bite him with their big teeth, they scratch him with their sharp claws. They took from him the Big Man Stone. He remembers the shouts. He remembers the screams. They ran him from the village.

Old Kra looks out of his cave at mother Omo below, down slope. It is not his village any more, they took it. He turns from looking down the slope at the Omo. He looks inside the cave now. He looks at his own self. For many days he is getting thinner, he is getting sick. He can't hunt like a young man any more. He scrabbles around in the dirt for snakes and worms and roots. He thinks of Big Wife Number One. He remembers her comfort. The memory makes him cry salt tears down his leathery old face. But he also remembers how Big Wife Number One found roots and special herbs that made all pain go away.

Old Kra makes a fire in the back of the cave, where a smoke hole goes through the roof at the back, so he can breathe easily but no-one can find him, not Brother Jackal, not Brother Leopard. Old Kra drinks tea with roots and herbs like Big Wife Number One taught him, and Old Kra sees shadows dancing on the back wall of the cave.

Crazily they dance, and like all dancers they tell a story. The dance-story is easier to understand than words. But he finds this crazy dance hard to understand at first, because it is more complicated than any dances he's ever seen, about where Brother Pig or Brother Gazelle will be in the rainy season, or how the World was born of the Big Sky Water. There is more to this shadow dance than that. But after many hours, many draughts of the tea that Big Wife Number One taught him to make long ago, the dance begins to make sense. This is what the dance says. That long, long ago, longer than many, many sun-rounds, there was a village bigger than the one below next to the Omo. Many times bigger than Old Kra can imagine, with a ladder leading up to the stars and angels climbing up and down on it from all over the Big Sky Water.

And the dance says more: that Old Kra was more than a Big Man, many times more—a great warrior, maybe even an Emperor. Yes, Old Kra ruled all the stars in the Big Sky Water. But bad things happened and Old Kra is Emperor no more.

"Why are you Emperor no more, Old Kra?"

At first, Old Kra thinks he spoke these words himself. Talking to yourself is a problem of living in a cave with no-one to talk to except the memory of Big Wife Number One in Big Sky Water. But Old Kra looks across the burning fire and sees a figure loom up. It is Big Wife Number One. Now, Old Kra accepts this. When you are old and thrown out of the village, you live with ghosts, live with your dead relations and your ancestors.

"The Empire has gone, many sun-rounds beyond counting," says Old Kra.

"Too true, Old Kra," says Big Wife Number One. "But you are still an Emperor to me, even in Big Sky Water"

"That makes me glad," says Old Kra. "Old Kra has nothing much to be glad about."

"Old Kra…" says Big Wife Number One, standing up and walking across the flames. The flames rise up and dance around Big Wife Number One, but they do not burn her. Old Kra sits back, not daring to move. Maybe ghosts can do that, he thinks.

Big Wife Number One steps through the flames. She stands over him while he sits on the floor of the cave. Big Wife is an old woman. Her dugs hang down, five-and-five, flappy and loose. Her legs and belly are fat and misshapen from the birthing of many kits. But Big Wife Number One still stands tall and proud. Old Kra thinks she looks like a queen. Especially from this angle.

"Big Wife Number One," he says, "always looks like the Empress of all the stars in Big Sky Water."

"Old Kra says the nicest things," says Big Wife Number One. She lies down next to Old Kra and with one mighty breath blows out all the flames in the fire. Old Kra says nothing. Maybe that's another thing ghosts can do, he thinks. But in the darkness of the cave he puts his arms around the big fleshy body of Big Wife Number One and she feels every bit as real as he remembers from the old times long ago when they were young and the grass was tall. Old Kra pulls her close.

"Old Kra is crazy like an old Lion" says Big Wife Number One.

In the night, Old Kra has strange dreams. He is in a place he's never seen before, not in all the dreams the Goddess has shown him. It is a stone place, next to a great water, like Turkana. The waterside is made of stone, and there is stone all around, huge, many times higher than a man, stones with lights in them. Old Kra thinks these stones with lights are the caves of a great village of cliffs, and then it comes to him—this is the Empire. It is night, and there are stars in the sky. A great silver line, like the web of a giant spider, strings straight as bowstring to the Big Sky Water.

Old Kra turns to look across the great water and sees a great moon hovering above it. But he knows that this not the yellow moon with the friendly face of the Hunting Master, but a great building, a cave, made by the Emperor.

Made by his own self.

But not by his own self.

Old Kra is confused.

He turns to look down the long stone edge of the waterside. Many tall poles with lights run along edge of the water. Old Kra sees a woman walking towards him, along the stone edge.

"Look down at yourself, Old Kra," says the woman. He looks down. He is dressed in strange robes. They fit close, in tubes round his arms and legs. Then he looks up at the woman. Old Kra is not scared of any woman, not even Big Wife Number One. But this woman meets his gaze, which he thinks impertinent. He makes a move to slap the woman down. But he cannot move. Not even a finger.

"Down, tiger," says the woman. "Time for some straight talking." The woman points at a seat looking over the water towards the strange moon. Old Kra sits down. He cannot help himself — it is as if he has been commanded. The woman looks him in the eye. The woman is beautiful and fierce like Big Wife Number One was when Big Wife was a young woman with full dugs, five-and-five, and needed taming. But the woman is dressed in strange robes, like those Old Kra is wearing.

The woman says many things with her mouth, and many more things straight into Old Kra's head. The woman says this will save time. Old Kra is frightened now, frightened like he has never been. He pees himself.

The woman becomes angry. "You did *what*? I'm ashamed of you," she says. The woman waves her hand and Old Kra is dry. "After all this time; after all these years; after all we've done together, that you've come to this... this... de-generacy. Yes, I knew it was a risk, to break the continuity of memory. That's something only a non-linear life table can cope with, I'm afraid — for you, it would have driven you mad." The woman cries out: she looks up at the sky, her eyes wet with tears. "Oh, Solomon," she cries, "why didn't you tell me it was so difficult?"

The woman looks directly into Old Kra's eyes: Old Kra thinks he might pee himself again with fright, be tries hard to hold himself in.

"Anyone would think you were stupid," the woman says. "And that's the tragedy, because I know you're not. I chose you. I made you. And despite your dreadful state — *despite* it, mind — you are doing a tolerable job. The Pitheks are fine now, their evolutionary course is set. Our job is almost over, thank goodness.

"But the Pitheks haven't got there yet, and it is vital that they are not killed. Vital. The whole plan depends on their survival. You have another task, now. You must lead the tribe away from the Pitheks as their seer, their prophet. Take them away, far to the east, where a few of your kind still live. Modestly, to be sure, but at least they don't smell quite as badly as you do—you ape, you great shit-stained, piss-soaked oaf."

The woman's eyes are like huge green lakes, and Old Kra is lost in them, so lost he cannot move. The woman takes a deep breath. "I'm sorry to bind you like this," she says. "I've had to make this Xspace in a hurry. You remember it, of course, don't you? *Don't you?*"

The woman paces up and down, up and down, like Brother Leopard. Her voice rises to a scream: Old Kra sees veins like cords on her neck, her fists bunched. Old Kra cannot speak, cannot reply.

"You mean to say you can't remember *this*? Xandarga Station? The Harbor District? This is the bench, the very bench where we first—we did—we *will*—we... oh, what's the bloody point?" The woman storms until she blows herself out. She sits down next to Old Kra, slouching, arms folded like a truculent kit. Old Kra finds that he can move, and he is boiling up with his own rage at this indignity. No woman ever talks to him like that, not even Big Wife Number One. He rises and tells her now, but his voice is different, strange, like he is, suddenly, the Emperor of All the Stars.

"No subordinate of mine, of any gender, of any species, has ever taken that tone with me," he says. "By rights I should have you taken to the brig and flogged." Old Kra puts a hand to his mouth. His head goes funny, blurry: he sits down again and puts his head in his hands. The woman smiles.

"Oh, Ruxie—thank goodness you're still in there, somewhere."

Old Kra doesn't know anyone called Ruxie. Perhaps it's the name of the Emperor.

"We haven't much time," the woman says. "Quick, now, into the shadows, they're coming."

The woman grabs Old Kra by the hand and drags him into the shadow of a giant cave further away from stone edge of the water. Suddenly the whole place is full of people: tall, bright, in strange robes, laughing, drinking from cups made of stone water. The woman points at two people, a man and a woman, walking to the bench where they'd just been, sitting down, and talking, and kissing, and talking some more. It dawns on Old Kra like the rising Sun on a brand new day after an eternity of darkness that this man, this woman, is the two of them, Old Kra himself and Big Wife Number One, but in the old days, or as if in some other guise remembered through a mist.

"I understand now, Xalomé," he hears himself say. "What should I do?"

The woman looks at him, gives one last, bittersweet smile, and vanishes without another word.

He wakes on the floor of the cave, in the morning chill, the fire now a heap of gray ash. Big Wife Number One is gone. Old Kra sees a glint of something shiny in the ash. He scrabbles around in it, still warm, and pulls out—he can't believe it—the Big Man Stone, the one the villagers ripped from his own fingers. He rubs some of the dust and ash from the pattern of the crescents and circles on its face. As he does so he hears a woman's voice in his head.

This is a monument almost as old as the Universe.

A Sigil.

A Talisman.

A Warning.

Look at it. Take it with you. The Pitheks will need to see it one day, still far in your future, to know when their time has come.

Old Kra holds the Big Man Stone up high. He comes out of his cave and walks down the mountain side.

Chapter 2. Pontiff

Gascony, France, Earth, June, 2073

And I say also unto thee, that thou art Peter, and upon this rock I will build my church; and the gates of hell shall not prevail against it.

Matthew **16**, 18

The church bell clanged noon.

"Class dismissed," said Jack.

In truth, the six youths had begun to gather their things and rise several seconds before Jack had spoken, and had started to file towards the door of the classroom, what had once been a ground-floor office in the Mairie. Summer was here, and even if there weren't already plenty to do on their family farms, teenagers could always find many reasons to bunk off in the sunshine. Not that they weren't interested, far from it. But education was just one among many things on offer in a bustling farming community, and was often considered an optional extra.

"Doctor Jack," sandy-haired Serge had asked: "what was it like, here at Saint-Rogatien, when you first arrived here with Doctor Jadis?" The whippet-thin, weasel-faced youth had assumed the mantle of unelected leader of the village school senior class. He was by far the smallest, but he made up for it in boldness.

"Yeah, Doctor Jack," the other five chorused, each one a hulking, dark-haired monolith like the others. "What was it like?" It occurred to Jack that they were all boys. He hadn't seen a girl in his senior class for—what?—three years, at least. But he never tired of telling them how different things were just half a century before, just as they never tired of hearing his stories of what they called the Old Days. It was something they invariably demanded at the end of morning classes, and they listened with absolute fascination, if not in complete silence. It didn't stop them jumping up as one when the bell went, even if he were in mid-sentence. But that's just teenagers, Jack reasoned.

So they listened, rapt, as he'd told them how the world was once absolutely heaving with people, who travelled from place to place in trains, like we do, although their trains weren't always hauled by coal-fired steam engines, like ours. To this, incomprehension—the closest rail station was Blagnac, a day's fast gallop away, and none of the boys had ever been more than six or seven miles from where they'd been born. But they were intrigued that people felt the need to rush around all the time when there was so much to do right here. What interested them more than trains was that people in the Old Days had also driven around in things called *cars* that hadn't needed horses to pull them.

"Or *cattle*," joked Patrice, the butcher's son, pointing to Marcel Lecroix—by far the biggest of the lot—whose even bigger blacksmith father plodded around the district on an enormous cart hauled by four oxen, a vehicle that occupied the entire width of most of the lanes it travelled along at a top speed of two miles per hour. They all laughed, even Marcel, and in the subsequent high-spirited fisticuffs they might have forgotten Jack entirely had Serge not said "but Doctor Jack—tell us again about the *planes*."

So Jack had told them of a *flight* he'd made in a *plane* from a place called *America* that had taken less than three hours, even though it had crossed the *ocean*. Uproar.

Where is 'America'? Is it further than—say—Marciac?

What's an 'ocean'?

Can you really have a machine that *flies*?

How fast did it go? Oh, said Jack, more than a thousand times as fast as Lecroix *père*'s ox-cart. And this was the best part—*it had no pilot*.

The boys were stupefied by all of this. Drone hyperjets (or indeed any aircraft, however humble); any habitation larger than a smallish town; any number more than a couple of dozen; and geography beyond the nearest market square: all might as well have been science-fiction to them. Either that, or a recollection of history so remote as to defy comprehension: of the Romans, say, or the Egyptians, or even the makers of Saint-Rogatien's hillside, or the buried city of Souris Saint-Michel. But if that were the case, Jack reflected, putting on his broad-brimmed hat and picking up his things, he was in their eyes just as much of a fossil as these ancients. A *living* fossil: a holdover from a past age.

And that, Jack reflected, was the real reason that the boys found it all so absorbing—testimony from the horse's mouth. Given that so many people felt so little need to read anything, oral tradition had once more come to the fore. The storytelling urge that had dominated human discourse for most of human history, in which the past few hundred years of literature was, to take the longest possible view, something of an anomaly.

After calling in at the boulangerie as Jadis had asked, he ambled the quarter-mile down the lane to their back gate. The back lane had once been neatly tarmac'd, but the asphalt skin had long since worn away, and the long line of grass and buttercups between the two wheel-made ruts had spread across the entire width of the lane. Erosion had deepened the lane, too, so that for much of its length it was a gully between two high verges, a cool and grassy corridor. In winter, though, it became an impassable, icy torrent, stripping much of the soil and vegetation: this was the only thing that stopped the lane becoming completely overgrown and impassable. Walking with his long, measured strides, Jack remarked to himself with pride that he could still do it, still walk tall. But he missed roaming the countryside, and wondered when it was that he had stopped doing so. Perhaps it would be time to venture abroad and see the world once again—see how the Plague (my! Was it really almost twenty years ago?) had changed things.

Any dispassionate observer would have seen in Jack a neat, distinguished elderly gent, albeit with a lean frame essentially unaltered since youth, if thinner and greyer. Yet apart from Serge, all those boys in his class were taller than he was, and wider, and the eldest was only thirteen. They all had hands like steam-hammers, and a couple of them had rather ferocious-looking teeth. Jack had to confess, it sometimes made him nervous. Taken together, they were of a type fundamentally different from his own: a new breed. In that case, he really *was* a living fossil.

What saved his class—and all the other hulking villagers like them—from a default sense of ominous brooding, was a generally happy-go-lucky demeanor that tended to throw all that suppressed violence into perspective: even if that, too, could go a little overboard. He remembered a few weeks ago at dusk wandering down this same lane to find one of his recent graduates, trousers round his ankles, humping away at a girl dog-fashion, right in the middle of the road. Jack, being a product of a certain era and upbringing, edged carefully past the grunting four-legged mass while pretending not to notice. Just as he was tiptoeing away, and imagining that he'd got past scot-free, both girl and boy offered a cheery greeting—"Hi Doctor Jack, how's it going?"—as casually as if they had been reaping, rather than sowing.

When he'd got home after that incident he'd been irritable and buttoned-up until Jadis had wheedled it out of him, and once she had, she'd teased him unmercifully, that what irked him more than the fact of conspicuous fornication in the street was his own embarrassment at having witnessed it.

"And anyway," she'd said, putting down the chicken she had been plucking and turning to him, a feather-flecked hand on his chest, "we used to like that sort of thing, once upon a time? Didn't we?" Framed by a mass of unkempt hair, her eyes smouldered with memories of long ago. The Spinney. The Nest. And, well, perhaps not so long ago. Maybe a couple of weeks, in fact. In their orchard.

Yes, he'd said, but we wouldn't have done it in public — would we? No, perhaps not, she replied, eyes sparkling — but it was the thrill that one might be discovered that added to the *frisson*.

But that's just it, Jack said — this routine coupling could have no *frisson* if the participants were plainly quite unperturbed about being discovered hard at it, in broad daylight, in the middle of the highway. To this, Jadis had no answer.

Jack laughed as he recalled a joke Avi had once told — that the reason people didn't have sex in the street in Tel Aviv was that people would stop and criticize their technique. This, he reasoned, was a joke made by Jews in self-acknowledgement of a tendency to pry and to gossip. But, replied Jadis, the joke wouldn't be funny at all if people really did have sex in the street. Would it?

If Jack were some kind of relic in the eyes of the villagers: and if this label were meant kindly, as a mark of respect, then Jadis' status was more ambiguous. Busy as she was trying to keep the farmhouse running, she rarely ventured outside: even her ritual morning round had fallen into decay. To the villagers she had become remote, but more than that — a figure unattainable in theory as well as in practice. For as the only woman for miles around who could pretend to any semblance of an education at all, let alone higher

learning, Jack suspected that she was increasingly seen as a
bearer of occult knowledge, a witch, even: an impression
deepened in recent years as she had been called upon to
serve as a kind of unofficial village doctor. To many villagers, especially the younger ones, Jadis' name was mentioned
rarely, and with awe, as if her name itself bore invocative
power, either to heal or to destroy. Only Serge dared refer to
her by name, as 'Doctor Jadis'. The others would go to some
lengths to avoid intoning these sacerdotal syllables, using
some circumlocution as 'Madame Jack' or 'The Farmer's
Wife' or just 'The Doctor'.

Jack accompanied her, as often as he could, on late-night
mercy missions to tend the dying, or to bring new life into
the world. She seemed quite unaware that her careless use of
the French that they'd both learned half a century ago was
seen as impossibly quaint, ornamented and antique against
the increasingly loose local *patois* that Jack had been accustomed to using as a teacher and occasional Mayor—an argot
that seemed to have grown up since the Plague. That, together with her piercing eyes, her flying, silvery-white hair
and artless, animated manner, rendered her a creature apart,
a shaman, a priestess. She seemed not to notice that their
neighbors viewed her as some kind of demiurge. Not that
Jadis wouldn't be amused by it—no, she'd think it was an
enormous joke—but that the knowledge might, in the end,
disturb her, make her change her behavior, so that she
would become yet more reclusive. And this would only
make matters worse.

The irony—that Jadis really *was* the guardian of occult
knowledge—had been preying on both their minds of late.
This was the Sigil, still wreathed in its transparent vacuum
shell, still packed in its crate, still covered by a tarpaulin in
the stable, now buried under a stack of hay bales and a
writhing disorder of tack, buckets and other farmyard para-

phernalia, all but forgotten. But he and Jadis were getting no younger, and they'd have to unearth it someday. Jack had a feeling that their life's work together would never be complete until they had plumbed the Sigil's mysteries. The problem was that now the machinery of high-tech academia had more or less fallen away, all they could possibly do was just look at it, as they had before, with no hope of further progress or insight. Just describing it seemed somehow inadequate. Having therefore no idea of the direction that research into the Sigil should take, they had no notion of where to start, and so, as is often the case with such problems, it was shelved, put aside, in the face of other, everyday concerns.

And then there was the Plague itself.

It had occurred to Jack quite recently how rarely this event was mentioned nowadays, how little it seemed to influence their lives, as catastrophic and cathartic as it had been for anyone who had lived through it. His contact with the younger villagers should have told him, however, that all his students had been born after its passing, and, to them, the Plague was as mythical a part of the Ancient World as cars and planes. And those villagers who had experienced the summer of '54 at first-hand — an ever-decreasing number — tended not to dwell on it, for its reminiscence rekindled memories of agonizing death, multiple bereavement and two or three years of grinding hardship that had claimed many more lives, through epidemics of lesser diseases, violent confrontation and bald starvation. Like veterans returning from the Western Front, they sought solace in living from day to day, piecing together a mundane, quiet life as best they could, and, most of all, not looking back.

He passed the field-gate and pushed it shut behind him, his mind a swirling disorder of all these and other memories and impressions. He thought about those contrivances called *cars*, and that his students were right — they really had been the most unbelievable things. In particular, he thought about a day that he and Jadis had raced off in one of these selfsame contraptions, so he could show her Souris Saint-Michel for the very first time, setting in train a series of events that would lead them to the Sigil. It had been forty-two years ago, to this very day. Then the occasion had been Jadis' Markham's twenty-eighth birthday. And today was her seventieth.

The village baker, Amélie Foucault, had baked a surprise birthday cake for Jadis. Madame Foucault was a shaggy-haired woman who, like most people in the village, was built along the lines of what Jack tended to call a brick shithouse. But why *was* everyone so big these days? It hadn't occurred to him before, but the parishioners of Saint-Rogatien increasingly reminded him of Domingo — in proportion, if not in erudition. Jack suspected that Madame Foucault's cake was less a gift to a regular customer than a ritual offering, to ensure fertility or a good harvest. But he kept these thoughts to himself.

Apart from the inviolate sanctuary of the Spinney, most of the garden had been given over to cultivation, now just beginning to come into fruition. They'd just enjoyed the last of the asparagus — a hard crop in their clayey soil — but one of which they were particularly fond. They were harvesting the first strawberries and gooseberries, making sure that they preserved at least as many as they ate. Shoots of young maize and squashes were just getting into the swing of having been transplanted from the greenhouses, and fresh green cucumber vines were essaying their first trails across the dry ground. The dark masses of potato plants rose knee-high: Jadis had already dug up the first of the earlies, egg-sized and golden, a welcome, succulent freshness that contrasted with the husks of the last of the winter store. It looked like a cornucopia of such easy plenty: but Jack knew (because his own back told him) that it had been the product of a half-century of toil.

The *potager* gave on to the herb garden with its billows of sage, lavender and rosemary, and then the orchard. He passed through the ranks of mature apple and nut trees, each one shading a kinetic retinue of chickens, ducks and geese, all involved in a constantly shifting stand-off with one another, the goats and the ever-present horde of Horribles.

As he rounded the eastern end of the house and walked into the front yard, he saw two horseman making their way up the long drive. One was small and stocky, with a long, grey, hooded travelling cloak, riding a neat palomino mare. The other, in contrast, was as enormous in height as well as in girth, enveloped in a billowing scarlet cloak, and riding an impressive dappled-grey percheron stallion of a size commensurate with its rider. This rider's hood was thrown back to reveal a bushy riot of snowy hair, silver against scarlet: a cross between a medieval knight and Father Christmas. Both riders wore long black boots, bandoliers and carried guns in long, leather saddle holsters.

Jack saw that they were, respectively, his own son Tom; and his old friend Domingo, whom the world of the past two decades would have now recognized as the ineffably remote figure of His Holiness, the Vicar of Christ. And yet here he was, in Jack's front yard. Truly, had the villagers known that Jadis entertained the Pope to tea, their heads would probably have exploded. But at least (Jack laughed inwardly at the thought) she'd never be burned as an agent of the Devil. Not with God on her side.

"Tom, *look!*" the Earthly Representative of the Divine Majesty called to his companion, on seeing Jack, "we are undone! We are caught red handed!" Then, to Jack, "We had meant our visit to be a complete... er... birthday *surprise.*"

Jack smiled. He could hardly imagine a less conspicuous entrance. The two horsemen plodded into the yard: Jack held their horses while they dismounted. Domingo patted the percheron and embraced Jack enthusiastically, before asking if the Lady of the House were At Home. He shambled to the kitchen door without waiting for an answer, his cloak flapping behind him. Presently Jack heard sounds of glad welcome from within, Jadis' sharp, excited voice a counterpoint to the rumbling bonhomie of the ever-welcome guest like summer lightning across a wall of cloud.

Tom, hanging back, took his turn. "*Bonjour*, Papa," he said, his face hard to read. "I'll just get these two settled, may I?"

"Of course," Jack replied, "if you can find room in the stable."

"Thanks" — Tom smiled, weakly. Tom pulled the saddles and panniers off the horses and led the beasts away. Jack followed him, ostensibly to help settle the horses, which would need rubbing down, feeding and watering, but really to reassure his son with his presence. Tom seemed nervous, as if he couldn't decide if the farmhouse really were home for him, and afraid of any conclusion he might reach. As it was, neither said anything.

As Tom had aged, he had assumed a reticence that eventually punctured the easygoing demeanor of his youth. Now an academic, he could be prickly and difficult, and Jack — being a somewhat reserved soul himself — sometimes found it difficult to get on with him. Especially these days, when years might pass between meetings (it had been a decade since Tom had last come home) and they approached each other almost as strangers.

At times like this Jack found it hard to parade the usual clichés that crowded his mind on such occasions — 'great to see you,' 'it's been a long time,' and so on — but could think of nothing more imaginative, and so ended up saying nothing. In truth, both men preferred it that way.

They walked towards the house, both smelling very strongly of sweaty horse.

"Papa, I'd like to stay here for a while," said Tom, as if in a flood, long suppressed. "I need a rest. To refocus, and to think about things. Maybe write. Let's call it a 'sabbatical'. The Fellowship has agreed. I have been working too hard, they said. So I am here. I hope you and *Maman* won't mind. But I do not want to spoil things…"

"Tom, you don't need to ask," Jack said. He looked at Tom: his son was still young, but at thirty-nine he hardly seemed to have changed since his twenties. Only his eyes had aged, and the skin around them; and his general mood had become somehow wizened and shrunken.

Not, thought Jack, that this was such a great surprise, in the circumstances.

In the Spring of 2055, Tom got his summons to complete his studies at Cambridge. The Plague had passed, and the University had managed to scrape itself together, if only on a war footing.

It was just what Tom needed. Shoshana's death had floored him completely, pitching him into an active and sometimes violent depression. He had once again become almost completely mute, and would wander off and be found — meditating, it seemed — half-clothed, in the middle of roads, impervious to the curiosity of passers-by. When it was impressed on him that this behaviour was unacceptable, he took to spending long hours sitting in the church: which had been fine while Domingo was still in residence, but the priest had had to leave at Epiphany, to journey back to Rome as quickly as he could.

After that, Tom would sit in the church alone, wordless and still for hours at a time, whence Jadis had to fetch him at sundown, sometimes after long and difficult persuasion. Shoshana had been carried off by what was subsequently found to have been a rare manifestation of the Plague. Tom, however, had blamed himself. After almost three months Jadis had reached the end of her tether.

"And does Tom think it hasn't affected *us*? Affected *me*?" she'd shouted at Jack, venting her frustration at her inability to intervene. So Jadis spent hours with her son cradled in her arms like a broken doll.

The invitation from Cambridge roused Tom from his stupor. The last thing he said when he boarded the train after the long buggy-ride to Blagnac was not a goodbye, but an apology. He was sorry, he said, for all the trouble he'd caused.

His last memory of his mother had been her smile. Don't forget Tom, we'll always love you, no matter what, she'd said. Always her smile, and her dark eyes.

The train journey was long and bitter—the stormy ferry crossing to England even worse—but Tom made the firm decision that it would represent a bridge between the past and the future. That Shoshana wasn't coming with him was a knife in his guts, but he'd just have to get over it. Hanging nauseous over the stern rail of the cross-channel ferry, he realized that since Shoshana had died he had lost the capacity to see the aura of anyone. Looking up, he realized it was not entirely true—*this* passenger was picked out in a faint puce—or was that just his sickly face? No—that passenger *there*, that girl, she has a halo of blue and gold. But it no longer seemed easily to him: he had to work at it. Not that he tried very hard, because he soon had many other things to occupy his time.

Once back in Cambridge, Tom had thrown himself into his work with a ferocity that surprised those of his classmates who'd also escaped the Plague. More surprising was that he no longer joined them in drinking sprees and girl-chasing expeditions, even though these were more muted anyway, given the imposition of a strict and increasingly monastic discipline on all students. Monasticism had initially been a temporary response to the crisis, but like all temporary solutions, it had acquired an inertial permanence, for the survivors derived comfort from strict regulation imposed from above, a haven from the chaos that had recently disrupted their lives. To Tom, cloistered by candlelight in his room, he felt he had to work doubly hard to make amends to his mother, and in memory of Shoshana, who had never got the chance.

He graduated top of his class that summer, but there had been no-one to greet him on the parched Senate House Lawn; nobody to take him for coffee or walk with him along the Backs. The prospect of travelling home was just too exhausting to contemplate, so he started immediately on the college fellowship he'd been offered.

The college was an amalgam of several pre-Plague ones, now re-established on ascetic lines, and known as the Petrine Fellowship. Even though there was no specific religious allegiance or division along gender lines, the head of the college was not called President or Master but 'Abbot' or 'Abbess,' and the Fellows swore vows of silence (at least while not teaching) and celibacy (whether teaching or not).

The reasons and mechanism for the Plague had remained an intractable mystery. However, the view in many quarters was that the Plague had been, if not a punishment for our sins, then a warning against committing any more. Both vows suited Tom, as they relieved him of the responsibility of enforcing them on himself. If he were not travelling for research purposes, he had taken all his meals in college, the only sounds being the minimal susurrus of knives and napkins and the slurps of several species gathered together on common purpose.

He drove himself, often working until dawn and taking only an hour's nap before resuming his daily duties. He hated the thickets on the margins of sleep where he might dream of times past.

The time when they'd made love the day before she'd died.

After a while the sensation dulled until it was more like an abstract painting, or a postcard received from someone else. But he could never quite shake off the reverie into which he was plunged each time he walked to the lab, for his route took him past the open door of the bakery in Bene't Street, where he caught the yeasty smell of new-made loaves.

By the time of his most recent visit home, to celebrate his mother's sixtieth birthday, Professor Tom Markham Corstorphine had become a rising star in the field of comparative anthropology, specializing in hominid religious practice. He had written an influential paper on Sand-Druid coming-of-age ceremonies, the research for which had taken him once again to Jerusalem, a long and wearisome journey by train and steam-packet. He'd hated every minute of it: apart from Jerusalem itself and a few religious enclaves in the Galilee, the Israel he remembered had become a wasteland, either barren yellow desert or stinking salt-marsh, where the sea had encroached on the ruined cities along the coastal plain. And because every time he paused from work, he saw Shoshana's deep purple eyes against the yellow-brown mountains.

He'd taken his frustration and hurt out on his students, who came to see him as a tyrannical martinet, much given to withering sarcasm. Matters had become much worse recently, with the admission to Cambridge of members of a hitherto unrecognized species of hominid, in addition to the eighteen or so already in residence.

People who regarded themselves as broadly belonging to *Homo sapiens* still made up the largest single species group in the student body, comprising just under half the total. But there were sizeable minorities of Tibetan and Mongolian Almai, Afghan Kaptars, Sasquatch, Pendek and the two known species of Sulawesian, to which could be added a smattering of Sand Druids and Menehune and a few others even more obscure, but which Tom made it his business to get to know, at least for background. Almost all the academics, though—the college fellows and the professors—were hominids. For example, he'd become good friends (inasmuch as he was any longer on friendly terms with anyone) with the Lucasian Professor at Trinity, widely regarded as a genius in transfinite hermeneutics, and the first Laotian Annamite to appear in Cambridge. Barely three feet tall and covered in golden hair so thick he never wore clothes, Professor Alexander Beetle ("my little joke," he said, "my birth name is hardly pronounceable by anyone, even me") he looked more like a mobile mop-head than a human being, but had, Tom thought, an unmatched delicacy of spirit.

But these new arrivals were different again, and to a degree that Tom found offensive. He became convinced that they existed for the sole purpose of humiliating him. After many long, lonely hours of meditation in his cell, Tom had distilled three reasons why he found these new creatures so particularly discommoding.

The first was that they were horribly gregarious. You could never get one of them on its own when you could have—say—four or five at once, all shrieking together. This made one-to-one conversation impossible and turned teaching into a circus. Tom had tried to tease them apart for supervisions, but they never let him. He'd remonstrated with their colleges. The colleges cited counter-complaints that Tom's efforts to separate them had infringed on their 'human rights,' so Tom would have to put up with it and teach them, and God help him if his charges felt the slightest whim to complain again.

The second was that these creatures felt that they had the licence to behave any way they chose in his classes. That they were sexually demonstrative was no particular surprise. Many hominids thought public sex no more shocking than, say, kissing, or even shaking hands (indeed, the Taimyri thought shaking hands a much greater solecism). The outright lascivious behaviour of some hominids in public was, if not the norm, then not much frowned on, either. No, it wasn't that—or at least, not very much. It was that these creatures had tried to importune *him*, three or four of them at a time.

At first it was verbal taunts and catcalls that he could ignore. But then came the awful feeling during supervisions that he was being *watched* rather than listened to, as if he were some prey item being stalked by a hungry pack.

Recently, there had been a couple of occasions when he'd been physically jostled and even subject to situations which could reasonably be regarded as sexually compromising, though he knew as yet too little of these creatures to know how much of their behavior had ritual content. This kept him from complaining to the University authorities. He might have done so had he been aware of any other academic similarly exposed—but he was not. So perhaps it was just him.

The third was their name. All hominids had some proud if unpronounceable name denoting their mythic and divine heritage. These creatures had no such thing, or if they did, they obstinately refused to tell anyone. Instead, they insisted on being known by the self-deprecating term of 'Jive Monkeys'. To Tom, this was the last straw, and the fact that finally convinced him that these creatures were here to get at him, personally.

After a while Tom had had enough and had agreed with the Petrine Fellowship that he take a sabbatical. In any case, his mother would be seventy and it was high time he went home for a spell. But still he hesitated. There were memories of home, which, even nineteen years later, had shells so thin that they might be broken.

It so happened that Domingo was passing through Cambridge on one of his occasional visits to the Astrometry Institute, and finally talked him round. Indeed, the priest had said, he, too, deserved a short holiday, as he was about to take a momentous decision and he wanted to meditate on it. The farmhouse was always a good place for reflection, and he had (he said) another reason for visiting the farmhouse in particular, aside from it being Jadis' birthday. Tom knew that Domingo loved to tease about secrets in his keeping, and so decided to let him spin his web without comment. But Domingo suggested that they travel to France together, and this appealed to Tom, for whatever else one might say, Domingo was always good company, talking so freely that it absolved him from most conversational duties. They could go first-class on the *Chemins de Fer de Saint-Christophe* direct from Cambridge to Blagnac via Saint Pancras and the newly re-opened Channel Tunnel, said Domingo, and then hire horses at Blagnac.

"We could creep up on the farmhouse: take it by surprise!" Domingo had said. Really, sighed Tom, Domingo did *love* his dramatic flourishes.

Domingo, for his part, had promised Jack and Jadis that he'd keep watch on Tom as much as he could, to be a kind of guardian angel.

But he had his own reason for ensuring Tom's health, and, where possible, his happiness—and that reason was guilt. It was he who had brought Tom as a baby to Jack and Jadis, a baby who had proved full of unexpected medical surprises that he, Domingo, was only just beginning to fathom. But even then, Tom's insistence that he had been at least in part to blame, left its mark on Domingo's mind. To be sure, Shoshana had perished from a curious inverse of the Plague, something which, when the dust had settled, turned out to have been rare though not unprecedented. But, then, who knew? Medical research had withered in the face of the Plague, as had so much else, so there was no way of falsifying Tom's beliefs. In the end the scientific realities hardly mattered. What mattered was that Tom blamed himself. And so, Domingo felt, he'd had the blood of an innocent life and the thought of another damaged soul on his conscience. Such was the heaviness of his heart when he finally arrived back in Rome in the early spring of 2055.

The Eternal City was in serious danger of belying its name. By the time Domingo reached the Vatican, Rome had been all but abandoned. Substantial parts of it had burned down, and most of the rest had become an eerie ghost town, made more somber by its vast, ancient ruins. By degrees, the remaining members of the College of Cardinals reassembled, and the election to choose a successor to the lamented Linus was a muted affair that passed unnoticed outside the echoing confines of the Sistine Chapel.

It soon became clear that Domingo himself was the leading candidate—perhaps the *only* candidate. His guilt, he felt, would hamper him, so he entered the lists with extreme reluctance, but his colleagues were adamant that he alone had the vision and energy to undertake what would very likely be the most difficult and thankless Pontificate of modern times. The Church had been thrown back to the early Middle

Ages, and it would take a churchman of rare devotion to reignite the spark. The Cardinals had liked Domingo's radical ideas, of taking the Church into the world, rather than waiting for the world to journey to the Vatican. Who'd want to come here anyway, they had said, to this grim mausoleum where walked only the shades of death and agony?

His first task was to choose a name. His real name was out: there had never been a Pope called Dominic, and he didn't want to set a precedent. In any case, his birth-name had been wished on him as a kind of mockery, and this was his one chance to select a name that would sit better with his own desires, his own mission. The effort of examining name after name, only to reject each in its turn, prompted a certain frivolity, a personal trait that endeared him to his colleagues, who reasoned that humor would have survival value in the current crisis. So it was in this mood that he had given some thought to Pope Pongo I: a name fitting for a Primate, he thought, cheekily, until decorum intervened.

In his youth, Domingo had been much impressed by the Blessed John Paul II who, like him, had been an outsider with an unwieldy birth-name. But as a name, 'John Paul' didn't seem to suit, not least because he couldn't help feeling that any true successor would have to have been called 'George Ringo'.

Jolting himself back to seriousness, he reasoned that nothing much else grabbed him. 'Benedict' implied a doctrinal conservatism that he didn't much like. To name himself 'Gregory' seemed unhealthily self-glorifying. 'John's, on the other hand, were two-a-penny. He knew it was just vanity, but he thought he needed a name that would signify difference, a new start, and yet with reverence to the Church in its youth, faced with many trials but full of vitality and potential. Something more *encouraging*, he thought.

His fascination with the more ancient byways of Church lore came to his rescue—emboldened by the choice of his predecessor, who had named himself after the second Pope, after Peter himself. He chastised himself for shame for not wanting to be called Linus III, but his feeling of wanting to break with the recent past proved the stronger impulse. In the lists of Popes from antiquity he found Eusebius, an obscure pontiff who ruled for a turbulent summer in 309, or perhaps it was 310, and later sainted. The word meant 'pious,' which was unexceptional enough. The Church at that time, in the dying days of the Roman Empire, had been riven by dispute about the conditions under which lapsed Christians, driven out of the Church following the persecutions of the Abominable Diocletian, should be readmitted.

Eusebius had been all for readmission and forgiveness—the predations of the Roman Eagle were hardly the fault of those persecuted. His opponents had other ideas, and in any case, they had the mob on their side. Faced with imminent anarchy, the Emperor had had little choice but to exile both the mild Eusebius and the agitating antipope. Eusebius was sent to Sicily, and was dead from starvation within a year. When matters had calmed down, a contrite Church brought his bones back to Rome. More than once had Domingo visited the crypt housing the Saint's remains, and had taken to heart the epigraph written by a successor, Damasus, detailing in eight lines virtually everything known about him.

And so it was that Papa Eusebius Secundus, Episcopus Romanus, took up his mission, his status as the first post-Plague Pontiff being his most unwelcome distinction. Like his ancient namesake, Eusebius's first task was to reunite his depleted and dispersed flock, and do so with love, whatever the cost.

He began by issuing an informal edict to his Cardinals—to leave the Vatican behind, to go out into the world, and to heal it. Were anyone to ask him why his own efforts were always that bit more painstaking, more heartfelt than those of his colleagues, he would, of course, have denied it. But his heart told him that he was driven by a need for atonement. He did it, he told his God in long penitent hours, for the sake of a young girl who had been offered the one thing she most needed in the world, the one thing that makes us human, and in her acceptance had been betrayed by it—and yet in the end she had been full of forgiveness.

For the next decade and a half, Pope Eusebius II travelled widely, founding and fostering new monastic orders. In ancient times, he said, monks had kept the flame of civilization alive by copying the works of the ancients. The modern world had more practical needs. So the first order he founded was the Society of Christophorines, whose devotion would be to the power of steam. Their religious duty was to build and operate steam engines to pump much-needed water; as well as locomotives, ensuring that the Iron Horse crisscrossed the continent, keeping trade flowing and maintaining a basic standard of living for what remained of the population.

The next body he created was the Order of Saint Adelard, whose task was to run the great nuclear furnaces of France, to maintain at least a minimum standard of electrical power. Domingo's critics were few, but some said that electricity, let alone nuclear power, was the work of Satan. Such accusations always triggered a mental juke box usually so deeply buried that he had forgotten it was there at all. And so it was that his inevitable response was "So what? The Devil always did have the best tunes," as Mick and Keith serenaded his mind's ear. Their advice was, usually, to Paint It Black.

The Pope travelled much further afield. His first voyage lasted almost two years. It started in May 2059, and after an Atlantic crossing beset by storms and pirates, took him to the ruins of Rio de Janeiro, whence he hopped northwards to the Caribbean and eventually Florida. The Americas in general had suffered greatly from the Plague. Central and South America had been reduced to a thin skin of trading ports around an almost wholly deserted interior, reverting to jungle and wildlife and—if the lurid folk-tales he learned from the one-eyed buccaneer he'd met in a Cayenne bar were to be believed—far worse things. Demons. Monsters. Anthropophagi who carried their heads beneath their shoulders, and who knows what else.

Things worsened as he travelled north. The East Coast of the United States and Maritime Canada had been completely deserted. New York was a ruin as impressive and as lifeless as the Circus Maximus, waves breaking against the stained glass and tarnished steel of the skyscrapers as Manhattan, like Atlantis, slowly sank. He heard that things were slightly better far to westward, and that the largest population centre in North America was Aberdeen, Washington, the administrative capital of the Shasta, a loose federation of Sasquatch tribes that extended from California to Alaska.

Taking ship once more across the Atlantic, he was briefly marooned on Lanzarote when his steam-powered yacht had not only run out of coal, but had lost its mast. A second ship, similar to the first but marginally less decrepit, took him to Dakar and around the Guinea coast to Lagos. He had hoped to see the Bishop of that city, who had been an old friend.

His wish was vain, for Africa was, if anything, far worse than the Americas had been. In truth, his heart had forewarned him of this. The population of Africa had been in decline for decades, suffering the consequences of disease, climate change, shamefully poor governance and general neglect. The Plague had hit Africa with the impact of a wrecking ball on a rotten watermelon. Apart from a very few widely dispersed coaling stations clinging to the fetid and malarial coasts, no human being was known to have survived in sub-Saharan Africa, as far as he could tell. Not one. Africa, once the birthplace of *Homo sapiens*, was now witness to its extinction.

That was not quite the same as saying that there were no *people*, but such hominids that might have existed were too widely scattered to contact. All that Domingo could do was ensure that each coastal station had a contingent of Christophorines before returning, by slow degrees, to Europe.

The steamer limped back up the coast until it reached Mauritania and the first signs of the Khalifa. The Plague had struck the mighty Islamic Empire hard and had ripped out its heart, claiming more victims than anywhere but sub-Saharan Africa. All that was left were sleepy coastal villages, and the rare, languid camel train that would penetrate the nearer oases. Climate change had struck these, too, so that the entire Sahel and Saharan Interior had now been abandoned to the white-hot erg.

It was when the Papal Barque crossed to southern Spain that Domingo noticed how crowded Europe was, at least by comparison with Africa. Andalusia, the region of his birth, had been among the least affected region of any part of the world, with fewer than one in six people falling victim to the Plague. Life continued pretty much as it always had. Still, the Pope easily resisted the temptation of scaling the mountains to the village where he had spent his earliest years. Instead, he embarked once again and crossed to the ancient port of Ostia, arriving in Rome in April, 2061.

Some of his brethren among the Cardinals had travelled even further than he had, and had equally interesting tales to tell, sitting and praying in the hollow remains of St Peter. The Plague had cleaned out a swath of steppe from Russia and Central Asia through to Mongolia and northern China, and had exacted a fearsone toll in India.

But the story was quite different in South-East Asia, from the Yangtze southwards through Indochina and the Malay archipelago to northern Australia, and outwards into the Pacific. The Orient was, according to one roving Cardinal, a necklace of hominid diversity like nowhere else in the world, almost like a world in itself. New species of hominid seemed to be emerging constantly amid the sorry, lingering remnants of *Homo sapiens*.

And so, hardly as he'd disembarked from the last one, Domingo set off on another, even longer expedition, eastwards through the Mediterranean and across the Black Sea to Georgia, the Colchis of the Argonauts where the Caucasus meets the sea. Thence northwards, across the Kazakh steppes until, after many adventures, he passed the Dzungarian Gates and into the vast, windy desert that northern China had become.

Turning south again, he found that the Cardinal had been right. To cross the Yangtze was to enter a different world, a land where hominids ruled. In streets and markets and temples and palaces from Kunming south to Kuala Lumpur he counted at least twenty different kinds of hominid, from the tiny, golden-furred Laotian Annamites to the fearsome Khong, the twelve-foot-tall, black-skinned, red-eyed trolls from the Burmese highlands. In the Indies the hominids mixed freely together in a permanent state of festive riot, a constantly shifting network of alliances made and unmade, with hominids of all kinds and colours parading the crowded streets of the vibrant, revitalized cities in a never-ending array of dazzling finery. But always, at the bottom, was *Homo sapiens*, reduced to a pitiful and servile state: the menials, the sweepers, the untouchables, the unseeables.

The anarchic brilliance of the Indies was such that Domingo wondered if he'd ever be able to form any kind of coherent memory of it. He was thinking along these lines as he leaned on the stern rail of the *S. S. Venture* as it puffed out of Batavia on the first leg of a voyage that would take him to Egypt and thence Europe. He looked round and discovered he had company. It was the Captain, who introduced himself and invited Domingo to dine with him in his cabin.

"The Plague was the best thing that ever happened round here," the Captain said, placing a well-chewed pheasant bone on a silver salver before it was whisked away by a stooping human. The Captain spoke in a kind of pidgin, a mixture of English, Chinese, Bahasa and a dozen other tongues. But despite its rich heritage, it was a remarkably simple language to learn and to pronounce, as it had been lashed together rather quickly to suit a wide variety of tongues and vocal chords. Domingo found it rather euphonious and had picked up the rudiments within a few days.

"How so?" Domingo replied, in a way calculated to invite further confidences.

"Well, look at it this way," the Captain said. "Here we all are, the underdogs, pushed into all kinds of holes and corners, and then—wham!—the tables are turned, are they not?" Domingo had to agree that they had. "And it's good riddance, too," the Captain continued. "Look what a good thing we've got going. *All* of us. The boot is on the other foot, for sure!" The Captain raised a glass to Domingo. "Cheers, Your Holiness!" he said. "Welcome to a brave new world!"

It was then that Domingo noticed the Captain's eyes, set in a broad, brown face. They were large, with yellow-green irises that almost covered the white sclera, and with oval pupils. He remembered seeing another face like that, once. A much smaller face, looking blindly up at him from a swaddle of blankets. Domingo realized with a shock that he hadn't seen Tom since that Christmas when Shoshana had died.

Towards the end of April, 2063, then, Tom returned to his cell to find much of it already occupied by a huge, weather-worn but otherwise familiar figure, long white hair tied back in a bandanna, barrel of a body clothed in a vibrant pattern of hibiscus, white on purple. All of a sudden he was a tiny child gamboling in the farmhouse yard, recognizing Domingo mainly by his smell — it never varied, his smell, and it smelled always of comfort and security and reassurance. Tom smiled — he remembered that he used to smile a lot more often when… when… oh, never mind.

"Domingo…" he said. He hadn't realized how much he'd missed his mentor until he'd said it. It was as if a lost part of his life had returned.

"We have some talking to do, Tom, you and I."

Soon after that meeting, the two of them had turned up at the farmhouse, to toast Jadis on her sixtieth birthday. Now another decade had passed, and they were here again, in the place that both of them would ever call home.

The party was not lavish, but it lasted well into the late evening, with much talk and wine and more talk, as can be understood by people suddenly reunited with long-lost children, parents and dear friends. There was even a cake, which Jack and Jadis had said was a present from the village boulangerie. 'A shamanistic offering,' Jack had joked, although Jadis had responded with no more than a quizzical frown.

The revels eventually came to rest in the sitting room, Jadis curled next to Jack on the same, desperately sagging sofa; Domingo in a cat-ripped easy chair and Tom cross-legged in front of the hearth, looking silently into the flames that were the sole source of illumination. The scent of burning apple-logs filled the room.

"We have been putting two and two together, Tom and I," Domingo explained, his dark shape punctuated only by the two points of light that were his eyes. "But we're not sure what the answer is yet."

Jadis sat up. "Oh, Domingo," she said, "do you have to be quite so mysterious all the time?"

"Not at all!" Domingo protested. "It is hard not to be...er... as you say, *mysterious*, when one is not even sure *which* two and two must be added, or even if they should."

"Jack," Jadis asked, looking up, "please say something to this silly man, would you? He is making absolutely no sense at all."

Jack just smiled, looked down and tousled his wife's hair. "Who'd like some Armagnac?" he asked. "I believe I still have a couple of bottles of the good stuff left."

Jadis sat up and hit him over the head with a cushion, whereupon everyone laughed some more, and Tom rose to help his father find a candle for a trip to the cellar.

After a long pause interrupted by the smoke and crackle of the apple wood, Domingo said with sudden seriousness: "Jadis, I apologise for this long absence..."

"Don't be silly, Domingo," she said, "I'm sure you've had lots to keep you busy." Jadis now lay curled on one side on the sofa, looking at the fire, her eyes bright coals from beneath her hair's shawl.

Speaking almost to himself, Domingo said: "Since I last saw you, all those years ago, you know, with Shoshana..." Jadis did not move. "I have travelled far and seen a great deal of the world," he continued, "and although many lives have been lost, there is still some hope for it. It is, however, a very different world from the one we've all known, those of us who've... er... been in it for any length of time."

"You mean us old *pantoufles*?"

"I speak only for myself, my dear Jadis," said Domingo. "The world is still wonderful, and in a sense it is renewed and we must take heart from that. There are relatively few...

er… human beings in it, though. If you went to eastern Asia, you'd think it a different planet entirely. But I have come to love it, despite—no, *because* of—these differences. I find them somehow… uh… invigorating."

"Where is this leading?"

"Well, it's like this, my dear Jadis—" Jack and Tom had now returned, with a dusty bottle and four assorted glasses.

"What's like what, my dear Domingo?" asked Jack, putting down the bottle before turning to riddle the fire. Tom picked up the bottle, poured four measures and handed them round. The sharp, prune-like aroma from the brandy combined with the general ambience of apple wood to make a scent more reminiscent of Christmas than Midsummer. Jadis sat up to allow Jack to resume his seat.

"Well, Jack, what *is* it like?" Domingo challenged, while raising his glass. Tom resumed his perch on the hearth, looking back at his father.

"I know what you mean, Domingo," said Jack. "I see it all the time, when I am teaching—*trying* to teach—some of the village teenagers. They speak a different language…"

Jadis laughed. "Don't they always?"

"But it's not just the language, it's them. Have you noticed,"—this to Jadis—"that people in the village are so huge these days? I thought it was just us getting old, but you know, I'm convinced it isn't."

Jadis closed her eyes.

"I have an idea. An explanation," said Domingo. "Like all such things you have to travel half way round the world to see what's right in front of you at home. The Plague seems to have spared the hominids. In all my travels, I have seen no case of a hominid falling foul of it. Only humans seem to have been affected, and many have still been spared, thank the Lord. Does that answer your question, Jack?"

"I'm not sure," said Jack. "Yes, people here have changed. They're bigger. But why? Perhaps they eat too much. Don't take enough exercise..." He paused, as if he'd been witness to a stunning revelation: "well, I'll be blowed."

"Hmm?" Jadis stirred.

"It's the Plague again. It didn't take all humans indiscriminately," said Jack, "only those without some admixture in their genes of something else, something... older."

"That's precisely it, Jack," said Domingo, "and I only realized it in the Far East when I saw the pitiful state of *Homo sapiens* in that part of the world. Over there, the earliest modern humans displaced the last remnants of *Homo erectus*. There was some admixture, but very little, and—I'd imagine—very little that was... uh... *viable*. But it was enough to get a few *Homo erectus* genes into the gene pool. And, fifty thousand years later, those modern humans with enough of this ancient DNA were spared the Plague. They are rather sorry and few, and easily cowed by the abundance of hominids."

"And here," said Jack, the light of the fire in his eyes, "we have a similar story, but with Neanderthals. How could I have missed it? They were here for an eternity before modern humans, especially in Gascony. Those who survived the Plague must have had a sizeable amount of Neanderthal blood in their veins. That would account for a great deal. The ancestors have come to claim their own."

"It is true," said Domingo: "the builders of Saint-Rogatien live here once again. What our dear friend Avi would have called the *avoteinu v'imoteinu*, the forefathers and foremothers, implying a skein of continuity unbroken into the deep past."

The pause in the conversation lasted longer than ever, as they all gazed into the dying fire, lost in their own thoughts. It was, eventually, Domingo who spoke.

"Might I change the… ah… subject?" he said.

The brooding reverie broke like a bowstring on a hot knife. Jadis sat up.

"Yes… of course," she said.

"Well, as I mentioned, Tom and I still can't make two and two add up," said Domingo, "and we think we know why. It's the Sigil. Neither of us have seen it for almost twenty years. Have you done anything with it? Published?"

"Of course we haven't, Domingo," Jadis said with a sigh. "We couldn't—wouldn't—do it without you, or without Tom. But we have no labs any more. No Institute. And we don't know where to begin."

"Ah, well," said Domingo, "now that Tom and I are here for a while, we might turn our minds to it, mightn't we?"

Jack and Jadis looked stunned.

"Well, yes," said Jadis," but don't you have other duties now? In Rome?"

It was then that Domingo dropped his biggest bombshell, a secret he had not revealed even to Tom.

"It's like this," Domingo explained. "Rome is not what it was, even after twenty years of restoration. My colleagues and I have decided… well, *I* have decided, and they have kindly agreed… that the Basilica of Saint Peter, while it is a pleasant place to visit, is not really convenient for living. So we've made it into a museum. So people can enjoy visiting it, and offer a welcome stream of…ah… *revenue*. That way, everyone is happy."

"But where will you go?" asked Jadis, anxiously: "Won't you have any kind of base?"

"Of course I shall, my dear Jadis. I should like to move the… er… Holy See to my spiritual home. That's if you'll have me. *Super hanc petram aedificabo ecclesiam meam*. Or words to that effect."

"Oh, Domingo, you really are a very silly man," Jadis replied, closing her eyes once more and leaning against Jack: "you *know* the answer to that." As if hosting the Vatican at her kitchen table were the most natural thing in the world.

Much later still, Jadis rolled over and embraced Jack from behind. "Thank you for a wonderful birthday," she said, sleepily.

"Oh, I think you should thank Tom and Domingo for that," said Jack. "It was as much of a surprise to me as for you."

"No, not *them*," she said. "I wanted to thank you for my *present*."

"Eh? What was that?" They had long ago given up the habit of birthday presents.

"*This*," she said, pulling him round into her arms and kissing him, and when she'd finished, burying her head in his chest. They lay there, like that, for a long time, forging a link with eternity.

In a small room across the hall, Domingo rose and unpacked a leather satchel which until recently had bobbed by his side, on the flanks of the percheron. He spent some minutes in hopeless contemplation, and then knelt at his old oak *prie-dieu*. He prayed, first, for guidance.

Then, for strength.

And finally, with silent fervour, for forgiveness—for forgiveness in advance, for what he would do next.

For withdrawing from the leather satchel a wooden box lined with the deepest blue velvet; for opening it; for removing the brown and weathered skull roof packed within.

For grasping a handful of herbs and dried flowers from inside a pouch of soft cloth; for placing them with great care within the upturned skull.

For taking a lighted candle from his bedside and setting fire to the herbs. And as the smoke rose, for chanting words hardly heard for millennia, far more ancient than *Agnus Dei*, but having much the same intent.

Bless us, Holy One, All High. Who took up the sins of the world, *qui tollis peccata mundi*.

Chapter 3. Child

Lower Egypt, Earth, *c* 45,000 years ago

Something wicked this way comes.
William Shakespeare — *Macbeth*

Clouds don't look like that, Dogfinger thinks. "Green-Eye," he shouts. "Look at the clouds!"

His sister stands up. Green-Eye is taller than Dogfinger. Dogfinger has nine summers. He is still a boy and runs naked. Green-Eye is older than him. She has twelve summers and bleeds with Mother-the-Moon. She has worn clothes for a year. She says she hates her new tunic. She says it is scratchy. Ma says her tunic makes her look grown-up. Green-Eye tells Dogfinger that she doesn't want to grow up. Next year she will be married to Crow-Knees. She will be called Bride of Crow-Knees. The year after that she will have children of her own.

Crow-Knees is the brother of the Chief. Crow-Knees is a very old man, says Dogfinger. He has twenty-four summers. Twenty-four summers is *not* old, says Green-Eye. It *must* be old, says Dogfinger. Dogfinger cannot count as high as that. Twenty-four is more than all the wheat-stalks in Pa's field. He knows. He tried counting them once. He lost count after sixteen.

Green-Eye is tall as a reed. She can stand up in the gully where they play. The gully runs from the village between two dry stubble-fields. Green-Eye's feet are in the mud at the bottom of the gully. Her toes dig into the ooze. The ooze is green and brown and squishy and warm. Her toes are dirty but her hands are clean. Green-Eye is so tall that her head is above the rim of the gully. Dogfinger is smaller than Green-

Eye. He lies on his belly on the gully slope, peering over the edge. Green-Eye puts her hand to her face. She shields her eyes against Father-the-Sun. Dogfinger gets onto his hands and knees. He stands up on the gully slope. He jumps up and down. He points at the clouds. They are brown and dusty and close to the yellow land. That is not how clouds should be, Dogfinger thinks.

Green-Eye looks at the brown, low clouds. Green-Eye says one word.

"Stoners."

"What are Stoners?" asks Dogfinger.

"Stoners are bad men," says Green-Eye. "They come to do bad things."

"How do you know, sister Green-Eye?"

"When we lie in bed," she says," I hear Ma and Pa. They talk of old things. About how Stoners used to come in the old days. Pa says Stoners are coming west again. Coming here, to the Great Delta. The land is dry. Stoners need food and water, like us."

"I remember! Stoners are demons! Grandma says so!"

"Grandma is right. But demons need to eat. We eat cows. Demons eat cows and people and crops and *everything*. Even the Earth itself. Stoners would eat Father-the-Sun and Mother-the-Moon and the stars, too, if they could. Stoners are locusts in the shape of men. Pa says we should move south, away from the Stoners. But Ma wants to stay in the village. Ma says she cannot walk far, because she is going to give us another brother or sister soon. Pa and Ma argue in the night."

"I've never heard them."

"That's because you're asleep. *And* you snore!"

"I don't!"

"*Do!*"

"Don't!"

"Do *too!*"

Green-Eye sticks out her tongue at Dogfinger. Dogfinger jumps down onto his sister. Dogfinger is small but he is strong. A hunting-dog bit off the little-finger on his left hand when he had only five summers. Dogfinger wanted to wrestle the hunting-dog. Before that he was called Eye-Patch, because of the brown birthmark round his left eye. Now he is called Dogfinger. He is very brave.

Dogfinger and Green-Eye roll down into the gully together. The children are covered in mud. They look at each other and point. They laugh. Then Green-Eye sits up. She looks hard at Dogfinger. Dogfinger sees her two eyes. One eye is brown. The other is green.

"Pa is right," she says. "We must leave the village. We must warn the people of the Stoners."

The children help each other to stand in the gully. The gully is slippery. They climb out. Sand sticks to the ooze on their bare feet. They stand on the edge of the gully. The brown cloud on the horizon looks closer now. Dogfinger and Green-Eye stare hard. They stare into the cloud. Dogfinger sees men like tiny gray dots, all moving. Dogfinger and Green-Eye listen hard.

Dogfinger hears the tramp, tramp, tramp of marching feet.

Dogfinger hears the clank, clank, clank of stone armor.

Dogfinger hears singing, in time with the marching feet.

"Green-Eye!" he says, "It sounds like Ma and Grandma and the other ladies. They sing, when they pound the grain." Green-Eye does not laugh. She tells Dogfinger to keep quiet. She tells Dogfinger to hold his breath. Several breaths pass. Dogfinger can feel his own heart beat.

"Stoners," she says. "I was right. This is an end to play, little brother."

"Aww, but you *said*..." he whines. Green-Eye turns and looks down at her brother. Green-Eye is not smiling any more. Green-Eye is not laughing. Green-Eye's face—one green eye, one brown—looks angry.

She looks like a grown-up.

"Dogfinger," she says, "this is important. We must run home, now." She starts to spring, like a young gazelle, long and lean and coltish. Dogfinger thinks she has returned to play. Dogfinger thinks that her angry face was only a game.

"Last one home is a baboon's bottom!" he cries, and launches himself forwards. But try as he might, Green-Eye, with her longer legs, is always in front.

Dogfinger's house is on the edge of the village. It is round. It has walls made of mud. The walls are very thick. Dogfinger helped Pa mend the walls in the spring. He loved the feeling of the mud and cow dung between his fingers as he squished it into the walls. Dogfinger's house has a roof made of reeds. Dogfinger helped Ma cut new reeds to fix the roof. He loved the feel of the pliant stalks between his fingers as he passed them to Ma. The house is warm in the cold winds of winter. It is cool now, in late summer, when Father-the-Sun is high, and the wheat has been cut. It is dry when the first rains of spring flood the land. Dogfinger loves his house. He was born there. He knows nowhere else. Dogfinger's house is the center of his world.

Green-Eye runs to the garden gate. The gate is made of thorn branches, in between two thick thorn hedges. Green-Eye waits for Dogfinger to catch up. Green-Eye bends over. Her hands are on her knees. Her straggly pale hair covers her brown face. She is panting hard for breath.

Green-Eye stands up. "Dogfinger," she says, "I must go into the house. I must tell Ma and Pa and our little brother and sisters that the Stoners are coming."

"What shall I do?" says Dogfinger.

"You must run into the village square," gasps Green-Eye. "Run as fast as you can, Dogfinger. Shout that the Stoners are coming. Shout for people to run away, into the fields. Shout for the Chief. Shout for Crow-Knees. Whatever you do, shout. Shout, as loud as you can!"

Dogfinger does not run. He does not shout. He stands, looking up at his sister. She looks angry again. He is confused. This is not a game any more. Dogfinger starts to cry. Green-Eye crouches down, so that she can look him in the eye. Green-Eye puts her hands on his shoulders. "Little brother," she says. "Now you have to be a big man. Be brave, like you were with the hunting-dog."

"A game?" he asks, "A game of 'Fierce Dogs'? Grrr!" He wrinkles up his nose. She laughs. He bares his teeth, like a fierce dog.

"A game. If you like," she says. "Go on, now." She stands up. "Well, what are you waiting for?" She smiles at him. He turns and runs into the village.

Dogfinger runs. He runs as hard as he can. He reaches the village square. The square is full of people. The people are running about, this way and that. They look frightened. He sees his cousin, Bride of Fish-Skin, carrying her new baby.

"The Stoners are coming!" he shouts. "The Stoners are coming!" Bride of Fish-Skin ignores him. She looks scared. Dogfinger sees Old One-Leg, hobbling on his crutch as fast as he can, a small animal-skin bag across his shoulders.

"The Stoners are coming!" Dogfinger shouts. "The Stoners are coming!" Old One-Leg doesn't notice Dogfinger. Dogfinger's voice dies in his throat. No matter how loudly he shouts, the villagers shout louder. He cannot be heard. He stands still, in the middle of the running people. All around is noise. The shouts of men. The screams of ladies. All around is smell. The smell of fear. The smell of burning straw. The houses beyond the village square are on fire. There is another smell, like roasting meat. Dogfinger is frightened. He starts to whimper. He wets himself with fright. Pee dribbles down the deep mud brown of his leg. It feels hot.

"What are you doing here, Dogfinger?" says a kindly voice. A fat lady looks down at him. It is Bride of Cattle-Egret. Dogfinger knows Bride of Cattle-Egret. She helps Ma pound the grain. Dogfinger looks up at Bride of Cattle-Egret. The lady bends down to him. She has a friendly, round face. Her round eyes look worried. Dogfinger can smell her fat arms and see the swell of her big warm bosoms swinging under her tunic. He thinks of his Ma. He starts to cry. Bride of Cattle-Egret starts to cry, too.

"Why are you crying, Bride of Cattle-Egret?" asks Dogfinger.

"Run home, little Dogfinger," she says.

"But my sister, Green-Eye," he says, "she told me to run here and warn the village. The Stoners are coming!"

"Sweet Dogfinger—you are too late," says Bride of Cattle-Egret. "Run home. Run home now!" Bride of Cattle-Egret squeezes his shoulders. She stands up, turns, and walks away. Dogfinger does not know where she is going. Bride of Cattle-Egret disappears into a haze of smoke. The smoke makes him cough. Dogfinger turns and runs back the way he has come.

The way home is not easy. The road is full of people, running, some this way, others that. He bumps into people.

"Watch where you're going," a man says. It is hard to see through the clouds of thick, gray smoke. Dogfinger trips over things. He stumbles.

He falls onto something soft. He does not know what it is. He struggles to get up, pushing with his hands. His hands slip on something hot and squishy. Dogfinger gets to his feet. He looks down. His hands and arms and the front of his body are covered in sticky red stuff.

It is blood.

He looks down. Dogfinger looks down, where he fell. It is a dead lady. She has no tunic. He does not know who the lady is, because she has no head. Her belly has been split open. He sees a tiny red child in her belly, and lots of gray squishy tubes, and lots of blood. Dogfinger feels giddy and sick. Dogfinger starts to run home, through the smoke. Dogfinger hopes he doesn't fall over again.

Dogfinger reaches the garden gate. He knows something is wrong. The thorn hedge is on fire. Dogfinger sees his house through the flames. The reeds of the roof are on fire. The mud walls are cracking in the heat. Dogfinger sees two big men go into the burning house. They are Stoners. Dogfinger stands in the street. The two Stoners come out again.

Dogfinger cannot move. Dogfinger thinks his feet have been stuck to the ground. Dogfinger cannot take his eyes from the door to his burning house. Dogfinger sees what happens, through a shifting curtain of flame. He hears the sizzle of burning reeds. He hears the crack of burning thorn branches.

The Stoners come out of Dogfinger's house. They wear helmets made of stone plates, sewn onto a kind of bonnet. They wear long tunics of gray, stone plates, like fish scales. They look like giant fish, with legs. They are laughing and shouting.

With one arm, one of the Stoners drags a man from the house. The man is struggling. It is Pa. Dogfinger wants to shout, but his voice has gone. All that comes out of his mouth is a dry rasp. In the crook of the Stoner's other arm, Dogfinger sees his two baby sisters. They are twins. They have three summers. They are screaming, silently. Dogfinger cannot see his baby brother. The Stoner puts down the twins and hits Pa on the head. Pa goes limp.

The second Stoner comes out of Dogfinger's house. In one arm he holds Dogfinger's baby brother. Dogfinger loves playing with his baby brother. Dogfinger's baby brother is called Hoopoe, because of his crest of crazy hair. Hoopoe has just learned to walk.

In his other arm the second Stoner holds Green-Eye. The second Stoner makes Green-Eye watch as the first Stoner bashes the twins on the head. Blood spouts from their mouths and eyes. The first Stoner throws their bodies into the burning house.

Then the first Stoner makes Pa stand up, pinning his arms back. The first Stoner makes Pa watch as the second Stoner throws Hoopoe into the flames. Then the second Stoner takes a long flint knife and cuts off Green-Eye's tunic. Dogfinger can see her thin legs and the little points of her new bosoms. Dogfinger wonders why his Ma is not here.

The first Stoner makes Pa watch as the second Stoner lifts up his stone tunic, grabs Green-Eye by the hair and makes her bend over. Dogfinger does not understand what the Stoner is doing to Green-Eye. He knows that it is a Bad Thing. Then the second Stoner grabs Pa, so that the first Stoner can do the Bad Thing to Green-Eye.

Then the first Stoner takes some rope and ties Green-Eye's hands together. The first Stoner makes Green-Eye watch as the second Stoner takes a long flint knife in one hand, grabs Pa's tongue with the other, and cuts his tongue off. Then the second Stoner reaches under Pa's tunic and cuts off Pa's willy. The Second Stoner shoves Pa's willy into Pa's mouth. Then the Stoners make Green-Eye watch as the Stoners take turns doing the Bad Thing to Pa. After that, Dogfinger cannot clearly see what the Stoners are doing, because of all the blood, and the flames, and the smoke. But

Dogfinger still cannot move. When the smoke clears, Dog-finger's house and his family are gone.

It is night. Dogfinger is lying down in the gully where he plays with Green-Eye. His arms and chest are crusted in blood. The smell of smoke is in his hair. The insides of his legs are slick with his own poo. His eyes and chest ache from breathing smoke. Dogfinger thinks he has woken from a bad dream. He wonders why it is dark.

Dogfinger wonders why Green-Eye does not come.

Chapter 4. Exile

Mount Carmel, Earth, *c.* 125,000 years ago

I have been faithful to thee, Cynara! In my fashion
Ernest Dowson—*Non Sum Qualis Eram Bonae Sub Regno Cynarae*

The party had begun to wind down, and Mr Khorare, suddenly bereft of duties or of need of attendance elsewhere—the Old King having retired to his chambers—took the opportunity offered by an open window onto the terrace to fulfil an urgent need for a lungful of fresh sea air. His most earnest wish, the desire of decades, had at last been granted, at least in principle. But whether it could be realized—ah, well, that was, as ever, a matter of adroit politics, as well as time. Mr Khorare was a master of both media, but that was of scant comfort.

The terrace was a vast expanse of creamy-white travertine fringed with a tastefully colonnaded rampart, jutting from a cliff, a hundred meters sheer over the Mediterranean Sea itself. Tasteful it should be, because he had devised it himself. The waves could be heard, a dim roar from far below. They could not be seen, however, except to one who wished to lean dangerously far out, over the parapet, and into empty space.

The giant castle—the palaces, stores, armories and the city itself, housing a greater part of the population of the Kingdom that Mr Khorare had served, faithfully, for precisely fifty years—towered even higher above the terrace; bastion on bastion, rampart on rampart, and extended eastwards and over and beneath and around the Mount Carmel massif for twenty unbroken square miles. The heart of the Kingdom Under The Mountain, easily the rival in size and sophistication of any city in the world, including—Mr Khorare had to admit—the now-fading memory of the Very Great and Ancient City of Axandragór, now lost, it seemed, beyond any hope of his seeing it again: given that the fulfilment of Mr Khorare's desires now lay in the opposite direction. Mr Khorare crossed the terrace and, resting a richly sleeved arm on the parapet, gazed across the western sea, over which the Moon was now setting, bathing the castle in a magical, pearly light.

I shall be following you soon, Sister Moon, he sang to himself.

It had taken this long, but, despite everything—despite early problems; despite many occasions when he'd narrowly escaped death; despite the frequent brutality of the Stoners themselves—this was a place he had come to love. Even though he must leave it, and soon. Now that he had contrived an interview with the Old King, albeit brief, before his patron abdicated in favor of his arrogant, unfeeling, belligerent son; before the King, may the Goddess forbid—died of old age or, as seemed increasingly likely, by intrigue, as a result of the impatience of the Crown Prince.

But what the King had actually *said*—well, that had been reassuring and breathtaking in like measure, and, Mr Khorare had to admit to himself, entirely characteristic of the wily old monarch he had served for so long.

Mr Khorare tried not to be torn in two—or in three—for in addition to the duties of his current home, and his pressing need to leave it, he still harbored a fond memory of the place whence he came. He was, in truth, the only one of his kind currently living here, and the only one generally known to most of the inhabitants. He longed for company. Even after all this time, he longed for news.

But that in the press of daily round he might occasionally forget his home and origins was brought to him forcefully earlier that very evening when, in his capacity as Chancellor of the Court of the King Under The Mountain, he had been introduced to one of the very rarely seen members of his own race. This was an emissary from his old home city, seeking permits and guarantees to trade in the Kingdom. Mr Khorare had been eager to interview the man who, like him, was — had been — a trader in fine textiles, and was looking for a market for his wares. That such a market now existed there was no doubt, but Mr Khorare found little solace, now, in the fact that there would have been none were it not for his own advice, his own intervention; his own careful work among the courtiers and the royal household over decades. Were Mr Khorare to have boasted that he'd civilized this Kingdom single-handed, he had ample justification for that claim.

Not that the emissary appreciated any of this. In fact, Mr Khorare found the visitor rude and uncouth, and concerned only with prices, tariffs and percentages, of which he talked loudly and brazenly even in the company of the nobility of the Kingdom, as if these grandees — many of them close friends of Mr Khorare — were servants or savages who might conveniently be regarded as invisible. The emissary had been a great disappointment, an embarrassment, even: Mr Khorare hoped that he himself had not been too much like that in his former life, but admitted to himself that perhaps, in some ways, he had. Mr Khorare buried his feelings of revulsion beneath his need to interview the trader and find out as much as he could about his old city. Perhaps, even, his family. His kits. His wife.

"The old place has become a bit of a hole, to be honest with you," the emissary had said, helping himself to more of Mr Khorare's private store of single malt: "the sea floods the Grand Plaza and most of the major thoroughfares at least twice a year. The sewage system can't hack it, so the whole place is slowly sinking in its own shit. Nobody actually *lives* in the City nowadays. Anyone — anyone of *consequence*, that is — has moved inland or into the Archipelago. The city itself is infested with pithekines and other riff-raff from the interior. In fact, just last year..."

Mr Khorare could no longer restrain himself. "Excuse me Sir, but in your... er... particular line of business, did you ever come across the House of Khorare?" The emissary looked at him blankly, at first, as if Mr Khorare had uttered a profanity in an unfamiliar language. But the wheels behind the emissary's blankly acquisitive, selachian eyes began to turn, and a memory stirred. Mr Khorare soon had cause to wonder whether nostalgia really was an emotion that should be indulged very often. Or at all.

"Khorare? Khorare? Ah yes, *Khorare*. I remember now," said the trader. "It was a scandal from my Father's time. Way back when, Khorare was the biggest and richest textile trader in the City. But he just disappeared — on a business trip, maybe, or just after a bit of stuff, *if* you know what I mean" — here the emissary leered and sniggered in a most unattractive fashion — "and was never heard from again. He'd never put his affairs in order, and the legal disputes dragged on for years. Eventually my father picked up the business for a song..."

"What happened to his family?"

"That's the best part of all. His wife was apparently a bit of a goer. Loved nothing more than banging away on a bit of illicit prong-o, and none too discriminating about what it was attached to. Khong, Yettins, Pithekines, even Floresians, if you can believe it: you name it, she opened her legs for it. As bad as her old man had been, or worse, to be honest with you, *if* you get my meaning. Been putting it around for years, she had, or so the stories went, when her old man was away.

"Well, when Khorare disappeared for good she went on a bit of a bender and made a biggish dent in her husband's fortune. Holed it below the waterline. When she was down to her last *zuzim* my Old Man picked up the Khorare palazzo for peanuts. He'd had the business anyway, so why not? She tried to claim tenancy but of course my Old Man was having none of it. He told me once that she came on to him, flashing her dugs at him, but by that time she was just a raddled old slapper, so he told her to sling her hook. Haven't a clue what happened to her after that, or her kits. Quite a brood, apparently, and evidently not all of what you might call provenanced parentage, *if* you take my meaning.

"Of course, what with the way things were going, the Old Man soon had to sell the old heap on—he got out just before the excrement well and truly hit the proverbial ventilator in the property market, *if* you take my meaning—so I expect the old palazzo is crumbling into the or-*dure* even as we speak, with five pithekine families fouling every room and swinging from the rusty old chandeliers. Nice whisky this, I have to say, Your Excellency. Can't say I've tasted better. Cheers!"

Mr Khorare had given the emissary the rest of the bottle, left instructions for him to be accommodated, and returned to the party, keen to assuage his conflicting thoughts and surges of emotion—his frank revulsion—by dint of assiduous and correct adherence to service and protocol. It was not as if he could afford to be on anything other than his best form. The party was, after all, given in his own honor: a half-century of service to the Kingdom was rare, even unprecedented. Not a few palace staffers, however, wondered whether Chancellor Khorare was enjoying himself, however, given the unwonted sharpness of his tongue.

Mr Khorare returned to the Grand Ballroom just in time, mere seconds before the sinus-jarring bray of auroch-horn trumpets that announced the imminent arrival of His Majesty, Hrothgar the Hideous, King Under The Mountain, Hammer of the West, God-Emperor of the Sunset Seas and so on and so forth in like fashion, and Mr Khorare's oldest and best friend. Mr Khorare was at the edge of the crowd when the royal palanquin appeared, a massive cedar-trunk and mammoth-ivory construction, borne by eight huge Yettin eunuchs, upon which was mounted, rather in the manner of a carnival float, the necessarily capacious and reinforced throne bearing the corpulent figure of the Old King himself.

Hrothgar appeared to be clothed in a suit of ill-fitting, ill-tanned leather. Either that, or he was naked, and the crumpled and hairy skin was his own. Mr Khorare was debating the matter with himself when a third option occurred to him — that His Majesty might have been availing himself of the latest Stoner fashion, led by the Crown Prince Hygelak and his circle, namely clothes sewn of the pelts of the people that Stoners called 'Thinskins'.

The Thinskins were a hominin race, primitive and as yet rather rare, that had recently appeared on the south-western, aethiopic fringes of the Kingdom. Taller but more slender than Stoners, the tenderness of Thinskin flesh, it was reputed, more than compensated for their weakness in battle: their skins, being almost hairless, were easy to tan and made marvelously supple leather. The scarcity of Thinskins in general made them highly prized as delicacies and out of reach of all but the wealthiest Stoner nobility. It was the *female* Thinskins, it was again reputed, that were especially succulent, most particularly in the thigh, rump and loin, and gave the best skins, being even smoother than the skins of the males.

At least, after they were dead.

When they were alive, it was said, by those in-the-know, they gave excellent sport, if one could put up with the screaming, but there were—again, it was said—ways round that.

But no, reasoned Mr Khorare—if the King were wearing a Thinskin pelt, it was a singularly bad one, not like the smooth finery of the Crown Prince Hygelak, lately aped by the fashionable. Hrothgar tolerated the current vogue for Thinskin flesh, but without bestowing openly royal favor on it. "Frankly, Khorare," he'd once said, "it's a little too insipid for our taste. Give us a well-hung haunch of bison any day, what?"

When the Crown Prince Hygelak came into his own—well, the Thinskins in the Kingdom and for hundreds of miles around would soon be hunted to extinction. No, Mr Khorare reasoned—the Old King was naked as the day he was born, a fact that became alarmingly apparent when the eight enormous Yettins stooped, lowered the palanquin to the flagged floor of the ballroom, and the King rose from his throne. All eyes were averted, all heads were bowed, all bodies were prostrated on the floor, as the King puffed and wobbled his way through the parting, shuffling crowd, towards where Mr Khorare stood, head bowed.

Mr Khorare's first view of his sovereign was of a pair of very large and hairy feet. A hand under his chin forced him to stand, to raise his gaze, over the knobbly royal knees; the flabby royal thighs; the royal nether regions (happily buried in several folds of the royal spare tire); the gigantic royal belly itself; the floppy-breasted royal barrel-chest; the royal bull-neck; the royal multiple chins; and, finally, the scarred and twisted royal visage itself. "Frankly, Khorare," said the King, in a quiet voice from a grizzled face, whose principal features were the wicked glint of eyes from within a sea of scarred skin and knotted muscle, the bright but tiny sparks separated by a truly monumental nose, "what's the point of wearing anything at all if our subjects don't even dare look at us, eh? Might as well go around in the buff, what?"

"Quite so, Your Majesty," said Mr Khorare.

"Fifty years, what?" The royal grip on Mr Khorare's chin was firm, despite the pudginess of the hand exercising it. "Seems like only yesterday when we picked you up after that little fracas with the Yettins in our Mesopotamian dependencies, what?"

It did seem like only yesterday when the then Crown Prince, dismounting from his coelodont, rounded him up on that remote hillside. Mr Khorare had expected to be spitted on the spot, or, if not then, later. But no—Mr Khorare had been treated as a long-lost friend, or, at least, a visitor long expected. He still remembered riding in the royal column of troopers mounted on coelodonts, rumbling in stately fashion along the ever-more populated westward roads through the seemingly endless savannah that was Mesopotamia, passing column after column of chained Yettins, and slaves and beasts of many other species, until his eyes were greeted by that unforgettable sight, that incredible silhouette—the pinnacles of the Kingdom Under The Mountain itself, raised sharp and shadowy against the sun, setting over the Mediterranean Sea. He remembered, too, his sharp intake of breath at the sight, and the then Crown Prince's voice, so close: "welcome home, Mr Khorare. Welcome home."

Mr Khorare had long puzzled over the nature of his welcome—that the King (as he soon became) had found him and brought him home as a treasured prize, a wise counselor, and not as a slave or—as was so often the case—live meat, on the hoof. He had his suspicions, though, but these were never articulated, the result being that he'd spent five decades watching his back, waiting for the shift in royal politics that would see his inexplicable good fortune evaporate as snow in summer, culminating with the sudden knife in the guts. But it never had, and now, fifty years had passed as if in the wink of an eye, and here his sovereign stood before him, once again.

"Yes, Sire," said Mr Khorare. "It does seem like only yesterday."

"I expect you've wondered, Khorare, about the reason for your singular run of survival," the King continued—not relaxing his iron grip on Khorare's chin for an instant, "when so many of your colleagues have ended up as eyeball-and-testicle soup?"

"Sire?" Mr Khorare felt his knees go numb, and his heart swap places with his stomach. Perhaps his run of luck was now up: he had outlived his usefulness and must accept his fate.

"Take heart, Khorare." Said the King. "We were led to you through some good fortune of our own. The same place where we still get that excellent single malt. Need we say more?" Khorare was flustered, and felt his face redden. The King shook it, and roared with laughter. "*Nice legs*, eh? Nice *Thinskin* legs? With us now?"

And then Khorare remembered the remote reed-cutter's hut, and the remarkable divine being that inhabited it—the same being who had, it seemed, governed his life, his journey. The Genie of the Talisman—the amulet he still wore, close to his chest. She had, it seemed, been looking out for him in more ways than he had suspected. He allowed himself the narrowest of smiles. He did not dare, however, to wink.

"Nice legs. Indeed, Sire," Mr Khorare agreed. "Very nice indeed."

The King released Khorare's chin with a flourish and looked straight into his Chancellor's almond-shaped, yellow-green eyes. The two men were evenly matched in height, for all that the King weighed more than twice as much. The

King's voice dropped, so that what he said next could not be heard by anyone except the two figures, standing in the eye of the still-prostrated crowd.

"We should offer you a gift, for your service, Khorare," said the King, "and something—*someone*—tells us that it should be more than the customary removal of non-essential body parts, or speedy passage to the life beyond. What, then, Khorare, is your desire?" The moment had come. Khorare found that his mouth had turned to sandpaper. Somehow, from some deep reserve, he found the words—the resource—to continue. He swallowed.

"Your Majesty is most kind," he said. "Should your Majesty wish to release me from my long service, then my desire—my most *earnest* desire—is to continue on the westward journey in which I was engaged on the occasion of my very first and propitious meeting with Your Majesty. On that day that seems like only yesterday." Mr Khorare bowed his head, hoping that he had not overstepped the mark. Even after all this time, he never really knew quite how he stood with this shrewd, intelligent Stoner emperor. Hrothgar had the knack of keeping everyone guessing, of divide-and-rule, and this had been the key to a long reign, coextensive with Mr Khorare's own position as the King's most trusted advisor. But Khorare had the sense that Hrothgar, too, felt that his time was nearing its end, an instinct that prompted him to be more forthright in his request than he might otherwise have been.

The eyes of the King Under The Mountain, when he chose to loose their gaze from the folds of his face, were huge and round, each one a deep brown well of unguessable wisdom and sorrow. After a long interval, in which Mr Khorare felt that he might be swallowed in their peaty depths, the King spoke.

"Your wish is granted, old friend. And if things are going the way they're going, you'd better get on with it."

Mr Khorare had had many opportunities to review this scene in his mind in the weeks that followed. He was doing so now, aching with nostalgia and regret, standing on the deck of the small but perfectly formed sloop *Exile on Main Street*, the boat he'd commissioned with the full (though discreet) support of the Old King, as it approached the coast of the country the Captain assured him was Rhoneland.

"Goddess, I wish I was coming with you, but *someone* has to hold the fort. Literally, what?" the King had laughed, reviewing the final plans for the boat with Mr Khorare and deciding on its name. *Chantilly Lace* and *Paint It Black* had been rejected as being too enigmatic; *Lady Jane* and *Ruby Tuesday*, too explicit. Mr Khorare had, however, been able to compliment the King on his inventive choice of names, the origin of which the King had been unable to explain clearly.

The talisman hanging at his chest appeared to throb with life as he neared his destination. This was sufficient assurance, thought Mr Khorare, that his path was the correct one, though precisely how or why this should be he was at a loss to articulate, still less, understand. He'd had many debates with the Captain of the *Exile* about this, now so long ago. But now, he knew, all arguments were settled, all debates resolved. There were tears in his eyes as the coast before them resolved from a thin line into a shore bustling with gulls and small boats. Tears of joy, tears of gratitude for the generosity of the patron he'd left behind, and whom he'd never had a proper opportunity to thank. The King had intended to come down to the dock at Caesarea for a final supper aboard the *Exile*, to toast it on its way, but he had failed to arrive. Just before they weighed anchor, a crewman told Mr Khorare that they should make haste: a battle was raging in the Castle, between the King's guards and those loyal to the

Crown Prince. There was even a rumor that the King had fallen.

A pilot and customs-yacht drew alongside. Formalities were quickly completed, and the pilot bade Mr Khorare welcome to the Port of Massilia.

Had Mr Khorare had any expectations at all of the port and city of Massilia, they should easily have been exceeded within the first few minutes of his arrival.

It was stunning.

As the *Exile on Main Street* tip-toed into the yacht basin, Mr Khorare at the prow, all he could do was stare outwards, jaw agape in frank wonderment—outwards, and also upwards. The boat was dwarfed by the vastness of the ships that crowded in around it, so that the little sloop had to bob and tack round the floating behemoths, the pilot and the captain in frequent conclave, leaving Mr Khorare with nothing to do but stand and stare. There were ironclads, four funnels apiece, blue with hugeness in the ocean haze. There were luxury liners, even greater, each one an immense city afloat. There were elegant three-masted clippers and schooners. All were served by bustling quaysides crowded with passengers and baggage offloaded, and loaded again, and gantries, and cranes, and stevedores, and touts, and hawkers, the throng of them all like tiny black ants against the ships they served.

There were paddle-steamers, too, the sight of which drew Mr Khorare to the rail more than once, his hands clenching and unclenching as he forced a memory to emerge, as a bird from a long-dormant egg. He had sailed on some such boat, he thought, from the Great and Ancient City of Axandragór—now more myth than memory, as if it had been a tale told by someone else, a nameless traveler at a roadside inn, lost in the darkness of immeasurable time. But the talisman still throbbed—no, it *ached*—against the skin of his chest.

More impressive than the busy flotilla by far was the city itself that surrounded it: a ring of towers, each a sharp, extended pyramid of stone and metal and glass, twenty—no, thirty, no (Mr Khorare counted the ranks of bronzed windows upwards, with mounting incredulity)—an amazing *forty* stories tall, or even more. Nothing—not the lost memory of decadent Axandragór; not the recent recollection of the sprawling ramparts of the Kingdom Under The Mountain—nothing had prepared him for this. Mr Khorare felt his hands, tight around the rail, go numb.

"Yes, it's quite something, Your Excellency" said the barrel-chested Stoner pilot, urgent at his elbow.

"Yes," Mr Khorare croaked, his throat quite dry. "It is," and went below.

Once in the city itself, Mr Khorare, who had no shortage of funds at his disposal, paid off the *Exile*'s crew and bade them good speed homewards, and set out to find suitable accommodation. His first lodging was a spacious suite in a grand old hotel, two blocks back from the waterfront. He stayed there for more than a month, during which time he found himself up against two momentous questions that had been advancing towards him, like a slow tide, for what seemed like his whole life. They now faced him like a cresting wave. Where was he going? And why?

He suspected that his destination lay somewhere in this country, somewhere in Rhoneland, but the closer he approached the question, the more elusive it seemed. The talisman burned and tugged at his throat, insistent. Clearly, his quarry was near—but what was it? Would he know it when he saw it?

And if he did—what then?

Nights found Mr Khorare in his suite, clothes and the remains of meals scattered around him in uncharacteristic disarray, staring at the talisman, desperate for resolutions to all these questions. But no inspiration came. Days found him in more positive, constructive mood, exploring the environs of the old hotel, during which expeditions he found a real-estate agent keen to show the well-heeled foreigner a wide selection of prestige apartments that might be made available for his use on a long lease. Until he stumbled on the answers to his problems—answers which would no doubt obtrude themselves randomly on his consciousness, in their own time, and which were, therefore, not subject to timetables or schedules—he might as well make himself comfortable in this unendingly marvelous city.

And so an apartment was procured. Once he had moved in, Mr Khorare ascribed the fact that it was the penthouse on the thirty-seventh floor of one of the city's tallest pyramids to some kind of reaction, first, to the often subterrene life of the Kingdom Under The Mountain—and possibly even to the low-rise sprawl of Axandragór before that. But no, he thought. There was more to it than that. The apartment was no mere cave perched high on a cliff. It had all the most modern amenities—flushing water closets; gas-mantles for lighting and even cooking; a speaking-tube to alert the concierge on the ground floor; and even a pneumatic tube port that could be used to direct capsules of mail to the building's mail-room and thence anywhere in Rhoneland—a country, he was to learn, of remarkable cultural refinement, as well as geographic extent. In addition, Mr Khorare was thrilled to discover that a team of servants was at his disposal. Cooks, valets and footmen were there to fulfil his every requirement. There was even a chauffeur to conduct the steam-powered *barouche* housed in the underground garage, on call twenty-four hours a day, at his own, exclusive disposal.

Mr Khorare lost no time having the apartment redecorated to his own, exacting tastes, as well as finding outfitters whose skill and sense of adventure would equal his own. All this activity entailed many trips in the *barouche*, crisscrossing the entire extent of the vast city. In the course of which he made many friends, and thanks to his own diplomatic skill, as well as the exoticism of his race, and (he was not so naïve not to have realized) his seemingly bottomless purse (which he increased still further through shrewd investments directed by a business contact of his tailor), he soon became tolerably well-known among the Stoner cognoscenti of Massilia as a connoisseur, an arbiter of taste.

How different it all seemed from the Kingdom Under The Mountain! Where there was once surly resistance to his esthetic ideas, there was now fascination, followed by acceptance; where there were once conversations conducted in monosyllables, there was voluble intercourse; where there was once the ever-present threat of severe, physical sanction, there was, it seemed, perfect amity and freedom. The clothes, his new friends, his *salon*, his trips to the theater, the opera, to concerts and to galleries—Mr Khorare loved it all. He had many causes to give thanks to the Goddess, or to Fate, and—in those rare moments of dyspeptic discontent—to imagine that after all these years of exile in a barbarous Kingdom, he deserved it.

Being the cosmopolitan soul that he was—and, perhaps, because his mind was forever engaged in the consideration of stuffs, and silks, and fine wallpapers and porcelain, it took him a while to realize that whereas the citizens of Massilia were, beneath their fine words and accoutrements, Stoners little different from the warriors and pirates he'd known for most of his life, their servants (one would never be so *gauche* as to have called them *slaves*) were of a different race entirely—taller than the Stoners, or indeed himself, with relatively flat, hairless ebony-black faces, and a slender carriage of dignified erectness. It took him a long time to realize that he knew this race well, but he made the connection very suddenly, as if from nothing, late one night after a house-party as he was dismissing his butler, Raull, for the night.

By that time — he had been living in his apartment for almost a year — he had come to know Raull very well. Raull had been his companion on many shopping expeditions; his guide to the Massilian social scene; his bulwark against social solecism; his sounding board; his inexhaustible fund of knowledge; and his *confidant*.

"Thinskins!" he found himself uttering — exclaiming, really, entirely without volition. He sat down, confused and embarrassed. Raull was at the door to the grand salon, on his way to his own quarters. He turned.

"Sir? Y'm'tokkin'?"

Mr Khorare had yet to surmount his occasional incomprehension of the fluidity of the Massilian vernacular, so much more freely flowing than what he now realized were the antique cadences of the language spoken in the Kingdom Under The Mountain; clipped and courtly, of a formality that belied the savagery beneath.

"Yes, Raull — I mean, no. Not really. Oh... What *do* I mean?" Raull hovered in the doorway even as his master wavered on the threshold of decision. "No, Raull — think nothing of it. You may go. Good-night!"

"G'night, Sir, m'tank'a." And he was gone.

How different Raull seemed, how they *all* seemed: his stolid cook, his elegant footman, his chauffeur, the pretty young scullery maids, the concierge so many floors below — from the creatures which, in the Kingdom Under The Mountain, were treated as pack animals, as vehicles for the most depraved sport, and thereafter, as the choicest meats, and — he gasped to think of it now — high-fashion leather. For a split second he looked at Raull, his poised, exquisitely mannered, refined and cultured Raull, and saw a flayed and butchered carcass. The thought made him recoil, shuddering. Had his long sojourn in the Kingdom Under The Mountain corrupted his sensibilities to such a hideous degree? Yet Raull was a Thinskin for all that, as were all his other servants. He resolved to discover all he could about Thinskins — their origins, their natural history, their habits, their dreams, their beliefs, their aspirations. He felt, all of a sudden, that this should be something like his mission. But he didn't have a clue where to start, and, somehow, he knew, this wasn't a topic suitable for discussion with one's servants. So, what with one thing and another, he put it out of his mind and carried on much as before.

It wasn't until many more months had passed, and Mr Khorare was returning from the first-night party of an experimental play at his favorite theater — a play that he found only moderately entertaining, for all that he'd partly funded the production and advised on the costumes and set design — that the subject came up again. Having dismissed his chauffeur and the steam-*barouche*, he wafted, slightly intoxicated, kaftan flowing, through the grand doors of the building and nodded a brief (if sincerely meant) greeting to the concierge. Now, normally, he'd have expected no more than a mumbled good-night in return — the hour was late, after all — but the response on this occasion pulled him up sharply.

"Haraddzjin Khorare of the Very Great and Ancient City of Axandragór!" the concierge said. "What are *you* still doing here?" Khorare turned round and stared at the concierge, from whose lips this startlingly stentorian ejaculation seemed to have emerged.

"I beg your pardon?"

"It's a fair question, isn't it?"

"It's... *what*?" The concierge fixed him a round-eyed, Thinskin stare. He noticed that she wasn't the usual concierge, but a much younger person, a female, presumably from the night-staff. He couldn't remember having seen her before. Mr Khorare noticed three further oddities. First, that her skin was pale, like a Stoner's, rather than the usual thinskin black. Second, that whereas custom dictated that all servants, whether male or female, had shaven heads, this duty concierge had an abundance of long, black hair that flowed from her head, down her back, and even over her face, like an impudent waterfall. Third, that she spoke in the same archaic language as he did, himself. Nothing like the protean speech affected by Massilians of all classes. Perhaps she was new in town and hadn't become accustomed to it. Mr Khorare decided that a diplomatic approach was best. It was, after all, what he was good at. He turned towards the concierge's desk and proffered a hand.

"I don't think we've met. I'm Mr Khorare. Penthouse suite. And you are... Miss....?"

"I know perfectly well who you are, thank you," the concierge said. "I've just told you, haven't I? And if you haven't worked out who *I* am by now, it hardly matters. But time is short, Khorare, and yet here you are! Going to plays, having parties, deciding in earnest tones the height of next season's hemlines, and generally fannying about, when evolution waits for no man. Not even you. To be quite honest, I'm disappointed. Yes, *disappointed*." Mr Khorare stared at her, open-mouthed. The concierge looked down, suddenly embarrassed, so that her hair completely covered her face. But, recovering her composure somewhat, she looked up again, raising her arms and pulling the hair away from her face, as if they were theater curtains.

"I'm sorry," she said, flushing and looking at him once again, her eyes full of beseeching sympathy where before they had been all diamond hardness. "Got a bit carried away." She stood up and, deferentially, indicated a door behind her. "Would Sir like to come into my office? What we need," she said, turning, "is a drink."

Of all the surprising things that were to happen that night, perhaps the most surprising of all was the drink he was offered — a malt scotch as medicinally peaty as anything he'd left behind in the Kingdom Under The Mountain. He'd always regretted not bringing any with him on the *Exile* — an abstinence borne of a desire, possibly misplaced, to look only to the future.

He took the drink from the concierge's hand — pale and slim, in which he could feel every knuckle and sinew, but clothed with skin as soft as a pelt — he took just one, tiny sip, and... without really knowing how... the small, cluttered cubbyhole of an office... hardly bigger than a closet... had grown, spread out, *whitened*... into a vast, wood-paneled *salon* with two button-backed leather sofas and a matching chair (in which he was seated) facing a fire in a gray stone fireplace... and a view of snowy mountains, up close... just like... just like he saw... just like he saw when...

He took a longer draught. It seared the back of his throat. He coughed. Laughter came from the sofa ahead of him and to his left, the figure silhouetted by the snow-blinding panorama behind.

"The reed-cutter... you... how?"

"Took you a while to catch on, didn't it?" she said. "Honestly, I've had to deal with some silly men in my time, and you are, without doubt, one of the silliest. But never mind. The project is almost complete, and you have only one more thing to do. Only one. Even if it's taking you several lifetimes." Mr Khorare felt ashamed, and confused, on account of not being quite sure why he should be ashamed, and these emotions together fuelled a mild resentment which he did his consummate best to conceal.

"My apologies," he said, "but I hardly thought of you in years — decades."

"Evidently." She sat back. He still could not see her face.

"The talisman?"

"He shoots — he scores!" She sat up. He could make out a penumbra of loosened hair like a halo, and her questing hands, each trying vainly to rein it in. "At last!"

Silence fell between them. Mr Khorare did not know what, if anything, he should say, and the duty concierge did nothing to help him (he could not help but think of her in this way — what else could he do?) But the wheels of his mind turned, silently, bringing images to him of the naked, wrinkled skin of the King Under The Mountain; the leather suits affected by the Crown Prince; his loyal butler, Raull (who'd be waiting up until his master's return); the abundant, nut-brown cleavages of the scullery-maids as they bent down to tend the fire, or sweep the floor; and, thence, of a resolution — wilfully neglected, he realized, by dint of the constant distractions of a life spent in dedicated pursuit of the superficial. He leaned forwards in his chair, cradling the scotch in both hands. He felt the chill of the heavy tumbler even as the tang of the vapors furled around his nostrils.

"Thinskins..."

"Hmm...?"

"I was to have found out about them. But I'm still not entirely sure how. Let alone why. And perhaps — well, perhaps that's why I... well, I admit it, I wanted to, but never got round to it."

"The road to hell, they say, is paved with good intentions. But your curiosity, Khorare, is commendable. After all, it's only natural for a person to take a keen interest in their creations."

"My... creations?"

"Don't look so surprised, Khorare. Here you are, thinking that your contribution to the well-being of the world has been to clothe it with ever greater refinement and taste, when what you have actually done is create a race of living beings of a beauty and elegance that only someone like you can confer. Being one of them myself—at least, some of the time—I can only offer my humble thanks, my undying, eternal—"

Khorare stood up. Whisky sloshed onto the floor. "Now look here, whoever you are, this is preposterous! What..."

"Sit *down*, Khorare," she said, with commanding firmness. He was gripped by invisible arms, gentle yet immeasurably strong, that pressed him down into his chair. "Time to talk turkey. Don't you remember anything, Khorare? The mouth of that shark that tore you to pieces? And how you woke up in the marshes, miraculously pieced together? All the King's Coelodonts, and all the King's Men?"

Khorare spoke with difficulty. "Yes... I remember."

"Good. That's a start. Well then, what follows, logically, from that wholly remarkable occurrence?" Thoughts swam in Khorare's mind: they bounced and leaped, breaking the hitherto untarnished sheen of his consciousness. Painful thoughts, of his youth, his father, his wife... and thoughts he could have sworn weren't his own, but framed in the minds of his father, and his grandfather, and back, and back, and a long journey, and a cave, and great cities he'd never seen, and hermitages in the desert, and creatures from out of the clouds, and a long, silvery thread stretching, taut, into the sky, and a quayside at night, and a woman walking towards him, a woman who looked remarkably like...

"Well, I'm blowed."

Another pause, longer, while his thoughts settled back into their usual equanimity. While his eyes could re-focus.

"But what have Thinskins got to do with all this?" he asked. "With any of this?" The sun went behind a cloud for a spell, so he could see a shadow of her face, her glinting eyes. She was leaning forwards, now, chin in hands, elbows on knees. She wore faded denim trousers and a huge, shapeless hand-knitted jersey that might once have been a mildly offensive shade of purple. Her feet were bare. He had the impression that she was one of those lucky people who could get away with wearing combinations of clothes that would have looked ridiculous on anyone else. He remembered models like that, in his fashion house. He wondered, idly, what she looked like naked, and wondered—less idly—why such lubricious thoughts had long ceased to cross his mind. It was then, only then, that he appreciated how old he was. Far older, he realized, than people of his race were accustomed to live—and yet he felt in the peak of health. Clearly, he was being kept—maintained—for a purpose. For as long as it took.

"The Thinskins," she said, waving a recalcitrant wisp from her face, "have everything to do with it. You could say that they are what—all this—is all about." She spread her arms wide, to indicate the tastefully spare salon, the furniture, the wooden floor, the panorama beyond.

"You—we—need them for a task, a great task that still lies some way off, in your subjective future. But they might not have existed at all, had you not become, to all intents and purposes, immortal. That's something that distorts the continuum like anything, especially for baryonic matter, just for starters. You wouldn't believe how much thermodynamic finagling I—we—have had to do to achieve that, not to mention the..."

Most of this passed straight over Mr Khorare's head: the one word that remained, reverberating around the inside of his skull, was—

"Immortal? Me?"

"Honestly, Khorare, how much persuasion do you need?"

"Well, I guess... but for how long?"

"How long has this been going on? No time at all. Or about fifty million years, give or take. Does it matter? The fact is, that without the many tiny things you've done in your infinitely extensible life—most so tiny you won't have realized their significance—Thinskins might not have evolved at all. Or turned out differently."

"Things? What kind of things?"

"Random acts of kindness, mostly. It's a brutal world out there. It doesn't need much to make a difference."

Another long pause. Fifty million years? He couldn't conceive of such an interval of time. He certainly couldn't remember having lived through it all. Perhaps that lack of memory was crucial—he wondered if to remember even a tiny fraction of such a long life would weigh one down into a kind of immobility. Such a power of recall—it would, indeed, be disabling. However, even with such desperate rationalizations going on in his head—really, a kind of damage limitation—Mr Khorare had the distinct sensation that he had become disembodied, and was floating among the rafters, looking down at them both. Deep down, he knew—he must have known—that he could not die. The whole shark incident was evidence enough for that. But when evidence is put before your eyes that is at once so stark, and so outrageous, you tend to put it out of your mind, put it beyond thought.

But something else now occurred to him: that perhaps he owed his long life at the court of the Kingdom Under The Mountain to that assumption of immortality, that whatever might befall him in the service of that bloody throne, whatever pains he might be forced to endure, he would always have come back. Looking back at the decisions he made, at their occasional recklessness (cloaked, always, in diplomatic niceties), he wondered whether that security had given him a confidence that he might otherwise have lacked. And that was, he reasoned, a reassuring thought. It was high time, then, to attend to the matter in hand.

"This... task," he began, "this task that the Thinskins have been appointed to perform. What is it?"

"Never mind," she snapped back. "You don't need to know."

"But..." He bit his lip. There was something in her answer, in its harsh alacrity, which troubled him. But if his long life as a courtier had taught him anything, however, it was that there were no such things as problems. There were only... opportunities.

He was in.

"I don't think you know it yourself, do you?" he asked. He smiled, sat back, and took another sip of the whisky, warmed in his hands.

"I do!" she protested, sitting up sharply. "Or... or at least, I *did*. I'm *sure* I did." Her owlish eyes dulled, then, as if she had turned her sight inwards, inquiring of some deep, inner resource. The moment, however, was fleeting. Swiftly, she gathered her composure, so that Mr Khorare was now no longer sure whether he'd really hit on something, or if the concierge was engaging in an elaborate game of double-bluff. "Anyway," she continued, "there's probably a benefit in *not* knowing certain things. Anticipation of some things might throw the game, and that could be disastrous, at this stage. I've this feeling... just a feeling... that when the time comes for this task to be performed, I'll fly right in there, blind, which sounds scary. Heavens, it *is* scary. But there's such a thing as rushing in where angels fear to tread. But in reverse, so to speak. But anyway, where were we?" She looked up at him, staring directly into his eyes, as if all the foregoing had been a soliloquy.

"Whatever the Thinskins are meant to do, *you* have only one more thing you need to achieve. Just one, but it is of crucial importance. You must *not* get it wrong. Now, listen carefully..."

The world swam. Universes collided, coalesced, pulled apart. He awoke on the *chaise-longue* in his own salon. The million tiny lights of a brilliant evening cityscape shone up at him through the picture windows. He must have just dismissed Raull for the night: his peripheral vision caught the sight of a disappearing foot and a closing door. He could remember nothing of how he'd arrived home—nothing at all, after bidding his chauffeur good-night. Perhaps he'd taken that same elevator journey so often, he thought, that it had become no more than a spinal reflex. That, and the well-rehearsed evening pleasantries customary between master and butler, at close of day.

No wonder.

What was more puzzling was that he could not recall the thoughts with which he had evidently been preoccupied, to the exclusion of all else. If he was certain of anything, though, it was of an impending change in the weather. He started to make plans to leave.

He soon became so engrossed in his arrangements that he failed to notice the fading taste of single malt whisky on his tongue.

Chapter 5. Astrometer

Cambridge, England, Earth, Spring, 2073

If the laws of the Universe are kind, they will never be found.
H. P. Lovecraft — *The Shadow Out Of Time*

The Yahoo cruised uncaring above the woes of the world, looking instead upwards, at the stars, as it had done for many years beyond its scheduled expiry date. It mapped, and patiently, it recorded. Doppler wobbles of distant suns, each suggestive of a planetary system. And, by focusing its well-spaced and extraordinarily acute eyes, it took pictures of the planets circling other, closer primaries. Each one vague, suggestive and pixellated, but planets nonetheless: each another, distant Earth.

Twenty years earlier, it had been the capitalized, acromymized YAHOO, the Yerkes Automatic Heliospheric Optical Observatory. Such is the hubris of scientists that this was now generally unremembered, and the YAHOO was now just Yahoo. It — or rather *they*, being a matched pair of identical spacecraft — had been launched on a pair of giant Ariane XV boosters from French Guiana in 2050. Although a combined NASA-European initiative, most of the mission specialists had been based at the Merlin Technologies Astrometry Institute on the old Madingley Road just outside Cambridge, and received feeds directly from the twin spacecraft, placed at widely separated Lagrange points in the Earth's orbit, coordinated to act as one gigantic interferometer, a single telescope mirror more than a hundred million miles across — capable of detecting planets the size of the Earth around nearby stars.

Four years later the Plague struck, sweeping away most of the engineers who had built the spacecraft and the scientists who had hoped to profit from the resulting data. And yet on the mission as a whole, the Plague had had remarkably little effect. Apart from a blip in the late summer of 2054 — the Plague Year itself — data streaming down from the spacecraft were routinely received and managed.

Only the personnel had changed.

Over the years, most of the scientists had been quietly replaced, as they had left or died, by others equally capable, but who were, in addition, members of the Order of Saint Adelard. Long before, the Yahoo had attracted the close personal attention of the man who would one day become Pope Eusebius II. So even had he not wanted to visit Tom in Cambridge from time to time, Domingo would have had ample reason to have called on his faithful band of astrometers.

He was doing so now. Thanks to the ministrations of the Chief Astrometer and his colleagues, Yahoo's image-enhancement software had been upgraded to allow not just the detection, but the rough mapping of Earthlike planets out to several dozens of light years, together with spectroscopic detection of atmospheric constituents, including — potentially — oxygen and water, the signs of life.

This raised a number of theological problems for the Pope, who suddenly realized that his own staff was in real danger of discovering life elsewhere in the Universe. To document the Lord's Creation was in itself a laudable aim. But Domingo had yet to work out a formal response to the discovery of alien beings, and was as yet unready to answer even the most obvious challenges that his flock would face were alien life actually discovered. Consider:

Would Christ have died for the unknown but possibly repellent residents of (say) Epsilon Eridani Three?

Would death and resurrection mean anything at all to any immortal hive-minds that might dwell on Canopus Six?

Would any evanescent plasma beings that just happened to be floating around Zeta Cancri even *require* salvation?

After many hours of prayer, thought and consultation, Domingo came to realize that the situation was just *Undique humanitas* all over again. It had been hard enough to convince *Homo sapiens* that other hominids were as deserving of Divine love as humans themselves. Now the tables had been turned, and, if anything, the hominids tended to be narrower and more prejudiced than humans had been. So how would the world react were he to stretch *Undique humanitas* to encompass any intelligent life in the cosmos?

He realized, tentatively at first and then with greater enthusiasm, that for all its early trials, *Undique humanitas* had actually worked. He had never shied away from a challenge, and he would not do so now: if Giordiano Bruno had been forgiven for positing a plurality of worlds, then there should be no reason why intelligent life on Earth was any more deserving of love than were it to occur anywhere else. Why is the Universe here, he was fond of asking himself, if only so he could laugh at the rejoinder—why, where *else* would it be?

Once he had resolved that particular issue, he became as excited as any schoolboy at the possibility that life might be detected elsewhere in the cosmos, and looked forward keenly to meeting the Chief Astrometer, Father Tikko Bray, who, he had said, had some potentially interesting news. It concerned the discovery and subsequent characterization of a system of planets around Lacaille 9352, a star in the Solar neighborhood so nondescript that earlier searches had largely ignored it.

"Tell me about your new star—your *Nova Stella*," said Domingo on a warm day early in the spring of 2073. Domingo could hardly resist a joke, especially not one in Latin.

"Hitherto there has been little to tell, Your Holiness," said Father Bray, smiling in response. "Lac 9352 is a dim, red-dwarf star, about half the mass of our Sun but very much dimmer, not quite a dozen light years away from us. Despite some early interest in possible planets, it somehow dropped off the menu, as it were, what with one thing and another. I have another interest, of course, your Holiness…"

"Which is…?"

"I'm sorry to say it concerns the Sin of Pride. The star is too dim to be seen without a telescope, for all that it is relatively close in space. It was not known to the ancients, but instead discovered by one of ours. De La Caille was an eighteenth-century astronomer and Man of God, Your Holiness. I number him among my distant relations."

"In that case, Father Bray," said Domingo, "*ego te absolvo*. Please continue."

"Of course, Your Holiness," said Father Bray, evidently somewhat relieved. "The star has two planets much like our own Earth. One orbits at around the same distance from the star as the Earth from our own Sun. But being as the star is so dim, this planet is frozen and lacks any atmosphere we can detect. The other, however… yes, the other, orbits much closer in, rather like Venus or Mercury. It is—well, it's… *interesting*."

"Interesting? In what way?"

"Well, Your Holiness, it's too early to say precisely, with any confidence. For all that the stellar system is relatively near to us in space and the star itself intrinsically dim, the planet is small and rather close to its primary for us to get a pure signal, untainted by stellar influence. Yet we have signs of an atmosphere rich in hydroxyl radicals. This, as Your

Holiness is well aware, means water and oxygen. We think there is appreciable nitrogen, too. We have some rough images—*very* rough, I'm afraid—suggestive of surface features that rotate with the planet. If I may..."

Bray pressed a remote, and a grainy image of a rotating, alien world appeared in the air, just centimeters in front of what had until recently been a portrait of the late, lamented Linus II. In the dimness of the blood-red star, the blues of the ocean were deep purple, almost black: the greens of the continents dark and somber. Scaphes of white ice rode the polar regions.

Even to Domingo's untutored eye, it was clear that these masses moved in tune with the planet's rotation. "So they are not clouds or atmospheric features..." he said.

"That is correct, Your Holiness," said the astrometer. "The planet appears to have separate continents and oceans. But as you can see, in some ways it is not very Earth-like. Lac 9352 isn't our bright, yellow Sun. The planet's year is very short, some fifty-five days, and the proximity to the star means that the planet is almost tidally locked, so that the days are very long indeed. A day on this planet would take more than a month."

"And yet, Father Bray, and yet," said Domingo. "The day is separate from the night, and the water from the land. What price the additional Days of Creation? Or has it stalled? Did this Eden go... ah... *awry*?"

"As to that, Your Holiness, we cannot yet say," Father Bray continued. "However, this is the best candidate for Earthlike life we've yet seen in twenty years of searching. The presence of oxygen speaks greatly towards an atmosphere very far from equilibrium. This suggests the possibility of photosynthetic organisms, perhaps even the presence of some kind of plant life, in which case—if one might speculate—there might be birds of the air, things that crawl, and so forth. But any more than that, well, that would be beyond the evidence."

And so it was that Father Bray and his colleagues continued their work, warmed and encouraged by Papal approval. Further meetings followed, in which the astronomer-priest and his employer reviewed further progress on the Lac 9352 system, such as it was. Images were improved, but not by much; further data came in, adding decimal places to numbers that were already accurate. But there was, as yet, no further news of birds, or fish, or whales, or of things that crawled. Creation had, indeed, stalled.

Domingo was beginning to think he might inquire of Father Bray whether there might have been any progress concerning the several other candidate systems that the Yahoo had been observing. As he himself had reasoned, even in our sleepy corner of the Galaxy, the sky was teeming with stars, brimming over with planets, all furnished by the Creator for our exploration, instruction, and delight.

A few miles away, in the center of the Cambridge, Professor Tom Markham Corstorphine of the Petrine Fellowship was preoccupied with more corporeal concerns.

Morgana had been the first of the Jive Monkeys he'd been able to distinguish from the mocking, menacing collectivity. Perhaps it was because she was slightly taller than the other two, whom she held somewhat in thrall. Other than that, they had all looked identical: very long, shiny black hair, big, accusing green eyes, and skin the colour of polished teak. Telling them apart had been essential if he were to impose any kind of order, to ask each questions individually during supervisions that veered crazily to the edge of anarchy. And they did their best to make that job as difficult as they could.

He did wonder why the three of them bothered to come to supervisions at all—none of them seemed to care a hoot about Sand-Druid religion, or the ceremonies of the Tungusi

Kaptars. Except that he *knew* why. They hung on his every word, like cats ready to pounce on a hapless rodent, for any suggestion of sexual innuendo, at which they would all screech with laughter and, increasingly, direct unwelcome suggestions at him personally.

He squirmed when he recalled the disastrous discussion about circumcision among the Sand Druids. Unlike all other Jews, who circumcised their sons as tiny infants, Tibestians waited until the *Bar Mitzvah* at thirteen — when they did it in public, using a hot blade of polished obsidian, without any kind of anaesthetic. Now, he just knew that any mention of genitalia would have them in fits so loud that the lecturer in the class next door would remonstrate with him afterwards, and even as he opened his mouth to speak he wondered why — *why* — he hadn't skipped that part of his notes, and gone on to something less controversial.

In the event it had been worse. *Much* worse. After the predictable disarray at the mere mention of penises, Morgana had looked him in the eye and asked "Have *you* been circumcised, Professor?" And before he had managed to collect himself sufficiently to respond, the others had joined in: can we look? Oh, *please*. We must take a *look*... it's *research*... and before he could do anything, they had pinned him to the desk and had started to pull off his clothes... I bet he's got a *big* one... *oooh*, he *has*... we'd like to get our teeth into *that*... and despite his efforts to fight them off... they hard started to take off their clothes, too... he was starting to panic, to feel sick... and, despite himself, to become *aroused*... redoubling their interest... so that when he screamed for help, the lecturer from next door arrived with several worried-looking students to witness what looked like a gang-rape in progress, although it was not, by then, clear who was raping whom, or if it wasn't just an orgy.

After that Tom flatly refused to teach any Jive Monkey, threatening their colleges with criminal proceedings if they insisted. The colleges responded with counter-charges of racism and breaches of hominid cultural rights, implying that Tom had put them up to it, inflaming them with talk of genital mutilation, *leading them on*.

It was then that the Abbot of the Petrine Fellowship had called him in and very gently suggested that Tom do his best to get to the end of the academic year and then take some time out, a sabbatical. The only reason that he had not lost his fellowship, the Abbot implied, was that Tom had friends in very high places. His parents. And places higher even than that. And, for the moment, he'd have to keep teaching the Jive Monkeys.

That evening, after he had dined alone and disconsolately in Hall and had returned to his cell, he heard a soft knock at his door. It was Morgana.

"Go to hell," he said.

"Look, Professor Corstorphine—Tom—we're… I'm… well, we heard what happened, and…" He was amazed she'd managed to smuggle her way into the college past the Porter's Lodge.

"You heard me," said Tom. "Leave me alone."

"… well, we're sorry," she persisted, ignoring him. "We didn't mean… I want to explain…"

"I'm not hearing any more," he said, and shut the door in her face. But her expression, just a split second before the door closed—somehow sorrowful, contrite, but with a barely controlled inner indignation—gave him pause. And it was more than that. It was her aura. He realized that it pulsed in dark colours indescribable to human vision. And that no aura had blazed brighter than a candle flame for him since Shoshana had died. Without wondering to ask what this might mean, he knew he just had to see it again, to know more. He pulled the door ajar, and within an instant she was inside, and in his arms.

Morgana was a mote at the centre of a great ultraviolet mandala, and it was then he noticed for the first time in his life that he, too, had an aura that matched hers, interlacing, interacting: it was the most glorious sensation imaginable. This must be how Shoshana had felt when he waved his hands through her body field, too... but it was too late now. Too late to turn back, even if he could. For now there was more than radiance: there was communication. He felt that someone had started talking to him in a language that he hadn't heard before, but which he felt he had understood all his life.

Her lips on his were like red hot coals, her tongue a solar flare inside his ready mouth. Each frenziedly unbuttoned the shirt of the other, and it was then that he became conscious of her brazen non-humanity.

And it was beautiful.

Beneath her perfect, brown breasts, each finished with a prominent, ebony nipple, there was another smaller, breast, with its own nipple, and beneath that, a still smaller breast... she had ten in all, paired, five each in two tracks that ran down her front, each path curving outwards towards her hips. It was weird, he knew. But he had never seen anything so exotic, so... lovely. Her green eyes flashed at his, defiant, and he read each nuance of her slit-like pupils as if it were speech.

Now do you see? That's why we made such fun of you. Because you are one of *us*, and you refused to admit it.

Worse, refused to admit your *manhood*.

If you'd only known, you'd have shown us and serviced us all—each one of us in her turn, in front of the others, according to her rank—*before* talking to us. It would only have been polite, to grown women, such as ourselves. *That's* how we acknowledge dominance. *Then* we would have listened to you. We would have been quiet as lambs. But instead you ignored us.

Insulted us.

But I for one, as the senior female, am prepared to forgive, on behalf of us all. If, that is, you observe the *Proper Forms*. And with that she raised the hem of her long skirt.

She wore no underwear. Between her legs, up as far as her navel, and almost from hip to hip, she was extravagantly, outrageously furred. Not the sparse springiness of pubic hair, but *fur*, rich and luxuriant. He hesitated, so she kissed him again, and with one hand unbuckled his belt and reached into his trousers. He had already hardened to beyond the point of pain. She weighed his balls in her hand as dispassionately as if she were judging fruit in a produce show, before running her fingertips along the underside of his shaft and squeezing the end, sharply. The pain was agonizing and wonderful.

"Tom—*please*..." she said, as if any acquiescent girl, but her eyes said something different, imperative: now, you *know* what you must do, to command my respect, and that of my subordinates.

With that she turned away from him and knelt on Tom's narrow bed, flipping her skirt up across her back and pointing her exposed backside at him, in accusation, in challenge. Her hair fell forward around her shoulders, exposing a single raised ridge of sharp, black hairs, running down from the nape of her neck to the small of her back, like the clipped mane of a pony. Even from this angle, he could see the tufts of fur between her legs, and that she was hugely engorged, to an extent far greater than would have been possible for any human female. Her aura now enveloped her like two bright violet wings: he saw that it radiated from within her body, and that her swollen vulva was its bright centre, its conduit, gushing torrents of white-hot radiation towards him. She was like a flower, marked with lines and arrows that only bees can see, arrows pointing to the hidden treasure of nectar.

He climbed onto the bed behind her to do her bidding, and drove into her. He felt himself swell even more to fill her, and her tissues responded, ring-like waves of hot, liquid pressure squeezing him and letting him go, compressing and releasing, and always drawing him inwards. The more he thrust, the more their twin auras danced in the air as one pulsating thing, until he became one tiny point inside her ready to burst. But he found he could not. He became bigger and fuller, tighter and more painful and pulled ever deeper inside her, until he thought he'd pass out, when her aura said

You May

and he exploded in an actinic fury of golden-tinged purple and then velvety blackness.

He had no idea at all whether she too had climaxed. For without a word she rose, dressed herself and left without looking at him, her aura following her like a deep, inky cloak. As the door closed behind her it said

I am content.

Honor has been satisfied.

For the remainder of the academic year, the three Jive Monkeys were as demurely attentive and studious as he could have wished.

That evening, however, Morgana left him eviscerated. For as much as he glowed with sexual satisfaction that crowned anything he had ever experienced, he felt he'd been emptied, *used*. Not only had he betrayed his vows, he'd betrayed the memory of his love for Shoshana, who had loved him too — unlike this creature, whose attentions were solely concerned with the niceties of the etiquette of ritual. Not love, or even lust—but politics.

When, some hours later after he'd bathed and dried and, still unsatisfied, bathed again; when the wash of hormones inside him had passed, he brought back the language of her eyes and her aura, when it had said that he was one of *them*; that he could not deny his origins. His soul rebelled: he was a human being, no more, no less, and not a hominid.

But was he? He knew that he was not Jack and Jadis' biological son, that he had been adopted. He had never sought to investigate his origins—and why should he? The farmhouse had been his world, self-sufficient and bounded by a love he now realized he'd taken for granted. Yet Morgana's argument had still made sense. *Visceral* sense. The instant bond he'd felt; that despite its utterly alien character he had still grasped each precise tic of her body language; and that their auras had actively *interacted*. Even more, the act had seemed so natural, so easy, despite the strangeness of her anatomy. There had been no thought that he might have been too big for her, as there had sometimes been with Shoshana, and all his girlfriends before that. On the contrary, he fitted inside Morgana like a key in a lock.

He remembered that he, too, had a stiff ridge of black hair running down the back of his neck. He recalled, with a pain that now brought ears to his eyes, how Shoshana had loved to run her fingers along it, delighting how each stiff tuft of hair bent under her touch and immediately sprang back.

Shoshana...

No, another part of him protested, more loudly as it knew it was weakening, he could not be one of these *things*, these... *Jive Monkeys*. The thought was horrifying. *Bien sûr*, it's a shock, the rest of him reasoned. But you *liked* it, didn't you? He realized that he had.

To the outside world, however, he would continue to paint himself, resolutely, as a human being, in the hope that he would, one day, convince his soul. After all, there were important parts of him, held with iron affection, that he would not relinquish. A human being he would remain.

The morning after Morgana's cathartic visit, Tom was roused from a miasmic dream in which Shoshana had stood before him like a painted doll in some kind of *dirndl*, and he was shooting at her with a small-caliber pistol. The bullets disappeared into her long skirts and she was yelling at him angrily. "Get yourself an eyeful, mister," she screamed: "where you gonna find knockers like these, eh? *Where*?" squeezing her magnificent, snowy-white breasts over the top of her bodice and thrusting them at him, flaunting them... and not just one pair, but five. Then the Shoshana-*thing* had turned round, lifted her petticoats and thrust purple, monstrously protruberant genitalia at him.

Surfacing to the sound of rain pummeling his small window-pane, Tom knew this could not have been. He had known her every silken surface. What if she'd been tricked out, like Morgana had been, with some kind of baboon's arse? No way — that was a machine optimized for one thing: routine, peremptory, *contractual* copulation, and that was all. No scope there for intimacy, for love. The thought of it revolted him.

A rough shake to his shoulder. The college servant, a Pendek in the robe and cowl of the novitiate who, while utterly silent, was clearly determined that Tom should wake up, and once he'd pressed the letter into Tom's hand and indicated a cup of herbal tea on Tom's nightstand, he left — walking backwards to the door, crossing himself as he did so.

Tom sat up abruptly in bed. He felt terrible. His limbs were sluggish, obeying only with sullen reluctance his commands to stir themselves, as if they were schoolchildren and it was Monday morning. His throat was dry, and his head pounded to what felt like the opening ceremony of the international festival of gong-makers. His eyes focused groggily on the envelope, which bore only his address. The letter inside was from Domingo, in his neat, precise hand and as full of mysteries as ever, but with an uncharacteristic note of urgency that brought Tom instantly to his senses.

My Dear Tom,

he read:

It is time that we talked about the Sigil. We have put it off for too long, I fear. Matters have lately progressed in an exciting but possibly unwelcome direction and we are in danger of being overtaken by events. I think it of overriding importance that you should be fully informed of these new developments. Please come the instant you receive this letter to the Astrometry Institute. A hansom will be waiting for you at the Porter's Lodge. I shall greet you on your arrival. In haste—

The previous evening at around midnight, about two hours after Morgana had left Tom in a state of anguished and fretful disarray, the Chief Astrometer, Father Tikko Bray received some disturbing news of his own. That Lac 9352, the small, distant object on which weeks of attention had been lovingly lavished, had literally winked out of existence.

Within twenty-five seconds of receiving the paged message, Father Bray had dressed, in the total darkness of his cell in the Institute compound on the Madingley Road. Muttering snatches of Vespers as he ran across the yard to Mission Control, he found that two colleagues had already arrived, and were already busy with the monitoring equipment.

"We first noticed an unusual darkening on the planet's face," said Father Frederick, the older of the two, a tall, grizzled Almai astrometer who had taken Orders late in life.

"But it wasn't our instruments," added Father Jonas — a Sulawesian, barely half the height of his colleague, very thin, red-eyed and covered in jet-black fur — "we were calibrating them against a target star the whole time — the darkening was really happening, as we were watching, and..."

"And yet the darkening wasn't even, the same all over," Frederick's gruff voice interrupted, "there were huge variations on the planet..."

"... like something was casting shadows on it..." said Jonas in counterpoint, counter-tenor.

Father Bray's eyes darted from Frederick to Jonas and back again. "Hold it!" he demanded. "Not so fast! Whatever it was, it's nothing to do with the planet. These shadows, or whatever, came from the star. We already know the star is variable..."

"Yes, Father," interrupted Jonas. "But not all *that* variable. And certainly not so variable that it vanishes altogether. We got that, too. Here, look at these pictures from the wide-field camera."

A wide monitor, integrating images from Yahoo to present a picture of what the Lac 9352 system would look like from a few light-minutes away. Or, rather, two pictures. Yesterday's had the star, a small and sullen disk, the planets as smaller, star-like points. Today's had nothing — nothing at all, apart from the background of stars. If the planets were still there, they could not be seen; but that the star itself had disappeared was unarguable. Bray muttered a profanity too low for the others to hear.

"There's more?" he asked.

"Yes," growled Father Frederick. When we saw that, we looked back at the logged recordings and pinpointed precisely when the star vanished. Then we studied them in closer detail and strung them together to make a kind of time-lapse movie. We think it's extraordinary. We don't know what to make of it at all. That's when we summoned you, Father."

"Thank you," said Father Bray. "You may play the film now."

When it ended, Father Bray sank into his padded Mission Control chair, dark eyes staring from a bloodless face.

"I think I should call His Holiness," he said, before rising hurriedly to find a toilet cubicle, wherein he was violently sick.

Father Bray had composed himself early the next day, when His Holiness arrived, dripping wet from the Spring shower now sheeting down outside, and accompanied by a man who seemed his opposite in every way. Where the Pope was enormous, Professor Tom Corstorphine was compact; where His Holiness was expansive, his companion was quiet. He looked ill, actually, and Father Bray wondered why he was here at all.

"Professor Corstorphine is a good friend of mine," the Pope explained, answering the unasked question. "He might also have an interest in what you are about to reveal, I think."

Father Bray beckoned to Father Jonas, whose lithe, black fingers waved at a holographic panel against one wall of the control room. The room lights and the other monitors dimmed in response, giving the watchers the impression that they were floating in space, looking down on the great red disk of Lac 9352. Although a midget compared with the Sun, it was still a star, and all stars are mighty indeed when seen at close quarters. At first it seemed much as it always did, like a roiling mass of angry tomato soup, with the occa-

sional cluster of dark spots and a few flares and prominences.

"We're seeing it in enhanced visual, with a little of the
UV fed into the blue end," noted Father Jonas. "Now, watch
closely." A time code and other data flashed by in the bottom right-hand corner of the image. What they were about
to see would take less than ninety seconds to elapse.

The first sign of anything odd was an added dullness to
the stellar North Pole (to the bottom of the picture) that
slowly built up in intensity and definition, until it looked as
if the whole north-central sector of the star was in deep
shadow. Another, similar shadowing soon followed on the
eastern limb (to the left of the picture), joining and fusing
with the northern shadowing until it looked as if the entire
bottom-left-hand-quadrant of the star had been occulted, or
eclipsed. Except that the eclipse only deepened, and was
joined by several other spots of darkness on the remaining,
unshadowed parts of the star's face.

After a minute the star was completely black. It evidently
still existed, from a few remaining, fitful flares, and the fact
that it masked any stars behind it. But then it appeared to
break up, its black remains fragmenting against the still
darker blackness of space, until — after the full ninety seconds — absolutely nothing was left. Lac 9352 had ceased to
exist.

-=0=-

The Trans-Europe Express burst from the Sangatte end of
the tunnel, dragging streamers of acrid, ashy smoke which it
would not shed completely for several miles. In a private
compartment near the front of the train ("being the Pope has
its privileges,"), Domingo pulled open a vent. Curling scuts
of soot flew in, soon replaced by fresh air.

"Steam trains in the Channel Tunnel—what mad pursuit, eh Tom?" Domingo laughed recklessly, offering the basket of croissants to Tom, who refused. "They used to be powered on gasoline. Or was it electricity? But *steam*! It has taken the Christophorines fifteen years to upgrade the ventilation, and *still* it's like pea soup in there. What struggle to escape! What pipes and… er… *tunnels*?"

Tom permitted himself a half-smile and poured coffee for both of them. Since leaving Cambridge they had talked relatively little, and nothing at all of the monstrous revelations at the Astrometry Institute. That a star—a whole star—could disappear before their very eyes, literally dismembered, by—*what*? The whole thing was just too stupefying to contemplate.

And then something stirred in Tom's mind—something that he had forgotten for twenty years. Not surprisingly, as it had been blotted out by the subsequent trauma in which he and Shoshana had narrowly escaped being atomized in the War of the Last Days. A tall, thin, freckled seminary student called Fearon Brimstone, who'd mentioned something about disappearing stars, and the Astrometry Institute, and his theory that there was something Out There ready to 'bite us on the bum'. Haltingly, he explained all this to Domingo.

"So whatever it is," Tom concluded, "this phenomenon has been known about for some time. Why did nobody hear about it?"

"I know the work to which you refer," replied Domingo. "And there has been much of a similar nature published before and since. The first report of a disappearing star— disappearing, that is, in unexplained circumstances, and leaving no trace—was in 2031, I think."

"But…"

"But why has nobody taken any notice?" said Domingo. Tom nodded. "Because," Domingo continued, "there was no way to explain it, no mechanism. And phenomena without mechanisms tend to just lie in the literature as curiosities until someone can come along and tie things together."

"What we saw — what we have just seen" said Tom, hesitantly, "I understand that this is the first close-up, real-time demonstration of this thing — this *phenomenon* — in action?"

Domingo nodded and sipped his coffee, not taking his eyes off Tom. "I believe, Tom, that the star was destroyed by the coordinated action of alien beings. I can think of no other, natural explanation, and neither can the Chief Astrometer."

"So it should get noticed *now*, shouldn't it?"

"I very much doubt it," said Domingo, "because, now we know what's happened to that star, how do we tell anyone? *Should* we tell anyone? And if we did, what then? We should have replaced complete ignorance with something that strains credulity to the limit. If given the choice between ignorance and he whole, pitiless truth, most people go for ignorance."

After that they were silent for a long time, each lost in his own thoughts.

Domingo felt himself chastened. Be careful what you wish for, his thoughts declaimed. He had earnestly hoped that, one day, alien life would be discovered that he might welcome into the Fellowship of Christ. But that such beings could exist whose purpose was to consume stars — well, that would require some modest reflection.

But then, he reasoned, he'd made a fundamental error, of assuming that such alien life that one could detect across the gulf of space must, by virtue of that detection, be intelligent. These star-swarming behemoths had not intellects vast, cool and unsympathetic, because they had not intellect to begin with. They were no more rapacious predators than the ichneumon wasp whose young devour the living meat of their hapless caterpillar hosts from inside.

Tom's mind registered little but shattered amazement. The discovery of vast entities that swallowed stars formed a resonant, gothic backdrop for the newly ignited personal battle over his own nature: a battle fought in sodden marshes of metallic despair that left him cold, cheerless and utterly exhausted.

The Trans-Europe Express thundered across the flatlands of Normandy, the bright Sun climbing above a bank of woolly grey clouds. Tom gazed at it, flying in the eastern sky, as they passed Chartres. He was grateful that it was still there, and wondered if great black shapes might, one day, be converging on it from out of the depths of space. His blood turned to ice: he turned to Domingo, and noticed for the first time how old his mentor looked, how lined his face, and wondered if he, too, felt the same horror.

Suddenly Domingo spoke, breaking Tom's reverie: "You know, Tom," he said, "as I believe I mentioned, we really should have another look at the Sigil."

"I haven't seen it since before the Plague struck," said Tom. "I'd be hard put to it to recall it in detail. So that I could draw it, for example."

"The same goes for me, Tom. And that's why we must see it anew. Too much has happened, in both our lives, and we need our memories... ah... *refreshed*."

Domingo explained that lately he'd been obsessed with the Sigil's three circles, and wondering if they had anything to do with the final fate of the Plague victims.

"It seemed too great a coincidence," he explained, "that the circles in the Sigil are the circles of end-stage Postembryonic Oolithic Petrosis. I started wondering whether the Sigil was some kind of document of this disease striking in early times, or maybe a prophecy."

"But what about the crescents, and the radiating lines?" said Tom.

"I know, Tom, it's futile, but I can't help thinking about it. Mind going round and round in circles, and circles can never be squared. It could simply be... well..."

"Yes, Domingo?"

"You never had the misfortune of watching any human soul succumbing to the Plague, did you, Tom? Even when you — we — were in Israel?"

"No, I did not."

"Well, I'm afraid to say I did. Perhaps I am suffering from nothing more than my own reaction to seeing my superior, a human being of great gentleness and humility, being mercilessly crushed, and crushed again, into that small compass. A circular compass, in what must have been unspeakable agony and mortal terror. So, you see, I tend to imbue circles with a great deal of... ah... significance."

But Tom recalled, as if it had happened to somebody else in a long-vanished age, of a discussion around the farmhouse table. It must have been in '54, just before the Plague, because he remembered Shoshana's pale face and wide purple eyes when she said of the Sigil's makers that:

"They wanted to ward them off, at all costs... to find a way of chasing the dragons away..."

"Tom?"

"It was something she said. That Shoshana said," said Tom, realizing that he'd voiced his thoughts aloud. "We were all at the farmhouse, just before the Plague. We were talking about the Sigil..."

"...and the Chinese legend that eclipses are caused by dragons," Domingo continued, "and how Shoshana said that the Sigil could be an expression of that same impulse. To chase the dragons away."

Domingo looked across at Tom, who, with the mention of her name, felt crushed, the betrayer, still alive, undeservedly, eking out a kind of un-life for so long as he could retain the memory of her. Tom saw that there was a moisture in the old man's eyes, as if he, too, felt some complicity in Shoshana's passing. Tom knew it was deeply uncharitable, but he didn't want Domingo to get away with it, with even a tenth of the anguish that he felt, all day, every day—even now.

"In which case," said Tom, his voice flat to the point of sarcasm, "Shoshana was closer than any of us knew. And that would be *some* small crumb to show that she had not died *utterly* in vain. And again, *in which case*," his eyes flashed at Domingo in reproach that was close to rage, "What would have the Plague to do with it—with any of it?"

"Why—nothing of course!" replied Domingo, as if he'd been slapped. But he then hesitated, as if he had reached a conclusion in undue haste. "But, my dear Tom, please forgive me."

"I know, Domingo. I should apologise." Even so, Tom was determined to allow Domingo no quarter. He would rather focus his pain on somebody else than open up, even to Domingo, because he was convinced that the latter course would expose his being to an overwhelming tide of guilt and shame that would then destroy him.

He was *human*. But if he were human, how had he killed her?

But if he *weren't* human, how could he have loved her?

But, on the other hand, if he *were* human, how could he have found sex with that alien *thing* so horribly magnetic? His mind spun crazily in futile circles of its own.

Domingo looked closely at Tom. "My old friend," he said, "I believe that each of us in his own way, has reached an impasse."

Tom looked dejectedly up at Domingo from the banquette opposite, his eyes vacant. Domingo parted his arms fractionally and without further encouragement, Tom crossed the compartment and sat next to him, burying his form in the older man's enveloping scarlet cloak.

Domingo was cast back to the time when he bore Tom proudly to the arms of his adopted mother. Why? Was his impulse pure? Was it to ease Jadis' burden of childlessness or, more to gain her approval, to bask in her sunshine? If the latter, it would have been a grievous error. Domingo wished more than ever that Tom would take him into his confidence. But perhaps Tom had not experienced enough for him to realize that acceptance is the wisest course. Not like Shoshana, who died untimely and cruelly, but at peace.

Part of the problem—not that it *was* a problem—was that unlike Shoshana, Tom had grown up in an atmosphere of unconditional love, which exacted no tribute. In such a situation he might have felt that no spiritual journey was required of him, because he could live his entire life in Eden. Pity, thought Domingo, that happy lot falls only to creatures without souls, for which the notion of love is meaningless, and for which acceptance requires no struggle.

"But whether the Sigil has anything to do with the Plague or not," Domingo said, more to himself, for Tom had fallen asleep in his lap: "we must go back to the farmhouse and see it again."

For the farmhouse, he continued to himself, is not just a sanctuary for both of us, but contains two of the most nimble minds I have had the fortune to encounter in my long life. Minds that once achieved fame on the remarkable intuition of one, and the penetrating insight of the other.

Like their discovery, Domingo thought, these two minds have been idle for far too long. *That* is the reason why we must go home: to crack the code. For we may not have very much time.

He looked up at the Sun and realized that a dozen light-years is but a mote in the eye of the Creator. No, not very much time at all.

Chapter 6. Hunter

Western Desert, Earth, *c.* 45,000 years ago

He took his vorpal sword in hand
Long time the manxome foe he sought
Lewis Carroll — *Jabberwocky*

Something beyond his senses alerted him to the plain fact that he was not alone.

He kicked out the small fire in the dell beneath the roots of the thorn tree where he'd made his den. He flattened himself on its slope, peering over the edge. He tried not to think of another time — another life, far away — when he'd been in such a position. Now was not the time to count the Father-the-Suns, the Mother-the-Moons, all that had circled since then.

Neither was it the time to count all the things he'd learned in the meantime. How to hunt. How to kill. Beasts, from mice and frogs, to that single coelodont that had fed, housed and clothed him for months. And men too, men much bigger than he was. Stoners. Others. None of his own kind. Well, not unless he was really desperate. People whose brains he'd guzzled, still warm, straight from their skulls.

There was a spike standing proud on the western horizon, small but hard against the setting sun. He squinted into the reddish haze. It was no more than a speck, but it was growing, even as he watched. It was coming his way. There was nowhere to hide, except in the dell itself. His thorn tree was the only one for at least half a day's walk around — and the water-skins hanging from the branches gave the game away. He was suckered. He was caught.

Oh no, he wasn't. The more he watched, the more he was convinced that the speck was alone, not some Stoner scout, not the advance guard of an army he'd soon see stretched from one horizon to the other. He'd been in situations like that, too, many times, and he'd escaped to tell the tale, if only to himself. A single wanderer, however, would be an easy target. Easy meat. And easy other things, too—marrow, bones, teeth, scraps of clothes, pottery, flakes of quartzite—anything and everything, to keep himself a step ahead of death. Half a step, really. That was all he needed. Half a step. The rock-hyrax he'd caught that morning would help. Maybe a whole step, then. Brained with a lucky stone. He hadn't eaten as much for weeks. He slavered at the very thought of eating it later, after dark. Roasted hyrax, turned on a spit.

He loosened the gazelle-horn throwing-knives in his belt. He hoped it wouldn't have to come to that. Still with half an eye on the horizon, he strung his wooden bow with Stoner hair, winding the strands tight. He probed the ground around him for arrows, each with a sharp of Stoner bone for a point. He could only find three, and two had missing fletchings. He'd long since run out of bitumen to fix things, and the last asphalt seep he'd raided was long away.

Oh, well, they'd have to do.

The speck had grown noticeably larger in the time he'd taken to grab his gear. It was still small, but it now had the shape of a man. But the more he watched, the harder it was to see it. One minute it had grown enormously, so that he recoiled, almost dropping his bow and nocked arrow: the next, it had receded almost to the vanishing point. He forced his eyes closed, squeezing out patterns behind his eyelids— opened, and refocused. The speck jounced around, now up, now down, now bigger, now smaller, now gone altogether— now reappearing in a different place.

A mirage. He'd seen plenty of those. The problem was that they made it even harder than usual to shoot straight. And this was the liveliest mirage he'd ever seen. A mirage that played games with the mind as well as the eyes.

"Put the bow down, boy," said the mirage.

The voice was so close that he dropped the bow and arrow with the shock of it. In a reflexive flash he pulled out a horn dagger, turned towards the noise, and bent his knees to spring. He sprang. He hit the ground with a crunch. He tasted blood in his mouth.

"That's the ticket," said the voice, now from above. The voice was deep, but dry, like the boom of the wind ricocheting through the ruins of monuments. A shadow stood over him, blotting out the sunset. "Now, might I trouble you — if you're not too busy, that is — to get an old man a drink of water?" The voice extended a hand. The hand was long and pale, but old and leathery. He grabbed the hand, which pulled him, straight off the ground, and on to his feet. The voice was commanding: the hand, amazingly strong.

Father-the-Sun fell like a stone into the west. He saw nothing more of the visitor than a silhouette.

"No matter," said the deep, dry voice. "You're somewhat surprised, I see." The shadow raised a hand. He saw a deep sleeve fall, exposing a thin, bony arm. "I can get it myself."

The young hunter knew no more.

He woke from a fevered dream in which he was underwater. A girl stood above the surface, wordlessly shrieking, but he could hear nothing. He knew that the girl was older than him. His sister. If only he could remember her name.

He was on the ground, in the dell beneath his thorn tree. His small fire in the roots had been rekindled: in the deep night, it was the only spark of light. The rich smell of roasting hyrax filled the small space. A figure, robed, hooded, crouched over the fire, turning the spit. He sat up.

"Who…?" he asked.

"*Me*?" said the voice. "If only all questions were that easy. My name is M!shay. Some people call me M!shay Ha'Shala/Mal. But plain old M!shay will do." The young hunter had never heard such sounds as these. There were real names here, he was sure, but the sounds within them — clicks, grunts, growls — were like dogs at bay.

"Shay. Shala-mal," he tried.

"Well, it's a start. 'Shay' will do, if that's all you can manage. Here, have some soup." Shay extended a bony hand, bearing a skull bowl filled with a dark liquid. The young hunter could smell the roots he'd collected, mixed with blood and hyrax liver. He gulped at it, spluttering at the heat. No matter — he was starving.

"The real question — the *big* question — the Question of the Age, if you don't mind my saying, is not my name, but yours."

"My… name?" He had not been called by his name since… since… since, well, since his life had ended and his life had begun. In all the Fathers-of-Suns and Mothers-of-Moons since, he had been too busy just surviving, alone in the desert, to ponder matters as inconsequential as his name. And besides, he had not spoken more than two words together, to anyone, for longer than he cared to remember.

"Well, let's try to guess," said Shay, squatting back on his heels. "You have a deep brown birthmark around your left eye. So, according to the traditional nomenclature of your tribe, you might be called… oooh, *I* don't know… something like 'Pop-Eye'? Or maybe 'Eye-Patch'? Perhaps? Mmm? You might help me out here." He paused. "Look, don't all rush at once," he prompted. "I'll be here all week."

Eye-Patch.

Memories, stirring. Honey-sweet scent of a mother's flesh. First steps. The smell of meat drying in the sun.

Hands, hands to put him down, hands to raise him up.

Tall, tall stalks of grain, of reeds, taller than he was.

Threshing, threshing grain, motes in sunlight, women standing in a circle, pounding, singing, always singing.

"No?" said Shay. "Well, you seem to be missing most of the fifth digit on your left hand. Unfortunate. An accident, maybe, in youth? Perhaps a narrow escape from a wild animal? An event worthy of commemoration, surely?"

"Name... my name?" The young hunter raised his left hand before his face, silhouetted it against the bright fire. He saw that his little finger was just a stub. He saw it as if for the first time.

A snarl of teeth across his vision.

Too fast, too fast.

Pain.

The voice, from the shadows to his right, only its long, pale hands visible, as they turned the spit, the voice said:

"I have looked long and hard for you, *Jjadhazev*. Dogfinger."

"Dogfinger..."

A gully between two fields.

Bright sun.

A girl, tall, squinting against the horizon.

She had one green eye, and one brown.

And all the Stoners he'd killed, whose blood he'd drunk, in all the Mothers-of-Moons since, were all in her long-forgotten name.

Green-Eye.

Revenge.

Dogfinger sat up, and looked at his mysterious companion. "How did you know? How? *Why*?"

"Let us say I've had... *help*."

"Help? Who? Mister Shay, there has only ever been me."

"Yes, Dogfinger. Yes—but not quite. There has always been you, alone. And you have done well. See—you were once a boy, but now look at you! You are a man. But it's not just you, you know. She watches over us. Over us all. *HaShekhna*."

"You are a riddler," said Dogfinger. "Nothing but a riddler, a riddler and a schemer. I should kill you now, old man, as I have killed all the others. I'd have the hyrax all to myself, and add your eyeballs, too."

"Oh, would you? Really?" said Shay. He put up one finger, a single digit into the air, and Dogfinger felt his arms, legs and tongue go numb. "I shouldn't advise it. And before you ask me where I get such power...? Oh, I see, you are struck dumb. So I can say my piece without interruption, can I? Good. By *Hashekhna*, I have been dying to get this off my chest for years."

And so Shay told his story, about being a wandering conjuror of his tribe, a beggar, a thief, the lowest of the low, kicked along the street. "*Shala/Mal*, in the language of my tribe, it means a beggar," he said. "But to me it means more. Ever since, when I was thrown off the walls of the City on the Heights for buggering a goat, and enjoying it, though not half so well as the goat, I fancy; and thinking that the best thing I could do was die, she was there. *HaShekhna*, that is. Not the goat. That was a 'he'. *HaShekhna* stood over me, pulled me up, scolded me. She became a mother to me, a sister, a lover. She took me to places. Oh, such places..."

Dogfinger recovered his voice. "She? Places? Talk, riddler."

"And there was me, thinking *I* had the speaking part," Shay sighed, turning the spit once more.

"I'm sorry, Mister Shay."

"Thank you. And 'Shay' is quite sufficient, without any spurious adornment. I can remember what she said to me.

'Get up, you silly man.' That's what she said. And then, she said, 'I've probably fucked it up, like I always do, but I cannot always be everywhere at once.' And then, *Jjadhazev* — ah, and *then*. She entered my very *soul*. She spoke to me from *inside my head*. She told me that I had to find you — *you* — and take you to safety. 'I hope I'm not too late,' was all she said.

"And then she went, just like that — *pouf*! The gap in my soul seemed immense, and I fell onto the ground again. I knew she was *HaShekhna*, the ancient Goddess of my tribe. But when again I woke, I had such powers, such *powers*. No-one will call me *Shala/Mal* again with such… scorn."

"Mister… er… *Shay*… can I ask a question, now?"

"Of course. That's why I'm here. *Hashekhna*, she said — guide this young man. Be his mentor. Be as a father to him. So, please, ask away. Whatever you want."

"What's 'buggering' mean?"

Shay was silent for a spell. "I can see you have still a lot to learn, *Jjadhazev*" he said. Then he turned his finger in the air, just like *that*.

Dogfinger saw a flash of infinite space.

And then it was morning.

The early chill, just before the dawn. Dogfinger was wet through with the desert dew. Father-the-Sun had yet to crest the eastern horizon. Several bright stars still shone in the blueness of the western vault. Dogfinger panicked. For a moment he forgot where he was. Then he cursed — he'd forgotten to spread skins out, pieces of pottery, anything — to catch the dewfall.

"Don't worry, *Jjadhazev*," came the voice. "I've done it already. Come, drink, enjoy — later, we'll talk."

Dogfinger looked up. And then, for the first time, he saw the face of his strange new companion. The face, framed by a dirty ash-gray hood, of M!Shay Ha'Shala/Mal, unfrocked elder of the Annakhnu of the City on the Heights. It was the strangest face that Dogfinger had ever seen. The face was tall, but narrow, with a lipless mouth surmounted by a tall, narrow nose. The face was parchment-white, ivory-white, as white as his own face was brown as the earth. The face was framed by straggly hair the exact color of ostrich egg-yolk. But strangest of all were the eyes. Large, shaped like almonds, with round irises as egg-yolk yellow as his hair. The face of a ghost. Dogfinger shrank back. As he watched it, the eyes stared back at him, unblinking—all, that is, for the wipe of nictitating membranes that rolled across them, shrowding them for a long, glutinous moment in a chalky caul, before retreating, exposing the eyes once again to full and disconcerting acuity.

"Here, take the cup," Shay said. Dogfinger, too stunned to argue, took the skull-cup from Shay's white hand, and took a draught of cool hyrax stew. "It's time we were on our way."

Dogfinger struggled to his feet. He could feel a light wind blowing over the lip of the dell. It dried the moisture on his body, cooling him.

"Where are we going?" Dogfinger asked.

Shay slung Dogfinger's water skin over his shoulder and walked with deliberation over the lip of the dell and headed towards the west.

"You'll see when we get there," he said.

The journey took only two days, but to Dogfinger it seemed like years. Dogfinger had walked far and wide in the seven years of his exile, but never in this particular direction—straight across the furnace-heart of the Erg. He toiled, struggling to follow Shay up the steep, shifting slopes of the dunes, trying not to topple and slide down the far sides of the great waves of sand.

Dogfinger rarely wore any more clothes than his moccasins and a quiver of arrows, but he was grateful for the broad leather hat that Shay had made him wear against a molten sun, and the rough cloth bandanna across his face that deflected most of the flying shrapnel of sand from his eyes. He was thankful, too, for his own moccasins: the heat of the sand burned into his feet, but the soft leather on his soles made all the difference between pigeon-stepping across the sand and not going anywhere at all. But the sand scored at his calves as he walked; it burned his ankles as his feet sunk in; the sun scorched his shoulders and his back. The muscles in his calves ached and stung as he slid down the farther sides of dunes. His tongue seemed to swell to twice its usual size inside a mouth that seemed to have been coated in red-hot gravel.

Shay was quite unperturbed by any of this. He drew his dirty-gray robe about him and stepped at the same, unvarying pace, loping up hill and down without distinction. It was only at the end of the first day that Dogfinger noticed that Shay's feet were bare. Bare, gnarled as white old roots, disfigured with ancient scars, but completely free of any recent cuts or blisters.

At the end of the first day, they huddled together in a foxhole in a country as bleak and barren as anywhere Dogfinger had ever been. It looked like another world — only the familiar stars barrelling above told him that they were still under the same celestial vault he had known all his life. Only after Shay had squatted on the ground, kindling a small fire with some resinous twigs he'd brought with them; taking out the water-skin and handing out scraps of greasy, day-old hyrax meat, did it occur to Dogfinger to wonder how Shay had found this place so unerringly. They had left the Erg behind several hours earlier, the land grading into an entirely flat surface, free of any mark whatsoever. There were no stones, no trees (nor indeed any plant life of any kind), no skeletons of dead animals. Not even any distant mountains whereby one might orient oneself. The land was utterly flat. And yet Shay had walked to this scrape in a dead straight line, looking neither to right nor left. Dogfinger stopped chewing the rubbery meat long enough to begin to frame a question, but Shay glanced at him from beneath his hood — his eyes catching the last of the sunlight — in a way that told him, as nothing else might, that he should remain silent.

Putting down the remains of his meal, Shay reached into an inside pocket of his robe and drew out a soft leather drawstring bag. He placed the bag carefully on the ground, spreading out the opening with both his long hands. After a few moments he reached in and withdrew a lamp made from the skullcap of a Stoner, the inner surface of which had been charred black and greasy with the passage of years. From another small pouch Shay took a handful of herbs and dried flowers, placing them with great care within the up-turned skull. Dogfinger could not be sure — and didn't dare ask — but it looked as if Shay was arranging the herbs and flowers in particular, exacting patterns. Then Shay took a lit twig from the fire and ignited the herbs. As the smoke rose, he chanted words that Dogfinger had never heard before, although he had the impression that they were very ancient.

The syllables that Shay pronounced were indecipherably glottal, guttural and barbarous, as gentle as thunder, as euphonious as an avalanche. But as Shay spoke, Dogfinger had the unsettling sensation that he knew what they meant. Softly, inside his head, was the voice of a woman. It could have been his mother. And seemingly with his mother's voice, the voice said:

Bless us, Holy One, All High. Who took up the sins of the world, *qui tollis peccata mundi.*

Shay did not speak again until the late afternoon of the second day. His words were just as enigmatic then, too. He turned to Dogfinger, grasped his sun-sore shoulders in both hands and looked him straight in the eye.

"*Jjadhazev*, listen to me. *HaShekhna* might think you're some kind of Big Shot, but *I* think she's a soft touch. Me? I'm not so sure. You might think you're the *Moshiach*. But wisdom is more than about killing. Remember that." Shay turned away before Dogfinger could reply.

On the second day of their journey together, Dogfinger and Shay walked westward across the hard-pan until Father-the-Sun had set in a red ball before their feet. And still they kept walking. Dogfinger followed Shay closely and carefully as the last light of day was extinguished and all around was completely dark.

Unable to see anything except the ghostly folds of Shay's robes a yard or so ahead of him, Dogfinger's other senses sharpened. The air became cooler, yes—night in the desert could chill one's bones—but it became moister, too. He could smell the green of growth, burgeoning all around him. And he could hear things, too—more than the careless desert wind, but the rustle of vegetation, the rattle and clack of tall stalks beating on one another. The chirp of crickets.

It felt like he had come full circle, back to his village: he was a boy again, playing with Green-Eye in the irrigation ditch between the fields, and all he needed to do was climb out and walk home to his mother's embrace. But no—he knew that could no longer be. In any case, he could not afford for his mind to wander. It took all his concentration to keep up with Shay's pace, unrelenting even in this utter blackness. If he missed his footing and fell, he might lose Shay and be abandoned, without any bearings whatsoever, in this unknown place. Shay's pace did not slacken until they walked into some darker blackness, Shay pushing Dogfinger's head downwards so he wouldn't crack it on a lintel—they had walked into an interior space, a dwelling. How

Shay had been able to reckon his way, without twist or turn or any doubt whatsoever, remained an enigma.

Shay knelt down on a dry earth floor and took out his small belongings, igniting the herbs and dried flowers in the upturned skull as he'd done the night before, and chanting the same, ancient ritual obeisance. By the small, flickering light, Dogfinger — still standing — saw that they were in a small mud hut, with two sacks of wool on the floor, either side of the skull-altar fire. Shay looked up at Dogfinger who was aware, for the first time, of the round reflections at the back of the old man's eyes. Like a cat. Now he understood how Shay could see where he was going, even when he — no mean tracker in the dark himself — was almost completely blind.

"Take a pew, *Ijadhazev*," Shay said. And without another word, the old shaman curled up on one of the wool sacks like a baby and fell asleep immediately, his face hidden by his hood. Dogfinger tried to follow his example, lying down on the vacant wool sack. At first the softness of it was uncomfortable, and even disconcerting, to one who'd spent every night, as long as he could remember, curled up in the crook of a thorn-branch or a scrape in the ground, or stretched out on the hard desert soil. But the fatigue of the two-day desert march soon claimed him, and he slept.

Dogfinger awoke to the grayness of early morning and an uncomfortably full bladder. Without thinking, he rose and went outside to relieve himself against the wall of the hut. So desperate was he to urinate that he failed to notice, at first, that the hut was just one among many, huddled closely together between thorn-branch stockades of aurochs and goats, stands of crops and the scattered shade of trees — acacia, palm and other kinds he did not recognize. There were people, too, going about the usual early-morning errands of any village, and one stopped to look at him. It was only when the warm and welcome relief spread throughout his lower body, and Dogfinger arched his back so that he could shake the last drops from his penis, that he had the uncomfortable sensation of being watched.

Now, usually, whenever this happened, his reflexes would spring into action, and he'd turn to face the perceived threat, antelope-horn dagger in hand. This time, it felt different. That he was quite naked was nothing unusual, this being Dogfinger's normal state. More worrisome was that he had let himself be caught unarmed. But the feeling of being under surveillance was different from, say, being looked up and down by a prowling leopard: not so much danger, then, as a kind of embarrassment. And yet this was not the shame of being caught doing something naughty, as he'd felt as a boy. Well, not quite. For in this not-quite-shame was something entirely new — fascination. He turned to face his adversary, and as he did so, he felt his balls shrink into his body.

His adversary was a species of human being he'd seen many times, long ago, in his home village, but never yet since. He had not, however, been old enough, as he was now, to appreciate such a creature for what it really was.

Standing before him was a young woman.

The first thing that struck him was the color of her skin. Not deep brown, as he himself was, but almost white. And not, then, the dead parchment-white of Shay, but a smooth lusciousness like a she-goat's new milk. This pure-white skin was freckled all over as if she'd been sprayed with honey. Her hair, though — now, that was *truly* extraordinary, being very long and *bright orange*. Her wide eyes were as brown and as dark as his own. The contrast with the pale face that surrounded them made their stare seem impudently inquisitive.

"Well, take a look at *you*," she said. "And be *careful* with that thing, won't you? It's not just for pissing through, you

know." She giggled. Dogfinger looked down and discovered, with equal parts horror and wonder, that his penis was
as stiff as a branch and standing away from his body. He
turned, to see the woman walking away, a sway to her walk
as she balanced an urn on one hip, rucking up one side of
her woollen skirt so that he saw the back of one thigh, as
white and smooth as the rest of her. The urn must have been
very heavy, if full of water, Dogfinger thought, yet she carried it with an elegant ease. He felt heat in his face, and not
the heat of the rising morning. He turned, ducked, and entered the small hut which he shared with Shay.

"Some of us are... er... *up*, bright and early," Shay said
from his bed, looking up at the slowly shrinking erection of
his young *protégé*. Dogfinger sat down sharply on his own
woolsack, trying to conceal an expression of mingled confusion, frustration and rage.

"Where are we? Who are these people?" he barked at the
old man.

"Easy now," Shay said. "If it's any consolation, which it
isn't, I understand how you must feel. You left your village
hardly more than a tadpole, and now you are a fine figure of
a frog. A bit unkempt—perhaps a little on the scrawny
side—but well, you'll do. A lily pad and a few lessons in
croaking and you'll cut quite a dash, I fancy. In the meantime, such reactions in the... um... southern regions are only
to be expected when one comes face to face with unfamiliar... er... *stimuli*."

"Southern regions?" said Dogfinger, "I thought we were
going far more west than south. And you haven't answered
my questions. First—where are we?"

Shay sighed. "Would knowledge of the name make any
difference?"

"The day before yesterday you seemed to think names
were important."

"*Touché*, my lad. We are, as you see, in an oasis. In my language it is called *Baj!ra'adhzt...*"

" 'Ba-yit'? 'Be-reshit?'" Dogfinger rolled the strange, angular syllables around in the mouth. It felt like trying to gargle with knuckle bones. Shay laughed — itself a weird, guttural sound.

"It's a fair start," he said. "But you need to try and say both words simultaneously. In any case, *Baj!ra'adhzt* means both 'home' and 'beginning': which, as you'll see, I hope, is most apposite. A little history, if you will — in ancient times much of the rest of this region was like this — fertile, farmed, tilled — but the desert has slowly swallowed it up, a little more each year, until only a few oases like this remain. My people once roamed far across these lands, made a great empire.

"But hubris comes to us all, even the Annakhnu of ancient days, and the few of us who remain live somewhat farther to the west of here, in huts such as these, in the lee of the far greater mansions our ancestors — the *elda enta geweorc*, to coin a phrase — and whose means of construction most can now only surmise, even were some few to distinguish them at all from natural features."

Shay sat up. Dogfinger heard the old man's bones creak and saw a fleeting grimace across the strange, elongated face. Shay must have registered Dogfinger's concern. "Don't you worry about me, *Ijadhazev*," he said. "Just a bit stiff after our little excursion, that's all. But to the present. *Baj!ra'adhzt* is, as you've seen, somewhat off the beaten track. Stoners don't know it's here, and wouldn't be able to get here even if they did."

"Stoners?"

"Indeed. Need I say more?"

"But who... these people? That woman?"

"That *brazen hussy*, you mean? Her name is Moonrise, and her temper is as fiery as her wholly improbable hair. Just like her to judge a man by his… ah… accoutrements."

"So… you heard?"

"It's only a little hut, *Jjadhazev*. And if you *will* run around as naked as a baby, waving your… er… *advantages* around for all to see, like some crude advertisement, you're going to attract attention, aren't you? Now, help me to my feet, will you?"

Dogfinger obliged.

"Now then," Shay said, stretching, "I'm off to find some clothes for you, and some breakfast for both of us. Don't move from this spot until I return. Agreed?"

Dogfinger nodded. Shay looked unconvinced, and ventured into the gathering heat muttering something about the ingratitude of young people, and how they weren't what they used to be. He had the feeling that he was meant to discover that answer for himself.

At first Dogfinger found his woollen kilt and shirt—the customary clothing worn at the oasis—irritating and constricting. He said little to anyone, and listened only slightly more.

After a while, though, he got used to his clothes, and the regular farmyard chores he was assigned by the others at the oasis. He even began to enjoy them. As life became routine, he found that his mind wandered, more than it ever had, to daydreams of what life might have been like at home, long away, had he reached manhood there, undisturbed by the Stoner raid. He'd have been working alongside Pa, perhaps, tilling and sowing and herding and reaping. And maybe he'd be looking forward to marriage, as Green-Eye had been. Funny, that, he thought—the thought that he himself might be in such a situation had not occurred to him until now.

Perhaps it was no surprise, given what Shay had referred to as 'stimuli'. Virtually all the residents of the oasis were young men and women. There was nobody younger than Dogfinger, and very few older than twenty-two or twenty-three summers or so. The reasons — the tragic, heart-stopping reasons — soon became clear. Everyone at the oasis had a story to tell: of rape, and mutilation, and murder, and of narrow escapes from Stoner raids on their respective villages all across the delta and as far south as the Cataracts of Cush. Of parents forced to watch the slaughter of their children before being slaughtered themselves — or being carried off by the Stoners to some unknown fate. The oasis was a refuge. A very few had found it by accident, but most, it seemed, had been led there by Shay.

Few had any more idea of the world beyond the oasis than Dogfinger did himself. But his mind, ever quick to anger, slower to reason, began to work on new paths. The people at the oasis, he wondered, were probably all that was left of humanity that had not been enslaved or killed by the Stoners. Not that Dogfinger came to that conclusion in such a measured way. Initially, what he felt was rage — intemperate, and volcanic. It was not Dogfinger's fault that many of the other people, especially the men, felt the same way. Tempers were often short, and fights broke out. Dogfinger seemed to be at the center of most of them.

That he won far more often than he lost seemed only to goad his persecutors. To taunt Dogfinger became a kind of sport — the older youths would jibe at his eye-patch, his missing finger, the fact that he was the youngest, until he could no longer contain his fury. His most potent adversary was Kingsnake, a man of twenty-one summers who, by reason of a cunning mind and superior bulk, had accreted a small group of men whose intent, it seemed, was to gather the fruits of the oasis to themselves, deserved or not — the food, the water, and especially the women. No-one dared speak out against Kingsnake and his gang, and when Dog-finger whispered about it to Shay in the depths of the night, the old man's response was that he was too far above such playground squabbles to get involved, and that if Dogfinger didn't like the other tourists at this resort, he should either sort it out himself, or find an hotel more to his liking.

One occasion, an hour before nightfall, about three months after Dogfinger had arrived, was typical — distinguished in Dogfinger's mind only by the cataclysmic event that followed immediately afterwards.

He had been herding the goats, spending the past week camping out with them in the dry pastures on the outer fringes of the oasis. The task was not arduous, but dull. Dog-finger had the distinct sensation that he was given such dead-beat jobs because nobody else wanted them, and be-cause he was the youngest and smallest and never com-plained. Not that he was displeased: for one whose company had been himself for almost as long as he could remember, solitude was always the best of friends. The trouble began, as it always did, after he'd handed the goats over — on this occasion to Heron-Wing, a tall and very thin youth only a little older than he was — and returned to the village. If asked, he could not have remembered how he'd gotten there through the wide fields, or what he had been thinking about, but when he looked up, there was Kingsnake and two of his cronies, hardly less bulky, blocking the gate through the vil-lage's thorn-bush perimeter. Dogfinger tried to sidle past, and succeeded — but he was not out of trouble, as the gang followed him into the village centre, accreting more mem-bers and onlookers as it went, and taunting Dogfinger all the while.

"How's your Ma, Squirt? Butt-fucked by any Stoners lately?"

"Yeah — chinless wonder. Bet your Pa was a Stoner."

"And if not your Ma, maybe *you* like to fuck Stoners, you fingerless fucker?"

"Bugger 'em up their hairy asses, don't you?"

"We all know you think you've got the cock for it."

"Oh, yeah, we've all seen how you love to wave *that* around"

Such taunts might, once, have riled him. But their constancy had worn him down so that now he felt only the mildest irritation. In truth, he was *bored* of being followed around by these idiots.

An image came to his mind, then, of being tracked across the savannah for several days by a leopard. Dogfinger was bored, then, too. Just tired of being followed. So Dogfinger had climbed the tree in which the leopard was lurking and ripped its head off with his bare hands. He couldn't have had more than ten summers, then. Now he had sixteen: and Kingsnake, while formidable, was no leopard. Dogfinger's only worry was that he'd rather not kill Kingsnake. Not straight away. But if he didn't, Kingsnake would only raise his game. So what was to be done?

Well, he thought, he couldn't just do *nothing*.

At the very center of the village, in the open grove of palms that served as the village square, Dogfinger turned to face his adversaries. They were all there, arranged in front of him: Kingsnake, with a bruiser of almost equal bulk on either side, and more of his gang arranged behind. Crowds of people were all around them, among the trees, forming a circle around the impromptu arena. The air was thick with anticipation, with fear. Dogfinger could sense that this was an important moment in the fortunes of the village; a moment of bifurcation, when the community would take either one course, or another. He hadn't asked to be put in this situation, but now that he had, he felt that the fates of the world had converged to this single point, and it was his choice, his privilege, to act.

Quick as thought, Dogfinger sprang forward, burying his head just beneath Kingsnake's ribcage. Kingsnake staggered back, bent double, winded. Before Kingsnake or any of his gang knew what was happening, Dogfinger had pulled back, clenched his fists together and brought them up, hard, beneath Kingsnake's chin. Kingsnake's head snapped back with unnatural suddenness. The crack of his neck as it broke reverberated around the square. Kingsnake's body slumped, lifeless, before Dogfinger's feet. Dogfinger stood above it, arms spread, knees flexed, hands tingling, blood pounding in his chest and head, waiting for the assault that would inevitably follow.

But none came.

Instead, the crowd of villagers erupted with anger, setting on the rest of Kingsnake's gang before they could make good their escape. A crowd which just a dozen heartbeats earlier had been tense and quiet was now a seething anthill of rage. Amid roars and screams, daggers were drawn, and people started to fall. The sand of the square was soon stained with red.

Dogfinger found himself at the fringes of the melée, trying to engage with one of Kingsnake's gang, who was doing his best to evade him. Dogfinger felt a hand gripping his right forearm, yanking it behind him, painfully. He spun round, loosening the enemy's grip while simultaneously bringing his left hand down hard on his assailant's collarbone—and found that it was Moonrise, the young woman with the remarkably red hair. Her jaw was set with a grimace of pain, her wide, dark eyes afire with determination.

"Let him go, Dogfinger," she screamed above the din. "You must come with me, now." And without another word she gripped his arm again and pulled him away from the square at a run. They did not stop until they had reached a stand of tall rushes above the broad, sandy beach that surrounded one of the many lakes around the oasis. Moonrise pulled Dogfinger down into the rushes—her mouth met his before their bodies hit the dark, wet ground.

At first he struggled, fearing another attack. But if it were an attack, its tactics were like nothing he'd ever encountered before. The more he fought, the more she moaned, and the noises she made seemed more like pleasure than anger. Dimly, he remembered noises like that coming from the part of the hut where his Ma and Pa slept, separated from him and Green-Eye by a rush screen. Before he could work out what to do, Moonrise had gripped his head with both hands, and had plunged her tongue into his open mouth. He let his own tongue explore her mouth in response. He relaxed, and as he did so, Moonrise grabbed his left hand and pulled it up and inside her shirt, folding it around a breast. He had never felt such softness. Not even the freshly exposed internal organs of slaughtered animals, as he plunged his bloodied hands into their carcasses to rip them out—had such lustrous vibrancy, a sensation overtopped only by the dim pulse of her heart's beat.

Moonrise released her mouth from his, moaned once more and threw her head back, exposing her neck, white against the crimson infusion of her cheeks and parted lips. Dogfinger kissed and bit at her neck, took his hand from her breast, feeling it vibrate and recoil as he did so. With the same hand now away from the hot aura of her flesh, he rucked up the cloth of her skirt and ran a hand up a thigh as endlessly smooth as the fabric above was coarse. Her flesh, just above the knee, was at first firm and cool in the pungent afternoon heat of the reed-brake, but became broader, warmer and more yielding as he progressed, curling his fingers around and inward until his palm came across the tight-sprung curls of her sex. Moonrise parted her legs slightly, allowing Dogfinger's hand to come to rest between them. His palm fitted round the inward curve of her body, where he felt his fingers drawn inward, more, and further still, to her moisture, releasing a rich, powerful odor as he did so. An odor to overtop the seething fecundity of the damp, root-choked soil on which they lay. An odor of need; an odor of something lost that will never be found, no matter how feverish the search.

Moonrise groaned softly and bit hard on his earlobe, breathing hard and hot into his ear, and reached downwards to grab onto his penis, which he now noticed had become excruciatingly hard, its tip stinging against the inside of his kilt as it rubbed against it. Moonrise pulled it free. "I want you inside me, boy," she said, her voice dark, quavering and thick. Dogfinger pulled himself above her, lifting the hem of her skirt, as part of the same, sweeping choreography that demanded that she spread her legs apart for him. Kneeling above her in the green nest of rushes, he was entranced by the neatness of her red fur, counterpointed and contrasted by the clarity of the skin that surrounded it, and the marvellous scent that rose from her sex that made him throb with a pleasure so intense it almost frightened him. She reached down with a hand, her fingertips grown ruddy with arousal, and with great gentleness where there had been urgency and force, guided him inside her. He felt a feint of resistance, but no sooner had he thrust further in, to a region of delight beyond any means for him to express it, than he came. Confused, terrified, he pulled back, seeing his own juices spread and spill over her thighs. She pulled him down beside her and sighed, more with resignation than pleasure.

"You've never done this before, have you?" she said. But her voice that could as well have been spiked with frustration and anger was softened with concern. Dogfinger said nothing. "Oh, well. Plenty of time to learn," she said, and lay back among the reeds. He lay down beside her. The noise of crickets as Father-the-Sun descended; the scent and warmth of her flesh, and the soft sound of the breeze in the rushes and wavelets lapping on the shore below; all conspired to lull him into a smooth and even state somewhere between sleeping and waking.

But they didn't sleep.

Instead they began to talk, at first softly and quietly, then with increasing animation. Dogfinger told her of his history, telling her things that he'd never told anyone, not even Shay — the details of his last day in his village before he fled, as clearly as he could recall it. Moonrise then narrated her own tale, different in each grisly detail, but in general terms much the same as his, and of everyone else at the oasis — of the increased Stoner raids; of the arguments about whether they should move; of their helplessness before the brutality of the thick-set, stone-armored warriors.

"Shay found me," she said, "Wandering along the sea-coast, far to the north. He brought me here. At the end my feet were burned so badly that I couldn't walk, so for the last few days he had to carry me. By then, though, I wasn't much of a burden."

"How many summers had you?"

"Twelve. The Stoners raided when the village had turned out for my older sister's wedding feast. I was to have been married the next year. I can remember everything about the man to whom I'd been betrothed — what he looked like, the sound of his voice, everything. Except for his name. Isn't that strange?"

"Shay," said Dogfinger. "He said something to me, just as we came to the oasis."

"Hmm?"

"A warning. That I wasn't the big shot I might think I am. That winning was more than about... killing." Kingsnake's dead face, an expression of shock painted indelibly upon it, rose in his mind. "That I wasn't the... one of his strange words... *Moshiach*?"

"Messiah," she replied. "Shay says that to everybody."

"But... why?"

"I've given up trying to understand Shay," she said. "He seems like this crazy old man, bringing humans to his refuge like a crow obsessed with collecting shiny beetles or sparkly pebbles. Why does he do it? He's *driven*. Something about a goddess, he says."

"*HaShekhna*?"

"That's the one. But the dear old thing, batty though he might be, he's saved our lives, hasn't he?"

"Yes, sure, he's strange," he said. "But isn't there a purpose to it? Are we humans just his toys, or are we free to leave? Take our chances with the world? We can't stay here for ever, can we? Shouldn't we break out, to take the fight to the Stoners? To take back what is ours? For the sakes of our families? Our... our... self-respect? I had more of that when I was a lonely hunter in the desert, living off rats and roots, than I've had here, with food and clothes and other people, with..." Dogfinger stopped, stunned by his own elo-quence — he'd said more words together in this one speech than at any other time in his life.

Moonrise sat up, and her expression on her red lips, her burning eyes, was, at first, unreadable. Triumph? Desire? Both? She pulled him closer.

"Shall we have another go?" she said. Within seconds he was inside her, pushing into depths so warm and liquid that at first he could not feel his way, but as he moved, the tissue inside her folded and corrugated so that he could feel its arousing rasp as he moved back and forth. She spread her legs as wide as she could, moving them upwards, canting him forwards above her as she did so; and wrapped her calves across his shoulders, pressing his sides with her thighs, forcing him inside her as deeply as he could go. Her voice rose into a strangled pitch of pleasured sound as he felt her wetness spread across his own thighs and belly. He pushed deeper, now, and harder, and found that he was now in control of her emotions and his. She climaxed in one last spasm, raking his shoulders with her fingernails, and fell back with a whimper.

"Now," she said, through full, red lips, her brown eyes closing with one, last, insouciant sparkle, "*that* was more *like* it."

In the months that followed, Dogfinger found that whereas people had once been dismissive towards him, they were now deferential. Where they had once ignored him, they now sought his advice. Slowly, almost without his being aware of it, his vote was not only registered by the other refugee villagers, but became the decider, the casting vote.

Dogfinger moved out of Shay's hut and in with Moonrise. Their marriage was celebrated for days, crowned in the early spring of the following year by the birth of twins. Nobody objected that Dogfinger named them after the twin siblings he'd so cruelly lost, for everyone had similar memories, and these new births were seen as harbingers of hope unlooked-for.

These children were followed by many others, born of women all over the oasis, and fathered mostly by Dogfinger. It was the tradition of many tribes, including that of Moonrise, for the chief of the village to impregnate as many women as possible, so that the strength of his seed would be spread. Dogfinger was at first startled by this, but was persuaded by Moonrise's acquiescence, if not her overt encouragement. After one such birth, Shay offered Dogfinger a monosyllabic word of congratulation (accompanied by a sly wink that spoke volumes) before setting out on yet another trip of retrieval, to add more stray humans to his collection.

"I shan't need to *schlep* my carcass around for much longer," he said, "now that you've been jumping on all the village girls with such gusto. I must say, they do seem so terribly obliging. But there's no accounting for taste."

Five more years passed. Five years in which the village at *Baj!ra'adhzt* turned from a refugee camp into a prosperous township, whose business was punctuated with the screams and whines and wails of children from what seemed like every house. One day close to the beginning of the dry season, when the cold of the desert at night would creep from across the oasis and into every heart, Shay returned after an absence of almost a year. Dogfinger had wondered where the old Annakhnu had got to, or indeed if he'd see him again, until a knock came on the lintel of his hut, as evening fell.

Dogfinger drew back the cloth curtain to see, silhouetted by the full moon streaming into the house, a man desiccated, sandblasted, as if the winds of the desert had sculpted his very flesh. Across his shoulders he carried a ragged boy of perhaps nine summers, a boy who was in hardly any better state than he was.

"Well-met by moonlight, proud *Jjadhazev*," said Shay, before his knees buckled. Dogfinger caught the boy as he toppled from Shay's shoulders—and Shay, shortly after. He looked into the child's eyes, and all his own history came back to him in a sudden rush. A history much like his own. He had been the same age as this child when disaster had overtaken him and his family. Now was the time, he resolved: *now*. The time had come for action.

Moonrise hurried through from the hut's other room, accompanied by the twins and two smaller children. She took the boy from Dogfinger's arms.

"This child needs feeding," she said, her voice pointed with worry. "I have some broth on the go."

"Chicken soup," said Shay, tottering, resting on Dogfinger's shoulder for support. "It solves everything. Might I beg a cup for my own agèd and unworthy lips, O Fair Bride of *Jjadhazev*?"

Moonrise smiled. "Coming up," she said, before disappearing amid a flock of offspring. Moonrise had ripened: her thighs and hips were broad, her snowy breasts swung loose and full beneath her shirt, and the roundness of her belly indicated continued fecundity. Shay looked up at Dogfinger, who was gazing at his wife with undisguised adoration. "You've done well, young man," he said, "although, personally, I don't think I could put up with the *noise*."

It proved to have been Shay's final trip, but one. More than wind and sand was eating away at his increasingly emaciated frame. Less than a month after Shay had returned with the boy across his shoulders, Dogfinger called on the sage, to find him comatose, sprawled on the floor of his hut, in a pool of his own excrement. Shay didn't seem to know quite where he was, nor the identity of the small but well-knit man with the birthmark round his eye who picked him up, cleaned him, and took him to his own, warm and well-ordered home, where he was cared for by a voluptuous woman with surprisingly orange hair and a lot of noisy children.

Shay's recovery was slow, but steady, and by the time that Moonrise gave birth to her fifth child, he announced that he was ready to move back to his own house. Dogfinger and Moonrise objected, but Shay's response was just as strenuous.

"Are you kidding?" he said. "Look at you. With seven souls in this hut, what you clearly need is an old fart like me cluttering up the place. For sure, like a hole in the head." He would not be gainsaid.

Indeed, once Shay had returned to his old quarters, and Moonrise and several other village women had cleaned it up a bit, Shay returned very much to his old self. After the festival of the vernal equinox, by which time Moonrise had fallen pregnant again, and at which Shay insisted offerings were made to *HaShekhna*, the old man summoned Dogfinger to his hut.

"My last trip into the world, *Jjadhazev*, was most instructive," he began. "If I have been adding fewer new acquisitions to my collection—oh, yes, I know what people say, and I don't mind—it's not just because age has taken its toll. It's because there are fewer souls to save. The Stoners have completely cleared this entire region of humans, as far south as Cush and far to the east, beyond the great delta. There are none left alive. None more to be rescued.

"I fear that the only free humans in the world are here, at *Baj!ra'adhzt*—at least as far as I can tell. If *HaShekhna* had not instructed me, so long ago… well, I dread to think…"

Dogfinger remained silent. He knew Shay well enough to interpret his dramatic pauses as just that, and not invitations to interrupt.

"I tell you that there is hope, *Jjadhazev*," Shay went on. "Yes, *hope*. I have seen and heard about many other kinds of people in the world, on my travels—from giants, twice the height of a man and covered with white fur, to small, sly, dark men with the eyes of cats, who can work great magic, though I have this only by reputation, I might add.

"But no matter what their differences, they all say the same thing—the Stoners are in retreat. It might seem hard to believe, but they, along with all the other kinds of men, are sliding into extinction. All you need to do, *Jjadhazev*, is reach out your hand and take what's yours."

Dogfinger thought of Shay's final acquisition, the small boy. A boy very much like himself, once upon a time.

"The time is now," he muttered. Shay said no more.

The following morning, it was found that Shay had disappeared. A search party was sent to scour the oasis. It was Dogfinger who saw him, a wavering speck, disappearing on the western horizon. Disappearing over the edge of the Earth, a reflection of how he had first come into Dogfinger's life, rising above Earth's rim, so long before. Dogfinger kept this secret to himself.

And so it was that in the refuge of *Baj!ra'adhzt*, which means both 'home' and 'beginning,' a boy once so feral that he could hardly recall his own name grew into a loving husband, a proud father, and a great leader.

But most of all, he grew into a man.

Chapter 7. Witness

Gascony, France, Earth, June, 2073

Then felt I like some watcher of the skies
When a new planet swims into his ken;
John Keats — *On First Looking into Chapman's Homer*

First, they had to work out how they were going to study the Sigil in reasonable comfort. The day after Jadis' birthday party, they opened the doors to the stable to assess the upcoming task. It was greater than any of them had anticipated.

When the Sigil had first taken up residence, the barn was a well-lit laboratory, with clean concrete floors, polished benches and plenty of lighting. The intervening years had not been kind. The concrete floor was still there, of course — scrubbed daily by Jack and whatever help he could get, in the course of mucking out the cows and the pony, and now Tom and Domingo's rented horses. The percheron seemed to occupy about half the space all on its own and looked distinctly cramped and unhappy.

The lighting had lasted as long as they could keep the solar panels and wind turbine in adequate repair, but an accumulation of wear and tear had meant that it worked at best intermittently, when it worked at all. In any case, the scarcity of light bulbs rendered as superfluous any efforts to keep the panels in trim. But light bulbs could now be obtained from the Far East, albeit at great cost, so now the machinery would have to be mended — another job to add to Jack's endless list of Augean tasks. The lab benches had been scavenged when more immediate uses for valuable slabs of hardwood had seemed more pressing.

The Sigil itself, mounted on a sturdy plinth inside its evacuated transparent plastic case, and packed in a crate, was too heavy and too fragile to move without lifting gear they no longer had. In any event it was buried beneath an accumulation of farmyard clutter. Just getting at it would demand an excavation almost as archeological as the one that had brought it to light in the first place.

Even without this impending dig, there was no way they were going to get close to the Sigil unless the livestock were put into one of the fields more or less full-time. Now summer had arrived there was no reason why this could not be done. But it took another week for Jack and Tom to renovate a crumbling storm-shelter for the animals close to the field-gate, where they could be fed and watered, freeing up the barn once more.

Tom reflected that the farm was slowly slipping into general dilapidation as his parents got older. But even a day here at his home had cheered and freshened him, blown away some of the brooding disquiet of Cambridge. Perhaps he could extend his sabbatical more or less indefinitely. Working here alongside his parents, putting the farmhouse to rights, digging in the dirt of this hallowed and ancient place, had always been a source of immense satisfaction for him.

Domingo, on the other hand, seemed to chafe at the delay and added his mighty frame to speed the work as much as he could. But while Jack and Tom were busy, he took the opportunity of a trip to the village to assess the logistics of moving the Vatican to the hilltop. Jack told Domingo that he could probably take over the top two floors of the old Mairie. His own duties as village schoolteacher teacher and sometime ex-officio village headman barely occupied two ground-floor rooms of the cavernous, crumbling, once-handsome pink-stuccoed building.

And so, several mornings later he and Jadis took a turn around the village. The thought of resuming her daily walk in Domingo's company filled Jadis with so much excitement that she practically bounced up and down with the eagerness of a little girl promised a trip to the funfair. It took her back to days of contentment long ago, when the then black-haired Domingo had first appeared in their lives.

Not that there was any chance of a tranquil wander, just the two of them talking, without interruption. The village itself saw to that.

Their first stop was the *Sanglier D'Or*, still a café of sorts, but now more like a tavern from an earlier age, the village's centre for news and gossip. Always bustling with life, its clientèle included a motley assortment of travellers from far and near — from tinkers to mendicant friars — pumped by the regulars for tales and ballads and word of things happening far away. News of Domingo's arrival had reached the *Sanglier* long before he had, so he and Jadis found the bar packed with spectators. Indeed, these now spilled out into the Place Etienne Geoffroy Saint-Hilaire, to make a welcoming committee fit for the return of a conquering hero.

"It's the Pope!" the cry went up. "The Pope and the Doctor! Make room! Make room!"

On hearing this general acclamation, Yvon Rossignol, the latest innkeeper of the *Sanglier*, made his corpulent way to the front of the throng.

As a relatively recent arrival, Rossignol had hardly ever seen Jadis; and the news of the Pope's arrival had been colored by stories of how, as plain Father Domingo, he had pulled the village together in its moment of crisis almost twenty years before. If the tales he'd heard were to be believed, Jadis was a white witch, a priestess of great power with the uncanny ability to restore life, whose healing arts had touched every family in the village and for many miles around.

"She brought my twin sons into the world," recalled one bright-eyed patron, whose account was typical. "Breech births! My Bernadette nearly died, a goner for certain, but the Doctor brought them into the light and saved her life, too! And all my sons and daughters after that!"

Left unsaid was the general assumption that she had some direct line to the core of the Earth, and was in mysterious communion with the long-dead ancestors of them all.

For some years Jadis had wondered at the source of the eggs, the hams, the produce, the bunches of flowers and especially the small dolls made from wheat stalks left anonymously by her kitchen door. After a while it had dawned on her that these were presents for services rendered. It never once crossed her mind (as it had Jack's) that these were votive offerings. She had turned into her own cave-painting.

And Father Domingo, said the locals—*our* Father Domingo, mind—has become the Pope himself. And he's here, in Saint-Rogatien! Where the Doctor had mended the ills of the village, rumor had been current for some time about how Domingo was doing the same to the rest of the world.

"Truly, he is a master of the fates of us all," a hooded and grizzled Christophorine had said one night, sipping a foaming pint of ale, recounting inflated tales of Domingo's travels to a rapt audience of locals.

"He is that—nothing less," said a colleague bearing the cross and lightning-bolt blazon of the Order of Saint-Adelard, his face scarred with radiation and chemical burns that would have been the signs of sorcery were they not carried by a man not so plainly touched by holiness. "They say he has been to the ends of the Earth… and *beyond*," he declaimed dramatically, raising a *pastis*. "He meets the creatures of Satan head-on, they say, and faces them down!"

Rossignol's first sight of the old friends, as they crested the hill and walked slowly into the cobbled square, did not disappoint. The Pope was a giant of a man, his bearded face framed by a long, snow-white mane, his hood thrown back, his scarlet cloak lifted into a swirling train by the gentle breeze, his chasuble richly decorated with a splendid design of red and green parrots, beautiful dark-haired girls with floral head-dresses, and muscular young men riding great blue waves on yellow planks. If this really was the Pope himself, he knew how to make an entrance.

The woman who walked so confidently next to him, despite being hardly more than half his size, seemed at first a pale shadow, in her long, grubby grey coat, floral skirt, sandals, market bag and floppy straw hat. But he could see that hiding behind her flowing grey hair was a face of all-consuming intelligence, concentrated in two large, penetrating eyes. He would not bear that gaze too long, Rossignol thought. She had the kind of eyes that could see right through you, if you'd let them. Perhaps cast a spell on you. But when she smiled, she seemed like the freshest village girl.

When they found the village all out to greet them, the Pope laughed heartily, and the woman laughed too—but when she saw the extent of the crowd, she took off her hat, lifted her arms and gathered her hair on the top of her head. Rossignol gasped as the lithe slenderness of her figure. This white witch must have been a captivating beauty, perhaps not so long ago. She looked—what—seventy? But she moved? Ah! Like a girl at her first dance.

Rossignol now found himself at the front of the crowd, pushed before the two dignitaries. Standing up to his full height of five-foot-three, he bade them welcome in the gravest voice he could muster, and bowed as low as his globular frame would allow. Domingo bowed even lower in response, his nose almost touching the ground, and the crowd hooted with mirth. Domingo helped the innkeeper to his feet, and fearing he might have made fun of him, embraced him like a brother.

"My good innkeeper, I thank you. And as I have the pleasure of so many ears at once, I have something that might prove of interest to all." The crowd hushed in an instant.

"Now, I would not wish to discommode any of you, my old friends. But although I have traveled to many places, I have always thought of Saint-Rogatien as my true home. Ever since I first arrived here in... er... *when* was it, Jadis?"

Then the woman spoke for the first time. She looked up at the huge man, smiling at the Representative of Christ on Earth if she were indulging a pet dog, and talking in the kind of French that Yvon's grandma would have found quaintly antique.

"Verily, methought 'twas of twenty hundreds of years and of twenty of nine."

"My old friend and colleague Dr Markham is quite... er... *correct*," continued the Pope, whose French, while in the high style, was at least this side of medieval. "I first came here... ah... forty-four years ago. It was different world back then, eh?" General laughter.

"And I love this place so very much that I have chosen to make it my home again: *et que sur cette pierre je bâtirai mon Église!*"

Deafening roars of approval.

"Now, my friends, I would not wish to keep you from your errands. However," — Domingo looked over the crowds to count several hoods and cowls — "I should very much appreciate the offices of my Christophorine and Adelardian Brethren, and the good Priest of the Parish, if I may..."

And so Domingo was carried off to organize the Vatican in exile. Jadis felt slightly deflated. She did not wish to have coffee alone, so she went to the boulangerie and chatted with Amélie Foucoult's daughter Camille, exchanging a half-dozen fresh duck eggs for two loaves, still hot from the oven. Jadis reflected that Camille, a strapping girl of nineteen, was the first child she'd brought into the world, with inexpert midwifery, that first, bitter winter after the Plague had struck. Jadis complimented Camille on the excellence of the birthday cake she'd made for her.

"Why, *thank you*, Doctor," blushed Camille, as if Jadis had blessed the bakery with a spell for its continued success. She leaned forward conspiratorially and, asked, half-whispering: "Is he really… *you* know… the *Pope*? You know, from *Rome*?"

Jadis confided that he was.

"But Rome must be so *grand* compared with our village, mustn't it Doctor?" gushed Camille. Jadis confessed that she'd never actually been to Rome herself, but for all its re-ported refulgently grandificent omnipulence (Camille found the Doctor hard to understand sometimes, she used such long words) the Pope had always thought Saint-Rogatien a *much* nicer place. And so they parted in mutual satisfaction, the one with bread for the next day and a feeling that her first patient hadn't turned out so badly; the other with the vague sense that she'd touched the hem of greatness.

Ten days after Domingo and Tom's arrival, the barn was now clear of animals. Jack and Tom fixed the solar panels and turbine as well as they could, but in the end they had to call on professional help. Laurent Gaspard, the farmhouse's regular electrician, had escaped the Plague, but had perished in the dire winter that followed, when, up on a church stee-ple fixing a lightning conductor, he'd slipped on an icy tile and had fallen to his death. It was his son Pascal who now carried on the family business. A basic electricity supply now existed thanks to the ceaseless efforts of the Adelardians, though its coverage was nothing like as extensive as it had been before '54: so Pascal Gaspard could afford to be only a part-time sparks. These days, he was really only interested in breeding beef. Jack managed to tear him away from his beloved herd of prime Limousin to get the barn lighting at least partly functional again. This meant a great deal of cursing, trying to source components (not just light bulbs) and digging holes in the adjacent field, tracing buried cable and patching the places where it had been gnawed through by dormice.

After that it was only a matter of shifting the detritus of decades to disclose the Sigil. Straw bales that were once stacked ceiling-high were shifted to the other end of the barn, lifting clouds of floury, sour-tasting dust, quantities of owl pellets and the desiccated corpses of unidentifiable small mammals that the Horribles had stored for rainy days that never came. Jadis was amused and delighted at the quantity of *objets trouvés* that were unearthed in the process, including her favourite border fork (mislaid, '68); a basket once used by Micawber, the dog (discarded after his death in a road accident, '61, but which Jadis could never persuade herself to cast onto the bonfire, and now much chewed by mice) and — amazingly — several boxes of very dusty but still functional light bulbs.

The first day of July was scheduled as the day when the tarp would be removed, and the Sigil revealed. The day was fiercely hot from the moment the Sun broke the horizon: the family attended to their chores as quickly as they could and then broke for breakfast at eight o'clock. Then it was to the barn. Not a word was spoken, and the tension rose with every step they took across the egg-fryingly hot yard, the remaining fragments of weathered tarmac already starting to soften and bubble.

For Jadis, the feeling was uncannily like that she'd had when the Sigil had first been discovered, in the shaft beneath the summit of the Great Pyramid at Souris Saint-Michel: that each time she'd covered it up and returned to it, she'd half-hoped that it would not be there, or have turned into something else.

Domingo's feelings could be summed up as an angular disjunction of hypotheses. His mind was so full of the many different ways he'd sought to explain the provenance of this object, and the diverse theological implications implied by each, that he hoped he'd be able to see the Sigil simply as it was, unadorned by his preconceptions.

Jack had thought relatively little about the Sigil until recently. He'd been far too busy with the mundane matters of organizing the farmhouse and the community of Saint-Rogatien to concentrate overmuch on science. Lately he wondered if his avoidance hadn't been deliberate, and, rather despite himself, he was beginning to wonder whether he'd become a little superstitious about the thing.

As if, he thought, it had been the Sigil that had called him to Souris Saint-Michel, or even to France in the first place, even before he'd got his doctorate: the long-sought focus of all his desires, the grounding for all his instincts.

No, that wasn't it, surely? His trip to France had been to give Jadis some space while she completed her finals — hadn't it? But what if it were a mixture of both — moving away from Jadis as he had been drawn into the orbit of the Sigil? He knew that this line of reasoning (if it could be dignified as such) was entirely ridiculous.

But it could have been worse, even than that: that the Sigil that had tugged on his soul from his youth, when he'd walked the hills and valleys of Britain and felt the landscape start beneath him, like the struggles of a caught leveret felt through a poacher's sack. It wasn't the Sigil's fault that he'd started out in England, rather than Gascony. If he'd come from Timbuktu, he'd still have been drawn *here* — pulled by the Sigil in its quest for its own revelation. In which case the Sigil had had nothing in particular to do with Jadis, except inasmuch as she'd also been snared, right from the start, by Jack's unconscious quest. No wonder, then, that he felt his boots drag with each step he took closer to the barn. The distance from the kitchen door was hardly twenty meters, but it could have been twenty miles, or twenty parsecs.

For Tom, inevitably, memories of the Sigil were tied up with those of Shoshana. He had only ever seen it in her company, and she had been party to the last serious discussion that anyone had had about it. As for the Sigil itself — the bald, physical reality of it — he had no particular memory or expectation.

The barn was dark and cool after the yard. Jack pulled the doors open and disappeared into the sharp shadows to switch on the lights. The interior was flooded with a soft yellow radiance more like that of mellow eventide than bright early morning. Jadis imagined she'd turned up for a barn dance a little early, and half expected people to barge in after her, with musical instruments, barrels of beer and strings of bunting and fairy lights.

Under the lights, strung on chains from the gnarled and cracked oak beams high above, the floor was bare except for a trestle table, four chairs of assorted sizes and types, and a few oddments kicked into corners that nobody had got round to clearing up. And, at one end, the Sigil, under its blue tarp.

The four of them stood over the shrouded object, each waiting for the other to make the first move. Jadis could hardly believe that they'd worked themselves up into such a state. She was convinced that they'd been feeding off one another, and that had each of them been alone, they'd have simply marched in and pulled the tarp away.

"Well?" she demanded: "Are we going to wait here all day? Some of us have things to do!" And at that she stepped forward and dragged off the tarp to reveal—a wooden packing crate like any other. The others exhaled at once, as if they had expected a monster rather than some ordinary household object. Released from immobility they crowded round, helping Jadis prise open the lid and remove some of the polystyrene packing chips. In a few moments they'd exposed the surface of the Sigil's hard plastic prison, and in a few more, they'd removed enough packing for the Sigil to be clearly seen.

Jadis peered at it through its casing. No, she thought—it's still there. It hadn't gone away, as she'd secretly hoped. The object was much smaller than she'd imagined, as it had expanded over its unseen years to fill her dreams. It was no more than a gray tablet, maybe twelve by three centimeters, and a centimeter thick. If you looked very carefully indeed, you could just about discern the faintest tracery of engraving on its face. After a minute or two, the whole pattern would become evident, and you'd see the three perfect circles, the crescents, and the fine, straight lines that radiated outwards from the central circle to the corners and edges of the bordered inscription.

Funny, she thought, it was the unnatural smoothness and flatness of the object that had first drawn their attention. The inscription itself had only become apparent a little while later, so fine were the lines in which it had been wrought. Jadis remembered the headaches she'd got whenever she found herself staring at the inscription for more than a minute or two. Silly me, she thought—she'd thought then that the headaches were part of the menopause she'd been going through at around the same time. Nevertheless, she'd got into the habit of looking only at photographs of the Sigil. These were just as good as the real thing, for no matter how they recorded the object — X-rays, UV, infra-red, in the visual, magnetic resonance — the pattern of lines and crescents and circles showed up, just the same.

Domingo bent closely over the transparent casing and found himself tracing the Sigil's lines with mental fingertips. The line's edges looked almost as sharp as those of newly cut paper. He wondered at the remarkable evenness with which the inscription had been drawn, and with that, began to imagine a startling possibility. That what they were looking at was not something individually hand-crafted, but mass-produced. And if so, why stop at just one? For the moment, he kept these thoughts to himself.

For Jack, hanging back, it was the tablet itself, rather than the inscription on it, that resonated most strongly with his sense of what belonged in a landscape, and what didn't. This lump of nameless material most definitely did *not* belong, not in *any* landscape. No matter how hard they'd tried, the Sigil's matrix remained defiantly unidentifiable. He remembered a talk he'd had with a physicist who confessed herself baffled by the way that any gravitational detectors went awry whenever they came close to the Sigil.

"It's *weird*," she'd said.

"How so?"

"Well, it's not just random gravitational anarchy," she said. "Put a detector a few hundred meters away from the object, and you know something's up. The readings get more... well, more *deviant*... the closer you get, until they reach a peak about half a millimeter above the surface of the object. But then... well, it's *weird*, that's all." The physicist had smiled, nervously, revealing an array of perfect teeth, but her gray-blue eyes had shown nothing so much as *fear*.

"But then… what?" Jack had pressed. The physicist had been a rather striking blonde from the University of Uppsala, he remembered, wryly, though he couldn't quite recall her name. Frida? Agnetha? Something like that. He wondered idly what she was doing now. If she'd married. If she'd had kids.

If she'd survived the Plague.

Back then, she'd just looked embarrassed, as if to discuss the Sigil any further would somehow have compromised her professional integrity.

"Well, closer to the object than that, the gravity field plunges to… well, there's no getting away from it. It plunges to zero."

Jack was stunned.

"That's right," she'd said, this time with more confidence. "It's as if there's nothing there at all. This material… well, it's like a *hole*. A hole in space-time."

Jack remembered relaying this information to Jadis later that same day, or perhaps in one of the days following. He felt he had to pick his moment. They were in the kitchen. She had grabbed her mac and market bag for a trip to the village.

"That physicist…" he began.

"The blonde? The rather *good-looking* one?" Jadis had teased. Jack remembered how he'd flushed. Agnetha or Frida or whoever it was had indeed been rather attractive.

"She thinks the inscription basically isn't there," he'd said. "Much ado about nothing."

"Well then," said Jadis. "Nothing for us to worry about, is there? What do you fancy for supper?" And his wife's long legs had carried her out the door with the insouciance of a gazelle.

If only the Sigil *had* been nothing to worry about. Were he to admit as much, it had haunted his thoughts from that day to this. Had the Sigil woven threads through his whole life just to bring him here, only to leave him mystified? Had they avoided studying it simply because of its nature, strange almost beyond conception? Beyond imagining? Jack felt that a dead end was not the answer. It *had* to mean *something*. But what?

"Domingo," asked Tom, in a voice so quiet that it was barely audible, yet which quavered with an emotion hardly controlled: "would you mind stepping back, I…"

"Yes Tom, of course… of course," replied the big man, standing up straight and turning round to look at Tom, whose eyes now blazed with an alien radiance.

"*C'est incroyable. Incroyable!*" Tom fought to catch his breath, his face bathed in wonder and terror. Domingo moved towards him, solicitously. "*Non*, Domingo, I'm sorry, I'm okay, really… I'm okay."

"What is it, Tom?" Jadis asked. "What can you see?"

In truth, Tom could hardly describe precisely what he had seen on the stone, except that it was so completely un-expected that he was temporarily winded with shock. When he'd last seen the rock all those years before, it was just that—a stone, with the feint, elegant lines of the Sigil in-scribed on it. But sometime between now and then, either the Sigil had changed, or he had.

Or maybe it was that he'd long ago discarded his iShades habit, and was looking at the inscription with his naked eyes, for the first time. This time, for real.

When his mother had scooped the last of the polystyrene chips from the Sigil's case, it was as if she'd uncovered a bank of bright ultraviolet runway lights that blasted into the backs of his eyes.

Squinting, he saw that the radiance was not general, but coincident with the lines of the Sigil. For him, and him alone, the pattern was etched in lines of purple fire that cast every-thing else into shadow: the contrast was so strong that this alone was all he saw, freed from its matrix. But, even as he watched, the pattern lifted from the matrix and tilted towards him in space. It grew, unfolding into something altogether more complex, drawing him into a new realm of sensation in which the barn, Domingo, his parents, and even his own body, faded into a ghostly background. The Sigil that evolved before his astonished eyes was to the engraved inscription as the finished mansion is to the architect's floor plan.

The central circle rose from shadow and grew into a violet sphere before his eyes. It seemed to fill his vision. The violet softened to pale blue, and then to yellow, as the sphere contracted to an apparent size of around a meter in diameter. Flares and prominences shot out from its surface into a turbulent, million-degree plasma. The sphere rotated before his eyes, like a giant, hot globe.

It was a star.

Tom could have sworn that he was a disembodied spirit, floating in space above the stellar corona.

And then it was joined by two other spheres, rising from the circles to right and left. Like the central star, they developed from an incandescent violet, although their fates were different. The star on the left condensed to a sullen red, like a pool of magmatic sludge. Tom thought of Lac 9352, the star whose terrifying fate he'd seen for himself. The star on the right also condensed, but the purple turned to an icy blue-white of an almost unbearable brilliance.

For a while all three blazed before him—red, yellow and blue-white—rotating, spitting out sparks, disgorging rivers of plasma into one another's orbits to create a dazzling, multicolored aurora. And then the stars on the right and left turned black: he could see spots on their surfaces that spread like hideous cankers hundreds of thousands of miles across, until the stars were eclipsed, each one giving vent to a final coronal blast of a power that would vaporize planets—before they vanished. The spaces they had once occupied were blacker than their surroundings, traversed only by a few stray and lonely photons. Floating above the voids, Tom thought that if only he were able to glance directly into them, he'd see dark tunnels that stretched forever. Except that shapes began to move within the blackness itself, still darker than the pitchy voids they inhabited, writhing angrily like maggots squirming over a rotten corpse.

"What do I see, *Maman*?" said Tom. "I can see the pits of hell opening up beneath my feet."

The dark shapes climbed out of the stagnant pits where stars had once stood, rising like two horribly fluid, ebony cobras, until they fragmented into smaller, black shapes that moved in formation towards the central star, from right and left. The shapes were much smaller than the stars, and their precise forms were hard to make out. But the formations in which they moved were all too recognizable. They were crescents, like the two crescents in the Sigil. They fell on the central star like soldier ants on a tethered goat, diving into its surface, breaking it up into shredded masses of livid orange fragmented by black fissures that looked hair-thin, but which could have accommodated the whole Earth millions of times over. Within minutes the central star had disappeared, and all that was left was yawning, eternal night.

Disoriented by the sudden and complete blackness, Tom staggered and fell backwards, bumping into Domingo. Trying to stand, he turned, vomited on the floor, and, tripping over his own feet, caught his head on the edge of the table with a crack. He toppled like a falling tree. By the time he'd reached the floor he was out cold.

He awoke to an intensity of pain that made him wish he were dead. He was vaguely aware that it was evening.

"Tom—it's me," said Jadis, her voice seeming simultaneously close, and yet coming from a wintry distance, as if she were calling to him from across a snowbound field.

"*Maman*? I'm sorry, I don't feel so well." Jadis saw her son's face turn green and whisked the bowl into place just in time for him to be sick in it, after which he turned over and slept solidly for thirty hours.

He was still feverish when he awoke two mornings later, but he felt well enough to sit up on the sofa in the sitting-room, when he told them all what he had seen. Jadis and Jack were aghast. Only Domingo seemed to understand, but perhaps that was because he had also witnessed the destruction of Lac 9352.

Tom could understand why they'd be so shocked, but what puzzled him more than anything else was that none of the others had seen the visions he'd witnessed. When it became clear that all they'd seen was the naked Sigil on the rock, he became irritable, then angry. The last thing he said was that if everything he did prompted people to make fun of him, he wouldn't give them the benefit of his company, and went to his room. In any case, he still had a pounding headache, and wished to lie down with his eyes shut.

Domingo, Jack and Jadis met in worried conclave in the kitchen late that evening. They'd all had very long days, and, much against their better judgment, were forced to leave Tom to his own devices. Jadis had worked hard with the animals and in the garden. Tom felt well enough to do some weeding for an hour or two in the late afternoon, but would exchange no more than a sullen monosyllable and did his best to keep out of Jadis' way—a fact that distressed her more than she was prepared to admit.

Jack had spent the day mostly in the village. He'd had a class to teach, and also to welcome the visiting Mayor of Seissan who had come to bask in reflected Papal glory. There had been a seemingly unending stream of such people over the past couple of days, when Jack's mind had become a helpless, torpid mass with Tom at its centre. His son had seemed so terribly unhappy: the communications they'd had from the Petrine Abbot explained some of it, but the essence of the problem was clothed in characteristically Cantabridgian circumlocution. And as Tom was unwilling to say any more, Jack felt tied, helpless — literally, unable to help.

As for Domingo, he spent much of the time in deep discussion with his expanding retinue of monks, making seemingly endless plans for moving people and equipment to the old Mairie, and yet all the while worrying about Tom. What was to be done, if he wouldn't talk? What *could* be done?

"Jack, Jadis, we must do our best to excuse Tom," Domingo began. "He has been under the most incredible strain at Cambridge. What with all that... ah... business with those East Asian hominids, and the destruction of the star we witnessed together, at the Astrometry Institute, I rather think he has had enough. Our homeward journey together was rather...ah... *fraught*. He is consumed with preoccupation; he will confide in no-one, yet it is plain that coming back here has brought back memories of Shoshana, for whose death he feels responsible."

Jadis's eyes were pools looking into space. "Oh, my poor boy," she said, and hurried from the room. The two men could hear her small, confident steps fading across the hall, and the creak of the treads as she climbed the stairs. Jack and Domingo remained as silent as expectant fathers outside a maternity ward, barred from the secret ministrations of women. Presently, Jadis returned.

"He's locked the room, but all is quiet. He's asleep. I managed to peep through the keyhole. Don't worry, Jack, he's breathing. I'll go up again later and..."

"But what was all that about disappearing stars?" Jack asked Domingo: "Is that... true?"

"Yes, I rather think it is," said Domingo. "This should probably go no further than this room, but I have a strong feeling that Tom's interpretation of the Sigil is the correct one, whatever one might think about the manner of its... ah... communication. He and Shoshana were quite correct— it is a *warning*. There is something in space that consumes stars, and it is not very far away from the Sun. I dread what the next few years might bring. You might as well know, but I am arranging with my more... ah... *technically minded* brethren to wire up the Mairie so that we can be in real-time broadband contact with the Astrometry Institute." He laughed, nervously. "So if we *are* in for the End of the World, we'll hear about it here first. We owe it to ourselves to be prepared spiritually, even if there is nothing practical that can be done.

"And that, my oldest and best friends, is what most worries me about Tom. He is boiling with anxiety, but bottles it up inside, with no... er... *release valve*. Confession has a value that goes beyond the perfunctorily religious, I think."

He paused, weighing words in his mind before speaking further. "Shoshana Levinson was worried about things, too. She'd had a rotten life before coming here, and then it got worse, because of what was... ah... *eating* her inside. She told me about it, too—or as much as she was prepared to—a little while before she died. And I believe that when that moment came, she had achieved some degree of... ah... *equanimity*."

Silence reigned while the ghost of Shoshana Levinson took its place at the table and then, with a sigh, evaporated.

"I never knew...," Jadis said.

"I am sorry, Jadis," Domingo replied, "but I am honor-bound to keep confidences... ah... *confidential*. In any case, were I a doctor, as you seem to be nowadays, I'd recommend that sleep is probably the best medicine for Tom, at least for the present."

"Yes. Let Tom sleep," said Jack. "It's clear that he needs it. Heavens, we *all* need it."

Jadis, unable to sit still, rose again to boil a kettle. "Domingo," she asked amid the flurry of cups and jars and spoons, "did Tom *really* see all that—what he says he did? Was it generated by the Sigil? Or did he imagine it all?"

"It is very hard to say," Domingo replied. "We have, I think, two options. Either Tom's account was brought on by his own mental strain, amplified by having witnessed, with me, the destruction of a star. Believe me, the experience of seeing an entire star dismantled in less than two minutes is every bit as cathartic as you might suppose. The other option is that Tom saw something external and real that we didn't, which, in the end, boils down to much the same thing."

"But we don't always *know* what Tom is seeing, do we?" said Jack: "Remember how we hardly even thought about him being blind, because he seemed to get around without vision?"

Jadis put three mugs of hot tea on the table. "And wasn't he blind again when he came back here?" she added. "After they had escaped from Israel... and then..."

"Jadis?"

Her face lit up with revelation. "Yes! He really *did* see what he says he saw! He *did*!" She leapt up, her hair flowing around her excited face like a wheeling shoal of silvery fish. "Don't you remember, after he and Shoshana came back from Israel and he regained his sight? How he said that everything had what he called an 'aura' about it? Perhaps that's what he saw in the Sigil—an aura that only he had the ability to see, an aura that contained real, encoded information."

"But Jadis.... *how*?"

"How should *I* know, Darling Jack? How *should* I? It's an artifact, perfectly crafted by creatures with advanced technology, goodness only knows how long ago, only somehow—somewhen—it found its way up our pyramid at Souris. We have absolutely no idea who made it. If there are dragons that eat stars, perhaps the Sigil was left here by little green men with three legs. Who knows what it can do? What properties it might have? Honestly, perhaps the Sigil is a dragon's egg! The deeper we get into this, the more glad I am that we never published the thing."

"No, that's not what I meant," said Jack. "Well, only partly. What I *meant* was how *Tom* could see these things, but we couldn't?"

"If the things he saw were real, not just symptoms of stress, well... I..." her brow furrowed, her large eyes crossing slightly in inward concentration. She looked up. "I don't know, Jack—I really don't."

"Well, in any case," said Domingo, perhaps a little too breezily, "it rather puts paid to another idea I discussed with Tom: that the circles in the Sigil somehow represent the end-stage of the Plague."

Jadis shuddered.

"We talked about it on the train," Domingo continued. "Tom was quick to point out that this idea doesn't account for the crescents and... er... *lines*. Especially now we know that the crescents are equivalent to the dragons of Chinese folk-astronomy—if we accept the remarkable evidence of Tom's eyes."

Jack sat up and looked at Domingo with a curious expression of concentration, as if he were reaching for something only just out of mental range. As if he'd had antennae, they would have been humming. "Domingo," he said, "I don't think you should throw that idea away quite so quickly. I know it seems ridiculous, if you'll pardon me, but, you know, it makes a kind of sense."

"How so, my dear Jack?"

"As to that, I have absolutely no idea. None whatsoever." The pieces in Jack's brain clicked into place. "I shall have to sleep on it."

Jadis finished her tea. "Sound like the cue for turning in. Domingo—would you pass me those cups, please?" Domingo stood up, passing the cups to Jadis with deliberate care. He felt drained, worn out, suddenly feeling every minute of his seventy-three years, and yet that he still had one duty to perform before retiring.

"Domingo, are you okay?" Jadis asked.

"Me? I'm remarkably well, thank you, Jadis, when all things are... ah... considered. However, I have some unfinished business with my maker. Good-night!"

Domingo would be kneeling at his *prie-dieu* until the early hours, pleading for guidance. His prayers were becoming increasingly ragged, desperate even, as he tried to solve all the mysteries that crowded his head at once, each clamant for urgent attention and immediate resolution.

What were the dragons? Were they coming this way? What was the Plague? What was the source of Jack's hunch, that the Plague had a connection with the Sigil and the appalling events depicted therein? And, while we were on that subject, were those events history—or prophecy? And who had *composed* the Sigil? How had they come by all that information? What was their purpose of leaving it *here*? Were there others? And why *now*? Why? Why? *Why*?

None of it made any sense at all. At three o'clock in the morning he awoke to find he was still there, kneeling, uncomfortably chill, his hands clasped together, his back aching, his legs full of cramps. His knees were acutely painful, both from the pressure of his weight, and because his blood had pooled around them. He struggled to his feet, crossed himself and hobbled painfully to bed. He had fallen asleep even before the sharp pins-and-needles sensation in his legs had subsided.

Across the hall, Jack and Jadis were under the covers, each one enjoying the familiar warmth of the other, the sanctity of the darkness and their own thoughts, and yet each wishing the other would break the silence. They, too, had unfinished business. It was Jadis whose resistance broke first.

"Jack…" she whispered, "what *are* we going to do about Tom?" He turned towards her and pulled her head into his chest, running his fingers through her hair, caressing her cheek. Her skin was dry, soft and warm, perhaps a little too warm, and he could feel that she was tense. He felt her lashes flicking and flittering against his fingertips as her eyes moved this way and that, searching for reasons, for answers.

"I don't know," said Jack. "Just keep on showing him that we love him, I guess, and by being patient. He seems so, well, I can't think of the word."

"*Alienated*?"

"Yes, *alienated*." They parted, and Jack sank onto his back, looking up towards where the ceiling would be, were he able to see anything at all. Human eyes naturally crave the light, and faced with gloom, Jack's created a show of tiny auroral sparks that danced before him. Perhaps Tom had seen something similar, albeit grotesquely magnified. But Domingo was right — if it were only Tom who had seen the dramatic display of cosmic carnage, how would the rest of them know if it were real or not?

"I wish I knew how to get to him, Jack, to get my little boy back," said Jadis, "but he's somehow buried himself under a shell."

"But he's not our little boy any more, is he?" Jack whispered to the dark shape of his wife. "He's a grown-up. Maybe he needs space and time to sort it all out by himself."

Jadis continued, as if she hadn't heard. "There was poor Shoshana, no-one knew how or why she died, and he blames himself... I can understand that, but really, dreadful things do happen..."

Jack had felt Shoshana's loss as keenly as Jadis had, mainly by virtue of their own impotence to stop whatever it was that was slowly killing her. Domingo's revelation about her last days had brought it all back. But that was past, and Jack's emotion was now more empathy for his unreachable son than grief for someone long dead and who could no longer suffer. For Tom, any effort to break with the past, however strenuous, seemed to run into a roadblock.

"He seems to be having such a dreadful time in Cambridge," said Jadis, "with these... these... what are they called? Jive Bunnies?"

"'Jive Monkeys,'" Jack laughed, quietly. "I know, they sound like they should be rather fun, with a name like that." Jack remembered hominids who had seemed 'rather fun' on the surface—quite comical in fact—which on closer questioning turned out to have eaten your friends, but only after torturing them in the most degrading and dehumanizing ways.

"Well, whatever they're called, I think they need teaching some manners," she said.

"But that's the point, Jadis. They said the same thing about him."

"And then watching a star being eaten by *more* aliens. No wonder he needs a rest."

"As do I," said Jack, pointedly. But he could tell that she was in one of her moods in which she was over-tired, still taut as a bowstring, and would remain quite unable to sleep unless she'd resolved some inner conundrum. She sat up. He heard the swish of her hair against her shoulders.

"But I don't understand it, Jack."

"Hmm?"

"*Why* doesn't he understand these... these Monkey thingies? Tom's an expert on hominid cultural differences. An authority. He's practically written the book on it. So why did he fail to understand these ones, in particular?" She sank down again, onto the bed. "I just don't get it."

Jack said nothing. But the cogs and wheels in his mind meshed again, and found purchase. As usual, Jadis was way ahead of him.

"I've always had a feeling about Tom," she said. "Well, more of a niggle than a feeling. You know, that he's one of a kind. More than just all that business with his eyes. He was always so alone at school, quiet, reserved. But he was *happy*, wasn't he? I just wish he'd talk about it more. Let it go. I hope he knows that whoever *he* thinks he is, we'll still love him, no matter what."

And, thus decided, she turned over and fell asleep. Jack was still awake when she had begun to snore.

Jack nodded off a little while later, subsiding into a half-dream in which everyone seemed perfectly ordinary until you saw their green, cat-like eyes.

In another room, Tom woke from sleep to find that the bump on his temple had gone down a bit, and no longer hurt quite so much. He'd made little sense of the dream whose shreds were now dissolving like mist before sunrise, but the last image had been of Shoshana, asleep. She had opened her eyes, which got larger and larger and bored into him accusingly. They turned from blue to purple, blazed like stars, and then became two black holes that covered first her face and then, like an expanding burn in a photograph, the entire scene. No, Tom, *NO*, her eyes said. You're not going any further until you get yourself some *menschkeit*. Pull yourself together!

Tom sat up abruptly and then quickly wished he hadn't. His head started to throb again. *Bien sûr*, he might feel confused, conflicted, angry even, but he had no right to take it out on other people, and especially not here. Part of the problem was that he really did want to talk, but apart from his natural tendency to say as little as possible, he was afraid of exposing too much of what he was convinced was his own guilt, and this itself was conflicting.

Another problem was that he felt, now, that he'd been spoiled: perhaps just a bit too lucky. Shoshana had had to fight to get to the farmhouse, the end of a journey that she had almost paid for with her life, several times over: a fare that had been—finally, cruelly—collected. And he had lived his whole life here, cost-free. The Shoshana in his dreams had been right. Even if he revealed to no-one the potentially debilitating anxiety about his own identity, he really did have to pull himself together. To grow up. And as he made that resolution, he imagined Shoshana looking down on him with love, her eyes blue once more, streaked with purple; her wide, full lips parting in a smile to reveal her crazy, loveable teeth, her soft hair falling down over her honey-coloured curves. Yes, he said. Shoshana, I shall do this for you, so I can continue to merit your affection.

So, that was that, then.

But there was also an important, practical aspect to all this. After an absence of a decade, he noticed that his parents had suddenly become elderly. They were as fit as any septuagenarians had a right to be, and probably a whole lot fitter, but he felt that the effort of the farm was becoming too great, and it was beginning to slip away from them. He would prolong his sabbatical indefinitely. The University could hardly complain—he was, after all, right on top of

Souris Saint-Michel, for all that nobody had actually visited it for years.

And there was the Sigil. With what he now knew about stellar extinction (his mind was already pacing out the problem in scientific terminology), it was time to write it up. He would ask his mother about it in the morning. He felt that they had to get on with it, in case they were... how did Domingo put it?

Overtaken By Events.

As he slid into sleep, he realized that those three words could describe his whole life. At every turn, he'd been prey to external influence, buffeted around like a rag doll in a hurricane. Shoshana had arrived, blowing him off his feet. She'd departed—likewise. And then they had both been blown off Masada, and then there had been the whole stomach-churning episode with the Jive Monkeys in which he had been a follower, when he should have been a leader. *Tiens*! He was almost forty years old. It was time he took control of his own destiny.

The following evening, Jack and Jadis ambled up the back lane, hand in hand in the sunshine, towards the village square. It felt like years since they'd done this—just to go out, simply for the pleasure of it, with no particular errand in mind or appointment to keep. But Tom had said he'd settle the farm down for the night, so why didn't they take some time off? Jack felt a sensation of relief, of a load slipping off his shoulders, whose weight he'd hardly noticed until it had been removed.

They found the Place Etienne Geoffroy almost deserted. The silent, old buildings under a rich blue sky of almost alien clarity looked like a cityscape by De Chirico. The boulangerie had closed for the day, and most of the *Sanglier* regulars were still hard at work on their own farms. In fact, when they wandered into the shade of its cheerful blue-and-

white striped awning, they saw that they were the only cus-
tomers. Yvon Rossignol was happy to attend to their every
need—which was herb tea for the Doctor, and a *pastis* for
Jack.

"My pleasure! On the house! We don't see you much
these days. Busy on the farm, eh?"

"Ah! But things are going to change, Yvon," said Jack:
"my son Tom is back and is showing signs of wanting to
take over. Respite for a *vieux pantoufle* like me. I have to say
it's welcome."

"*Change,* eh? Let's drink to the younger generation!"
beamed Rossignol. The clash and clang of pans within beto-
kened the arrival of Madame Rossignol in the kitchen. The
innkeeper's face turned dark and anxious. "Please excuse
me," he said, waddling into the shadows—"duty calls!"

The two of them sat there at the round, rust-pocked café
table, remembering the first time they'd sat there, on their
honeymoon. Each replayed the moment in their mind: Jadis
felt her eyes moistening. She'd been pregnant. Funny, she'd
almost forgotten that, and how much she'd enjoyed it—the
feeling of pride, at a life growing inside her. The irony bit
her now, that she spent most of her time away from the farm
attending the births of others, and yet she'd never borne a
child of her own. She became conscious of an ache in her
lower abdomen, a sympathetic echo of times past both sweet
and bitter.

Inevitably, her thoughts turned to Tom, who had, it
seemed, decided to emerge from beneath his long, black
cloud, and who just that morning had volunteered himself
to write up the Sigil for publication. Although she felt a rueful pang at this, she was grateful, for she knew now that
she'd never get round to it herself. Not any more—it was not
just the farm, and village life, but that she'd got out of the
habit of thinking along academic lines, and she was easily

distracted. *Damn it*, she cursed herself, *it's because I'm an old woman!* The true source of her pang, then, was the recognition and acceptance of her own mortality. As long as she'd kept putting off writing up the Sigil, she'd had a ticket to forever.

"Drink up," said Jack—"I have something to show you." Hand in hand—for they were on their honeymoon, once again—they left the café's shade and ventured into the scorching afternoon heat. They picked their way carefully across the worn, sun-drenched cobbles to the sanctuary of the churchyard gate. She knew where he was leading her. Past the ranks of well-tended graves (so many more than they had been then, almost half a century before); past the welcome, fragrant shadows of the giant yew trees; to the limestone parapet on the other side. The view seemed hardly to have changed. But in those days the vista had been one of morning, and the sun had been at their backs. It now hung before them like a great blood-red ball, bruised on the Earth's western rim.

Jack reached out for her hand, although his eyes were fixed on the far horizon. She could feel the tension running along his fingers like electricity through a cable.

"Somehow," he said, "somehow, we have to make sense of it all. We can't just leave it all to Tom. Not that he couldn't do it, far from it—but because *we* are responsible."

She thought back to that horrific night when they'd seen that yeti, interviewed on the Zenge show, confessing to the murder of Faye and Primrose and their friends, and when she'd begged Jack to understand what they'd unleashed on the world. If it hadn't been for Saint-Rogatien, the way it changed everyone's understanding of history, the hominids might still be hidden, and Faye and Primrose and many others might have lived to climb other, greater mountains.

And if it hadn't been for Jack's feeling that something unusual stood here, a gigantic monolith from an almost unbelievably remote antiquity, none of that would have happened. Souris Saint-Michel might still have been a dusty footnote to the career of a long-dead cleric.

Domingo might not have come into their lives.

And if it hadn't been for the fact that her dear Jack could never quite articulate his intuitions, her life might have drifted away from his own. Their first date might have been their last. There'd have been no Nest, no accident... no Tom.

Rainstorms. Brainstorms.

Jadis stared straight ahead, at the sinking star. She wondered how many more times she'd see a sunset. Indeed, she wondered how many more times there would be a sun to set. Or to rise. The ancients had spent a great deal of time, thought, ritual and bloody sacrifice in an effort to guarantee that very thing. How we arrogant scientists had laughed at this naïve presumption—that anything humans could do might influence the majestic clockwork of the heavens in any way, or be influenced by it.

And yet the Sigil had been a product of a science which, while indescribably ancient, was presumably far greater than theirs, seemingly designed with that very end in view—to propitiate the Gods, to keep the stars from going out.

Jack had had this insight too, she knew, affirming Domingo's wild surmise that the Sigil and the Plague were connected. But as he had with his sense of the landscape long before, he had no way to constrain or articulate it. Jack had needed her then. And he needed her now.

It could be that the world needed her.

The Plague and the Sigil. The Sigil and the Plague.

Circles, circles.

Let's just look at the facts, she said, and take an appropri-
ately long view. The Sigil, irrespective of its own inherent
antiquity, had been buried in the Pyramid more than a hundred thousand years ago, a rough estimate based on the context of the layer in the Pyramid in which it as found.

A hundred thousand years. An interval way beyond our
normal experience. But when mapped against the scale of
the Universe, an interval as evanescent as a flash, seen
through the corner of one eye, of the scarlet hem of a gown
disappearing behind a mud hut. Turn round, and it would
be gone. On the largest scale, that of the Universe, we and
the Sigil exist at what is, for all practical purposes, the same
moment.

So far, so good. Now, consider this, she said to herself:
human beings evolve at more or less the same time that the
Sigil is deposited within the Pyramid and is then uncovered,
and again, at around the same time, a Plague arrives. It's
funny, she said, nobody has ever found any kind of infectious agent for Postembryonic Oolithic Petrosis. All we
know is that it is specific to people who can claim to be *Homo
sapiens*, with relatively little genetic introgression from other
hominids. In fact, we know so little about the disease that we
can't even tell if the victims are 'dead' in any sense we'd understand the term. She voiced this thought to Jack.

"Perhaps they're listening to us talk, right now!" said
Jack. Even though the sun was on their faces, they both shivered: the graveyard was full of Plague victims, brooding in
their caskets. "'That is not dead which can eternal lie,'" he
murmured, "'and with strange aeons even death may die.'"

"Hmm?"

"Just something I remembered from my student days,
tramping the hills. An old Lovecraft story…"

"Oh, Jack, you really are a very silly man!" She turned to
look at him then, her dark eyes glistening with that mixture

of love and exasperation one can only ever find in couples married for so long that each knows and tolerates every wrinkle and foible of the other. The way that she always tolerated Jack's strange fascination for anything Gothick. She could never understand how anyone could derive enjoyment from scaring themselves witless. But he kept half a shelf in the office to indulge what he imagined was his secret vice, and sometimes, when he couldn't sleep, he'd carry a candle to his creaking recliner and, feet up on his desk, take another midnight stroll into what the blurbs of the faded paperbacks would always say were 'eldritch realms of preternatural and chthonic terror' or some such tosh. She smiled. Dear, sweet Jack. The world might need her, but if it weren't for Jack, she'd long since have vaporized and vanished on the wind like smoke.

She still rememberd the first moment they'd met, when she'd breezed in late to his supervision, all a fluster from a bike puncture, trying to brazen out her embarrassment. How could one be late for a supervision? And a *first* supervision? But he'd only looked at her with those calm, blue eyes, his slightly lopsided smile, and she knew—she just knew, in that moment, with the kind of absolute certainty that is the currency not of science but of faith—that this man would be her rock, would make everything all right. Whatever happened.

They now held each other close in the cooling air: a breeze from the distant Bay of Biscay was making its way across the land, leaching out its warmth. Shaking the hair from her eyes, she looked up at him and said: all we have now is a correlation. No, not even that, a *coincidence*. There's too much we don't know, she said, rehearsing just some of the possible unknowns.

Are the dragons munching their way through this corner of space alone, or are they found more generally?

Does their activity change with time?

Are there more Sigils? Domingo thinks there might be.

And if someone found one in Cretaceous rocks among some tyrannosaur eggs—well, that would seriously weaken the link. And, taking the long view, is the Plague unique to humans? Maybe there's some unknown animal reservoir, or a virus, or something. The trouble is, she said, nobody knows, and since the Plague, nobody has had the means to find out.

"No," he'd said. "You worked that out long ago, don't you remember? The disease didn't seem to spread by any kind of agent."

"Yes. So I did," she replied.

As they watched, the sun sank behind the distant hills, and just as it disappeared, it shot a shimmering curtain of rays upwards, dressing a few shreds of otherwise nondescript clouds in a rich array of pink and gold. Jack and Jadis stayed a little longer to admire the display, then turned and walked homewards.

"I know it's just a coincidence," sighed Jack, as they walked down the lane, their field gate coming into view as darker blur against the deep blue of night, "and, yes, you're right. Perhaps Tom was right, too, to dismiss Domingo's wild surmise. It's just, well..."

Jadis had known him long enough to recognize the signs, or to know that Jack's hunches were always worth following to the end. She turned to him again.

"Jack—*tell* me."

"No, it's probably just daft," he said, "for all that it's been niggling me for years."

"What has?"

"Oh, all right. But it's more to do with the Sigil itself, rather than any connection with the Plague. Funnily enough—well, not *funny* really, but... well, it's all to do with

Tom's eyes. You see, I've seen eyes like his before. Just once. It's only in the past few days that I've made the connection."

It was now fully dark and the summer stars had begun to appear. Vega, Deneb, Altair. Jadis looked up at Jack—his head was a silhouette against the wheeling sky.

"Jack...?"

"You remember just after we opened up SSM and I flew off to the States?"

"Yes—you finally got to meet Ruxton Carr."

"Well, it's him. He had eyes like Tom's—big, green, cat-like pupils. And then, when Tom came into our lives, I thought I'd seen eyes like that before, but could never place them. Well, it's all clicked. After all these years! And just think about Carr. You remember when dear old Roger first told us about him, and that he'd set up two institutes?"

Jadis said she had. She remembered that she'd been pregnant at the time. How much had happened when she was pregnant. She missed it. Oh well, too late now. *Far* too late. But she snapped back to the present, and jumped into Jack's argument. But she held his hand more tightly, and warmed to the reassurance of his grip in response. Oh, Jack, I shall forever be just a child in your arms.

"I remember," she said, "one for landscape archae-ology—for you, and me, and Roger: the other for astrometry. And how everyone was puzzled by the choices."

"Yet in hindsight," Jack continued, "they shouldn't have been, because Carr had always publicly said that he backed 'The Future'. And what two, precise things are we having to study *now*? Interesting, eh?"

"I see," said Jadis "if it hadn't been for Carr's choices, we'd never have found the Sigil, nor known about stellar extinctions. Jack, that's amazing. It's been in front of us the whole time, all these years. How could we have missed it?"

"But there's something else, too, something that only I could have known about, because he told me at our one meeting. I remember it like it was yesterday. He told me that our work—yours and mine—was of 'the utmost importance,' and—get this—that 'it might even save the planet.'"

Jadis felt that Jack was talking more to himself than to her or anyone else in particular, for in two minutes he'd said more than he usually did in a whole day. This meant that he was really on to something, his mental bloodhound hot on the trail.

"Ever since I've been wondering how digging ever deeper holes underneath France could ever do anything to save the planet," he said. "But now there's the Sigil, and the links with the disappearing stars, and *somehow it all fits in together*. I'm *sure* of it."

"And the Plague too?"

"Yes, that too. God knows how or why, but yes... that too. I'm sure about that. Absolutely."

They were now at the back door that led to the *arrière-cuisine*. In the deep shadows, Jack's eyes sparkled like polished coals.

Chapter 8. Pilgrim

Massilia, Rhoneland, Earth, *c.* 125,000 years ago

The wicked, quaint fruit-merchant men,
Their fruits like honey to the throat
But poison in the blood
Christina Rosetti—*Goblin Market*

The last stage of Mr Khorare's journey—the most wonderful, and the strangest—began in a dawn of mist, when Raull toted what few belongings (just two small bags) Mr Khorare had chosen to take down to the lobby. No concierge was to be seen: the steam-*barouche* waited beyond the bronze-and-glass doors, its fumes adding to the fog, the chauffeur in shadow.

Mr Khorare and Raull embraced in the silence of friends, unsure that either would see the other again. Mr Khorare had reassured his servant that he would indeed return, but his business was such that a precise time of homecoming could not be given. He had entrusted the valet with his keys and his affairs, confident in his abilities to service all such needs with delicacy and discretion even in the extended (and perhaps indefinitely prolonged) absence of his master.

For himself, Mr Khorare knew that there would be no return, and no need, in truth, for any luggage aside from his own self and the talisman he wore in a soft leather drawstring bag, hung on a cord around his neck. To signify such to himself—if not the valet—he wore a grayish silk chemise that might once have been cream, or white, and a pair of faded knee-breeches of indeterminate color and fabric, but which might once have been velvet. He had discovered these at the back of his closet, and, surprised to have seen them at all, pulled them off their hangers to his face, greeting them with the same tears of joy that an owner might lavish on a much-loved pet whose disappearance, long before, is now no longer expected to be followed with prodigal reappearance. Once Mr Khorare had recovered his composure, his expert eye noticed the skill with which these weather-worn garments had been patched and mended: gussets almost invisibly stitched into otherwise irreparably corrupt seams, the near-invisible needlework of matchless quality and refinement. Mr Khorare could not remember having ordered such restoration, nor having paid for it—still less having undertaken it himself (would that he could!) But that his life was often punctuated with long lapses of memory was a circumstance to which he was now accustomed. So, now, he simply offered an inchoate thanks to whomsoever it was, and took the reappearance of his old, shark-shredded, battle-rent travel garments as a good omen.

The steam-*barouche* took Mr Khorare and his two bags (a small haversack and a smaller, leather belt-pouch) northwards through the morning fog to Massilia's main rail station. As they passed through the near-silent streets of early dawn, the white shrouds concealed the buildings on either side so that Mr Khorare lost all sense of where he was, or when, or how fast they might be going. But at last the twin pyramidal pinnacles, framing the main gate of the rail station like cathedral spires, loomed forth. The steam-*barouche* pulled up outside the gates, puffing gently, and the chauffeur gave a hand to his master as he alighted. Here, only the usual friendly valediction. No heartfelt farewell, as had been with Raull—the chauffeur had no reason to suspect other than that his master would return, the next day or the day after. Any more surprising intelligence could be conveyed to the servants by Raull at a time and convenience of his own choosing.

In any case, Mr Khorare had not the heart for any more good-byes. Those few he had made had drained him, emotionally—and in any case, his mission was now to look forward, not back. His ticket purchased in advance, Mr Khorare had only to find his train and board it. Before another quarter-hour had passed, he was comfortably seated aboard the *Princess of Aquitaine*.

The main concourse of the Massilia rail station was so vast that Mr Khorare could not see the ceiling above him—iron girders and stone pillars teetered upwards to be lost in the steam from the engines and the mist curling in from outside. The marble floor was peppered with people—mainly Stoners, with a few Thinskin servants and porters. Very occasionally, the roughly-maned figures of Yettins could be seen towering above even the tallest Thinskin. Every single one, though—Stoner or Thinskin or Yettin—seemed no larger than a crawling ant when placed against the scale of the station building. Mr Khorare was soon lost amid the crowds, just one brownian particle among hundreds, though his face was turned upwards to find the great black wall of the departures board, steam fuming from small vents as the pneumatically powered destination indicators whirled and flapped, pacing each new departure, each fresh arrival, as if the machine itself were the controller of time, rather than simply a herald of events posted within it.

Within the surging crowd below, Mr Khorare stopped, awed not only by the size of the board but by the wealth of possibilities it offered. In a moment, he could be on the *Northern Lights* that took three days to reach Far Yotunheim, realm of the Ice Giants; or the *Tundra Herald* that tracked the endless forests of Rhús as far as the High Frontier of Altaic Yettinland. He could climb aboard the *Sierra Mountaineer* that would call at the golden city of Carcassonne before traversing the Pyrenees and crossing Iberia to the Guadalquivír. Then again, he might hitch a ride on the *Flying Reindee*r which, arrowing through Rhoneland, would set him down at Calais Station for the boat-train interchange to distant, wild Britain.

In his relatively short time as a resident of Rhoneland, Mr Khorare had — of course — been aware of the Stoner Civilization at its apogee, the culmination of the best part of a million years of slow acculturation from nameless progenitor species. Such, though, was dry intellection. Not until he'd seen the great departure board had he been truly aware of its scale, which humbled even the extensive realms tributary to the Great and Ancient City of Axandragór, and made an impudent wart of the barbarous Kingdom Under The Mountain.

But more was to come. Amid the departure board was a notice advertising the imminent departure from Track 29 of the *Princess of Aquitaine*, headed for Bordeaux with connections for Poitiers and Rennes, but calling at a number of places in between, including the one now engraved on Mr Khorare's mind — the Great Pyramid of Xxántroghátrem.

The train itself, resting at Track 29 and fuming like a dragon but lightly at rest, was an awesome sight in itself. Starting from the immense, cylindrical engine nearest the barrier, fuming with brutal, barely concealed power, a chain of sleek, silvery carriages stretched into the blue distance, farther than Mr Khorare could clearly see. Each carriage was as tall as a house, as long as a street, and there were, according to Mr Khorare's own squinting count, at least thirty of them (a steward later confirmed that there were thirty-six, culminating in a traction locomotive of a similar impressive order to the one he'd already seen). Mr Khorare reached inside the leather pouch strung around his neck, and, warm from the talisman next to it, retrieved his ticket. His assigned berth was in Coach Fifteen, he read, somewhere in the hazy distance. He hastened to reach it before the train departed: indeed, he heard the guard's whistle as he stepped, winded and panting, onto the footplate. He followed the directions to his seat—a small cabin, in truth—up a winding *escalier*, deeply carpeted in rich crimson and with reassuringly thick brass-work handrails.

As he climbed, he was reminded of the stairs to the box in his favorite theater, the box reserved for distinguished personages, and patrons such as himself. But the time had long departed for memories of past glories—Mr Khorare's mind was canted resolutely forward. He found his perch on the third and topmost level of the carriage, and had had barely time to register the small but luxurious washing facilities; the roll-top *escritoire* with its lamps and pens and inkstands; the carved walnut side table bearing a bone-china platter loaded with fresh bread and ripe fruit, and, next to it, a neat stack of polished skull-bowls; the elegant *fauteuil* and *chaise-longue* before great crystalline picture windows on both sides—before the leviathantine monster he now inhabited jerked and lurched into wakefulness beneath his feet and all around him, and, with a boom and a roar and a clang, the glooming vastness of the station building began to slide smoothly back, away into history, revealing a landscape of pearly white light.

The next revelation to assault the bruised senses of Mr Khorare was the extent of the city of Massilia itself. The great train slid slowly through crowded suburbs, punctuated by the clipped spaces of parkland, dissected by streets, rail lines and long-tamed rivers and canals crossed by well-maintained bridges, and the frequent exclamations of pyramids. These were of various shapes and sizes, some four-sided, others three, or five; some as small as shacks, others towering far above the houses all around; some as gently sloping and voluminous as hills whose gentle slopes belie their height; others, like spires, steeply raked and needle-sharp.

Such was the townscape with which Mr Khorare had become familiar during his sojourn in Massilia. What, however, defied his expectation was that the landscape did not soon thin out into farmland or wilderness, in the same way that the massif of the Kingdom Under The Mountain soon gave way to cedar forests, tamarisk scrub and the open savannah of Mesopotamia. No—it continued, unchanging and yet endlessly varied. After an hour and a half, Mr Khorare realized that the entire country of Rhoneland was nothing more than a greatly extended city, a region that had been subdued by the Stoners for many hundreds of thousands of years. After an hour more, it came home to him that the course of every river had been altered, the better to suit its usage; the very hills themselves had been leveled, remodeled, even moved. The entire continent of Europe had been shaped by the massive collectivity of Stoner effort, muscle and will for time out of mind. Mr Khorare, awed, scooped some bread and fruit into a skull-bowl and subsided onto the *chaise-longue*.

He knew that he could not afford to get too comfortable as his station stop was no more than an hour away, so, with the tamed town-lands passing by below, he gave thought to his destination.

Mr Khorare had had no clear thought as to this, nor what he was to do once he'd got there. He had learned to let the whims of the world guide his fate. Hence it was—or so he imagined—no more than mere chance that had led him to pronounce the name of Xxántroghátrem when his wayward feet had guided him to a travel agent a few days before. The travel agent had suggested the present date, being one of pilgrimage to that greatest and most ancient of pyramids. Mr Khorare confessed, however, that he'd seen precious few other passengers on this train that might have passed for pilgrims—but then, he reasoned, he was late boarding, and his cabin was a private one.

In the days before his departure, Mr Khorare had made several trips to the municipal library, where he'd read—in very old books, themselves translated from still more archaic records—that the Great Pyramid of Xxántroghátrem was one of the oldest structures in Rhoneland, if not *the* oldest. The problem was that nobody really knew *how* old it was, nor the identity of the builders. The Xxántroghátrem of the title referred to *Róghadhr*, a mythical Stoner chieftain who had lived (if indeed he had existed at all) many millennia earlier, and whose name had become attached to the structure by virtue of several legendary exploits when the structure to which his name had accreted already labored under a toll of years beyond count.

The original name for the structure had been lost in remotest antiquity, and it was likely that the creators of the Pyramid had not themselves been Stoners. Despite their manifold achievements in subduing the very earth to their will, the Stoners regarded the long-lost builders of the Great Pyramid with nothing short of religious reverence. For not only was the Great Pyramid extremely old, it was also extremely large, dwarfing any comparable structure the Stoners had erected. The structure covered sixteen square miles, and its apex rode a full two and a half miles above the plain. Even the hardiest pilgrims took more than a week to climb its thousands of steep and teetering stairs, and only the fittest of that select group would find enough air at the summit to satisfy a ragged gasp.

And the Great Pyramid of Xxántroghátrem was just the start—a barbican, a gatehouse, to still further wonders. From the southern face of the Pyramid a wide road shot due southwards, the Great South Way, dead straight for ten miles, connecting the massive structure with something equally wondrous, underground. He could find no hint of what that something might be. When asked, the travel agent simply turned away as if Mr Khorare had suddenly become inaudible, and no book he could find so much as mentioned the matter. It was clear that whatever it was, Mr Khorare had to find out for himself. As if he had been drawn to it. As if it were his destination, the culmination of his existence.

Mr Khorare was pondering on this and related subjects when he felt a slight shift in the tenor of the vehicle in whose belly he was traveling. The note of the engine seemed to weaken and drop by no more than a quarter tone, but this was enough to alert Mr Khorare that he would soon be reaching the station that served the Great Pyramid of Xxántroghátrem. Hastily, he finished his meal and placed the skull-bowl on the table next to the (depleted) bowl of fruit. Picking up his baggage, he half-walked, half-swung down the tight, spiraling staircase until he reached the ground-floor footplate. Once there, he found the way barred by a clot of other passengers, mainly dressed in flowing robes of purple. There were men, and women, and small children, and much luggage, and a great confusion of noise. But it was only when the train had finally shuddered to a halt, the hydraulic rams of its brakes shrieking, and the doors had opened to admit a clear northern light, that Mr Khorare noticed. Every single one of the pilgrims was a Thinskin.

The secrets of Xxántroghátrem were beginning to reveal themselves.

The sun of summer climbed steeply into the blue vault. Mr Khorare alighted onto the platform and was immediately assaulted with heat and humidity, as if someone had dropped a sodden blanket on his head. He had not noticed, before, that his cabin had been climate-controlled, responding—perhaps—to the automatic sensation of his own warmth and boldily moisture, so that he would reside in comfort at all times. He had had a closely similar arrangement fitted to his own apartment in Massilia, and, having framed that thought, felt a stab of regret. But no, a second thought came — the time for regrets was past. Things were moving to a head. Shouldering his meager haversack, he walked briskly into the stream of people surging through the station building and into the small town clustered before the eastern face of the Pyramid.

The town of Xxántroghátrem was small. But then, reasoned Mr Khorare, any town not cowed into insignificance by the vastness of the Pyramid would have to have been extensive indeed. Even so, the conurbation, such as it was, was hemmed by the press and noise of humanity, almost all of whom were Thinskins. Mr Khorare had no choice but to dive into the crowd in the wide street outside the station, whereupon his vision became instantly restricted to the bright robes and animated people within touching distance of himself. His senses were soon all but overwhelmed by the acrid musk of Thinskin bodies, and the constant chatter and boom and shriek of Thinskin voices (Stoners being, as a rule, much quieter in all situations except the extremis of battle).

It was plain that Mr Khorare had arrived on market day. From glimpses between the tall, brightly-clad people he saw gaily decorated stalls on each side of the great street, selling all manner of things — fruit, meat, and cloth, and house wares, and cheap souvenirs. All such orientation as he could contrive was to be made by viewing at a steep angle, which view afforded Mr Khorare a clutter of pyramidal rooftops, and, behind them all, a vast canted wall, bright white in the late-morning sunshine, which occupied most of the sky.

The Great Pyramid itself.

No amount of reading or preparation had prepared Mr Khorare for the sight of the Pyramid, close up. He stopped, where he was, amid the crowd, transfixed. The crowd surged and flowed about him as were he were no greater an obstacle than a pebble on the bed of a great river. Occasionally he would be buffeted by a glance or a jolt from a passer-by, but nothing could tear his eyes away.

The Pyramid was so incomparably huge that it seemed to tower into the sky and overtop him, so that, at first, Mr Khorare had trouble retaining a secure footing. Mr Khorare's eyes scanned the bright face of the structure for some detail—anything—that would bring some ordinary sense of scale and proportion to his rescue. But as his eyes accommodated to the assault of blank, reflective whiteness, he noticed a line of black dots trailing up the median line, from base to apex. The dots were scattered, clumped, with more towards the base, and thinning out towards the summit. From where he stood, Mr Khorare could discern no movement, but that, he realized, was an artifact of distance. The dots he saw were people—pilgrims—ascending and descending the Pyramid's morning-side face.

Having recovered himself, Mr Khorare looked down and brought to mind that his travel agent had made him a booking in a small *pension* in a small side street just off the main thoroughfare. Reasoning that the latter was the great street in which he found himself, he let the crowd push him on once more, further away from the railway station, and deeper into the town. The names of the streets were, fortunately, inscribed in large signs at a high level, in the clear, angular characters of the Stoner language current in Massilia, so it wasn't long before he found the street whose name accorded with that in his memory. The problem now was how he should make his way orthogonal to the movement of the crowd, without, first, being carried straight past. However, the observation of the pell-mell movements of small children, weaving in and out of the adults as small creatures amid great trees on the forest floor, gave Mr Khorare an idea. Already almost a head shorter than most of the Thin-skins, even the women, he ducked down and made his way in a kind of crouching lope, dodging bodies and legs, and soon found himself in the shade between two market stalls, and, in rapid progression, in the street of his desire.

The shade here was welcome, as was the quiet: the side-walks were populated by relatively few pedestrians, and just one steam-*barouche*—a taxi-cab—had stopped kerbside, al-lowing a small party of richly attired pilgrims to alight. How such a conveyance could advance in this town at any greater speed than a pedestrian was a mystery. But when he looked up, the Pyramid appeared to close the end of the street like a great white wall. This closeness must have been an illusion, for Mr Khorare knew for a fact that it was at least half a mile away.

The party of pilgrims from the steam-*barouche* was headed, as chance would have it, to the *pension* in which Mr Khorare had been booked, so, hurrying to catch up with them, he joined the knot of people as they entered the build-ing. He waited, patiently, as the pilgrims completed their transaction with the receptionist, with much shouting and waving of arms and jostling of what seemed like a quite in-ordinate amount of luggage. When they had dispersed to the elevator, their luggage before them on a heaving trolley pushed by a harassed-looking bellhop, Mr Khorare found himself at the front of the queue. The receptionist looked up. She was a Stoner female of middle years and quite unpre-possessing appearance, but her dour face was quite trans-formed by the smile with which she greeted Mr Khorare, as if responding to a welcome quietness following the rumbus-tious fuss of the Thinskin pilgrims. Mr Khorare's immediate business was completed with polite expedition. But Mr Kho-rare, responding to the receptionist's welcoming smile, and perhaps a shared solidarity of reticence, felt prompted to start a conversation. To answer the question that nobody seemed willing to address.

"Madam," he started, tentatively, "I wonder if I might inquire…?" She looked up from her tickets and documents.

"Sir?" Her accent was polite and clipped, as something she wore as part of her job, conversing with tourists from all over Europe. Mr Khorare imagined that as soon as she went off-shift, she'd resort to the ever-changing fluidity that was the argot of Rhoneland.

"I'm not a regular… uh… pilgrim here…"

"Yes, Sir. I thought you weren't, but I didn't like to say."

"Where do they go—the pilgrims—after they have ascended the Pyramid, and come down again?" She looked straight at him, eyes wide.

"You mean, you don't know?"

"No, Madam, I'm afraid I don't," he said, "I've tried to find out, but no text I can find, no tourist guide, says anything about what lies underground, buried at the end of the Great South Way. Not so much as a name. When I ask, people turn away, or change the subject, as if I had made some impolite personal remark. It really is most perplexing. Might you shed any light on the matter? I do apologise if to do so might prove inconvenient or embarrassing. I should not want to cause you any discomfort." The receptionist flushed.

"Sir, I should have to explain something that visitors to the Pyramid usually know without anyone having to tell them, something to which they have become accustomed since childhood." She lowered her voice and leaned forward, as if about to vouchsafe a confidence. "It's a taboo, you see, and… well, really, I don't think I should say anything more. It's something that only Thinskins ever discuss, and then only between themselves. Do you plan to head that way?"

"Yes, I do." The affirmation just popped into his head, where only a vague cloud of possibility existed before. The talisman burned like a brand against his chest, its heat only slightly dulled by the leather pouch in which it hung.

"You have no plans to ascend the Pyramid, then?"

"No," he said. "The Great South Way is my course."

"In that case," she said, "we serve breakfast at 4 a.m. sharp, after which you should check out and follow the guests who've just checked in. They are going that way to-morrow. I'm sure they wouldn't mind an addition to their party."

"Do you think they'd be willing to... uh... take me into their confidence?"

"Really, it's impossible to say. But at least they'll know the way, and what to do, and perhaps furnish you with some assistance. Oh—before I forget—here's your room key," she handed over a thick metal disc like a large coin, engraved with complex, labyrinthine patterns on both faces. "It's room two-oh-five, take the elevator to the second floor. Is that all your luggage?" She gave a winsome smirk.

"Yes, Madam. It's just me."

"Well, have a nice day, now." She turned and disappeared into a back room. Mr Khorare was left quite alone.

-=0=-

It was not until the fifth mile of the Great South Way had passed that anything changed in its remorseless monotony. Mr Khorare had breakfasted in the dining room of the *pension* at a table for one, a discreet distance away from the loudly chattering party of Thinskins, before checking out. The morning receptionist was a Stoner woman, younger than the one with whom, the day before, he'd shared such confidences: so his uneasy loneliness was heightened, rather than eased, by any sense of conspiracy, however ill-merited.

He left the *pension* in the dawn's chill, trailing the colorful party of Thinskins as it draggled and honked like herded geese—heedless of the tranquility of a town as yet only slowly waking—through a warren of nameless streets, sometimes broad and well paved, but mostly narrow alleys of dirt in which the party was obliged to walk in single file, stepping gingerly over puddles and piles of refuse. The Great Pyramid of Xxántroghátrem was ever their guide, and, as they walked, its aspect, above crowded tenements and elegant public buildings alike, slowly changed: the blank eastern face, bright in the dawning sun, gave onto the southern face, with a promise yet brighter—the two gigantic facets separated by the razor-edged line of the south-east ridge. The journey was so bafflingly tortuous, and the turnings so unexpected despite the universal signpost that was the pyramid, towering above everything, that Mr Khorare found himself repeatedly grateful for having had the fortune to be following a party that was at the same time so well-informed about the route (which he should not have been able to have found himself) and so noisy in their prosecution of it (so that even if they passed out of sight behind some building or obstacle, he could still hear them, and so follow).

After almost an hour of walking through the mazy ways of the town, the south-eastern ridge faded behind them and the bright southern face of the Great Pyramid now presented its way to them, entire. Before long the party found itself at a small cluster of modest stone huts at the end of the broadest and straightest road Mr Khorare had ever seen. Standing at some distance from the Thinskin party while its members gathered in conclave, apparently in prayer (to whom, or for what, Mr Khorare remained frustratingly in ignorance), Mr Khorare could only wait. Wait, that is, until the party moved off down the immense thoroughfare, with himself trailing at a respectful distance. No chance of losing them here: this, the Great South Way, arrowed southwards with diamond-hard straightness, its surface a perfect jigsaw of dressed slabs, pristine, for mile after mile, and a full twenty yards wide. The town of the Pyramid ended abruptly here, just as the road started, giving way to a featureless emptiness of gently sloping countryside, with not a farm or a building in sight on either side of the road, as far as the eye could see. It occurred to Mr Khorare that this was the only part of Rhoneland he'd seen that could count as in any way deserted. Which meant, he reflected further, that this desolation was entirely deliberate. A wilderness, cultivated for a purpose.

That purpose was soon to become apparent. To step with deliberation along a straight road without distraction is, as Mr Khorare discovered, to set up a rhythm in which one's steps soon become entrained with one's breathing, and, before long, with the beat of one's heart. Although the heat of the day increased — there being no shade of any kind — Mr Khorare soon found himself bowling along with a welcome serenity of spirit and determination of purpose, even though he was as yet still ignorant of what that purpose was. The way, the way — that was all that mattered.

To step, first once, and then again.

To breathe, first in, then out.

Systole, diastole.

A small fragment of Mr Khorare's mind, detached from the rest, observed his generally calm and meditative mood, and speculated that were all pilgrims to have achieved that same, trance-like state by journey's end, then it was no wonder that definite reports from that destination were hard to come by.

As he walked, the knot of Thinskin pilgrims ahead of him faded into a colorful mirage-like blot, their chatter subsiding and, finally, dying, as distance and meditative purpose sucked it dry. The pilgrims were always at a fixed distance ahead of him, pursued, but never attained. At first, Mr Khorare paid little heed to the impression that the knot had broken apart; that a small piece of it had become detached, and was growing larger. As he paced, though, a disturbance clouded his mind. Had this fragment stopped, or had it reversed its direction, and was now approaching him? He was helpless to investigate, though, as his arms swung relentlessly back and forth, his legs and feet moved like mindless machinery, pacing the way.

Mr Khorare drew level with the fragment at the five-mile marker — the halfway point of the Great South Way — when the fragment spoke.

"We thought it meet that one of our number should accompany you, Excellency Khorare," it said. "We should be honored if you would join us."

Mr Khorare was less startled by the content of the Thinskin's message, and that he knew Mr Khorare's name and former office in the Kingdom, than the sound of the voice in which these words were articulated. It was quite unlike that of a Rhonelander, and had every cadence of the Kingdom Under The Mountain. At first, Mr Khorare found any answer at all hard to produce, in any accent at all.

"Did you...? Might I...?"

"Don't be alarmed, Sir, please. My name is Vortigern. Like you, I am a former resident of the Kingdom Under The Mountain." The Thinskin whose name was Vortigern put out his hand for Mr Khorare to shake. Mr Khorare, his diplomatic poise recovered, took the proffered hand and shook it, and responded with the most courtly greeting he could muster in the language of the Kingdom.

"Well met on the road, Friend Vortigern," he said. Vorti-gern bowed, rose, and the two men fell into step together, trailing the still-moving blot of pilgrims now on the horizon.

Chapter 9. Jester

Mount Carmel, Earth, *c*. 45,000 years ago

Not to go on all-fours. *That* is the Law.
Are we not Men?
H. G. Wells — *The Island of Dr Moreau*

"There was a Yettin, a Stoner and a Thinskin, and..."

"Crusher? *Crusher*! Put *down* the Royal Convenience and listen to this!"

"Your Most Exothermic Majesty is too kind. As I was saying, there was a Yettin, a Stoner, and a Thinskin, and..."

The big Stoner pulled his still-dripping penis from the Thinskin female tethered on its arms and knees, spat on its haunches, and took another bite from the bone he was gnawing.

"Hnnn?"

"We said, listen to this. It's a good one. Fucking get on with it, Catshit."

"My most panegyric obeisances, Majesty." Catshit, the motleyed jester, bowed low. "I shall continue, at the orgiastic pleasure of Your Egregious Tremendousness." He stood up to his full height, barely half that of the Stoner bodyguards in the hall. There were six of them. Add the Royal Convenience, and he himself, Catshit thought, and you'd have all that was left of the Court of the King. And only two—he and the King—still had tongues. The King had had a brutal way with dissent, in his time. But that time was rapidly fading, and there was no dissent left. Just a lot of very, very old jokes.

"There was a Yettin, a Stoner and a Thinskin..."

"We've already heard that part, Catshit."

"I crave the bounteous mercy of Your Most Meretricious and Ordovician Majesty."

"And you can get up off the floor, too." Hengest, King Under the Mountain, adjusted his bloated frame on a throne much too small for him. His belly sagged over its arms. Skeins of drool ran from the corners of his mouth as he chewed on morsels he'd picked from a nearby platter. Streaks of piss and shit ran down his legs, smearing the seat and plinth, and running across the dais. His blotched and bloated hands scrabbled blindly for the last few scraps of meat as his blank eyes, almost buried in the folds of his face, twitched this way and that, gazing around his hall. Catshit the Jester chose not to refer to his employer's mistake. An easy mistake to make, in his condition. But it was never good — never *safe* — to second-guess the King.

"There was a Yettin, a Stoner and a Thinskin…" The King sighed. The jester continued, quickly, his voice quavering. That it had come to this. "… and they were travelling across the savannah. After many days, and all sorts of exciting adventures with which I shall not tax Your Vertiginously Anechoic Majesty's patience…"

"We told you to get to the fucking point, Catshit."

"I am ever delighted to serve Your Most Thunderously Thanatogenic Majesty. As I was saying, the three companions — the Yettin, the Stoner and the Thinskin…"

A bone, with scraps of meat still attached, whizzed past his left ear. The King was blind, but his aim was still pretty much near the mark.

"… they found a vast palace, in the shape of a pyramid. They entered without resistance, and found that it was equipped for their every whim. Mountains of food — haunches of aurochs, sand-baked coelodont, mammoth steaks, succulent fatted Thinskin, offered live and fresh for the slaughter, and the choicest cuts; vats of mead and beer;

flagons of testicle-and-eyeball soup; as much fresh, young, willing Thinskin cunt as they could fuck in a lifetime, before sampling that exquisite savor that only just-fucked Thinskin flesh can provide..."

"Huh. *We* like our Thinskin cunt *un*willing. More resistance. It's the *fear*, you know. Brings out the flavor. *Oi!* Ripper! Gnasher! Slasher! Pay *attention*. And Crusher, we told you to leave the Royal Convenience *alone*. We should like another go at it before we retire. We should not like it *spoiled*." Grunts of flat assent echoed around the hall.

"Get the fuck on with it, Catshit, will you? We haven't got all day. Empires to rule. Cunts to fuck. You know how it is. The endless duty of government."

"As your Most Euxinic and Palindromic Majesty requests," continued Catshit the jester. "Anyway, after a gargantuan banquet, at which their every wish was fulfilled, the Yettin, the Stoner and the Thinskin retired."

"Oh, we *bet* they did."

"The next day, after further debauchery on their couches, they availed themselves of such further pleasures that the Pyramid Palace could offer."

"More fucking? We do hope there was more *fucking*. We *like* fucking." Three or four of the bodyguards laughed. The sound was ugly, like flints smashing together. Another of the bodyguards shambled over to the Royal Convenience, pulled up his stone-embroidered kilt, and rammed his cock hard into its anus. The Royal Convenience, bound as it was by its elbows and knees to a raised platform, emitted no more than the tiniest whine. The knees of the Royal Convenience were splayed somewhat further apart than its elbows, for ease of access, particularly for the immense bulk of the King. That, and stability, given the punishment to which it was repeatedly subjected.

"Your Psychotropically Tendentious Majesty will be pleased to learn that the fucking was free and abandoned," continued the jester, "involving various species of man and beast in as many ingenious positions as even the boundless imagination of Your Most Mandragorously Cumbrous Majesty might surely contrive."

"Tell us the one about the Thinskin baby buggered to bits by a bull mammoth in *musth*. We *like* that one."

The jester told him. The laughter that rang around the cave was sustained and appreciative. The bodyguard currently using the Royal Convenience used the cover of noise to drive harder into it. Its meager dugs flapped back and forth in time with the assault. Rivulets of blood and shit ran down the backs of its scrawny thighs. The bodyguard climaxed and withdrew, turning his attention away from the Royal Convenience as if it did not exist.

"Get on with the joke, Catshit," bellowed the King, as the laughter subsided. "The one about the Yettin and so on. The Pyramid Palace."

"I prostrate myself before even the most fleeting desires of Your Most Mendacious and Zymurgic Majesty," said the jester, kicking aside a few of the bones scattered across the filthy floor of the throne room. Just to make some space. "As I was saying, the three companions availed themselves of such abundant further pleasures that the Pyramid Palace could offer.

"The Yettin left early to track down a herd of coelodonts across the plain. The Thinskin left early to find others of his kind, and sailed off on some ridiculous pilgrimage to the west, seeking the Fabled Port of Massilia and the Pyramid of the Goddess..." The jester's voice turned a darker shade then, as if he were talking more to himself than the King. As if he'd been on such a pilgrimage himself, once. Certainly, that was the part of the story he loved to tell most. So much, that he often ran the risk of losing himself in detail that came to his mind far more easily than his other inventions.

Thankfully, the King Under the Mountain failed to notice his jester's reverie, being convulsed up with mirth. "Port of Massilia!" he guffawed. "*Pyramid of the Goddess!*" Tears of laughter spurted from his porcine eyes. His bloated belly shuddered and heaved. A further stream of piss dribbled from between his massive thighs, down his calves and over the scabbed, rotting stumps of his feet. "Go on, Catshit, go on! What happened to the Stoner? What happened to *him*, we wonder?"

"As Your Most Bohemian and… er… *Rhapsodic* Majesty commands," the jester said. "The Stoner chose to remain in the Pyramid Palace that day. There was always another dainty to try, another drink to sup, and the Thinskin cunt just kept on lining up for his attention."

"Go on, Catshit! Go on! Don't Stop! What happened next? We do so *enjoy* this part."

"As Your Most Corpulent and Hemispheric Majesty commands. Well, as the Stoner was just finishing off fucking his thirty-fifth or thirty-sixth Thinskin cunt, and just wondering whether he should stagger off for lunch, or simply rip the latest cunt's tongue and eyeballs out, then and there, for a snack to keep him going until teatime…"

"Yes? *YES?*" the King bellowed, his swollen breasts and sagging arms vibrating with the promise of yet further entertainment.

"Certainly, as Your Most Feculent and Necrotic Majesty pleases. Well, at that very moment…"

There was a scuffle in the shadows near the door to the throne-room. The jester had his back to it, so he could not see it. Neither could the King, being blind. Two of the bodyguards moved off to investigate.

"At that very moment…"

"*YES?*"

"… there was an earthquake. It was so violent that the Pyramid Palace collapsed instantly, and…"

"*YES*? What the fuck happened to the Stoner?"

"… and the Stoner? He was *crushed to death*." The jester finished with a flourish of his multicolored, tricorn cap. The King laughed so hard that his guffaws turned to wracking coughs. "Catshit, you have excelled yourself," he spluttered, before wretching, red in the face, and wiping dribble from his beard.

The jester bowed low. "One endeavours to give satisfaction, Your Majesty," he said.

"Oh, you do. You *do*. But now we need satisfaction of another kind. The Royal Cock stands to attention. Guards? *Guards*! You know what is required of you."

Four of the guards clustered around the King. Two hoisted him up by his armpits, their beefy hands disappearing into folds of fat. The two others bent down and wrapped their own well-muscled arms around the King's flabby thighs. Despite the hugeness of the bodyguards and the lengths of their arms, each one could only just barely encircle a royal thigh with both his arms, and even then not without burying his face in the enveloping mass of the royal gut.

With no sound apart from the occasional grunt of effort, and the shuffling of feet across the rubbish-strewn floor, the bodyguards lifted the King into position behind the Royal Convenience, lowering him gently on to his well-cushioned knees, so that at no time did the decaying stumps of his feet touch the ground. The Royal Cock emerged from between the mounds of fat. It was enormous, by any standards, but compared with the surrounding bulk, it seemed no more than a seedling sprouting from a cracked fissure between mountains of blancmange.

With a bodyguard supporting each of his shoulders, the King thrust himself into the Royal Convenience like a pile-driver. His belly spilled around the haunches of the tethered Thinskin female so that the jester could not really see what was going on. Nevertheless, the force of the King's movement drove the creature forwards, so that its knees and elbows strained against its tethers. Catshit the jester noticed how blistered the Royal Convenience's limbs had become, squeezed taut by the knotted leather thongs that held it in place, permitting only a limited range of movement.

The throne room was silent. Silent, but for the wheezy gurgles of the King *in copulo*, and for scuffles from the back of the room, where two of the Stoner bodyguards held a third, smaller Stoner, who was struggling against their grip. It was a Royal Messenger.

"Your Majesty! I have news of clear and present danger! The army of the Hated Usurper!" he shrieked, before one of the bodyguards smacked it hard across the side of the head. The messenger fell silent, head to one side at a crazy angle, eyes now lifeless, tongue lolling.

One of the two bodyguards swiftly decapitated the messenger, while the other chopped and jointed its arms and legs. The first then took a long knife and slit the messenger's belly open. Guts spilled out onto the floor. The bodyguard plunged in, ripping the messenger's ribcage apart like the pages of a book. When the second bodyguard tried to intervene, to take the messenger's still-beating heart for himself, a scuffle broke out.

Hengest, the Two Hundred and Forty-Fourth of that name, and the Twelve Thousand, Four Hundred and Seventy-First and Final King Under the Mountain, took no notice, but continued to take his evening's pleasure as he had always demanded it—in contemplative silence, and uninterrupted.

-=0=-

Zagrond lifted his muzzle to the air, nostrils flaring, and sniffed. Pale mucus slid from his cavernous nostrils. His long, prehensile tongue caught it before it fell. "The wind is before us," he grunted. "The time is now."

Horsa the Stoner, astride an armoured coelodont which, while gigantic, was a dwarf beside the mighty steed of Zagrond the Yettin, looked down from the bluff at the long, westernmost slopes of the Zagros as they fell away towards Mesopotamia, lost in the sunset haze. As far as he could see—in front, and from side to side—the land was carpeted with the signs of an army, poised to spring. Stoners and Yettins, arming, sharpening flint knives and hefting bone shamboks; repairing long coats of flint-scaled fish-mail; stringing horn bows with the precious guts of Thinskins.

Stoners and Yettins together, tending the vast corrals of armoured coelodonts, the ranks upon ranks of assault-mammoths and the teams of aurochs that would make up a supply train at least five miles long. Had Horsa but known it, it was an army the like of which the world hadn't seen for millions upon millions of years. The warm wind was in his face.

"You are right, friend Zagrond," he replied. "We move out in the hour before dawn tomorrow."

"You're no friend of *mine*, Stoner," came the gruff response. "You are only my *customer*. When the service is rendered, so shall the payment be due. Remember *that*, Stoner."

"I shall," said Horsa, wondering whether, even with a division of the spoils, that there would be enough to satisfy an army even a hundredth the size of the one arrayed before him. His scouts had told him that the slender assets the Kingdom Under the Mountain had controlled in his youth had long since been squandered by King Hengest—the dissolute elder brother he now intended to overthrow. There was little tribute, and less crops, the scouts had said. All the forests had been cut down or burned; the wells had become too salty to use, or had run dry; and desert had spread over once-verdant grazing land. Raids for the few wild Thinskins that evaded extinction had gone so far afield that they had become uneconomic to pursue, the supply-lines stretched to beyond breaking point. The only prize left was the brood-stock of Thinskins lately bred in captivity in the Citadel of the Kingdom itself, at Mount Carmel—a smart move by his brother, Horsa had to admit, which had bought the ancient Kingdom a little more time.

But that might be a prize that his Yettin allies might not need, or appreciate. Or perhaps they would—and fight his own, better-trained but wildly outnumbered Stoner force for access to it. In his heart, Horsa knew that Zagrond's scouts would have given the Yettin warlord precisely the same information.

"Very good, Stoner," Zagrond said. "We meet on this spot, an hour before sunrise." The Yettin swung his coelodont around, plodding uphill to his own camp. Horsa heard the mercenary's long white braids, beaded with Afghan lapis, clink and chime in the cooling air. The coelodont, each leg the size of a man, its immense horn like a shard cut from a mountainside, snorted its response. Horsa, on his own, lesser beast, remained motionless, alone with the clamor of his thoughts.

Strategy, on the hoof.

He could, of course, let the Yettins take the Thinskins, herding them all the long, rocky miles to the Pamirs and the far Altai, allowing him to keep the Kingdom, even if all its cupboards were bare. But what if the Yettins couldn't be bought off so easily? After all, Horsa had heard that plenty of manflesh existed beyond the Yettins' eastern mountains. Pithecanthropines—smaller and scrawnier than Thinskins, but far more abundant and easier to herd. Gigantopiths, too, and many other creatures he'd only heard about in travellers' tales: from the ruby-eyed, coal-black giant Khong of the jungle, to small, lithe monkey-dancers with the clever eyes of cats, whose females had five pairs of breasts. Fancy that! He smiled—perhaps he should change his plans utterly, abandoning the bankrupt west, and make his way to the mammiferous east?

No. The time for such idle speculations had passed. He had an injustice to avenge, and an army at his command, an army that had taken many years to assemble. West was his course, for good or ill.

But then—now *here* was a thought—what about *beyond* west, to Europe, the heartland of the Stoner civilization of old? Travellers from that region were scarce, and his own scouts rarely ventured that far. Europe was a desert of ice, some said, and the ancient pyramids of fabled Rhoneland stood in ruins. But there were hints—only *hints*—of great Stoner cities that still survived, deep in the Earth. Cities surrounded by herds of mammoth and bison and reindeer that stretched unbroken from horizon to horizon. Yes—he could let the Yettins take the Kingdom and everything in it, and he would go further, to Europe.

The trick then, of course, would be trying to convince his own commanders that any payment they might receive would be deferred indefinitely in the cause of a prize that was nebulous, if it existed at all. His plan, spun from delicate webs of wishful thinking, dissolved before his eyes. No, he sighed—the Kingdom Under the Mountain was where his future lay. Such as it was.

-=0=-

Hengest had retired, taking his coterie of guards with him, and the throne room was quite deserted. All, that is, for Catshit the Jester, and the Royal Convenience, still pinioned to its dais. Catshit—who wasn't *really* called Catshit, but had been so for so long that he could recall his true name only with difficulty—now performed a less public but still-necessary duty. His old, wiry frame scampered onto the dais, scattering the putrid litter of bones and other refuse. His slender fingers teased apart the thongs that bound the Royal Convenience's elbows and knees. The poor creature could not have untied anything itself, except, perhaps, with its teeth—for it had neither hands, nor feet.

Catshit still remembered that day—it couldn't have been any more recently than fourteen years ago—when it had been brought in, screaming with fear, the sinews in its neck knotted with hatred, after a long raid into the Nile Delta. It had been a 'she,' then, a defiant young woman. "I like my cunt with *spirit*," Hengest had said. He still had his feet and his sight, then, before the Sweetwater Disease claimed them. "I'll have *her*."

The removal of her extremities, along with her tongue, had been peremptory and swift. But they had gouged out her eyes, too. Catshit always remembered eyes. Partly because people kept reminding him of the oddities of his own—yellow-green, almond-slitted, like a cat's. But that young woman's eyes were equally distinctive. Distinctive, for their asymmetry.

For one had been brown; the other, a bright, emerald green.

But when she lost her hands, her feet, her tongue—and especially her eyes—she lost her being, in the fading eyes of the King. She was just the Royal Convenience, forever poised on knees and elbows at His Majesty's pleasure, and that of his courtiers and guests. A tool to be used, as neutral and neuter as a spear or a drinking cup.

Having untied her, Catshit braced himself beneath her and lifted her, as gently as he could. He stopped for a moment to re-balance himself: a *pietà*, crouched in the Throne-room's shadows, of a little dark man, the round tapeta of his eyes reflecting moonlight from the open doors onto the terrace, cradling the maimed, emaciated form of a royal servant even lowlier than he was. Its arms and legs were still flexed, stiff, frozen from having held themselves that way for at least ten hours each day, every day, for fourteen years. Catshit could see the scars, the scabs, the sores, the open wounds; the corrugations of its ribs, the pitiful flaps of its dugs, and its face — its poor, dear face; the sore, chapped lips; the sunken pits where its eyes had been; the masses of its hair, once full and rich and the color of the desert sand, now thin and lank and gray.

It looked up at him, then, as if it could see, somehow — see, even without its eyes. It stretched its arms towards him, knobbled stumps of wrists prodding the sides of his face. It forced a weak smile in its lined and sunken face: its thin lips moved, ever so slightly, as if it were trying to say something. This had happened every night, night after night, beyond count, beyond recall. Yet Catshit could never understand what it meant, until now. For now, his job was done.

He stood up, this human wreck lightly in his arms, and walked out onto the white travertine terrace. He could feel the patched motley of his pathetic jester's costume grow stained and warm from the fluids of abuse emanating from between the sticks of the Royal Convenience's legs. The wind from the terrace came straight off the sea. He could hear the waves crashing to shore, hundreds of feet below.

The terrace was no less a worn-out ruin than everywhere else in this dilapidated husk of a Kingdom, but he felt that it was somehow special, somehow *his*, and it was here, against the worn marble rail that teetered farthest out over the waves, that he had made his home—a heap of tattered blankets and those few trinkets that had somehow remained unlooted by the King's dwindling number of ever more brutish bodyguards.

Catshit the Jester felt, though, that he could forgive them such intrusions, for he had made greater thefts by far. For it was he who had arranged for all the wells of the Kingdom to be poisoned with rotten bodies, of which there had always been a plentiful supply. It was he who had commanded, pretending to be acting on orders for the King, to burn the remaining forests, and to irrigate the fields with seawater. This process of sabotage had to be so slow that nobody would see it coming, nobody would notice. It had taken at least three of his own lifetimes. Final notice had come in the form of the messenger, slain before the full importance of his message could be appreciated by the ailing King. The Kingdom that had lasted for more than two hundred thousand years was now no more than a rotten husk, hanging on a high branch by a slender thread. The slightest gust, and it would fall. And fall it must, if the stratagems of the Goddess were to be fulfilled.

Not that he planned to be there when the final blow fell. His task was complete, and he understood, at last, the message on those mute, ragged lips, a message broadcast with such silent yearning for more than a decade.

"I understand, Green-Eye," he said. "I understand."

He walked straight past the nest of rags that had constituted his home—and hers—and climbed up onto the parapet, still holding her mutilated form to his chest. He launched them both into space, and as they fell, he fancied that he could almost hear her whisper of thanks.

Chapter 10. Paramedic

Cambridge, England, and Gascony, France, Earth,
May, 2025 and November, 2075

Shortly before I left the Other Earth a geologist discovered a
fossil diagram of a very complicated radio set. It appeared to be a
lithographic plate which had been made some ten million years
earlier. The highly developed society which produced it had left no
other trace.

Olaf Stapledon — *Star Maker*

Her face showed nothing but blissful peace within the
halo of her long, dark hair. Lying flat on her back, her neck
was in a brace, her body rigid in a frame. The paramedic had
seen many accidents worse than this, but it always distressed her to see victims so young. Worse still, pregnant.
She thought of her own two young children, both at school
and happily ignorant of the abandoned carnage that occasionally troubled their mother's working day.

Escaping from the reek of the burning car, the police, the
fire engines, the crowds of people and the general mess attendant on all road traffic accidents, the paramedic and her
colleagues wheeled the gurney into the relative peace of the
ambulance. The driver switched on the sirens and the blue-
and-yellow-check van screamed southwards towards Addenbrooke's hospital.

Once inside the vehicle, the patient was briefly jolted into
consciousness and emitted a small, urgent sigh, as if she
were asking for something. The paramedic turned to look at
the patient's face, barred with blue from the flashing lamp
reflected through the window. She was amazed, having been
convinced that the girl was dead. But then, as she looked, the
patient opened two large, dark brown eyes, which looked

directly at her, just for an instant, but with frightening pene-tration. A moment later, the gaze softened, looked inward: the patient mouthed just one word before grimacing with pain and retreating once again into a coma.

"Solomon…"

The paramedic had not wanted to look again at the bruised and bloody mess between the patient's breastbone and thighs, a field of destruction against which her face made an even more poignant contrast.

Later, in the operating theatre, the surgeons had done their best. Dilatation and curettage is upsetting enough even when the mother is healthy. When the mother has suffered from multiple ruptures to her spleen, pancreas, liver and intestines, and is clinging to the slender web-strings of life, it is more like emergency field medicine. The uterus looked like it had been shredded, like a basketball run down by a combine harvester. Stitching it up took some hours. Luckily for the patient, one of the surgeons was currently on sabbati-cal from Los Angeles and arguably the world's leading ex-pert in the treatment of gunshot wounds to the abdomen.

It is possible that he saved her life.

Her baby was already dead, however, having taken the full force of the impact as the patient belly-flopped onto the bonnet of the car. During the course of this very complex procedure the third-trimester fetus was removed, one piece at a time, its remains swabbed out and discarded.

One would not have expected the surgeons to have re-moved every scrap of misplaced tissue, every particle of de-tritus that had penetrated the patient's body, and they did not. They can hardly be blamed for that, given the circum-stances. Indeed, they were as overjoyed as anyone else when the patient went on to make a good recovery from her inju-ries.

But some damage, while it seems invisible, can be long-lasting.

Cells from the lining of the ripped placenta had buried themselves in the uterine wall, beyond immediate detection. In the course of time, most of these were flushed out by the patient's immune system. A few, however—possibly not more than one or two—fused with host cells, making tiny inocula of chimaeric tissue, each an intimate ikon of grieving mother and dying child, sculpted on a subcellular level.

It is now known now that women, as they get older, often become chimaeras, each one bearing patchworks of cells in unconscious memory of each one of the children they have borne. Although scientists continue to see this as a conundrum in itself, theologians have come to regard it as evidence for God's compassion. This phenomenon was hardly known in those days, when the patient was recovering from her trauma. So she never knew that some tiny protoplasmic scraps of her never-to-be born child lived on inside her.

Try as they might, chimaeras cannot always obey the rules, and after fifty years of effort a small colony of the descendants of what had once been fetal cells finally broke free. Eluding the ever more placid sentries of an ageing body, they declared independence, and, finding no resistance, they started to send out new colonies throughout the harlequinade that was the re-patched, re-healed and re-sealed endometrium.

They meant no harm.

That's just what they did.

And so it was that in November, 2075, when Jadis was in her kitchen pickling the last of that year's cucumber crop, she felt a sudden stabbing sensation in her belly. It felt as if someone had kicked her. Hard.

Her mind went into a sudden giddy swirl, and just for an instant, she thought she was outside, in a walled garden.

Instinctively she glanced down and saw her frayed jeans where she had expected to witness a thin, viscid trickle of cherry-red blood running in a determined line across the snowy field of her inner thigh. Pulling herself together, she put down, with great deliberation, the pan of hot vinegar she was holding, and sat carefully at the kitchen table until the pain had gone away.

She had been conscious of a dull pain there for—what?— it could have been a couple of years, even. But she had dismissed it as a sign of ageing, and paid it no further attention. Only now had it intruded into her life and mind with such force. But she would dismiss this pain, too, as a symptom of the same incurable disease. Who was it who once said that the most you can expect in advancing age was to wake to a day free from pain? "Well, whoever it was," she said to herself, "they were right." She continued with her task, despite the fact that her mind kept wandering, so much so that she frequently came to senses to find that she had stopped, motionless, gazing at everything and again, at nothing.

The rogue cells inside her continued to breed.

She reflected on the pain as she continued her work. It dawned on her that it had grown steadily alongside the increased tensions in the farmhouse that had surrounded the seemingly endless, futilely circular arguments about the publication of the Sigil. That the pain had finally broken out to stand before her explicit, conscious scrutiny mirrored the plain fact that matters had now reached an *impasse*, in which the three men in her life wanted her consent to publish the paper that Tom had diligently drafted. But she had refused, without compromise. The more they pleaded, the more they pestered, the more she hardened her heart. But *why*, a part of her asked?

Two years earlier, when they had revealed the Sigil with such ceremony, she had happily consented to Tom writing it up for publication. No, her soul cried in response — not 'happily'. Her acceptance had, in fact, been both provisional and grudging, and something that had troubled her, being a tacit admission of mortality, of declining powers, of *failure*. Such an admission, tacit or otherwise, would have represented a violation of her very nature, for inside she felt she was still a young woman. It had never horrified her to see her hands and face as brown and lined, because she had always assumed they'd belonged to someone else. Furthermore, she had never allowed herself to fail at anything, for, to her, failure was an abnegation of the self, and on that point she would never give any ground at all.

Not that she would ever have couched her attitude in these precise, formal terms, either to herself, or to the outside world. On the contrary, she had focussed her anger and frustration into the sharp beams of logic. She could not just drop the news of the Sigil onto the world free from context, as she kept on saying to Tom during a period of what had seemed like several weeks over the summer, in which he had harried her constantly. No, she said, it would look ridiculous, as if they had arrived from nowhere to say they had discovered Atlantis. The Sigil could not be published, because they had no idea who could have made it, and why it was there — and that was that.

Tom's habitual response was that the chances of answering either question were utterly remote, as she well knew: and therefore that he might as well not have bothered drafting his report. In which case she might have had the grace to have made this clear before he'd even started. Tom would often finish this line of argument by stalking out of the room in search of some hard physical activity on which to vent his frustration.

At this point Jadis had always bitten her lip, as if wanting to say something more. Tom (if still in the room) always pressed her to spit it out, whatever it was, and have done.

Matters had come to a head when the three of them were sitting down to supper—it had been in September, just a couple of months earlier—and Jadis and Tom had started to circle each other in the same weary dogfight.

Jack simply pretended it wasn't happening. He had told Tom quietly, many times, to back off, that Jadis would come round eventually, in her own time. But Tom seemed compelled to harass his mother, the compulsion growing as Jadis became more entrenched.

"But why, *Maman*, why?" Tom had said. "Why can't we just publish it, get it done, move on?" Tom had said.

"You know very well, why, Tom, and please don't whine." She pulled herself up abruptly. She had never talked to Tom like this, not even when he was small.

"I just don't understand," said Tom, "I really don't. It's such a simple thing. Describe the artifact. That it *is* an artefact nobody can doubt. We put our doubts about the age on the table: that it seems to be older than any dating technique we know can measure. We put our doubts about its composition, likewise, on the table: that the cursed thing has resisted every known means of penetration. If nothing else, to show how hard we've worked. We need not even speculate about what it all means, if you don't want to. But we could show the world what we've found. Maybe invite comment. Invite help."

"No, Tom, *no*," she'd insisted. "And why don't you understand? All those years ago, she…"

This was the point.

"'She'? Who?"

Jadis hid her eyes beneath the gray shroud of her hair. She felt that she had crossed a line that had forever been there, for all that nobody had mentioned it. Inviolate, violated. Her answer came slowly, through her frustration, her embarrassment.

"It was… well, it was Shoshana, if you must know. In the first week she was here, I asked her, and she…"

"*Maman…*" Tom was a picture of a cold rage.

Jadis couldn't pull back now. Sensing a weakness in the cordon that surrounded her, she went for the kill.

"Yes, Tom, *Shoshana*. It was *Shoshana*. Remember her? Shoshana said that before going public, we needed to know more about who made it. It was plain enough to her, and she was a schoolgirl with nothing more than native common sense. Something that some people seem to have lost. *Some people who should know better.*"

"This really is the limit," said Tom. His face was white with anger, his green eyes flashing. "You know," he said, in a tone plainly calculated to wound, "I think I might as well just publish the thing under my own name and have done."

"You will do no such thing!"

"All right! I'll publish it with your name on it! The lead author!"

"Tom, the answer is still no." She gripped her belly and drew a long, anxious breath. "We *have* to know more about its makers before we can legitimately say anything. Otherwise it looks like a joke… a very, very sick joke. And do you want to make fun of us—of *me*?" She had wanted to apologise for raising an old ghost, but the argument had now gone too far. Tom pushed away his plate, snorted contemptuously and went for the door.

"If you want me," said Tom, looking pointedly at Jack, "I'll be in the shelter, settling the horses." The Sigil, now effectively abandoned once more and with winter approaching, the barn had returned to its accustomed use.

Jack helped Jadis clear and wash the dishes in absolute silence. Even from a few feet away, he could feel the pain and rage envelop her like a fetid cloud. To an extent, he agreed with Tom. They should just write it up and have done. After all, he and Jadis were getting old; it was important unfinished business; and, resignedly, he just wanted to clear his desk.

At first—years ago—he had felt that Jadis had been quite right in her insistence that one could not publish the Sigil without any idea of how it got there, or why. But as the years passed with that question still unresolved, and perhaps without any realistic hope that it ever would be resolved, he was coming round to the view that they should simply publish the Sigil, be candid about the problems with dating and provenance, and leave it at that, just as Tom suggested.

A datum for others to explore in the future. A mystery for others to solve.

So Jack screwed up his courage and just told her—maybe Tom's right, publish the inscription, be candid about its provenance, nothing more.

"Jack—I can't do it," she said. "I—I just can't."

"Sure, of course," he said. "But it's not an ideal world and we won't be here forever. We should really put our spin on it before anyone else comes along when we're dead and gone and does a hatchet job. You were there when it was uncovered. You deserve the credit."

"Jack…"

"In any case," he continued. "Tom's right. What does it matter who made it? You can't have all the answers at once."

"Oh really! There's no need to be quite so patronizing," she replied with some asperity, not looking at him, concentrating on the dirty dishes in the sink. Jack ignored her barb and tried another tack.

"Anyway, I think we owe it to Ruxton Carr and his people and the confidence they always had in us. Roger, too."

"Jack, that's not fair. It really isn't."

Jack decided to say no more, because he knew he'd hit home. In the last analysis, he felt, the Sigil could have been what the whole story had all been about, from the very beginning: the Institute, perhaps even their being together. And he knew that Jadis, in her heart, knew this too.

They said nothing further about it until they had gone to bed, and they'd heard Tom come back inside and lock up. In the darkness, Jadis felt that it didn't matter whether she met anyone's eyes or not.

"Jack, I'm sorry about what I said to Tom," she said.

Jack said nothing for several seconds.

"Jack?"

"Well, I rather think you should apologise to Tom... not me."

Silence.

"Jack, really," she said, "I know you and Tom are both right. Publish the thing as an announcement and, as Tom says, move on."

"Hurrah." Jack's tone was quietly sarcastic. It did not suit him — never had — but he was getting better at it as he got older.

"Jack, don't. Please don't make this any worse. It's just... well..."

"Hmm?"

Slowly she tried to explain what had been haunting her, the reason for her reluctance. She might — *might* — be prepared to live without having to identify the makers if the message of the Sigil could somehow be decoded, in a way independent of its origins. They'd had Domingo's eclipse theory, and then Tom and Shoshana's suggestion that it was a warning, and, finally, when they had unveiled the Sigil,

Tom's shattering, apocalyptic vision. And then there was Jack's quiet insistence that the Plague had something to do with it. The problem, she said, was twofold.

First, which option should they choose?

Second, how could their choice — any choice — be substantiated?

"But why don't we just lay out all the possibilities and leave it for someone else to worry about?" Jack asked. "As Tom says, just put it all on the table?"

More silence.

"We could do that, of course," said Jadis. "But…"

"But?"

"Oh, hell: it's all about Tom. It all comes back to Tom and what he saw in the Sigil. That's the most graphic evidence any one of us has ever had, but only Tom was capable of gaining it. Nobody else has — or, perhaps, can. We really need to put it in, but how on Earth can we? Tom's account can't be substantiated, replicated. And, apart from that, how do we — I — ask him about it? After everything that's happened?"

Jack turned to wrap her in his arms. She squirmed slightly, finding it hard to get comfortable. These days, she felt like she was no more than a loosely aggregated bag of bones, all sharp corners and unwieldy angles.

"So, Jadis, really, what you're really worried about," Jack said, "what it all boils down to is… is reproducibility."

"Darling Jack — what would I do without you?"

"Much the same as you'd have done otherwise, I suspect."

He noticed that her laugh had faded to a kind of gasping pant.

"But I wish Tom wouldn't keep on at me all the time," she said. "It's making me tired, Jack. So very tired. And…"

"Jadis?"

But Jadis had fallen asleep.

-=0=-

After two years of hard work, Pope Eusebius II had made the top two floors of the old Mairie into his Portable Vatican. The upper floor contained a very small flat for himself (what he called his 'Official Residence,' given that he also spent many nights in his old quarters in the farmhouse), and a chapel for the use of his staff.

The floor below contained two small offices, staffed by Christophorines, and what he liked to call his 'laboratory,' a chamber really no bigger than a large cupboard. This room contained, thanks to the diligence of Adelardian engineers, direct qWave links with the Astrometry Institute in Cambridge. It was as far from the glories of Rome as possible, but that's the way Domingo liked it. He could keep in touch with his Cardinals and Bishops remotely in a constantly convened virtual consistory. It was, he thought, an excellent and efficient way of working. And what he spent an increasing amount of time doing was watching the stars, as more and more of them winked out.

"News is not good, Your Holiness," Father Tikko Bray had said by qWave one afternoon in the early Summer of 2075. "Ross 248 and 154 have gone, Your Holiness. But you already know about those. But Wolf 359 seems to have dropped off our screens, too. These... *things*... appear to be converging on us, from all points in the Heavens."

"I understand, Father Bray," replied Domingo, thoughtfully. "However, I believe that Lac 9352 remains the only star we've had the misfortune to have watched actually in the act of disappearing."

"Yes, Your Holiness," replied Father Bray. "But that was two years ago, and several light-years further out."

There was a long pause.

"But now you have so much more data, Father Bray," Domingo went on, "and the case of Lac 9352 needs to be set in... ah... *context*. You understand that I can hardly put my name on a paper, much as though I'd like to. But let's look on the bright side. By not being directly associated, I can remain free to establish context in a manner that can be construed by those sufficiently charitable as... er... *independent*."

"Your Holiness?"

"Yes, I think it high time that *you* and your colleagues wrote something up. I really do. I think it might prove extremely helpful."

The world carried on in general ignorance of a note that appeared in October on an Adelardian-run astronomy pre-print engine by T. Bray and colleagues entitled 'Systematic stellar extinction in the Solar Neighbourhood'. Domingo had a printout sent down to the farmhouse, marked for Jadis' attention. Having not had a reply for some weeks, he called round himself.

He found Jadis far from her usual state of animated business. Instead, she was seated at the table, gazing into space, surrounded by pans and jars and half-pickled cucumbers and the tang of vinegar. There was a seam of pain in her face. She was clearly miles away, and before she knew it, Domingo was pushing a mug of tea into her hands.

"Domingo?" she said.

"The same," he said. "Now, Jadis, what's the matter?"

"Oh, you know, everything and nothing, much as usual," she said. "And especially Tom. And what to do about the Sigil."

"Publish it, of course." The words slipped out fractionally faster than he had intended.

"Oh not you, too." She stood up and turned away. She seemed about to launch into a tirade, but stopped herself, turned back and sat down again.

"Jadis," said Domingo, "I passed you a preprint from the astrometrists in Cambridge. About how more stars have been disappearing, and how the... er... *dragons* appear to be approaching our particular corner of Creation."

"I know. I read it—thank you, Domingo," she said. "I'm sorry for not thanking you earlier. It's just..."

"It is hard to take in, I admit," he said. "I prayed long and hard about it, to overcome what I felt was a feeling of utter denial. But it is useless to resist, I feel. We can only pray for equanimity and... uh... acceptance."

"Acceptance? Of what?" She looked at him, wide-eyed, reproachful, as if he were a villager who'd had the gall to interrupt her mid-sentence. He read anguish in her face. Domingo took her hands in his.

"Acceptance that the world is about to end," he said. "There. I've said it." Jadis sat motionless, seemingly unable to comprehend what her friend had just told her. "This is why you—we—really should publish the Sigil. Don't you see? The pattern we see in space is recorded in the Sigil. Documented."

She smiled weakly. He wasn't sure whether she had taken any of this in.

"Tom..." she began.

"Jadis," Domingo said, "you need not worry about the... er... *eschatological* aspects of Tom's vision. Not now... now that we have proof."

"No? What? No, that's not what I meant at all," she said. "It's just that I... it's... I don't feel particularly well, Domingo. Do you mind? I am not sure I can really talk or think about all... well, all *this*, just now. Is that all right?"

Domingo noticed that her movements were hunched, uncertain, like an eggbound chicken, whereas before she'd always been so easy and carefree. And she looked so pale, her skin like beige parchment stretched over prominent cheekbones, making her brown eyes stand out all the more. Strange: until now, he'd never noticed that she'd aged, and quite considerably so in the past year.

As he tramped back up the hill to the Mairie in the teeth of a strong autumnal westerly, bringing with it the detritus of leaves and maize stalks, rain, and the faraway smell of the sea, he wondered whether acceptance would come fast enough before an end which he felt was inevitable. He'd have to summon his Cardinals here, to Saint-Rogatien, in person, for what in his mind he was already calling the Council of the Last Days.

To an extent, he felt, it was a moment for which all clergymen prepare throughout their ministries. From the Pope down to the humblest shaman (and there were many times when Domingo felt more akin to the latter than the former) the function of any priest is to guide his flock through the great transitions of life: birth, marriage, death.

The imminent death of the whole world should be the same thing, only on a greater canvas. Really, just a matter of administration and logistics. He felt he ought to be comforted, that his own religion had detailed prescriptions for this very eventuality. And yet, and yet, no novice, no seminarian ever feels that it will be *they* who has to preside over the millennium, the rapture, the Last Days. He felt that if he didn't keep moving, keep busy, the responsibility would crush him.

That, and the terror of utter helplessness.

How similar he was to Jadis, he thought. Perhaps that's why Jadis looked so distracted. When he finally crested the hill, musing on Jadis' condition, he was met by an anxious monk in the hooded robe of the Adelardian novitiate, hurrying across the rain-slicked cobbles.

"Your Holiness," the novice said, bowing low. "I am requested to ask you to qWave Father Bray immediately. He has some urgent news."

-=0=-

Later that same evening, Jack saw the compost bucket in the corner of the kitchen full to overflowing. Tom had been busy with the stock all day. Jadis would normally have emptied it, but this evening she'd seemed more than usually absent, lost in thought. When asked what was wrong, she'd bitten her lip and turned away, shrugging off his glances, the touch of his hand.

It concerned him, but the immediate problem was hefting the bucket of peelings and other kitchen detritus down to the far end of the garden. He was astonished by the weight of it, and relieved when, after much puffing and heaving through the chill of the evening air, he'd upended the contents onto the compost heap. Placing the bucket carefully on the ground, he stretched himself upwards. He could almost feel his strained back muscles and bones clicking back into place. That, initially, was not the cause of his delight. For, looking up at the cold, high northern sky beyond the spinney, the night now washed by the rain into an unmatched clarity—he saw a shooting star. The briefest flash at the corner of his eye, and it was gone.

Now, he thought to himself: *that's* interesting.

It occurred to him that in all their years at Saint-Rogatien he'd never seen a single shooting star, not one. As he paused to consider this, he saw two more, much brighter this time, and then a whole shower. For several seconds, the whole sky was streaked with the silent trails of incandescent interplanetary debris, before fading quickly to nothing. Jack's eyes had by now accommodated to the bright show, so now he was plunged into darkness. This in itself did not unnerve him. He stood quite still, staring at the sky, waiting for the stars to come back into view, one by one.

Jack loved the stars. In his youth and early manhood they had been his constant companions as he tramped the hills and vales. Now, in his old age, living in a village in which artificial light was a rarity, they had become his friends once more. He turned to face the south, and saw the familiar figure of Orion march high above the roof of the farmhouse. White Rigel; Betelgeuese, baleful red; Bellatrix; the remarkably bright haze of the Nebula where new stars were, even now, being born. Further up he saw orange Aldebaran, and the exquisite ice-blue points of the Pleiades.

Looking downwards once more across the belt of the Hunter he found a bald patch of sky that looked like it shouldn't have been there. Perhaps he was a little rusty? But no, Orion was in the same place, and the other constellations, and all the stars shining evenly from a sky so clear that he could pick out the Milky Way from horizon to horizon. He was worried, disoriented, and fought to quell a tiny tendril of panic.

No. Start again.

That old stargazer's trick. He traced Orion's belt downwards and leftwards… but it was true.

The Great Dog had closed its Eye.

Sirius, the brightest star in the night sky, had vanished. Jack felt his legs go numb. He sat down abruptly on the upturned compost bucket.

-=0=-

Domingo walked to the qWave set, his mind sparking premonitions of disaster even as an Adelardian technician spoke briefly into the handset, passed it to him, and left the room, bowing. Domingo waited until the oak door had shut with a click before speaking. He sat a plain bentwood chair at a desk before the curtained window, three small qWave monitors on standby in front of him, each one a shimmer of light, no more than a coherent arrangement of air molecules. The only other light was the golden glow from a pair of candles in a sconce on the wall behind him, throwing his own face into shadow. Yet this simple room was qWired directly into the Astrometry Institute in Cambridge, and through that, the Yahoo spacecraft. From his Portable Vatican, Domingo had eyes in the sky.

"Father Bray?" he began. He was surprised at the nervous tremor in his voice.

"Your Holiness." The Chief Astrometer's voice seemed crackly and distant. Domingo became conscious of how warm the small room was, how oppressive.

"You have... er... *news?*"

"Yes, Your Holiness," the Chief Astrometer cleared his throat. Perhaps he was as nervous as Domingo. Or maybe it was just bad quantization on the line. "I pray, first, that Your Holiness is seated?" Domingo assured him that he was, and that he was anxious to hear the latest information from Cambridge. He hoped his demand did not sound too hoarse, too peremptory.

"Very well, Your Holiness," said Father Bray. "It's like this... the star Alpha Canis Majoris disappeared sometime in the early hours of the morning, Greenwich time. The latest Yahoo plate should be on your leftmost monitor." Silence on the line. Domingo looked through a porthole into the blackness of space where once a giant star had raged. All that was left was a set of superimposed crosshairs and a squirl of numbers against a field of faint, distant stars. He was absolutely stunned.

"Your Holiness?"

"Yes, thank you Father Bray, I heard you. Sirius."

"It is the first naked-eye star to have been, affected, as far as we know." To call Sirius a naked-eye star was, Domingo thought, typical astrometric understatement. Just nine light-years away, it was — *had been* — the most splendid jewel of the night sky and the fourth brightest object in the heavens, after the Sun, the Moon and Venus.

"Did you... ah... *capture* the process in action?" Domingo wondered how much more disturbing the destruction of a large, blue-white star such as Sirius would be, compared with the disaggregation of the red dwarf Lac 9352 that he had witnessed.

"I'm afraid not, Your Holiness. But it's definitely not there *now*, and neither is the neutron-star companion, Sirius B, and... oh, Your Holiness, something's just come in. Please allow me a second..."

"Of course, Father Bray." Domingo heard, faintly in the background, the exchange of sharp, excited voices. He could not make out what they were saying. Father Bray came back on the line.

"Your Holiness — I have just now heard from Cardinal Signorelli." Domingo knew that this indomitable Cardinal and his airship-borne expeditionary team were in northern Australia, searching for an unusual and very secretive tribe of hominids called the Potkurok. "The Cardinal's news is extraordinary," the Chief Astrometer continued. "He says that Alpha Centauri has disappeared." Domingo felt that no further surprises were possible.

"What — *all* of it?"   ·

"It seems so, Your Holiness... and I must apologise once more for a short delay while I...?"

"Of course." More hurried exchanges in the background. Pops and clicks. Domingo waited for almost a minute until Father Bray returned.

"Your Holiness—I apologise once again for the delay—yet I have now managed to corroborate Cardinal Signorelli's observation with real-time data from Yahoo. The central pair of stars—Alpha Centauri A and B—well, they've definitely gone. You can see the latest Yahoo image in your central monitor." Domingo looked through a second porthole into space, opening next to the first, the two hanging ominously over his desk. "We cannot see Proxima, either," Father Bray continued, "and have to assume the worst."

Proxima is—was—the lonely outlier of the Alpha Centauri triple-star system. It had another distinction, too. At just over four light-years away, it was the closest star to the Sun. Domingo could hear his heart pounding: he steadied himself against the edge of the desk in case he fell.

"Father Bray," he said, "I guess that it is fair to assume that we are... er... *next*." Domingo did not want to see what might open up in the third monitor—still blandly showing the default screen of the crossed keys of the Holy See—and, for the first time, began to appreciate the utter terror that Tom had felt when he first saw the Sigil, in all its hellish splendor.

"Pray for us, Your Holiness," said Father Bray. "Pray for us all."

"Yes, of course. I understand. And please convey my deepest thanks to your redoubtable colleagues, for continuing in such circumstances." He took a deep breath, gulping for air. "But before you go, Father Bray, I should like to know one further thing."

"Your Holiness?"

"I suspect you have a fair idea of the distribution of these... er... *dragons*, in space, no?

"Possibly, Your Holiness, but they are very hard to see. They can be detected from very slight gravitational effects, and lucky occultations of background stars, so one assumes that they are made of a very dense and dark material. There have been some reports of cometary activity in the Oort Cloud, which suggests that they are quite close, and…"

"Please, Father Bray, I do not wish to halt your disquisition, which is most… ah… *interesting*. But can you estimate when these… er… *entities* will be in the vicinity of the Sun?"

"My sincere apologies, Your Holiness. We have been discussing this very thing in some depth…"

"And?"

"Our best guess is that the path of the closest group of these… ah… gravitational anomalies… will intersect the Sun in five months time. If we were pressed, and strictly off the record at the present time, we'd say between the 17th and the 19th of April next." Domingo could hardly believe his ears.

"You know, that date…" he said.

"Yes, Your Holiness. I do."

"May God bless you, Father Bray. You may go." The Chief Astrometer offered the customary response and the line went dead.

Domingo sat quite still for a very long time, quite unable, at first, to assimilate what Father Bray had told him. The nearest and brightest stars to the Sun had all gone, and the dragons were now nibbling the outer reaches of the Solar System itself. But what struck him more forcibly than anything, even more than these cataclysms, was the timing. No, surely not. This had to be a coincidence. *Had* to be.

He looked up towards the curtained window, and even though his face was entirely shadowed by the candelabra, he felt the warmth of light on his face. Escape from bondage. Plagues. Angels, passing over. Hope.

Resurrection.

Slowly at first, and then with increasing conviction, he pieced it all together.

-=0=-

Tom dreamed that he was looking at the Sigil again. He was tiny and it was huge, like a vast sculpture, a monolith. The pattern of circles and lines was picked out in oxyacetylene flame against a charcoal-black background. As he watched, the flames burned down into the underlying matrix as precisely as any laser cutter and it fell to bits, a crazy three-dimensional jigsaw of angular blocks. Tom tried to spread his arms around them all, to stop them tumbling to the floor, but they just kept falling, falling with a regular rhythm, *knock, knock, knock*, and more and more, until he pulled himself through the surface tension of wakefulness to hear a gentle rap on his door.

It was his mother, with a cup of tea.

"*Maman…*" He sprang from his bed to take the teacup from her: it looked like it had become somehow awkward for her to carry. Tom was struck that she looked terribly old, and ill.

"Thank you, Tom," she said. "Thank you so much." She sat down on the edge of the bed, a small sigh escaping like the wheeze of an ancient accordion. "Tom, I apologize. For everything. Of course you can publish the Sigil. I won't stand in your way. No longer." Tom sat down next to her.

"*Maman* — why? After all this time, you…"

"Please, let's not have a post-mortem. Suffice it to say that Jack has convinced me. And Domingo, too. They are both of them very silly, much as I love them."

The rest came out in a confusing tumble about disappearing stars, bringing Tom smartly back to his disquieting experience at the Astrometry Institute, of watching the death of Lac 9352, echoed by his vision of the Sigil. Even so, he found it hard to take in that Sirius had disappeared. Yes, Jadis had said, Jack had appeared wild and breathless at her side in bed last night, having seen it—or rather *not* seen it—and could hardly get the words out. She had to cling to him, she said, to calm him: she had never—never in her whole life, their long marriage—seen him as agitated.

But anyway, Jadis said, she would need no further convincing, and so perhaps she was being small—petty, even—to hold things up any more.

"*Maman*, surely not."

"You know, it's not that I don't still have serious reservations about the whole thing." She looked straight ahead, as if Tom were not there.

"Hmm?" Tom sipped his tea.

"Yes. For, you see, it resolves nothing." She looked round at Tom: "we are still no closer than we ever were to understanding who made the Sigil, or why. Not really. It might as well have dropped from the sky. Although I have some ideas. Guesses, really." She coughed. It was a hollow, dry sound.

"Jack has been on and on at me about coincidences," she said. "How odd it is that Ruxton Carr funded two things that seemed as disparate as an archeology institute and an astrometry institute and, my goodness, what should we find? *Quelle surprise*, but the Sigil, and disappearing stars, and that they are somehow tied up together. What a coincidence it seems! But Jack has an idea that the Plague is all mixed up in it too, which I'm not sure about and…" She looked directly at him, into his eyes, unflinchingly, as if he were not her son, but a zoological specimen. Tom suddenly felt cold and pressed his hands round the tea mug.

"*Maman*? What is it?"

"Look, Tom," she said. "I know we haven't always got on recently, and I desperately don't want you to take what I have to say the wrong way. Really, I don't." Tom was silent. He felt that whatever was coming next would be another shattering blow, and that his mother had backed him into a corner with some species of emotional blackmail.

"Tom," she continued, "you never met Ruxton Carr, did you? Not even in all your time in Cambridge? And even though you were our son, associated with one of his largest and most long-term projects?"

"No, *Maman*, I didn't…"

"Well, I never met him either — but Jack did, just once, long ago, and he said something very odd to me, just the other day. That he reminded him of you. That you and Ruxton Carr had the same eyes.

"And, Tom — please don't mind this — everything has come down to your eyes, and how you see things, ever since you were a little boy, when you couldn't see anything. I remember the first time you saw, as clear as day. It was Fairbanks who… ah, well." Her voice petered out as she paused to draw breath in a jagged gasp, but in that instant, Tom saw a whirl of blinding light, and felt the comforting, furred bulk of his first and, perhaps, his truest friend. The one who said nothing, but somehow always knew.

"*Maman*…"

"And now, with what you and *only* you saw in the Sigil," Jadis continued, her eyes looking inward, as if Tom weren't really there. She paused again, and then turned the twin spotlights of her gaze upon him. "You have a gift, you see — a gift that I think Ruxton Carr had, too, which is why we — that's Jack and me — set this whole thing up in the first place. But you weren't related to him, were you?" The question seemed rhetorical.

Tom thought of auras, and how, despite himself, his own aura had meshed so compellingly with Morgana's. He shuddered, and his voice was strained and sharp.

"*Maman*, where is all this leading?"

"I'm sorry Tom, I don't really know. Everything these days seems so… well, mixed up, beyond my grasp." Her eyes lost their sparkle for an instant. "You may as well know. Well, I'm just getting old, I suppose." Tom put down his cup and moved forward on the bed to embrace her. He was shocked at how little there was to hold. The warmth and softness—the maternal *hugeness* he remembered, as if he were no more than a babe—had turned into nothing more than a starved sparrow. It comes as a shock, he thought, to know that one's parents are mortals. That they will get old and die.

"The fact is, Tom, someone made the Sigil," she said, softly, "and we haven't really thought much about them. We've always had the excuse that because the Sigil was the only sign that its makers existed, that we couldn't possibly make any headway. But that's not true. We can say something, even if we cannot prove it. Which is frustrating, but there it is." He felt the tremors of agitation course through her suddenly fragile body.

"If we can say one thing about the Makers," she continued, "it's that they already had a very advanced technology, far in advance of anything we could ever match. That gravitational business: that it seems to be some kind of hole in space-time. That it seems to be made of a material that nobody has ever been able to identify, though, once… one of the physicists thought it might be some form of metallic ice. He was laughed off the podium, I seem to remember…" Tom thought her mind was beginning to wander, to fade.

"*Maman?*" he prompted.

"Oh... sorry Tom... where was I?" she answered, pulling herself up. "Oh yes. So either the Makers were people of this Earth—hominids, presumably—or they weren't. Something from elsewhere. Little green men. So which is it? What would you choose, Tom?" She turned directly to look at him.

"I... well, I'd have to say that a hominid would be the most likely option," he said, nervous in the spotlight beams of his mother's eyes, "given that we have plenty of evidence for the existence of hominids stretching back millions of years... the early Sand Druids and so on... and that we have never detected any intelligent life elsewhere in the Universe."

"Go on, Tom."

"But if the Sigil's makers were hominids—*if*—they must have raced ahead of their fellows." He said. "We've always thought that the latest common ancestor of all the hominids we know about—including the Sand Druids, Almai, *Homo sapiens* and so on—lived no earlier than eight million years ago, around when the chimp lineage diverged, and..."

The penny dropped.

You see, Tom, you *see*?" said Jadis, picking up on Tom's argument. "That whenever people say we've 'always thought' something, I always suspect that we've 'always thought' wrong—made the wrong assumptions. Now, this'll be ancient history to you, but I still remember Jack's conviction that the landscape of Europe had been tamed and shaped for a million years, a fact that was as plain as day to Jack despite the fact that everyone had 'always thought' it was a wilderness. So, that's one thing. There might have been hominids with truly, breathtakingly advanced technology, living far longer ago than we've assumed possible..."

"But, *Maman*," Tom interrupted, "there's absolutely no evidence of that. Technology like that would have left a trace in the fossil record, surely?"

"Oh, Tom, you know better than that!" She smiled and bowed her head, her eyes, huge, peeping through the skeins of gray. "The fossil record leaves us virtually nothing. Who knows what might have existed, that we'll never know about? If it hadn't been the Sigil, we'd not even have suspected that its makers even existed. Why should we?"

"Yes, *Maman*, of course…"

"All right then," she said, with animation. "Absence of evidence isn't evidence of absence, but I'd concede that given that we have no evidence of technologically advanced hominids maybe, oh, ten or twenty or, damn it, fifty million years ago, we have to look at the other possibility." She drew breath, slowly, laboriously. "What if the Sigil-makers weren't hominids, but something else?"

"*Aliens*?" Tom was incredulous. "You mean to say that they really were little green men? *Maman*, you've always pooh-poohed that idea."

"Well, yes, but think about it. We finally—finally!—have evidence that we're not alone, don't we? We know nothing of ancient, advanced hominids, but we *do* now have *proof* that some kind of alien life exists."

"The dragons…" Doors flew open in Tom's mind. "Maman, you're right. So if there is one alien species, there might be others, and… and…"

"Tom, whoever the Sigil's makers were, and whenever they lived, I think that its makers were trying to speak—to send messages—using signs that we humans can interpret. Just as you… just as Shoshana said they had."

It had been Shoshana all along. Shoshana, dead for twenty years, still lived in the fact that she had brought reconciliation between Tom and his mother.

"Shoshana…" whispered Tom.

Jadis turned, creaking, to look at her son. "You loved her very much, didn't you?" She paused. Tom felt that her emaciated form was bracing itself for a final spurt, as if in the teeth of a gale that might blow her fragile form apart. He held her closer, to steady her.

"*Maman*, don't worry, I'm here."

"Tom, I must say this while I still have the chance. That you are my son, and you always will be, no matter what; and that I have always loved you since Domingo brought you the path through the snow on Christmas Day, no less, wrapped in swaddling clothes just like the baby Jesus. And I love you now, despite everything. And I love you because you loved that poor, lost girl. And I'll love you until the day I die, which I fear will not be long."

"Oh, *Maman*..."

"Tom, hear me out." She said. "Domingo is always droning on about 'acceptance'. He told me something about the end of the world being nigh or some such, which I did not accept until Jack told me about Sirius. The dragon-things — the aliens — are coming this way. Just as the Sigil-makers said they would, whoever they were, or whenever they lived. So now I accept it. The world will end sometime sooner or later, because the dragons are coming to eat the Sun. The Sigil was a warning about the dragons. A vision that Shoshana *imagined*, and you *saw*.

"No matter that you thought we were making fun of you, we — me, your father, Domingo — we never doubted the truth of that vision for an instant. So, really, you are the very best person to describe the Sigil. So now it's *your* turn to accept something, Tom — that the Sigil's makers might have something to do with *you*, though I can't imagine what. Whatever species you belong to, Tom, I suspect — only *suspect*, mind — it has a history longer than any known hominid. Did you ever get your DNA tested?"

"No, I..."

"Of course you didn't," Jadis said. "There was no reason to have done so."

Tom thought, with a shock, about Morgana and her crew of Jive Monkeys, and brought to mind a paper he'd seen in an obscure journal saying that a preliminary analysis of their DNA looked more like that of lemurs or tarsiers—not like that of higher primates at all—his assuming that the researchers must have got it wrong. Assumptions. How frail they were, and how fickle.

"There, that's all," Jadis croaked. "I don't think I can say any more." She collapsed into his arms, gasping for breath.

Tom saw a fleck of blood on his sleeve. It was the tiniest spot imaginable. But it was there.

Acceptance.

Shoshana.

Himself.

Chapter 11. Saviour

Rhoneland, Earth, *c*. 125,000 years ago

'The time has come,' the Walrus said,
'To talk of many things'
Lewis Carroll — *The Walrus and the Carpenter*

Mr Khorare seized the moment, as a warm wind rose and brushed against his face. "Please, friend Vortigern," he asked, "as we are both heading that way, would it be possible for you to tell me something of our destination?"

Vortigern smiled, but his eyes, which were disconcertingly blue-green in his ebony black face, looked straight ahead, as if wistfully, to the end of a road which might be attained only in physical fact, but not in spirit. His robe, a deep purple, billowed and flapped in the light breeze. It was a long time — at least a dozen paces — before he replied.

"As we are, as you say, both going that way, I think I might be able to tell you something of it," he said. "However, you should know, Excellency Khorare, that to say anything about the… the destination… is… how should I say? Unusual. My friends and I have talked long and hard about what we should say to you, should the opportunity present itself."

"You knew it was me? All along? How so?"

"Excellency Khorare — you are aware from our speech that we come from the Kingdom Under The Mountain, just as you do. When we saw you in the *pension*, we were thunderstruck. We debated the implications of your apparition well into the night." Mr Khorare could imagine the raised voices and extravagant gesticulations that constituted debates among Thinskins. Vortigern sighed, and continued.

"Your appearance — here, now — could hardly be a coincidence. There must be a purpose to it, and we hardly dare to presume what that might be, though we can guess it. But irrespective of that, the fact remains, Excellency, that your name is one of infinite respect and reverence to my people, the Inheritors."

"It is?" Mr Khorare's surprise was piqued with curiosity about the name that Vortigern had used. The *Inheritors*.

"Look back at the Kingdom, Excellency," Vortigern said. "Its rule. Its customs. At the indignities my people have suffered, and continue to suffer, and will, no doubt suffer, long after you and I have turned to dust on the wind." Mr Khorare did indeed look back, and it was as if peering through a keyhole into a country of distant memory. What he saw was most unpleasant. People hunted and kept as cattle, used for sport and all manner of depraved pastimes by the Court of the King, before being flayed, butchered for meat, their skulls used as drinking-cups, their fat rendered for lamp-grease, their skins tanned and made into lampshades or fire-screens or clothing for the wealthy and the fashionable, their guts made into ropes or bowstrings, their bones carved into toys for children, their teeth into gaming pieces. Mr Khorare flushed with his shame at his easy compliance with such atrocities, over so many years.

"I know, friend Vortigern," said Khorare. "I am deeply ashamed. I'm sorry that I…"

"Don't be. Sorry, that is," said Vortigern. "But for your steadying hand on King Hrothgar, matters would have been very much worse. Because of your civilizing influence, many thousands of our people managed to escape the Kingdom, to disperse both west and east, to more civilized countries — or make their way south, back to the High Simien, our ancient homeland in Aethiopia. Without you, we fear that our very species would have been diminished, even to the point of extinction.

"I had no idea that I..."

"If anything, Excellency, your influence is proven in the breach. Since you departed these past two years, matters have deteriorated alarmingly. The Old King was assassinated by the Crown Prince Hygelak on the very eve of your own departure, and the slaughter since has been... well, I need hardly describe it. My wife, my children..." Vortigern's eyes began to water, but his bearing remained otherwise poised and erect. "Suffice it to say that as many of us as could manage it escaped to come on pilgrimage."

"I'm sorry, Vortigern. Truly, I am."

"What's past is past, Excellency Khorare. But please, before I tell you of our destination, might you honor me with some account of your own adventures? And of how we come to be treading the Great South Way, both together?"

Mr Khorare told Vortigern something of his history; of his upbringing in the Great and Ancient City of Axandragór now far away; of his ill-fated voyage to Dilmun, and his subsequent meeting with the Stoner Prince in whose service he'd spent most of his life; and his wish, on retirement, given that everyone he'd known in Axandragór would have died, to move instead westward, rather than east, and see something of the wonders of the world before he died himself.

He knew that it sounded unconvincing, but if Vortigern thought the same, he gave no hint of it. To be sure, had he been attending closely, any percipient listener might have read a great deal between the lines. For Mr Khorare was careful to omit all mention of his curious meetings with the reed-cutter and her avatar, the concierge; the seeming fact of his own immortality; and the existence of the talisman in the leather drawstring bag hung about his neck—the talisman whose safe delivery to their mysterious destination seemed so inexplicably important.

Mr Khorare, his story having finished, paced onwards, the Thinskin at his side, his own fellow pilgrims still a blur a few hundred yards in the distance. Vortigern was silent, and Mr Khorare guessed—rightly, as it turned out—that he was measuring his words, assaying the weight of what he was about to say, and what he could judiciously omit. Mr Khorare was, of course, a businessman at heart, and recognized that information has its price, just as much as any bale of stuff.

"The destination—*our* destination—is, in many ways, a mystery," the Thinskin said, at length. "I have not been there myself, you understand, but from what I know, it is a kind of mirror to the Great Pyramid and the town around it."

"A mirror?"

"Yes, I know: the analogy is not a very good one," Vortigern said. "Suffice it to say that the destination is a city that lies under the Earth. A city dominated by a pyramid."

"So much is suggested from what I had learned, friend Vortigern, although I had not known of the underground pyramid. Am I given to understand that the destination is much like the Kingdom Under The Mountain?"

"In some ways, yes—in that both are subterranean. But the destination is greater, by far: it stands to the Kingdom as a lion to a lentil."

"Who created this underground city?" Khorare asked.

"That's part of the mystery—nobody really knows, not even the Stoners. Their tradition has it that it was built by their predecessors, much as we, the Inheritors, will be their successors. Thanks to you."

"*Me?*"

Vortigern slackened his pace. He was clearly uncomfortable about what he was about to say next.

"The Stoners have many legends about the underground city," he said. "Legends about its past. We, on the other hand, have legends about its *future*."

"But—friend Vortigern—you mean prophecies, don't you? Not legends? Legends are necessarily about things in the far past, which, while once real, have been obscured and made fanciful by the dimming effect of time, by the..."

"Excellency Khorare—*friend* Khorare—please bear with me on this. It is a concept that I find very hard to convey, and a great secret of our race. Were you a Stoner, you'd not have heard even as much as I have told you. But I assure you that I am cognizant of the distinction between prophecies and legends. *Quite* cognizant."

"And what, then, are your... *legends*?"

"Friend Khorare, there stands at the center of the underground city, a great pyramid, as I have mentioned. It is—of course—nowhere near as great as the Pyramid standing at our backs." Both men knew that the passage of several miles had hardly reduced the loftiness of the Great Pyramid behind them, even though the city surrounding it had sunk below the horizon.

"It is, however, far less accessible. Whereas hundreds of people ascend and descend the Great Pyramid of Xxántroghátrem every day, the summit—and even the slopes—of the underground pyramid are barred to us. We do not know what lies at the summit, but we suspect that something—or someone—lives there. We Inheritors precess around the pyramid in torchlight parades, cementing our legends, our traditions, our hopes, but we never set foot on its slopes. We *never* ascend it."

"Because it is sacred, a taboo?"

"That is what it has become. But to set foot on the pyramid is death. Real, physical death. At least for us. But the legends speak of a visitor, a traveller from the farthest east, a man who is neither Stoner nor Inheritor — a man with the eyes of a cat. A man, in short, like you. The legend says that this man will ascend the pyramid, with an *offering*, to... to *placate* whatever it is that lives at the nameless summit."

"And what then?"

"That, friend Khorare, is not known. But our interpretation of the legend is that the visitor from the east will, once at the nameless summit, make the appropriate offering, or obeisance, or at any rate do *something* — something momentous — to ensure that the Inheritors really will come into their own."

"Something...?"

"That's all I know, friend Khorare. That's all anyone knows."

The two men continued to pace southward. The Sun had passed its zenith point, shining directly into their eyes, and was now slowly edging towards the southwest. Mr Khorare was, by now, very hot, very sweaty, and footsore. The leather of his sandals was beginning to chafe. His discomfort perhaps explained why his initial reaction to Vortigern's story might have been one of waspish dismissal, even disdain, though he knew better than to give voice to his misgivings. Yes, he did have eyes like a cat, he supposed. And he did have what might be called an offering, which even now fretted in its leather pouch: Mr Khorare felt at times that the talisman was alive, like a mouse, squirming and struggling within its narrow cage. But legends of the future? That really was too much to credit.

As if reading his mind, Vortigern spoke. "I can appreciate your skepticism, friend Khorare," he said. "It must sound most exotic to one who confronts such matters for the first time, matters with which every Inheritor is familiar from early childhood. If it will help, I might let you in on another secret."

"Yes?"

"It is our scripture, the Book of the Goddess, a text so ancient that its origin is utterly obscure—a fact which, to us, only magnifies its holiness. Despite its antiquity, friend Khorare, you will never find a copy written down, for among the Stoners, the possession of this book means instant death. I myself have never seen it written down, and neither have any of my fellows. So children are taught it, by rote, line by line. Every Inheritor knows it off by heart."

The mention of the word 'goddess' triggered something in Mr Khorare. He felt it as a kind of analogy, a small red flower, blooming in the desert.

"Can you—are you permitted—to recite any of it to me, friend Vortigern? Anything concerning the Goddess of whom you speak?"

"Yes, I shall try. I cannot think it would do any harm, given that I am convinced that you, friend Khorare, represent the fulfilment of our legend, even if you are not so persuaded yourself."

Without breaking step, Vortigern began to intone, in a sing-song voice, a beautiful, keening song like a lullaby, full of unexpected if melodious intervals, and mellifluous ornament. For a moment, Mr Khorare felt that he'd been transported to the opera house back in Massilia.

The song told of a bright young goddess robed in red, who appeared among a nameless people, blessing them, hallowing them, and chiding them as both brave as lions, and yet as foolish as newborn lambs. Her countenance then became stern, warning her people to beware of imposters. Her discourse then, according to the song, concluded, as far as Mr Khorare could tell, in this wise:

For I am a Jealous Goddess, apparently,
And even though I've probably fucked it up

For everyone, as I usually do,
I'm not going just to lie back with my legs open
And be two-timed by a load of silly old men like you,
Lovely though you are, each and every one.
So you guys had better watch out. Grrr!

Vortigern finished his song with a keening ululation. He turned his face away from Mr Khorare, as if he'd just confessed some appalling misdemeanor, and was embarrassed at having done so. Turning to face straight ahead, and pointedly not looking at Mr Khorare, Vortigern cleared his throat.

"I'm afraid that I do not know precisely what it means," he said. "The language is ancient and—if I might say so—somewhat barbarous. But in its obscurity lies its holiness, I think, or so we Inheritors interpret it. For while it is recondite, it has the ring of authenticity held only by the most ancient, arcane things. I do not think that anyone could have made it up."

"No, friend Vortigern, I agree," said Mr Khorare. Indeed, Mr Khorare could hardly contain his shock. For beneath a veneer of what he hoped was interested, if detached, appreciation, Mr Khorare felt his emotions rip through him like a scimitar, a sensation of *deja-vu* of such disabling intensity that he almost crumpled to the ground where he stood.

For he had heard those words before—those words, *exactly*.

It was in another life, and in another time, but the words evoked for him a ruined temple, and a young goddess in red fading into golden flame: a young goddess subsiding into his arms. And a small creature by his side, hardly more than a pet, but standing tall for the first time, like the inheritor his descendants would, one day, become.

It was then that Mr Khorare's whole life coalesced about him, the hitherto vague clouds condensing to a needle-point, a finality of purpose. It took no more than a second, but he felt a new steeliness come into his eyes. He turned those eyes ahead to see, beyond the fuzzy knot of pilgrims, a cluster of monumental stone buildings rising on the horizon, in the middle of which was a great, yawning gate, giving on to a void of blackness.

The nameless destination, at last.

-=0=-

Torch in hand he climbed, leaving the bright round of pilgrims far below, marching round the pyramid in concentric circles, in alternating directions. From this height he could see only the points of their torches and the patterns they made, as whole things that would have been invisible from ground level. Magical mandalas of flame they made, circling the pyramid. But he could spend no more time or energy marveling at the allure of these patterns. For time was running out, now, and in any case, the slope of the pyramid was steep and stony, deserving of his full concentration, the slope increasing in pitch as he climbed. The soles of his sandals slipped on the steepening scree, until he was crawling like a spider on hands and feet, the talisman in its bag swinging out, past the neckline of his worn chemise, dragging along the pyramid's stony surface. The entrancing songs of the pilgrims that had filled his ears on the lower slopes were now drowned by the rasps of his own breath and the beating of his heart.

The crawl turned into a climb, and the final ascent was as of a cliff, demanding that every step he took, every crevice and every handhold, was as considered as a move in a game of chess. But, finally, after an age, and when the palms of his hands were scratched, the soles of his sandals scored, its straps and buckles and the knees of his crushed-velvet pantaloons almost worn through, his face became level with the summit. Not a pinnacle, but a perfectly flat, featureless square no more than five or six yards on a side.

Featureless, that is, except for a plain door of wood, in a frame, standing in the center of the platform, hanging teasingly ajar. Through the crack, Mr Khorare could just make out a room whose windows looked out over a landscape of dazzling whiteness, punctuated by the jagged forms of conifers, with a range of mountains in the distance.

Mr Khorare scrambled onto the surface of the platform, dusted himself down as well as he could, and without a second thought, walked across the threshold.

The talisman sat on the coffee table between them, a trinket surrounded by tumblers and bottles and the remains of a meal. Mr Khorare looked down at it, the strange, gray object, perhaps stone, perhaps metal (for he had never thought, before, to inquire of its substance), at its finely drawn cartouche of circles, crescents and radiating lines. He had never studied it for long, for whenever he did, he'd always had the most unpleasantly vertiginous sensation of somehow being sucked into it, and the effort of tearing his eyes away always gave him a headache that lingered for several hours. He ripped his gaze from it now, refocusing on the hazy figure in the chesterfield opposite.

"No, Khorare," she continued. "Nobody really knows who made this city. Well, *almost* nobody." She gave a teasing smile, and tossed her head. "It was here before the Stoners came and built Rhoneland. When they are gone, it'll be here still."

"And the Thinskins? The Inheritors?"

"Oh, they'll be gone too, for a while," she said. "Despite all appearances, the Stoner civilization you have known is long past its prime, and will soon collapse into barbarism once again, taking the Thinskins with it—as the pleasantly tropical climate you have known all your life breaks up into deserts, whether cold, dry, or both.

"But before they fade out altogether, the Stoners will reoccupy this hidden city, and fastnesses like it, as refuges, both against the weather outside, and being fearful of what is to come. They'll take their model from something—somewhere—you know well, Khorare."

"The Kingdom? The Kingdom Under The Mountain?"

"Yes. Thanks to you, Khorare, the Inheritors will indeed inherit. But the matter will be decided in your old adopted home.

"Why, then, have I come here? So far westward?"

"Because, Khorare, there are only so many plates I can keep spinning in the air at once."

Khorare wondered why he could not see her face as anything more than a blur. That quick glance at the talisman must have done something to his vision. He felt himself growing fuzzy, fading. Perhaps he'd had too much scotch. He was aware that as she spoke she had risen from her chesterfield, and then, wending her way round the sofa, come to stand before him.

"Because, Khorare," she said, "the talisman had to be delivered here. At the top of this pyramid. And you've delivered it. So now your work is done."

She bent down, then, and Mr Khorare was dimly aware of the graded curves of her breasts pendant beneath her blouse, of loosened strands of hair across his face, a warm, welcoming scent of musk; her small, delicate hands on his cheeks, and the impression of her lips on the top of his head. The world, already distinctly vague, faded out, and when it came back into focus, Mr Khorare found that he was in a different body and in another country whose dry scent he thought he recognized.

Oh no, he thought—not again.

His second thought, once he'd risen, resignedly, from the rock on which he was seated, was that he should really do something about his clothes. This harlequinade of diamond motley. This three-pointed cap. *With bells on.*

Honestly!

What was the world coming to?

Chapter 12. Convergence

Gascony, France, Earth, Easter, 2076

Fortunately this early philosopher left descendants; and from these arose, in due course and by means of a series of happy mutations, a race of large-brained and non-simian creatures whose scanty remains your geologists have yet to unearth, and catalogue as an offshoot of the main line of evolution.
Olaf Stapledon—*Last Men in London*

The drove moved on through space. Most of the time it grazed on stars that were rich in carbon and other complex atoms, but which were otherwise small and dim. On the other hand, the recent consumption of several powerful energy sources had stimulated rather than sated—radiation in abundance, but these young, bright stars had been of relatively low metallicity. The white-dwarf star orbiting the biggest and brightest of the young blue-hot stars had, however, been a real treat for those of the drove that had got there first.

But what the drove wanted most were stars that had both size and reasonable metallicity, somewhere in between the abundant but small M and K-class dwarfs, all brewing elements for billions of years, yet each with its own savor, like stationed salt-licks for migrating cattle; and the O and A-class giants, too young and hot to have acquired much in the way of complex elements. Main-sequence F- and G-class suns were most prized—neither too hot nor cold, neither too rich nor too poor. As if they were some galactic Goldilocks, they drew the drove like a magnet.

The drove sensed a suitable star in the path of its current somewhat haphazard migratory route and converged on it from all corners of space. By the time it reached the star's

Oort Cloud, the drove numbered approximately thirty thousand individuals.

Not that any member of the drove would have thought this way, or even thought at all. Although some of the inhabitants of an aluminosilicate pebble orbiting close to the star had named them 'dragons,' they were more like sheep, cattle, or even whales, grazing mindlessly on the fruits of galaxies and nebulae, as indolently as were they plucking berries from bushes, or sifting krill from the sea.

Perhaps even to have thought of them as living organisms might have stretched a point. Generated during the inflation phase of the Big Bang, each member of the drove was a dimensionally complex knot of space-time whose size and shape in 3-space was consequently hard to estimate. But whatever its exact size, a dragon (for want of a better word) exerted a disproportionately large gravitational field, while radiating no discernible energy. Had astronomers but known it, the dragons of space made up a small but appreciable fraction of the non-visible mass from which the Universe was thought to have been constituted. In practice, a dragon was a mobile black hole with a hunger that could never be assuaged.

By January, 2076, the dragons were observed to have sucked star-like Saturn and Jupiter dry. Uranus had disappeared, too, by way of collateral damage. Now so close, the aliens were discernible (against a luminous background) as individuals, in the way they had not been during the remote observation of Lac 9352. Domingo would never forget the image of a swarm of black specks swirling around the King of Planets like a mockery of a shrouded gossamer ring, before a column of them plummeted like a spearhead into the Great Red Spot. It only took a few moments for the rich russets and browns of the Jupiter's cloudscape to be drained of all color; only a few more for the giant planet to implode and disappear into nothingness, as if it had never been.

By the early Spring of 2076, rumors of the end of the world were in general currency. The great cities of south-east Asia erupted in flames before settling down to sullen acquiescence. Hominids in isolated corners of the world worked themselves up into a frenzy of sacrifice. In a small community in the Negev Desert, a Sand Druid called Bob looked up at the sky, sighed, and closed his egg-yolk eyes for the last time.

The people of Europe, after south-east Asia the next most populous part of the planet, were suddenly on the move, even though there was no chance of escape, as all parts of the Earth were doomed equally. It is likely that they were spurred on by the meteor showers of extraordinary frequency and intensity — now, as they ever were, harbingers of doom.

As the rumors spread from house to house, from refugee to monastic hospitaller to mendicant friar, it became clear that the last of all harvests would be gathered in at Easter, and as time passed, the rumors became firmer and more consistent. The world would end some time mid-afternoon (Greenwich time) on Easter Sunday.

Messages came from the Holy See at Saint-Rogatien that this was in fact a sign not of despair but of *hope*, given that Good Friday coincided with the ancient Jewish festival of *Pesach*, celebrated with a ritual meal. Among Christians this would always be indelibly associated with The Last Supper: the last meal Jesus took with all his disciples before his death, and now the last meal that the peoples of the Earth would take with their families and friends before — before, well, who knew what?

The end now seemed certain, but the messages emanating from the ancient hilltop at Saint-Rogatien were of expectation, not resignation.

Throughout the winter, clergy had been gathering at Saint-Rogatien and finding accommodation where it could. Their number was swelled by people from many miles around — people who wanted to hear the words of His Holiness, Pope Eusebius, some time before the end. A tent city sprung up in still-snowbound fields; carts and caravans congregated in corrals under snow-laden trees. More and still more arrived as the land thawed in late March, until the farmhouse was an isolated eye of peace in the maelstrom of people. The early sowing season was disrupted — but if the crop was never to be gathered in, what did it matter?

Only a very few were agitated. Soapbox cranks and false prophets were far less frequent than one might have imagined, given the imminent apocalypse. Indeed, most of the migrants seemed to be at peace, and all were waiting for the promised outdoor mass on the morning of Easter Day itself, when the Pope, it was said, would address the crowd from the roof of the old Mairie opposite the church on the hill. In the meantime, there was a mess of people, all clothed in the slick brown of muddy slush; the screams of babies; the whimpers of children realizing that they would never go home; the press of beasts; the wild parties and bacchanalian festivals of people who had nothing more to lose; the queues for scarce food and stinking, hastily dug latrines amid the mired ground.

A harbinger of doom came on the very last day of March. The destruction of most of the outer planets had scattered moons and other small bodies like grapeshot all across the Solar System. Although much of the débris was yet too far from the Earth to have reached it since the dragons had laid the outer Solar System to waste, the gravitational ripples were felt much closer in, disrupting the courses of several Earth-crossing asteroids. Meteor showers were a nightly occurrence. Several objects had already made close approaches to the Earth, although none had actually made contact.

The first object to hit the planet was Mnemosyne, hitherto an utterly insignificant fly-speck of an asteroid, which struck the wide and empty North Pacific at a relatively shallow angle. The sea boiled, and the consequent tsunami inundated the coastlands from the Philippines to California.

The second impact, later the same day, was closer to home. This was another tiny Earth-grazing asteroid that had long troubled the Astrometry Institute on account of a long series of projected near-misses: the object was extremely small, but regularly approached the Earth within a few tens of thousands of kilometers. The gravitational disturbances from the outer Solar System had tipped its orbit just enough to raise the probability of its striking the Earth into the red zone.

As sunset on 31 March, Minor Planet 100039 Ziemelis streaked south-westwards across southern France and made landfall at the ancient Episcopal seat of Urgell, in Catalonia, just across the Pyrenées. The impact had the explosive yield of a small nuclear bomb. Urgell itself was obliterated in an instant.

Within seconds, the superheated blast wave had scoured the valleys of Andorra, atomizing everything in its path. The mountain wall shook and crumbled, but in the main stood firm, protecting Saint-Rogatien from the worst effects of the blast and the subsequent shower of white-hot rocks: yet an incandescent wake had been painted across the vault of a sky that looked like it had been split in two. The southern horizon was utterly black, a field against which the mountains could be picked out in ominous relief, making them look unusually close.

There were other changes, too. The strange gravitational eddies, slipstreams and wakes created by the passage of the dragons through the Solar System set up tidal stresses in the fabric of the Earth itself. The ground seemed to grumble from constant low-level earthquakes. Over the past two or three months the unquiet Earth had increasingly erupted into cataclysm. The Pacific Circle of Fire was alight: the last remnants of Tokyo and San Francisco had tumbled. The Sasquatch Confederation of Shasta was devastated by the resurgence of Mount St Helens; Yellowstone was a lava lake of boiling fury; the San Andreas Fault opened like a wound. Iceland had burst into flames and split asunder. Mount Tiede in Tenerife had slid into the Atlantic, dousing the already sodden Eastern seaboard of North America with a twenty-meter tsunami. What with the dust raised by the bolide impacts, the exhalations of the world's volcanoes forged a livid spectacle of the final sunsets.

Those with sharp eyes had noticed that the Moon, too, had changed. It had begun to vary in size through its cycle, as well as in phase. And those with sharper eyes still noticed craters and rills never before seen from the Earth, riding on the Moon's eastern and western limbs. The Moon had been shaken in its orbit: the lunar dark side would not be dark for much longer.

Comets, earthquakes, volcanoes and impacts. Heralds of doom, scrawled across the face of the deep.

The evening of 18th April was the Last Supper, celebrated both quietly and loudly, gladly and sadly, with acquiescence and with terror, in a thousand campfires around Saint-Rogatien, and in homes and hovels and caves and towers across the writhen world, as the Sun set for the last time. The final sunset was, fittingly, the most spectacular yet. The bloated orange ball of the solar disk, magnified by the richly refractive horizon, sank through palatial ranks of deep red and purple clouds and, as it finally vanished, launched penetrating streamers of saffron yellow above it to the zenith, painting in gold the undersides of the cinnamon cloudbanks.

Jadis watched from the door of the *arrière-cuisine*, propped on Tom's arm. When the Sun disappeared behind the church, she sighed and looked at her son. His own expression was hard to read: Jadis thought it might have been awe. But what Tom actually saw was always impossible to know — like trying to describe color to a cat.

"Let's lay the table," she said.

Very little further was said as Jadis, Jack, Tom and Domingo ate their simple, final meal, of bread and cheese with some of last year's pickles and the very first stems from the year's asparagus.

Domingo had blessed the meal as he had done many times before, in happier and less contemplative times. He had spent the day at the Mairie and alongside the parish priest, assisting at several services in which the congregation had spilled out of the church, into the square and down the adjacent streets; ministering, comforting and blessing a constant stream of supplicants, and helping as much as he could.

He should have been exhausted.

Instead, he was fired up with a potent mixture of eager anticipation and uttermost terror, as if he were a small child invited to dive into the pool from the high board. He couldn't sit still, and his chair creaked with a thousand tiny squeaks as he shifted his bulk this way and that. He kept stealing glances at Tom, as if in solicitation for a friend who had to reach an uncomfortable decision; and also at Jadis, who now seemed very sick indeed.

Jadis didn't know what to think. The pain in her insides was now so great that connected thought was very difficult in any case, but those thoughts she did actually manage mostly left her angry and frustrated.

The world coming to an end? What was one meant to think of that?

How ought one to react? Regret? Happiness? Horror?

She was even less prepared to give any quarter whatsoever to the illness that was now plainly eating away at her. On his many visits to her bedside in recent weeks, Domingo had blithered on about 'acceptance'. She thanked him for his kindness, but said that his visits were cheering in themselves, whatever he said: and that she wouldn't know what to do with such abstract concepts anyway.

Her one spark of hope came from Jack, who said very little, but who was always *there*, especially in the long and increasingly interrupted nights of the past two or three months; who would hold her close and stroke her hair, combing it with her ancient tortoise-shell plastic comb, rekindling half-buried thoughts of matters long past when her flesh had been young and full and incorrupt, to the extent that she had been quite capable of engendering more life within it. Had she any tears left to shed, she would have cried for that, for her childlessness was now her single greatest regret. In idle moments she found herself blaming Tom for this—and this shamed and horrified her. So she clung to Jack all the harder. Were Jack to die or disappear, she thought, there really would be no need to go on living, were she in an infinity of pain, or none.

Really, she thought, nothing had changed—for it came back to her as clearly as it had been yesterday, when she had been revising for her finals while Jack had made his first visit to Saint-Rogatien, and the pain of his absence then had been a bitter hunger. Rather like the pain she felt now, except that not even Jack's arms could ease it.

Jack was mostly worried about Jadis, against which the end of the world would always come a poor second. At dinner, he would reach over to her and squeeze her hand—small, bony and hot, like the body of a goldfinch—just to reassure himself that she hadn't vanished—or died. Whenever he touched her she seemed energized, becoming the center of the occasion, as she always had been—bright-eyed, excited, animated, the long, leggy girl he'd first met, with the wild, dark hair and matching eyes of quite disconcerting ferocity. The eyes—well, they were still there, large and round in her pinched, lined face, and as fierce as ever. But he was distressed that there was no means of easing her pain, and even if there were some palliative, he was not sure she'd have done anything more than ignore it. To have acknowledged help would have been to admit that she was gravely, even terminally ill, and this might have made matters worse, not better. As with all things, it was usually best to let Jadis achieve equanimity on her own.

However, he did wonder, trying to bury the shame of even thinking along such lines, that were she to die, what then? He suspected that the farmhouse would revert to being a place like any other, and not the center of his world as it had been for half a century. And once his heart had been torn out, he imagined himself an ant from a colony whose queen had died, wandering hither and thither without direction until he met his own random fate.

Tom had completed his paper on the Sigil a few weeks earlier and had sent it to *Nature*, courtesy of one of Domingo's qWave transmitters. He had received an acknowledgement, but nothing more, not even a polite yet curt notice of rejection. Not even the offices of that august journal were immune to the death of the Solar System. Tom viewed all this with resignation. He was glad to have got the thing off his desk—off all their desks—and in any case it didn't much matter now. If the world were to end, he was glad that he'd meet it here.

He reflected that his world had ended so many times already, and his reaction to each event had never been a credit to his own soul. His world ended first when he'd gained the gift of sight, and he had had to adapt, painfully, to the new world of light. Yet he had never trusted it fully, so that when Shoshana had arrived, ending his world for a second time, he had had to adapt all over again. And then there was Masada. And Morgana. And the first viewing of the Sigil.

And then—*then*—there had been Shoshana's death, for which he felt himself responsible though he could not work out precisely why this should be, even though he flagellated himself constantly in an inexhaustible (if now tolerably well-hidden) black pit of remorse. Oh, yes—Tom felt that he had already died a thousand deaths, like the coward he felt himself to be.

Yet, from all this, it seemed clear that ends were never as final as they first seemed, but were in the great scheme of things better regarded as transitions. In which case, perhaps the end of the world would not be such. But no, he thought, he had seen what had happened to Lac 9352: his only course was to compose himself with as much dignity as he could muster.

For *Menschkeit*.

For her sake.

Amid all this, Tom was still trying to make a further accommodation, to the conversation he'd had with Domingo earlier that same day, in which wave followed thundering wave of revelation, so that Tom had felt as bleached as a plank of driftwood washed up on a tropical shore. So much, he had thought, for taking back the reins of his life.

He had just bedded the horses into the stable, locking the door carefully behind him. What with the volume and press of people in the district recently, one couldn't be too careful. He looked up from the padlock and was startled to see Domingo's great bulk close by. Domingo apologised for making him jump.

"We have long tried to put two and two together, Tom, you and I," he said.

Tom looked into the older man's face, questioningly. It was richly lined, where one could see past the thick white beard and moustache, but the brown eyes were as deep and as wise as the bones of the Earth. The eyes lit up again as he continued: "I have a problem which I cannot solve alone, Tom," he said. "I'd value your help."

Tom was torn. On the one hand, he loved and trusted Domingo as a father. On the other, as sons and fathers might, he felt himself in constant danger of being trapped by the older man's guile, his greater experience, especially if he, as the younger and greener, were approached on the pretext of needing help, as if he were the wiser of the two. Domingo had done it again—here was an occasion when Tom could hardly have denied him.

So Tom suggested that they talk it over, whatever it was, in the Spinney, where they could be quiet, and enjoy the slanting rays of the afternoon sun through the branches of the trees. They sat on an old split-log bench of Jack's ancient devising, cracked, worn to a silver-gray smoothness after the ravages of many winters and summers.

"Domingo?"

"Yes. Tom." Domingo swallowed, as if—Tom imagined—he were going to ask a favor from a superior that he didn't expect to have granted. "I wish to... er... *solicit* your understanding, and also, possibly, your forgiveness. Concerning your origins and circumstances, and my part in them."

Tom was shocked, but not—if he were honest—entirely surprised. He thought he knew what was coming, particularly after his recent conversations with Jadis, and imagined that Domingo had cooked up whatever-it-was with his mother, perhaps as a last wish, a last attempt at final reconciliation, before the end. He thought he'd get his retaliation in first.

"Domingo," he said, "I'm sorry, but I have been through all this with *Maman*. How I have something to do with whoever-it-was that made the Sigil. I understand that you wish to make it up to me, but really, there's no need." He rose to go. Domingo placed a restraining arm of Tom's elbow as he did so.

"Please, Tom," he said, "indulge an old man in the last days of his life—of *all* our lives." His voice was stern. "I do not think you should have anything to lose by listening, and by listening, my heart would be eased somewhat." Tom sat down again and tried not to look like a sulking teenager. Guiltily, he remembered other times when Domingo had contrived to ease his pain. A boy standing next to a man in an aloha shirt, before the new grave of a dog.

"I offer no more excuses for the following," Domingo began. "If it pleases you, just think of it as a… er… well, a *story*. Some of it comes from the evidence of my own eyes. Rather more comes from my own travels in the Far East, together with the recollections of some of my colleagues. And some, my dear Tom, comes from *you*."

"Yes, Domingo. Of course." Again, Tom tried not to sound as if he were humoring his old mentor. He rather thought he had failed. Domingo cleared his throat.

There was, once, a species of people raised on this Earth (said Domingo), who were neither hominids nor aliens. Their own origins lay back during the Eocene epoch more than fifty million years ago. In that remote period, the Earth was as warm and lush as it had been during the reign of the dinosaurs. The Eocene world was an Eden, a jungle of riotous life from pole to pole. Indeed, the subsequent history of the world could be read simply as a tale of steady yet inexorable environmental decline.

If the Eocene marked the high fortunes of any particular group of animals, it was the primates, which evolved rapidly from small squirrel-like forms into a range of creatures like nothing seen since. Palaeontologists had long appreciated the diversity of Eocene primates, while acknowledging that only a tiny fraction of all those species that had ever lived had been preserved in the fossil record. Eocene primates colonized every niche that forests had to offer.

Some even colonized that most evanescent of niches: intelligence.

These creatures were remotely akin to what would become the nocturnal tarsiers of Borneo, although they gradually evolved an appearance almost indistinguishable from that of modern humans. This was no more than the well-known phenomenon of convergence, in which unrelated creatures, through the adoption of similar lifestyles, come to look similar to an uncanny degree.

Over a relatively short period several more-or-less related species of these primates had appeared, flowered and become extinct, until one species alone survived. This species erupted into a massive, world-girdling civilization that tamed the Earth to an extent that dwarfed the greatest achievements of *Homo sapiens*. In short, it transformed the world beyond recognition. This civilization and its *sequelae* ruled the Earth for the next several million years, against which the span of humankind looks trifling indeed.

Tom thought about the wilder and grislier excesses of Avi Malkeinu's tall tales, but chose not to draw that comparison aloud. Instead, he wondered aloud, as he had with his mother, how evidence for such a great and temporally extensive civilization could have remained unknown, even given the well-known roulette of fossilization, in which most species on Earth evolve, live out their spans and die without ever once troubling posterity with even a single scrap of bone or tooth robust enough to stand the test of deep time.

Ah, said Domingo, but these creatures *did* leave their mark—in the very face of the Earth, in its denudation and wholesale alteration. It was this civilization that was responsible for the climate change that withered the Eocene jungle. Had it not been for this mighty civilization, the Earth's climate would not have declined as severely as it did.

"It is ironic, is it not," said Domingo, "that Jack's recognition of the Neanderthal civilization that shaped Europe a million years ago was itself but a reshaping of a world that had been civilized for almost fifty times as long? Because, without these Eocene primates, there might have been no Ice Ages. This was what nearly derailed what I think—I guess— was their greatest plan."

"Their… greatest plan?"

"*Homo sapiens*. Yes, Tom, you looked shocked. And I apologise for my small dramatic… er… *flourish*." Domingo explained that nearly everything he had to say was pure guesswork, for all that it fitted the evidence. "A civilization that lasted as long as I suspect this one did must—*must*— have ventured into space. So if these creatures weren't aliens themselves, they probably encountered several extraterrestrial forms, over a very long period."

It was during this star-faring phase, Domingo suggested, that these creatures learned of the dragons from other species, or even discovered them for themselves. It became apparent from their researches that a biological solution might be engineered to combat the dragons, and that this would take a very long time indeed. But millions of years are easy to a civilization as ancient and stable as that of the Eocene primates. The task was to select a strain of primates and set in train a course of evolution that would produce a species that could combat the dragons in some unspecified way when they next arrived in this sector of space.

"Don't ask me how, Tom—I really *am* on… er… thin ice, here. And, unfortunately, as so often happens, even the best-laid plans gang aft agley at the last minute."

"Like mice and monkeys, maybe?"

Domingo laughed, chose to ignore Tom's attempt at gentle skepticism, and went on. Listen carefully, he said: this is the interesting part.

By around twenty million years ago or so, the final civilization of these once Galaxy-spanning creatures was on its last legs, fragmenting into smaller and mutually hostile factions. Their experiment had been going well for some time, but as a result of internecine strife and discord, they had created not one clear lineage of dragon-slayer but many—the hominids—and it was not at all clear, even to them, which if any of their several biological *protégés* would be of any use. So, knowing that they might not survive long enough to oversee their *Grand Projet*, they engineered the Sigil. It was, indeed, a warning—a prompt—for any hominids that might survive.

"Of course," said Domingo, "if we have learned anything from your mother and father's researches here at Saint-Rogatien, and later at Souris Saint-Michel, it's very hard indeed—even, perhaps, impossible—to pin the tool on to the toolmaker. So these primates whose existence I have… er… hypothesized might not have made the Sigil, but appropriated it from some even older civilization, perhaps even one elsewhere in the Galaxy. The strange… uh… *nature* of the artifact certainly suggests that might be a more likely explanation. In any case," he continued. "It hardly matters. Not now. That the Sigil exists is enough, I think, for us to discern its purpose."

Tom recalled an argument from long ago, an argument since suffused with a keening longing, loss, pain, and regret.

"A warning," he said. And then, after a pause, he whispered one more word: Shoshana.

Domingo grasped Tom's hand, then, and the two men sat in silence for some time, listening to the birdsong and the wind in the trees, and watching the sun in its stately fall towards the world's edge.

At length Domingo continued his story, painting a picture of a civilization now so decayed that its products, perhaps once the rulers of the Solar System, or of more than one, came to live humbly among the hominids, the products of their own technology, mingling with their own creations and writing themselves out of history.

Tom sat up straight and looked back at his mentor. For the first time he saw the lines of care, of worry—of age—in Domingo's face.

"And who are these remnants?" Tom asked. "Who are they?" In his heart Tom felt that he probably knew the answer, as his mother had done. Yet he had to hear it from Domingo's mouth, as much as he dreaded it.

"They are the creatures that now call themselves 'Jive Monkeys,' Tom—no, now, don't start, I suspect that this is not a complete surprise to you given what you already know, and your... ah... recent *experiences*."

Tom sat back, trying to drive from his mind the horrible yet fascinating image of Morgana, and more than that, of him and Morgana together. But why *should* he continue this futile denial? Why not just accept it as a fact of life and move on? His mother, with her penetratingly logical mind, had worked it out. If Domingo had worked it out too, whose insights into human desires and motivations were perhaps more profound than anyone alive, Tom knew that it must be correct.

"And, Tom," the old man continued, "this is why I have asked you for your time this evening, and have been so rudely... ah... *insistent*. For I have felt your pain over many long years. It seems that you are of a greater lineage than any of us, and we've forced you to... er... *slum* it."

"Domingo, don't..." The memory of Shoshana's purple eyes filled his mind's sky, as soon as he had taken off his iShades to see.

"But I'm afraid I must, if only—selfishly—to ease my own mind, my own heart, before the end. For it was I, as you know, who brought you to this hearth and home, to comfort the childlessness of a good friend who'd had an accident that meant she could no longer bear children—your mother. And know this, Tom, she loves you with the tenacity of a lioness. That is why the past few months—years—have been such a trial for her. And you too, I suspect."

Tom nodded.

"The fact is, Tom, that you are a... ah... 'Jive Monkey,' and neither you, nor I, knew it. Just like, I suppose, those with whom you've had such problems in Cambridge. I must apologise for that, too, for it's my fault. I didn't know it when I rescued you from that massacred village in Borneo forty-odd years ago. I could have—*should* have—made more inquiries, I know, but Jadis was desperate, and... well... we didn't really know anything about hominids in those days. In retrospect, I guess, we should have seen it.

"But it is, perhaps, the curse of a species that has inherited the Earth to assume that it is alone and has always been so, and will therefore see in every face, no matter how different it looks, a reflection of itself—because it can conceive of no other. Had we known your true nature, Tom, it would have explained many things that perplexed your parents, and, I have to say, me."

"Such as...?"

"Well, Tom, in short, it's your eyes." Tom heard his mother speaking, but Domingo's voice carried a greater authority and knowledge than hers. For Domingo had been aware of his own perceived failure and had been engaged on a long and penitential research effort, if not in atonement, then at least to understand. "One thing I have discovered is that Jive Monkeys are habitually born blind, and a certain altriciality of development means that they cannot see at all until they are around five or six years old. At this stage the Jive-Monkey visual system is remarkably similar to that of a human, apart from an unusually shaped pupil. But the visual capacity increases with age as new banks of rods and cone cells develop in the retina, permitting a fair degree of sensation in the infrared and ultraviolet..."

"Domingo, please, stop, please... I... understand," Tom begged. "And I forgive you." Domingo put his great bear-paw of a hand on Tom's slender brown fingers.

"Thank you, Tom," he said. "Thank you."

"But there is more, isn't there, Domingo? Shouldn't you be telling me more? If I am a... a... one of these creatures, then aren't there consequences—from any liaison with a human?"

Domingo paused for a long time as if he—even he—had not the words sufficient to say what he wished. "I expect that there might be, Tom," he said. "There might. But, I... honestly, I do not think I can say any more."

Tom could have sworn he saw a single tear well up in a wrinkle in Domingo's left eye, overspill the lid, and run down a line in his weathered cheek before disappearing into the eaves of his coniferously forested moustache.

The time for raging was long over. Shoshana's eyes, starred and flecked with violet, looked at Tom from out of the setting sun and, with a sudden flash of hardness, demanded that he be a *mensch*. This father-and-son game was not over. Not just yet. So Tom placed his free hand on top of Domingo's.

"Domingo, my forgiveness still stands." He smiled. Domingo nodded his thanks like a penitent. "But there is a question I must ask you, too."

"Tom, name it."

"Your stirring tale was of humans and other hominids as potential dragon-slayers. Did you mean that the long quest of the ancestors of the Jive Monkeys was to produce a species that could kill these things? The same creatures that we two, with our own eyes, saw destroy Lac 9352? Even when they could not?"

"Yes, Tom, but that was where the ice was at its thinnest... I didn't..."

Tom interrupted, his voice spiky and sharp as if chasing down a logical quarry before a roomful of hesitant, frightened undergraduates. "But that's just *it*, isn't it?" he said. "The whole business with the Jive Monkeys, though it concerns us closely, is a side-show. But if their ancestors were star-farers, why couldn't they have just blasted the dragons out of space with... oh, I don't know... ray guns?"

"Tom, I'm afraid I don't know..."

"... and yet you mentioned humans and other hominids as dragon-slayers," Tom continued. "You were quite specific about it. But no species on Earth today can launch anything more than a firework, and the dragons eat stars for breakfast and kick planets around like footballs. So where are these valiant *Saints-Georges*, when we need them?"

Tom rose to go, muttering that he'd promised to help his mother with the supper. That thought, too, struck him with a pang—she looked so frail, and yet defiantly denied the very suggestion of infirmity. Almost as a parting, Parthian shot, he turned again to the older man, still seated.

"And what's more, Domingo, *Homo sapiens*, which I expect was what you were getting at, has only just avoided extinction, and that by the narrowest of margins, effectively ruling them out of contention…" Tom stopped, quite still. He felt the blood drain from his face, and his knees weaken. He sat down again next to his old—his oldest friend. "Domingo—I must apologise," he said. "It's the Plague, isn't it? There is a connection, and…"

"I believe so, Tom. Or, rather, I *hope* so. I know you shot down that idea long ago, and you were right to have done so, given the evidence, or lack of it. But Jack thought there was a connection, somehow, and if it weren't for Jack's iron whims, neither of us would be here discussing all this, here, now."

"But… *how*?"

"I have no idea, Tom. None whatsoever," he said. "All we can do now is hope. And pray."

-=0=-

As he had done on so many nights of late, Domingo stayed up all night, praying and thinking. If not kneeling at his *prie-dieu*—in which his knees had now worn two great craters—he was pacing the confines of his narrow room in the farmhouse. On this night, he consoled himself with thoughts of the ancient midnight antiphon, on this, at the very darkest hour before the dawn.

cum rex gloriae Christus infernum debellaturus intraret

He thought again of the transitions that marked men's lives, and how he and his fellow priests were only the gatekeepers. Did they have a responsibility to be reliable guides to the world beyond?

qui tenebatur in morte captivus

His teaching insisted that they had, for scripture was quite clear on the nature of the next world and the terms under which it could be entered. He remembered how Avi had often needled him about this: the Jewish conception of the after-life, he had said, was necessarily vague, for who could say anything about a country whence none had returned? And yet, Domingo had countered, the Jews did not deny the conception of afterlife outright—and there was, after all, one who had come back from Heaven, to show everyone else what it was like.

advenisti desiderabilis quem expectabamus in tenebris

In that he had complete faith. But attendant on the incarnation and resurrection there had been salvation, too, and for that he prayed his hardest.

te nostra vocabant suspiria te large requirebant lamenta

Even then, he could not entirely dispel Avi's teasing empiricism, for it had resonated with him, too. After all, had he not been a scientist in his younger days? A cleric, certainly, and yet one who had been taught, even encouraged, to question received wisdom? In his thirst for more knowledge from the Astrometry Institute, despite its dreadful implications— was he not a scientist now? In that spirit, he had felt his mind increasingly drawn to the images of blood-spattered horror twenty years earlier when he had stepped into the isolation ward, deaf to the pleading of poor benighted Dr Al Hajj, to scoop the spherical remnant of Pope Linus the Second from beneath the gurney, and to insist on an appropriate container.

tu factus est spes desperatis magna consolatio in tormentis

The flight time of the Papal hyperjet from Israel to Rome had been less than an hour, and yet Domingo recalled it having been the longest hour of his life. Running from the storm as the fury of the Khalifa broke on the Mediterranean shore, he had sat in air-conditioned peace, with the sealed box at his side.

He recalled the *touch* of the erstwhile pontiff. The sphere had been hard and smooth—smooth enough to be slippery, almost as if it were alive. Handling it, he felt as if he were trying to restrain a wet and writhing otter, or a newly caught fish. When he had finally got a grip—with an awkward combination of hands and sleeves and forearms—he noticed that the sphere was noticeably warm. This was, perhaps, to be expected, in a corpse which until moments before had been alive. But not after several hours and days had elapsed, when, still just as warm, the corpse was buried with due ceremony. At the time, Domingo had been puzzled by this: but many other concerns had pressed on his time and his mind and he had put his perplexity aside.

It was only lately that Domingo had begun to think that the Plague represented a very strange kind of death indeed, perhaps much less final than the phenomenon usually associated with that stygian scythe: more, then, of a transition.

Billions had been swept away in the Plague.

Billions of agonized finality, each one initially in circumstances all its own, and yet ultimately all exactly like Linus the Second, in that the final product was always the same—the black spheres, each featureless and identical in size and colour with every other.

He'd seen clusters of them on his travels. A dusty square in deserted Nice with these ominous matt-black Plague spheres instead of the smaller, graven chrome pieces of *petanque*. Banyan trees in the East Indies, with collections of black spheres rolled calmly against their bases. Whole towns in China, utterly deserted but for the spheres, lying in the streets, in shops, in homes.

In recent weeks he had often cause to recall a curious line of Jack's whose derivation he could not place, and which Jack, skittishly, wouldn't reveal:

that is not dead which can eternal lie,
and with strange aeons even death may die.

All over the world, these black spheres were brooding. Waiting. But for what? Domingo earnestly hoped that if his intuition—and Jack's—was correct, that their condition was transitional, not final. And that they would not take much longer in choosing their moment.

-=0=-

Tom, like Domingo, could not sleep, either. Curiously, he felt, his insomnia had nothing to do with the promised cataclysm. The end of the world was far too stupefying a concept for him to even begin to imagine. He supposed that most other people felt the same, which was why there had been so few disturbances in the tents and campsites around the village. If one had no idea what to expect, not even in one's worst nightmares, it was pointless even to worry.

So why insomnia? Reason urged that he be at peace, finally, having scrambled after many hazards to a high, clear summit of equanimity, long desired, often denied. After all, he had achieved some kind of reconciliation with his mother, with Domingo, with the memory of Shoshana, and even with his own identity. And, as he always was these days, he had been running the physical side of the farm more or less single-handedly, and always went to bed in a state of welcome exhaustion.

At about four o'clock he gave up even pretending to sleep. Perhaps he'd go downstairs and make himself a cup of tea, and take it into the garden. It had been his traditional routine in Cambridge when the cramped confines of his cell closed in on him—to take a midnight stroll around the cloisters, the rhythm of his steps resonating with the waves of sleep. That is, until the pressure of work and other matters had become too much for him. But that was then. He rose, dressed and went downstairs.

He put the kettle on the range and, while it was heating, walked through the *arrière-cuisine* to the back door. He did all of this in darkness, as he always had, without thinking: against the pitch interior of the shuttered house, the night sky was a brighter curtain of slate-blue. He walked out on to the terrace—the same, had he known it, where Jack had first announced Souris Saint-Michel to the Dream Team.

The Earth grumbled and groaned beneath his feet, as it had done for several weeks. The constant infrasonic rumble had become an accompaniment to their lives so persistent that most now chose to ignore it, despite the threat it represented: that their small, fragile planet was trying to hold its course despite being tossed on a sea of unexpected and occasionally violent gravitational cross-currents.

But there was something else, too—something that only Tom could see. That the planet seemed to be generating its own aura, an aura that pulsed to the rhythms of the titanic forces now stressing the crust.

He saw it first on the edge of the *potager* as a faint blue-white glow against the near horizon, and traced it towards him as an illuminated network of thin lines that criss-crossed the terrace beneath his feet, as if they were phosphorescent sea-worms, and he were standing on glass. His eyes followed the glowing lines back to the *potager*, where they met other networks and formed greater branches and boles across the garden, through the field gate, and up the back lane to the village square. Picked out against the yellowish haze of the western horizon, he saw the luminous trunk join

others moving in from other directions, and they all converged on the graveyard behind the church where the trunks
fused into something like ball lightning, making strange
dancing shadows and silhouettes of the looming yews and
cypresses that shaded that part of the cemetery, on the very
peak of the ancient hill.

And then there was an almighty crack like thunder, followed by a sustained roar, as the graveyard buckled and
erupted. A shaft of white light, almost unbearably bright
against the night, stabbed upwards from behind the trees,
broad and straight, like the blade of a broadsword, fading
only by virtue of its increasing distance. Tom saw it taper to
a point and vanish above his head, at the zenith.

From the kitchen, the kettle whistled like a cock-crow.

Chapter 13. Usurper

Mesopotamia, Lower Egypt and Mount Carmel, Earth, c, 45,000 years ago; Souris Saint-Michel, France, Earth, c. 45,000 years ago and 1866 AD

Someone had blundered.
Alfred, Lord Tennyson— *The Charge of the Light Brigade*

Dust, dust.

The Yettin champion Zagrond wheeled, turning in the high saddle of his coelodont in a whirl of white fur, gray flint and blue lapis, as the gigantic, snow-maned animal reared, turned in mid-air and thundered to the ground in a yellow-brown cloud. Zagrond charged at Horsa again, head down, its vicious two-meter horn pointed straight at him.

For an instant, Horsa—his long shambok flailing in his right hand from its leather strap, reins grasped in his left—saw nothing but the point of his enemy's horn barreling towards him, surmounted by the fanged, bloody yell of defiance in Zagrond's face. At the very last moment, Horsa willed his own mount to step aside. His rhino, clanking, like he was, in flint fishmail, was huge, yet still puny compared with the might of the Yettin's mount.

Zagrond, startled by Horsa's feint, surged in a rage of spume and fur through a gap he did not expect. The ring of Stoners cheered, but their triumph was short-lived. As Zagrond passed by, his momentum too great for him to pull up without injury, he gave an almighty swipe at Horsa with his three-branched bone flail, smashing it towards the Stoner's head. Had Horsa not blocked the blow with his shambok, he would have lost half his face, ripped clear from his skull.

Bone flail met bone shambok with an impact that jarred Horsa's right arm so violently that the sinews in his shoulder strained and tore. The force of the blow instantly shivered both weapons into flying shrapnel. Blasted in Zagrond's wake, Horsa felt several fragments bury themselves in his hands and face. The Yettin whirled past like a hot wind. Horsa felt a stab of agony in his left eye. His vision was stained with red. His right arm was numb.

In the yellow distance, Zagrond slowed and turned once more in a screech and a fog of dirt, pulling out more weapons for another assault on the renegade Stoner chieftain. Horsa drew a narwhal-horn javelin from a saddle holster, and, transferring the reins to his weakened right hand, resting them in a knot on the pommel, hefted the weapon uncertainly in his left, waiting for the Yettin to return.

It was an outcome that Horsa had not expected, for all his contingencies and stratagems, and one he could not, now, afford to lose.

-=O=-

He had met the Yettin leader as they had agreed, at dawn after the evening of their last parley. With a wave of his hand, the Stoner army and the larger force of its Yettin allies moved off. Horsa could not help but gasp at its immensity. It seemed that the entire surface of the hillslope, all the way down to the valley bottom far to the westward, had moved at once on his command, as if the Earth itself had adjusted its blankets over the ground beneath.

The deep-cloven Tigris had been the first obstacle, revealing the first signs of strain between the always fragile alliance between Stoners and Yettins. They had come up against the lip of a steep-sided canyon where they had expected an easy ford. Several assault-mammoths, always in the vanguard, had slipped and fallen over the rim before anyone realized what was happening.

The regrouping of such a vast army had taken three days, until scouts had had the chance to discover a ford some miles to the northward. More days lost, but worse was to come. The ford had been held against Horsa's scouts by a small contingent of Stoners from the Kingdom Under The Mountain itself. Lightly armed and easily cowed, this distant outpost was easily beaten.

Too easily.

By the time the main host had reached the ford and was halfway across—a maneuver that Horsa reckoned would take an entire day—they were ambushed by a sizeable force of Stoners. They appeared from nowhere, as if the rocks in the water and the banks on either side had simply melted into men.

The Battle of the Fords of Tigris was fierce and desperate. Arrows rained down, slashing beasts and men. Mammoths, their legs cut from beneath them, toppled into the river, unbalancing more mammoths and troopers on coelodonts, raising great waves that swamped Horsa's contingent and Yettins alike.

Despite its cost, the ambush had been routed by sunset. The Yettins, impatient for the joys of battle, had come into their own: each of the huge, furred man-beasts had picked up a Kingdom Stoner in each huge hand and had ripped out throats with impressive fangs. But all surprise was lost, and all momentum.

The subsequent passage across Mesopotamia, between Tigris and Euphrates, was ominously quiet, but this time it was the land itself that conspired against them. Horsa's childhood memory of this land had been of lushness and ease, of homesteads amid rushes and fields of wheat taller than a man; lakes full of fish and fluttering with spoonbills;

the shade of frequent, bountiful palms. Such was the picture of this country he'd painted for Yettins more used to the enclosed world of mountainsides than this open, flat land. A country of plenty, with supplies to be found wherever needed, and grazing for the enormous contingent of beasts. Even if he knew in his heart that such a rosy image was unlikely to be borne out in reality.

But this land of plenty was now a pitiless, brown desert, utterly lifeless and uninhabited, with hardly a dry blade of grass for fodder — let alone palms, lakes, waterfowl and the rest. The only water revealed itself slyly, as quicksands, where the lakes must once have been, that mired yet more assault mammoths and troopers on coelodonts, weighed down with armor. Horsa realized with sickening shock how long ago his boyhood must have been, when he with his mother and her loyal courtiers had fled the rapine of the young Hengest. Whether this evil transition in the landscape had been the result of the depredations of the Kingdom, or the slowly worsening weather which, in the past twenty years, had led to six months per years of snowfall on the higher ground where his boyhood remembered hardly any at all — was not, at the moment, at the forefront of Horsa's mind.

Of more concern was the friability of his Yettin alliance. The Yettins were clearly beginning to suspect that Horsa had lied to them, deliberately: had led them into a trap. The worst thing, Horsa reflected, was that he had allowed *himself* to be fooled by his own childish expectations. That the innocence of childhood would have survived the ghastly betrayals of adulthood.

It was on the marshy banks of the sluggish Euphrates that matters had come to a head.

The Euphrates and the Tigris could hardly have been more different. Whereas the Tigris had ambushed them with sudden canyons, the Euphrates was slothful and meandering, and crept up on them by stealth. As they approached it, the flat land on which they had been traveling dipped so gently that they were unaware of it, until they found themselves in a country of tussock and tall reeds. Platoons became cut off from one another as their vision was obscured.

Horsa, at the head, found that he could no longer see his lieutenants to his right and left. He rode in a debatable land of pools and reedbeds, unable to see over the tops of the reeds, even mounted on a coelodont. The rhino, for its part, was swaddled girth-deep in mud and water, and was making heavy weather of it, snorting, and bucking its huge head. By the time Horsa had calmed it and looked up, he realized that he was quite alone. The world was eerily silent. Even Zagrond had disappeared.

He rode on, looking for what remnants of his army might still exist in this treacherous country, until his coelodont breasted a wave, scattering a clatter of ibises that flew up right in front of him. Now the last reedbeds had gone, and the Euphrates stood before him, wide, flat and blue. It was a relief, to be honest, to see a horizon uninterrupted by reeds. But this river was no mountain stream to be hopped at a bound: it was almost as broad as the sea. The farther bank could just be seen as a thin silver line ahead, parched under the westering sun before him.

As his rhino began to wade across, he began to pick out the motes of troops on rhinos, the smaller specks of footsoldiers, and the larger images of mammoths, all making their way across, in front of him and to either side, as far as the eye could see. The reeds had spread the army out, refracted it, so that it must have been five miles wide. The reeds had also slowed some parts of the army more than others—he, for example, had been at its head before they had strayed into the land of reeds, but now he was some way behind the leaders.

No choice now, thought Horsa, but to ride the shallow river to the other bank, and regroup. Horsa took some solace from this. Like all military men, he found comfort in being able, now and then, to subsume himself blindly to external constraint, absolving himself of all responsibility, all thought.

As it happened, their crossing point had been at the farthest extent of a vast meander, so whereas the eastern bank had been flat almost to the point of inexistence, the western bank was high. The final stretch of river was treacherous, with deep, fast-moving currents, and the farther bank was a broad, shelving beach. When Horsa's coelodont finally made landfall, shedding braids of water from its armor, Horsa looked down to see a motley selection of his own troops. They were in a sorry state. Many appeared to have lost their armor. Some were injured, a few gravely—bodies lay in disarray up and down the beach. Several were disposed in crazy angles. The stench of death lay thickly on the ground like a poisonous vapor. Only one man rose to greet him. It was his esquire. He took the coelodont's reins from Horsa and helped him dismount.

"What news?" asked Horsa, wondering how the army was to regroup.

"Very bad, Sir," the esquire said. "As you see, we had to fight our way across."

The story that the esquire told was grim.

-=0=-

Zagrond pounded towards him, bright white and blue against a rising plume of yellow-brown dust. Almost at the last minute, the Yettin let go the reins of his charging coelodont, raising both arms wide. He held a long, broad-bladed scimitar in each hand, poised to bring each one down at an angle and slice Horsa's head off with two diagonal cuts. Horsa weighed the twisted spike of narwhal horn in his left hand. It was heavy, reassuring. He tensed himself for the throw. The last thing he saw before the final strike was the inside of the Yettin's mouth, his array of teeth, the huge tongue, lolling, trailing gobbets of saliva. With one final heave, Horsa launched the dense ivory javelin at his adversary.

-=0=-

"It was the Yettins, Sir," the esquire said. "As we entered the reed forest, they doubled back. Some of us gave chase. We found them in rear, looting the supply train and making off back East."

"And what then?"

"We gave battle, Sir. The battle went back and forth, and the last tongues of it licked us across the river itself."

"You did well, it seems."

"Yes Sir, most of the Yettins will go no further. But, I regret, neither will most of our army. I've sent scouts up and down the banks to start a regroup. I took the liberty…"

"You are to be commended."

"Thank you, Sir. But we brought one just Yettin to account. A Yettin who killed many of us before he could demand to be brought to you for… for justice."

"Look up, Stoner," came a voice from ahead and above. On the grassy ridge above the beach was Zagrond, still mounted, silhouetted by the descending sun, surrounded by a crowd of nervous-looking Stoner spearmen, plainly afraid of being trampled by the Yettin's monstrous steed. Horsa shaded his eyes but said nothing.

"It is as your servant has said," Zagrond said. "We Yettins suspected treachery, Stoner. So we took our payment on account."

"But the contract has yet to be fulfilled, Zagrond," said Horsa. "The Kingdom still stands."

"The Kingdom, Stoner, as you well know, is rotten. It is poised to fall. Just one gentle push and all will collapse. A baby could do it. Even *you* could do it." The Yettin laughed. It was a horrible sound, like skeletons being crushed inside a giant fist. "Such prizes as there'd be would not satisfy our Yettin hunger: our Yettin thirst."

"You are without honor, Yettin. Be gone," said Horsa.

"Honor?" the Yettin cackled. "Honor? You are a beggar and a thief, Stoner, as you have been all the days of your life, cowering from a bully of a brother who dwells like a great fat maggot inside a rotten fruit, long bereft of value, with nothing but the other maggots for company. All entirely satisfactory, I dare say, if you are a maggot, and rotten fruit is to your taste. I, on the other hand, am a contractor, taking his due. Really, it is you who should read the small print."

"I cannot let such a slur passed unmarked," said Horsa, his temper rising sluggishly to the surface. A duel was the last thing he needed. He was uninjured, to be sure, but he was soaked through and weighed down by his armor; and he was exhausted. But the worst thing was that everything the Yettin said was true. He, Horsa, was nothing but a vagabond trading on the glories of a Kingdom that had in reality faded long ago, and which was now hardly worth the effort of claiming. He knew in his heart that he had deceived the Yettins—and his own men. But he could hardly admit as much in front of the remnants of his troops, who'd traveled so loyally and so far. Rank has its obligations, as well as its privileges.

"I thought as much, Stoner," replied Zagrond. "I suggest a joust. Shall we do it here on this dreary beach, or go slightly inland, where there is more room for a decent run-up?"

-=0=-

The narwhal-horn javelin left his hand with what he thought was agonizing slowness, compared with the break-neck speed of the approaching Yettin. The ground shook. So violent was Zagrond's final approach that Horsa could feel his own teeth rattle in their sockets. Horsa had aimed the javelin at Zagrond, but his left arm had not the strength of his right, and the javelin fell short. So rather than strike the Yettin, it pierced his coelodont through its right eye. The forelimbs of the gigantic animal buckled beneath it, pitching Zagrond forwards, through the air. The animal ploughed on through the dirt, carried by its momentum, its rider arcing above it.

As the animal came to a stop, half buried in dirt, Zagrond belly-flopped onto its huge, sharp nose-horn, which impaled him. Gray-brown innards streaked with blood dripped from the Yettin's wound, ran over the coelodont's head and dripped in viscous gouts onto the grass. Blood ran from the Yettin's mouth, frozen in an expression of horror, and dripped from the ends of his fangs.

It was only then that Horsa realized he'd been holding his breath. He exhaled — a hideous, gasping rasp of relief. There was nothing before him now but the Kingdom, his birthright. He'd take it alone, if he had to.

-=0=-

Dogfinger's eyes flashed open and he was suddenly awake. Father-the-Sun had yet to rise above the rim of the world, but he could still see — or, rather, sense — the body of Moonrise, his Bride, asleep with her back towards him. Hitching himself up on his right elbow, he traced the fingertips of his left hand over the sweeping curve of her hip, enjoying the contrast between the underlying hardness of her hipbone and the luxuriant fleshiness of her buttocks and thighs; feeling her skin yield to his touch, smelling its fragrance, released, as he did so.

"The time is now," he said, as much to himself as to her. "The men have gathered," he whispered to the darkness. "The scouts have plotted our course. We shall make our way north to the sea, and walk along the shore with the sea to our left. Then we shall meet the Stoner city, and take it."

"And I suppose you expect me to stay here with the other women and the children, waiting for your triumphant return? Hmm?" Her voice in the dark came suddenly.

"I thought you were asleep, Bride," said Dogfinger.

"Evidently."

"I wanted to leave without fuss, and... well, you are with child, as are many of the other women."

"Whose fault is that, may I ask? And yet you thought you'd leave me... us... behind?" She turned over to face him. He caught the twin glints in her eyes, fierce and hard. "You've had a sheltered life, Dogfinger," she said. She sat up. Dogfinger could just make out the fullness of her gravid body as she did so, the sway of her huge breasts; the swish of her long hair.

"Husband," she said, "I was older than you when I came to the oasis. I am older than you still. I know the world better than you do. It's bigger than you imagine. When — if — you finally get to the Stoner city, you're not going to come back, all this way, to fetch us, and then go all the way there again? Three journeys, when just one would do? Are you?"

"Well, I… I confess…"

"So you are taking us with you? Good. I think you'll find us all… prepared." She lay down again, but closer this time. Dogfinger could feel the velvet skin of her belly and breasts rub against him. Her nipples, now coarsened and baby-chewed, were hard against his ribcage. "However," she continued, "I think we might have to put off our departure for a day or two. It's not as if we have to keep an appointment, is it?" She bit his earlobe. "I mean, after all," she continued, "the Kingdom will still be there, when we get there." She ran her fingers down across his belly. He stiffened. "And after we've taken it," she said, "it will, presumably, need populating."

She heaved her bulk on top of him, her distended belly resting just under his ribcage. She braced her mighty thighs on either side of his hips. Dogfinger felt himself slide into the cosseting warmth between. Yes, perhaps, his expedition against the Kingdom Under The Mountain could wait another day.

Maybe two.

But no longer.

-=0=-

By the time it reached the Sea of Galilee, the greatest army ever seen on the surface of the Earth, or near it, for tens of millions of years, had been winnowed to fewer than a hundred Stoner footsoldiers, ragged and hungry. Horsa and his men paused by the shores of the lake to recuperate.

The passage across the steppe had been relatively simple. Horsa's band had met no further resistance, but hunger and thirst had begun to take their toll. When the soldiers reached the shores of the Sea of Galilee, they broke ranks, some running—others limping and hobbling—into its healing waters, ripping off their armor and diving in. Horsa hadn't the heart to stop them, and indeed raised morale considerably by ordering the slaughter and consumption of the last of their animals—his own coelodont. The land all about was barren, and they'd had nothing to eat for two days. There was time, now, for hurts to heal. The redness in his vision faded, the inflammation receded. Healthful swims in the lake and a rich diet of broiled coelodont liver prompted his strained shoulder to knit together.

In truth, Horsa felt happier as a leader of a band of brigands (for that was what they were) than a massive army. They could move more quickly, and perhaps penetrate the heart of the Mountain even before its inhabitants knew that they had been invaded. Burglary, then, rather than full-on assault. It was in that spirit that Horsa and his band, refreshed, crept up on the Eastern Gate of the Kingdom one evening about a halfmoon later.

Horsa remembered the splendor of the Eastern Gate as it had been in his childhood. He remembered the gigantic seated statue of Hrothgar the Great, the near-legendary King Under The Mountain who had ruled the known world perhaps eighty millennia earlier, towering above: the Gate itself opening between the statue's knees.

He remembered the immense stones, painted in gay colors, the flags and the banners cracking in the breeze; the perpetual market in the lee of the gate, the busy traders and throngs of people made as small as ants by the giant statue, people buying goods of every kind.

He remembered gawping beneath the awnings of the tannery market, at the richly furred Yettin pelts, piled high, contrasting with the darker hides of Thinskins.

He remembered running errands for his mother to the apothecary stall, to fetch Thinskin bone paste (a guaranteed cure for all known ills).

But most of all he remembered the delicatessen, with its jars of sweetmeats designed for the epicure—and with fabulous prices to match—for wild-caught Thinskins were scarce, even then. Bunches of Thinskin tongues, pickled and dried; deep-fried Thinskin ears and noses; pretty displays of crystallized Thinskin fingers and toes, almost irresistible to any five-year-old Stoner princeling; translucently-thin slices of ham from Thinskin heifers, freshly caught in the Nile Delta and 'newly violated' (he'd asked his mother what 'newly violated' meant, but she'd changed the subject); and, most of all, great, richly decorated stone jars of Thinskin eyeball-and-testicle soup, seasoned and prepared for the discerning palate.

He remembered his mother allowing him just a small spoonful of this most magnificent of all delicacies at a banquet. He remembered it as being insipid and tasting of nothing more than salt, and told his mother so. She laughed— how he remembered her laugh—and had said that it was something called an 'acquired taste,' which he'd appreciate when he was older. He'd never had the opportunity: his mother and her court took him into exile just a few weeks later.

Horsa had imagined the scene of his return for decades.

He had imagined himself a conquering hero, walking into the bustling market with his men, garlanded with Thinskin body parts by the oppressed citizens of the Kingdom, who would flock to his banner and overthrow the hated Hengest.

He had been bracing himself for the impact of what he suspected—*knew*—was the reality for several days, as his band passed through deserted villages, barren fields and homesteads laid waste, where once had been light and life. Nevertheless, the sight that greeted him as he and his band crested a knoll about half a mile from the Gate was heartbreaking. The Gate itself was unguarded, deserted, its stones drab and broken. Of the statue of Hrothgar, just the legs were left, trunkless, standing either side of the Gate. The head lay some distance away, on its side, its writhen expression half-sunk in piles of rubble and refuse.

Horsa decided to camp in the modest cave formed by Hrothgar's left nostril, and strike at the Kingdom the next day. He wondered, with resignation, if he was preparing to burgle a ruin whose treasures had long since been looted by others: that he was nothing but a vulture, a grave-robber.

The final day of Horsa's long-planned, long-desired mission of revenge dawned bright and cold. Leaving a small detachment of Stoners to guard the Gate, Horsa led his remaining men through the Gate itself and into the heart of the Kingdom.

Where once had been elegant halls, full of life and gaiety and business, were now dark caverns that reeked of decay and neglect. Piles of refuse lay everywhere; bodies, and parts of bodies, and skeletons, of Stoners and Thinskins alike, were scattered all across the floor. Remains of food, dried and furred with mold; shattered flints, broken weapons, plates, flagons. Horsa's heart sank with every step. The trail of desolation went on for hall after hall, for hour after hour. His men, who had awoken in good heart, fell into brooding silence. They had expected at least some sign of battle, token resistance, even a feint. If one is to lead fighting men on such an expedition with a promise of a battle at the end of it, Horsa reflected, that promise really ought to be fulfilled.

He was heartened, then, by a ghost of a sound, coming from a passage ahead. Some of the men had heard it too, and Horsa felt the spark of spirits reviving all around him. He rushed ahead to a passage leading sharply downwards from one of the seemingly interminable series of once-grand but now-deserted and gloomy staterooms, and signaled for his men to gather round him and be silent. He heard his own breath and the beating of his own heart punctuating — what? It sounded like screams of agony and rage, one merging into another, without cease. He remembered that sound from his youth, again from the market at the Great Eastern Gate.

It was the sound of herded Thinskins at bay.

This, if anything, was the prize, the spoils of conquest. Horsa beckoned his men to follow, stealthily, down the broad passage. They needed no further encouragement. A few minutes later Horsa found himself on the threshold of a golden opportunity.

A later commentator might have recognized it as the jaws of Hell.

The passage opened out into a broad cavern, the roughness of its walls thrown into relief by the guttering flames of torchlight. Before him was a moving mass of pale color, in shades from ivory white to a kind of livid pink. It took a moment for him to realize that the mass was a press of bodies, jostling, shifting — and screaming. This had been the source of the noise he'd heard from the stateroom above. Screaming not in words, because the screamers, having been raised in strict captivity, had no language, even had they tongues to frame words.

This, then, was the prize domestic Thinskin herd raised by his brother Hengest, bred in captivity in caverns deep beneath the Kingdom. It was his brother's last attempt to prolong the life of a Kingdom which, Horsa now realized with a feeling of wrenching emptiness, had been no more than a grinning death's head of contempt, existing on borrowed time — perhaps for millennia before he himself had been born.

As he looked more closely, first at one Thinskin and then another, he realized that this herd was hardly a prize worth fighting for. These creatures were no more than oversized, bloated maggots. Whimpering within rolls of fat, heads shaved, dead eyes staring, lips slack and drooling, Horsa saw gelded cattle where once had been men; creatures without ears, without noses, without eyes, without fingers, without hands. And all, without exception, howling without cease.

In that moment Horsa felt a sensation he'd never felt in his life—pity. Not just for these wrecked and wretched specimens, bred for their meat and their pelts, but for himself, and even for Hengest. They were, every one of them, prisoners, witnesses to the fall of a once-great civilization. The Thinskin herd filled the great cavern from wall to wall, and Horsa could just make out, in the distance, the figures of Stoners assigned to guard and protect this last pitiful vestige of a Kingdom's wealth. A cry went up from the guards—Horsa's band had been spotted. Arrows flew: one of his men went down. Several Thinskins in front of him collapsed, pierced by flint-tipped shafts.

Horsa's men broke ranks, then. This, they realized, was the last throw. There was no Kingdom here, just booty to be swagged before a hasty retreat. He saw his men, to his right and left, diving in, grabbing at Thinskin arms and legs, slashing with their bone daggers, slaying, and then raping before slaying, and then eating. Thinskin heifers were down on the ground, each pinned by two or three of his own men at a time. Stoner heads came up, faces grinning, blood running down their faces.

Horsa saw the Kingdom's guards barge and trample their way through the crowds, but not, he saw, to fight his men directly. No, Hengest's men had also realized that the game was up, and were now trying to corral Thinskins for themselves. Fights broke out over Thinskins between the guards, between his men, and between his men and the guards, as if no distinction were now to be found between one Stoner and another, between guard and invader. He saw one young Thinskin heifer pulled in two, her guts slopping onto the cave floor and lapping up the legs of her assailants. Some of these stooped to gather the offal, but did not get up again, for they, too, were slain in their turn by Stoners jealous of these dubious prizes. In another place, he saw Stoners — guards and invaders together — sitting down for an impromptu banquet of raw, tender Thinskin flesh.

Horsa could watch no more. Not because he was especially disgusted by the actions of his troops. Thinskins were legitimate spoil, after all, and he could hardly deny his men their booty after such a long and costly campaign. But because he had business of his own. He picked his way through the growing carnage in search of his elder brother Hengest, the last King Under The Mountain.

Horsa scurried like a ferret through a maze of passages, all the while trying to dredge the memory of the Kingdom when, as a small boy, he'd run along these same alleys. But that was then, and whereas there had once been light, and kindly servants of whom to ask directions, now there was drear, lone darkness.

At length, however, he came across a broad way that he would once have recognized from its contents. This had once been the Way of Trophies, a hall lined with prizes from ancient campaigns; lapis armor from ancient battles on the Yettin frontier; weapons, armor and banners from even further afield; the Cush, the High Simien. As a child, he remembered the Court Jester, Kraator, taking him by the hand and explaining where it had all come from and why it was there.

He remembered being particularly frightened by an image of a black, red-eyed troll which the Jester had explained was called a Khong, from lands far to the East and South. Horsa remembered looking up, then, into Kraator's curious yellow eyes and seeing an expression which he did not then understand, but now realized was an picture of loss, of longing for something only just now brought to mind after a long lapse of memory.

"I saw one of these, once, long ago," the Jester had said, "a Khong."

"Did you? What was its name?" lisped the infant Horsa.

"Its name was Axaxaxas Mlö," replied the Jester.

Horsa laughed. "What a funny name!" he said.

"Yes, Highness," the Jester said. "Perhaps that's why I remember it! Come on, it's time for your bedtime story."

These memories now crisped and bleached like shreds of gibbeted skin before the sun, and Horsa found himself once again in the Way of Trophies as it had now become. It was as black as night, the way now lit by the sullen glow of torches in sparse wall-sconces, burning low and guttering with soot. If any trophies remained unlooted, they were impossible to see in the mirk. The gloom deepened as Horsa went on, towards what he now realized was the Great Chamber of the Kings—so dark, now, that he could no longer see the ground beneath his feet. This was awkward, he soon realized, as he kept tripping up on refuse scattered in his path.

A greater darkness loomed up before him, which he reasoned must have been the doorway to the Great Chamber itself. There seemed to be no trace of a door: the monumental, square-topped arch grinned dark and open, like the nasal cavity of a skull. Night must now have fallen outside. Had this not been the case, the Chamber would have been lit by the great windows giving directly onto an ancient terrace that looked directly over the sea. But all was as black as charcoal: Horsa was amazed to think that he'd been underground for almost a whole day.

Horsa paused on this, the last threshold, and drew breath. The stink of the place was overwhelming—of rancid grease, and rotten meat, and feces, and desperate decay, and corpses that should have been buried centuries ago still walking impudently beneath an astonished sky. He took one step forward into darkness.

Then another.

On the third, he brought his boot down with a crunch onto some hard, knobbly object. As he raised his foot, the object came with it, grasping weakly at his calves. He suppressed a spike of panic, realizing that he'd stepped in the chest cavity of a desiccated corpse, his boot caught in its ribcage. He shook the obstacle free, cursing, and in the next moment knew that all surprise had been lost—and also that he'd reached his quarry.

"I knew you'd get off your pimply little arse and come here eventually, baby brother," boomed a voice from the shadows ahead of him, "but you're a little late for the party, don't you think?"

"You have squandered the last vestiges of honor in our house," replied Horsa. "All pride... all... self-respect. Come out of the darkness and fight, Hengest." To have replied at all was Horsa's greatest error, for his voice allowed the blind King to get an accurate fix on the new intruder.

"Ever the insufferably pompous little shit, I see," sighed the King. "A snot-nosed little wanker you were then, and a snot-nosed little-wanker you remain. Do us a favor, please, and fuck off." Horsa hefted a narwhal-horn javelin, aiming at what he imagined was the source of the voice. He pulled his arm back and launched the missile into space. He heard a kind of wet crunching noise in the distance, followed by a gasp and a gurgle. But before he could learn whether his javelin had hit home, a heavy object whistled through the darkness and cracked him smartly between the eyes. Stars flashed before his vision, and then — nothing.

-=0=-

Dogfinger's first view of the Kingdom Under The Mountain was from the south, as its topmost pinnacles were picked out by the first rays of a new rising sun.

Unable to sleep, he'd crawled from the bison-hide bivouac he'd shared with Moonrise, untangling himself from her snoring form. The air was fresh: a cool wind was coming off the sea. His people were spread out, with careless lack of vigilance, in small supine mounds all along the beach, almost as far as the eye could see. He heard the mewling of a newborn baby, somewhere in the distance, away south.

The exodus from the refuge of *Baj!ra'adhzt* had been relatively uneventful, and they had met no resistance whatsoever along the way. The first push, across the erg, had been brutal, but they had overcome it, even with the long trail of women and a seemingly endless parade of children, and things had become much easier once they'd reached the coast. After that, it was simply a matter of walking with the sea to their left, until they reached the Kingdom.

But journeys are uneventful only in retrospect. Dogfinger had expected a Stoner ambush at any moment, and spent long hours planning contingencies with his immediate circle of lieutenants. Even after he'd retired, he'd lie awake for hours, despite the gentle chidings of Moonrise (who was, by that time, nursing another baby, born on the journey) that he really should turn off his brain and get some sleep.

"The country is quiet, Bride," he'd say, "*too* quiet."

"It's not like *you* to be suspicious, Husband," she said, her voice punctuated by the soft slurping noises of the nuzzling infant. "It doesn't suit you. Do you not think that this silence is nothing but the absence it seems to be, and not some cunning Stoner stratagem? Do you not remember what Shay said before he left? That the day of the Stoners had passed, and that all we had to do, now, was reach out and take what was ours?"

But Dogfinger only grunted in acknowledgement, turned over and stared at the wall of the tent.

As soon as he had left the tent on that new morning, Dogfinger stretched to his full height, and spread his arms. It felt good to be free, and to be doing something. He walked straight to the shore, bent down in the surf and splashed the cool foam on his face. Then he turned to face the north, and saw the city for the first time. He'd seen nothing like it in his whole life. Its scale simply defied description. An entire mountain, rising from the sea, fortified with gates, and ramparts, and towers. He was seized with panic—here they were, no more than a mile or two from the Kingdom, which they'd stumbled on almost without knowing it (having camped under cover of night the day before), and presumably within sight of any sentry that might choose to peer from its battlements.

His people were sitting ducks.

The men, the women, the children, the last hope of humanity against the Stoners. *His* children. *His* wife. But as he thought of Moonrise, he reflected that she'd been right. Yes, they were probably almost within bowshot of the Kingdom—but if that were true, they'd have been dead by now, or taken prisoner. He squinted in the new dawn, looking more closely at the mountain. It was perhaps a little far to be sure, of course, but his sight was keen, and he could see no movement either on the Mountain or anywhere near it.

There were no brown clouds on the horizon.

There were no men like tiny gray dots, all moving.

There was no tramp, tramp, tramp of marching feet.

There was no clank, clank, clank of stone armor.

There was no singing, in time with the marching feet.

"Green-Eye!" he'd said, "It sounds like Ma and Granma and the other ladies. They sing, when they pound the grain."

Green-Eye had not laughed. But she had, at last, been avenged. Dogfinger looked again at the Kingdom, but to his eyes it was just a mountain again, a relic of a distant past he had no wish to revisit. He looked past the mountain now, at the waiting world. It lay open and ready before him, for him to take at his leisure.

-=0=-

It was time to rest, Dogfinger thought, putting down his flints and awls and sucking at the tiny cuts in his gnarled hands. He stood up, stretching the curled and tightened sinews in his legs, stamping out a sudden cramp.

The day was darkening, now, or it might have been the strain in his eyes beginning to tell, he wasn't sure. But the forests he used to see from this rock-shelter, down to the lakeshore where their winter camp now thronged with his children and grandchildren, seemed thinner than they had been when they had first come here, so many years before. The herds of bison now marched further to the south in the winter, and reindeer, once scarce, were seen every winter, in enormous herds. Dogfinger breathed the rapidly cooling air and pulled the bear-fur jerkin tighter around him.

Yes, he was sure that Father-the-Sun didn't come as far north as he once remembered, or rise so high in the sky. But yes—he remembered now—he had come from a distant land, where Father-the-Sun had been fierce and vigorous. But perhaps Father-the-Sun was old, like him. And, in truth, Father-the-Sun had died for him the previous winter, when

Moonrise had been taken from him—from them all—just as they'd looked into the eyes of their first great-grandchild.

It had been a girl, whose eyes opened defiantly and stared hard at him. Dogfinger smiled at the memory: for one eye was as brown as the earth, and the other as green as the sea.

Dogfinger opened his hand, where he stood in the evening chill, and looked down at the lump of mammoth ivory resting on his palm. To anyone else, it would have seemed no more than a roughly-shaped blob, and Dogfinger knew that many hours more work yet remained before the ivory in his hand matched the picture as yet fresh in his memory. Of Moonrise when they were young. Of white skin in the reed-brakes; of fecund and fleshy curves; and of impossibly red hair.

-=0=-

The old man wheezed his way down the slope from the *abri* at Souris Saint-Michel. The crew had retired for the day, but as evening fell, the man couldn't help have one last look around. The field season of '66 was drawing to a close, and he knew, in his heart, that it might be his last, despite the promise of that enigmatic back wall. Something lay behind it, he just knew it, but any investigation would now have to wait. Besides, he'd promised to help Marc de Chetalier in his orchard.

Negotiating the steep, rock-strewn slope would have been difficult for anyone, let alone an old man with a cane. As he descended the last slope he slipped, and nearly fell. Righting himself, he saw that the end of his cane had dislodged an interesting pebble from the spoil-heap. He stooped, creaking, and picked it up. It was a sculpture in ivory, no bigger than a brooch.

A sculpture of a woman, idealized.

Her thighs were fat, tapering to tiny feet. Her belly was grossly distended, and surmounted by improbably vast breasts. The face was blank, but was framed by scratch-marks that might have represented hair. Squinting more closely, he thought he could make out traces of red ocher.

He smiled, the kind of rueful smile gifted only to those who have lived long and eventful lives, and have only just accommodated themselves to the sad fact that all such lives are finite. For sure, he thought to himself, he'd seen sculptures like this before, and scholars were inclined to regard them as no more than sympathetic magic; votive offerings to fickle gods, pleading for fertility in a pitiless world.

Some went further, seeing in the abundant curves of these sculptures the first stirrings of organized religion.

Such vanity, he thought. Such vain castles of speculation.

Because, were one to take the time to look more closely, and closer even than that, past one's predjudices and assumptions about the unknowable spiritual lives of our ancestors, you could be sure that whoever made these sculptures were human beings, with the normal complement of human urges, dreams, and memories. This tiny image, he was sure, was a portrait of a real person. No, more than that—a portrait of the sculptor's *love* for a real person.

The names of the sculptor and his model were irretrievably lost. But the love—ah, the *love*. That had lasted not months, or years, but millennia, transcending death itself.

The Abbé Gaston de Bonnard pocketed the sculpture and tottered down the slope.

Chapter 14. Apotheosis

Gascony, France, Earth, Easter Sunday, 2076

For the growing good of the world is partly dependent on un-historic acts, and that things are not so ill with you and me as they might have been is half owing to the number who lived faithfully a hidden life, and rest in unvisited tombs.

George Eliot — *Middlemarch*

Disturbed by the stresses in the Earth in which many of them had been interred, the spheres stirred into renewed life. Not that they were really dead, for Domingo's intuition had been correct, as had been the suspicions of the massed ranks of scientists in the Khalifa who had tried to probe their secrets and failed. Were anyone left to appreciate it, it had been ironic that every one of those scientists had ended up as a sphere himself, united with their former enemies in a single, headlong rush to the zenith, as insistent as the migration of glass-eels from the Sargasso Sea.

Had the scientists managed to break open a sphere, they'd have been disappointed. For beneath the thick shell was nothing more than a gluey, protoplasm-like substance, its monotony broken by a few roving amoebocytes. This should not really have been a surprise, for the insides of a pupating caterpillar are similarly featureless, with no immediate, visible clue to the glorious transformation about to take place, when the cells within grow and divide, and something emerges as perfect as a butterfly.

Such clues as there might have been would have been genetic. It was indeed a wonder to the genetic pioneers of the twentieth century that the same genes that create a caterpillar also produce a butterfly. But there was a greater wonder still, unknown to all: that the genes of those human scientists held the key to a similar but quantitatively more profound transformation.

The genetic code is often seen as a language. The words that scientists use to express the manipulation of DNA — words like 'translation' and 'transcription,' and even 'code' — are evidence enough that this analogy is deeply rooted. If the genetic code *is* a language, however, it is one of a subtlety greater than any invented by human beings. Nature has transcended the apparent simplicity of the genetic code, written in an alphabet of only four letters, to create a means of communication of almost infinite nuance, in which meaning is almost wholly dependent on the context in which the DNA is transcribed by the microscopic machinery that reads it — and which is in turn created by that selfsame DNA.

Who can read the meaning of any given string of DNA, just by looking at it? Without the infinite recursion of context, it might contain the memories of trees, the autobiographies of the archangels, the key to all mythologies, a complete history of the future, or all of these things — or have no meaning whatsoever. In this ambiguity lies flexibility, for the DNA might be the instructions to make either a caterpillar or a human being — or anything in between. All living organisms contain genes that are substantially the same as in any other given organism. In the great scheme of things, relatively little separates the genetic complexions of humans and butterflies. It is the *context* that matters. Fragments of the same genes can be shuffled, placed against new neighbors, forced to form new and unexpected interactions — and generate new meanings.

So had human DNA been shuffled and tended, pruned and tweaked, over tens of millions of years, such that when the time was right, the human form might rearrange itself into a new shape. A sphere, black as space, a metaphor for the end of the Universe.

Or its beginning.

Although the spherical shells were resistant to anything the Khalifa could throw at them, they were not uniformly unquestioning barriers. For there was one, further signal, just one, that could penetrate them.

That signal had now been received.

The genes within the spheres rearranged themselves for one last throw, in a way analogous to the gavotte in which the genes in the human immune system rearrange themselves to create antibodies, customized to fight any conceivable infectious agent. The analogy was, however, remote, for this rearrangement manipulated the shape of matter itself, puncturing the fabric of time and space, opening tiny doors into the heart of the cosmos,

All across the world, the spheres responded to the call. As Tom saw it in the early hours of Easter Day, the spheres engaged in their own spectacular resurrection, hurling their brilliance towards the zenith point. And so it was elsewhere, from the deserted villages of China to the abandoned game of *petanque* that Domingo had visited in Nice. The radiance split the sky above the smoking ruins of Los Angeles, half-drowned New York, and the desert oases of Africa. The shade of Linus the Second broke free from his tomb and joined the downed hyperjet pilots of the Khalifa in one, final flight.

After the destruction of Jupiter, the plague of dragons had jarred the Yahoo from its focus. Had it been able to have turned its fantastic binocular gaze on the Earth at that moment, it would not have seen a quiet, blue-green planet, but a star: the center of innumerable incandescent shafts radiating into space. Once out in space, the rays gathered, as if they were so many geese finding their bearings before the long voyage home; swayed, and turned at last towards the beleaguered Sun.

-=0=-

Just before sunrise, Domingo realized, once again, that he had fallen asleep where he had been kneeling. Struggling to his feet, pins and needles shooting up and down his legs, he shook his head clear, padded across the hall to the bathroom and washed his face clear of the last shreds of night.

Haec dies.

This is the day.

He felt he should be rejoicing, but his heart was over-whelmed with dread. Have faith, he told himself.

Faith.

He swallowed, and calmed himself with a series of long, deep breaths. How peculiar, he thought—he had never before considered the matter, but for the first time in his life he actually felt *old*, as if his usually boundless energy were ebbing away into the ground. *Faith*, he told himself.

He shuffled downstairs, praying that each creak of the polished wooden staircase wouldn't wake the other inhabitants of the farmhouse, and left the house by the back door. He drove wet swathes in the long, dewy grass, yet to be warmed by the dawn. Pausing to unlatch the field gate onto the back lane, he looked anxiously up at the sky. It was a deep blue, like the velvety interior of a wooden case one might use to keep, for example, silverware. Or, perhaps, an upturned skull roof slicked with the millennial deposits of burned herbs. His eyes darkened. Hope, he felt, really *ought* to spring eternal.

A few stars could still be seen in the west, but they were fading rapidly. He turned now to the east, looking across the fields, and saw the Sun crest the horizon. He was about to sigh with relief—but caught his breath. For the sky did not lighten. It remained the same, deep, saturated blue of the late hours of night, as if he were viewing it through a polarizing filter. The Sun seemed larger than normal, and was clearly visible as a disk against the darkened sky. He had the briefly vertiginous sense that he had woken up on another planet and now surveyed an entirely alien scene. Reassurance, such as it was, came in the form of a few high, red cirrus clouds, the only blemish on the clear lapis bowl of the heavens. If not another planet, then, he felt he'd walked into a fresco by Giotto, the hagiography of Saint Francis, or some such. He decided to take heart from this comparison.

Haec dies quam fecit Dominus exultemus.

Today would be the day he would meet his Maker. One way or another. He set his face against the Sun, turned westwards once more and hurried up the hill to the square.

-=0=-

Jadis awoke with a start just before sunrise, imagining she'd heard a creak on the stairs. She was immediately assaulted with a pain so overwhelming as to be almost unbearable. It was not just her insides, this time, but every single joint, every nerve in her body.

"Jack... Jack?"

"Mmm?" Jack stirred.

"Would you be a love... and make some tea?"

Without a word Jack swung out of bed and padded out of the room. The dawn was just peeping through the southward window in the hall, the window that looked over the courtyard. It struck him, first, that no birds sang, because although the Sun had clearly risen, it still felt dark. Not that any thoughts of apocalypse entered his head, for his mind was now wholly occupied with Jadis and, he was almost certain, her terminal illness. Frankly, she was slipping away from him, a little further each day. With each new dawn she was thinner and more fragile, and he felt helpless to intervene. The first step in curing an illness is always to admit that something is the matter, and Jadis simply refused to do this, or even discuss it. But perhaps it was now too late for that.

In the kitchen, he found a half-filled kettle, still warm. He was not the only person in the house who'd had a troubled night, then—but it was Easter Sunday, and Domingo would presumably have left early, and Tom would have gone out to tend to the stock. Jack brought the kettle to the boil and filled two mugs.

As they cooled, he ventured just outside the back door to cut some mint for their tea. *Real* tea was a rare treat, saved for visitors. While he was in the back yard, he cut a sprig from the abundant hemp that had seeded itself just outside the back door a few years before, and now formed a curiously twining vine up the wall. Funny, he never knew hemp could climb like that. Neither he nor Jadis had ever been enthused by recreational drugs, and neither of them had ever smoked: but it was an attractive plant, so they just left it. But if Jack put some in Jadis' tea and added enough sugar, perhaps she wouldn't notice. At the very least, it would stop her constantly wanting to throw up, not that she ate very much these days, anyway.

The great ball of the Sun was now a degree or two above the eastern field, but the sky was as deeply blue as ever, the colour of cornflowers, or a child's painting. He felt, rather than heard, a crack like a distant gunshot, but coming from beneath his feet: the Earth, too was waking up to greet the new and final day.

Haec dies.

This is the day.

Having cut the mint and marijuana, and with the leaves in hand, Jack stretched in the new warmth. The night had been no worse than usual. Jadis had talked a great deal in her sleep and had woken up twice, disoriented, sweat beading on her brow, her eyes huge and frightened in her thin face. He could have sworn that once, when, tossing and turning in her dreams, when she had meant to chide him for being 'such a silly man,' the words had come out as 'Solomon'. No, *more* than once: the biblical name was repeated several times until she had willed herself back into deeper sleep.

Jack allowed himself a wry smile. 'Solomon,' eh? Fancy that. A name of proverbial wisdom. He rather liked that, he thought. He resolved not to tease Jadis with it in the morning. It would, he thought, only distress her.

The kitchen welcomed him again with the cool dark of waning night. He stirred the leaves into the hot water and added some sugar.

He really ought to have felt aggrieved about the whole thing, he felt, that Jadis could let herself die with no consideration for his feelings in the matter. But that was just it. Jadis had this over-inflated sense of duty that extended to not being a burden on anyone else, taking self-sufficiency to an extreme. As far as Jadis was concerned, either she wasn't ill — or she *was* ill, but she would get better if the symptoms were ignored for long enough. It never crossed her mind that this course of action might — would — destroy her in the end.

He smiled again, but this time with great sadness, because it was this relentless self-reliance in the face of all advice or evidence that led to the car crash that led to Tom, to…

For many years he wondered whether, had Jadis reached Addenbrooke's, their baby might have been saved, or if she'd have miscarried anyway. He recalled Marjorie MacLennane having made the same point, not long after the accident. Great heavens! This was more than fifty years ago, so why brood on it now? Well, it was something to do with the Plague, and something to do with Domingo, too, but he couldn't work out what. And then there was the farmhouse, where he stood, a place that had always seemed utterly changeless. Even when the world rushed and swirled around it, as it had lately, the farmhouse always remained inviolate.

A magic space.

But the Plague had honored no such boundaries. When they realized that the Plague struck *Homo sapiens* exclusively, he started to wonder. The Plague might well have claimed poor Shoshana—albeit in a form that had been extremely unusual.

Tom, they knew about.

Domingo? Jack wasn't so sure.

Jadis? Well, not all humans got the Plague, so perhaps she was in the lucky minority.

And himself? Ah, himself. Who knew? Perhaps, like many people these days, a smidgeon of Neanderthal blood ran in his veins, enabling him to recognize the landscapes of his longfathers where others could not.

He gathered up the mugs and headed upstairs. As he climbed, he was seized with an awful premonition, that he would push open their bedroom door to find that she had died. He stopped to catch his breath, putting the mugs down on a bookshelf in the upstairs hall.

-=0=-

Domingo arrived in the square to find it already full to overflowing with people. The press of supplicants, the hands thrust out to him, the pleas—demands—for blessings, for absolution; he heard them all, but after a short while they merged into a constant stream, like the sound of the sea in his ears. He made his way, slowly, to the church, where he'd assist the priest in some of the Easter offices. He made a point of not looking back at the slowly rising Sun, although he felt its welcome heat on the back of his head. Every other person, however, was gazing at its saffron disk riding in the unnaturally blue sky. Watching, open-mouthed, and wondering.

The rituals of Easter were usually of great joy to him. He realized, now, before the church heaving with a sea of people, that his previous comfort had been little more than the smugness of children who enjoyed a bedtime story they had heard already a dozen times—because they knew the ending. In which case, the solemnity of the antiphons and psalms seemed hardly more than a sham. In this unnervingly detached frame of mind, he wondered what the first Easter had been like, when Christ's disciples were convinced that their Lord was going to die a nasty, slow and, above all, certain death: and the genuine joy when the Resurrection, beyond hope or expectation, was made plain, even to the doubters.

That first Resurrection morning, he thought, has less in common with the way we came to celebrate Easter, with its ending already known, than with the rituals of the ancients, who made bloody sacrifices to ensure that the Sun would rise the next day: because they were gripped with a terrifying certainty that this would not happen were the proper forms not maintained. The Easter they were celebrating right now had that same *frisson* of terror, of uncertainty.

Part of him knew that the world would end today, in a few hours. But another, the greater, still hoped for some form of Divine deliverance. Easter was so close to Passover, as he and Avi had often discussed. We were slaves in Egypt, as Christ had explained to his fellow Jews at their own Last

Supper, but the Lord saved us, with his mighty hand, with his outstretched arm. Although Domingo found it hard to engage in the offices themselves, his prayers were as heartfelt as ever.

-=0=-

After Jack had left the room, Jadis slowly and painfully sat up in bed, swinging her legs very carefully over the side. When the giddiness had ceased and the spots before her eyes had cleared, she looked down at her knees, and all of a sudden she realized how bony and blotched they looked. Her arms, too. Indeed, every part of her. She felt truly, utterly, horrible.

Trying very hard not to be sick, she rose, very carefully, to look for her comb. This had always been an important part of life—sitting on the edge of her bed and combing her long hair—especially when Jack helped, even as her black hair had turned to gray. She'd be damned if she were to stop it now, just because she felt ill. The oversized faux-tortoiseshell comb was the same she'd had, for as long as she could remember. Remarkably, it had not lost a single tooth despite the daily punishment to which it had been subjected. She thought she'd left it on the bedside table, because this was where she'd *always* left it. But if so, she could no longer see it. Perhaps it had fallen on the floor. She slipped to her knees on the floor beside the bed. The twin impacts on her knees shot up her thighs like lightning bolts, and she just stopped herself from crying out. Gingerly, she lay down full length on the floor to look under the bed, but her comb was not there, either. Where had it got to? It was then that she realized that she was immobile, quite unable to get up. She started to cry with the frustration of it.

-=0=-

The procession made its way out of the packed church and into the square. The Sun rode high before it from its deep blue vault. The crowd parted, inasmuch as it could, for Domingo, the parish priest and the lines of Christophorines and Adelardians as they made their way across the square to the Mairie. The crowd surged forward once again, right to the building's iron railings.

Once inside the cool of the building, Domingo thanked the parish priest and his brethren. He believed that the time of judgment was imminent—and whatever happened, he said, he prayed that God would be with them all. They bowed, and left, taking up stations in the well-kept front yard of the Mairie, just inside the railings, a peaceful haven of ordered paths, box hedges and bay trees.

Domingo was alone again. He was relieved, but also frightened. Loneliness is a not a natural state for human beings, which is why enduring it had always been a test for people of faith. It was appropriate that in this last office—the last one of all—that he was not only alone, but that all eyes should be upon him. He thanked God for the opportunity that had been presented to him, that he should be in this position of command. He saw himself at that moment against the cosmos, and was humbled. Just one old man, alone, to present the eulogy for the world.

Painfully, he climbed the stairs to his private apartment on the top floor. Painfully, because despite the almost proverbial strength he'd enjoyed throughout his long life, he felt at last—as he had this morning—that age was beginning to tell. He was seventy-six, and his weight was a considerable strain on his knees, already bruised from his frequent vigils. He sat down to catch his breath and offered one last, small prayer for strength.

It was his favourite psalm, which he murmured under his breath, over and over like a mantra, as he went back into the hall and found the small winding stair that led to the parapet on the roof of the building.

nam et si ambulavero in medio umbrae mortis

he gasped with deep and unsteady breaths as he negotiated the steep and tightly curving staircase:

non timebo mala

as he reached the parapet and looked down—how far it was!

quoniam tu mecum es

Domingo was no stranger to making speeches—indeed, he had always quite enjoyed it—but now his mouth was dry, and nothing seemed to come out. The crowd below saw him, a robed figure on the parapet, and fell silent. There was no wind, even the birds of springtime were silent. It was as if the world waited on Domingo's next words. But all he could say was what was in his mind at that moment.

"My friends," he said, "although we walk together in the valley of the shadow of Death, we shall fear no evil, for the Lord is with us."

And then the sky boiled.

-=0=-

She must have blacked out, for the next thing she remembered she was in bed again, beneath the sheets, with Jack looking down at her, his brow furrowed.

"Darling Jack, it's me... I couldn't find my comb, and..."

"Hmm? It's right there, on your bedside table. Where you left it."

"Oh, really? I thought… Perhaps I was confused… I thought…"

"Let's prop you up," he said, "and I shall comb your hair. Would you like that?"

"Oh you silly man! Of course I would!"

So he gently lifted her into a sitting position on the side of the bed, propping her up with pillows so she wouldn't fall back, or sideways. He took the comb and began to tease her hair with long, easy strokes.

She closed her eyes and, at first, she saw all those combings past, all together, at once. And as he combed, she relaxed and began to make out each event separately. When they were younger, it had all been terribly erotic, and they had often ended up back in bed, which only made her hair all the more disordered. She laughed at that now. These days—and for many days before that—it was simply one of those silly rituals that bonded them together. Something they liked to do because… well, *because*.

Part of the reason Jack liked to comb her hair, he had said once (well, actually, a lot *more* than once) was because it was an inherently futile act, which tickled his sense of humor. She had the kind of hair that would never stay in one place for long, and that, said Jack, was one of things that had first turned him on when they'd first met. And after that, it seemed, her home had always been with him.

-=0=-

The spheres formed a cohort of billions, but in the dimension they now inhabited, they were but one vast, linked entity, as if each sphere had been a macroscopic quantum object, an instantiation of a single thing, a crystal with innumerable facets. From the human perspective, they were no longer spherical, but formed a shape impossible to describe except in purely formal terms, and even then only with mathematics not yet discovered by human beings.

In words, the description could only have been a mess of contradictions. In one sense, they united to form a point of infinitesimal size but infinite density. In another, they linked up to form a new, larger spherical shell, this one large enough to surround the Sun and the entire volume of space out beyond the orbit of Venus.

In yet a third sense, the effect of the spheres was to twist time and space into a series of knots of infinite curvature, linking every instant with all the others that had ever been, or would be; uniting every point in the cosmos with every other. In this way they recreated, in solar orbit, the moment of the Big Bang in the instant of inflation that had expanded it from a singularity to the size of a human fist. The dragons were sucked into this vortex and translated to the very beginning of time. But even in such exotic circumstances, matter and energy had to remain conserved. In destroying the dragons, the spheres had only ensured their regeneration.

-=0=-

She leaned back against him, and made her way to the very edge of sleep. How odd—she no longer felt any pain. None at all. She had to admit it was a blessed relief, and she now realized quite how uncomfortable she'd been for the past year, or more. Oh dear, she must have been most disagreeable to everyone around her. Especially poor Tom. She hoped they'd all forgive her.

Ah, but her mind was wandering again, and she was a cloud floating over a calm landscape before the foothills of a range of high mountains. How far it stretched, in all directions, with the yellow sun shining down on the snowy peaks from a deep blue sky. She wondered when or where she'd touch down, as she knew she would, and, thus distracted, she was only vaguely aware that the sky had changed color, from blue, to gold, and then to blue once more. This time it was the clear blue of any other spring day. She idly wondered whether they should get the early potatoes planted.

But what was this? The wintry ground came up to meet her, and she landed, gently as a snowflake, on the bottom of a high mountain valley. She got to her feet, looked up, and was only mildly surprised to see, on the ridge to her right, what looked like a hunting lodge, built on a monumental platform of dressed stone. There was a floor-to-ceiling window the entire width of the building, which was flooded with a welcoming yellow light. She looked up, then, and it was night, and the stars had begun to come out.

-=0=-

At the very moment that Domingo finished speaking, the dark blue sky fell to pieces. Fractal lines like lightning bolts split the heavens from horizon to horizon. More lines joined them, until, after a few moments, the entire sky had turned a uniform golden colour. Domingo looked up and gasped — as did every person in the square below. All thought was lost at the wonder of it. When Domingo had recovered his senses, he felt that they really had been transported into a fresco by Giotto, to a time when art was just waking from the Middle Ages. A moment before perspective had been achieved, when there was in effect no distance at all between any object in the Universe, when Man and God were at one and at peace, and all skies were golden.

The phase of gold lasted for a minute or two, just long enough for everyone in the crowd to have turned round to gaze in astonished awe, before it faded, to be replaced by the clear, pale sky of springtime, the yellow Sun gazing down as it had for billions of years, and as it would for billions of years to come. The birds sang again, as if they had experienced no more than a momentary interruption. Domingo's spirit soared — his God had heard his cry in the wilderness. His prayers had been answered.

Tears coursed unasked down his lined face. He stretched out his arms once again, to the sky and to the crowds.

"*Et misericordia tua subsequetur me, omnibus diebus vitae meae,*" he roared: "*Et ut inhabitem in domo Domini in longitudinem dierum.*"

I shall enjoy your mercy for all my days, and I shall dwell in your mansions of glory for ever.

And the crowd roared back: "*Amen!*"

Epilogue

We wonder,—and some Hunter may express
Wonder like ours, when thro' the wilderness
Where London stood, holding the Wolf in chace,
He meets some fragments huge, and stops to guess
What powerful but unrecorded race
Once dwelt in that annihilated place.
Horace Smith—*Ozymandias*

From the Private Journals of Eusebius Secundus, Episcopus Romanus.

This might well be my final entry in these journals before I leave, finally, to take up my long-vacant throne.

I have been reluctant to do this for many years, having formed a strong attachment to this old place, but the College of Cardinals has become more insistent of late. The Eternal City thrives once more, they say, but cannot truly live without its 'Supreme Arch-Episcopal Adornment' (their words, not mine).

In any case, I might not be long for this world, having almost matched the impressive longevity of the great Gaston de Bonnard, in which case I really should move back to Rome while I still can, so that my succession might be managed without too much fuss and bother: and in case I am tempted to climb one of the magnificent apple trees that Jack planted long ago, in search of riper fruit that hangs yet, only just beyond my grasp. Even so, once in Rome after so long a spell at Saint-Rogatien, I'll feel like an exile on Main Street. Perhaps, then, it might be appropriate to reflect on some larger matters, before I go.

The world changed irrevocably, in the Spring of '76, as everyone is now aware. However, just as a new generation grew up in ignorance of the Plague, a further has risen to maturity that would gasp in disbelief were one to say that the Solar System once had many more planets than it has now. Once we had assessed the damage, as it were, we found that Mercury had vanished, in addition to the giant planets consumed by the dragons.

Venus moved closer to the Sun: its clouds boiled, and its hellish surface was once again exposed. Mars, also, moved slightly closer, and was devastated by asteroid impacts. Its great volcanoes surged into life after perhaps a billion years of sleep. That, and the additional impact of two comets, shrouded that Harbinger of War in the mantle that Venus had shed, and its surface is now hidden from us. Some say that when the clouds part—in one year or in a million— Mars will look like another Earth, with blue skies and open oceans, and, perhaps, the blessing of life. Apart from that there are a lot of rocks about, until one reaches lonely, blue Neptune.

We should be fools to cry. Our Earth has been spared major devastation, although her orbital parameters have changed a little. My old friends the astrometers in Cambridge tell me that the shape of the Earth's orbit is a shade more eccentric, the tilt of the axis a few shavings of a degree greater, and the Moon is marginally further away from us. This might explain why the Moon is now to be seen fully in rotation, and why the summer weather is in general hotter and more oppressive than it has been for many a long year, and why the winters, while mercifully brief, are very cold indeed. But that could an old man talking: an old man often tempted to take his winter holidays at Nice, where is he once more a guest (albeit now one who settles his accounts) at the Hotel Negresco.

What has been the cause of much perplexity is that the year has lengthened by about two and a half days, which — what with the antics of the Moon — has made calculating the date of Easter a matter of some contention, still unresolved. Cardinal Bray implores me with some urgency that my first task when I get to Rome must be to convene a conference on this very issue. Probably before I have a chance to unpack, if he has his way.

Whereas I acknowledge that a return to Rome will be a blessing, in the end, it shall tear my heart to leave the house in which I now reside. I well remember my first visit, when I had the good fortune to have met Dr Jadis Markham, who became my closest friend and, I have to say, my confessor. Jadis died at the very moment of God's victory, and I am confident that she sits close to the throne of the Almighty.

After her death, many people wished to view her body and pay their respects, for there are many in Saint-Rogatien and the adjacent communes who would not have lived but for her ministrations. She lay in state, as it were, at the church, before Jack, Tom and I buried her in the Spinney, which was her favorite place on this Earth. I still sit there by her grave, on Jack's old bench, on occasion, when I wish to think through some particularly knotty point of theology, and I can still hear her voice whispering through the trees — 'oh you silly man, it's like this'. And the problem will have been resolved.

Jack's mortal remains now rest beside her in this quiet spot. After Jadis died, he felt he could no longer continue, as he said he saw Jadis in every tree and every hillside, in every country lane and on every horizon. His confession to me was perhaps a little unguarded, for he spoke with feeling and at length of Jadis as a young woman, full of vivacity and charm, and of their early days together. This is how we all should like to remember her, for that is when I first met her, too. Jack went back to Cambridge, with Tom, and spent two more years as an Emeritus Professor before he died, and his body came back here. Tom resides in Cambridge still, himself now a distinguished Emeritus Professor.

Jadis told me once, that her devotion to the health of her neighbors was a kind of penance for what she had unleashed on the world. She said that she knew it was ridiculous—if not presumptious to an outrageous degree—but she felt that had she and Jack not unearthed the Sigil, then none of this would have happened: the Plague, the dragons and so on and so forth. I confess that I had been inclined to dismiss this, until a curious incident not long after her death, when Jack and Tom were making the house ready for my installation. I happened to be a witness to the event, for I was helping them to arrange matters, as they had kindly made over the house to my stewardship.

We had assembled in the barn to essay a general clear-up, and found the Sigil, where it had been for so many years, concealed under its tarpaulin, since Tom had described it and drafted his paper for *Nature* which—thankfully, in the light of what happened next—was not yet published. The three of us discussed what might be done with the ancient artifact, and soon reached the decision that it should be transported back to Souris Saint-Michel, and stored in the old Museum there. In the course of this discussion we removed the tarpaulin and unpacked the crate, more for old times' sake (and in spite of Tom's initial reluctance), to look at the curious inscription. You may imagine our surprise when what greeted us was the bare, smooth surface of the matrix. No trace of the Sigil could be seen. It had vanished, as if it had never been.

Tom's immediate task was to withdraw the paper from consideration, and this was swiftly done. Without the publicity that would have then ensued, the existence of the Sigil was known to remarkably few people, of whom only Tom and myself are now alive.

Perhaps it is better that way.

Nevertheless, in the weeks following that peculiar event, Tom, Jack and I spent many evenings discussing its significance. First: was the Sigil real, or had we imagined the whole thing? The latter choice implied some kind of collective delusion, which did not strike us as likely, even taking Tom's peculiar experience of the Sigil into consideration. But if the Sigil had been a real object, then Jack and Jadis' ideas that the Plague and the visitation of the dragons were not coincidental, but connected, must have had some bearing in fact. The Sigil had been a warning—just as Tom and Shoshana had thought—and it had done its work, specific to the times in which we then lived, and not for all times or circumstances.

Several rather unpleasant implications might follow from this idea. First, that the Sigil was more than a simple notice of the approaching dragons, but that its providential uncovering had somehow triggered the Plague. After all, the Plague had no known, proximate mechanism, and even today, none has been identified.

In addition, it is salutary to note that the event that swept billions away, but which in the end saved the Earth, was sparked by the slenderest chain of events. I was not aware quite how slender they had been until Jack had explained them to me. Were it not for the excavations at Souris Saint-Michel, the Sigil might never have been found. But before Souris, there had to be *Le Dig* at Saint-Rogatien in which I was a participant, and that would not have been possible had not the work been funded by the prescience of one Ruxton Carr; and, in turn, had it not been for a morning in Cambridge long ago when a teenaged Jadis had walked into Jack's class five minutes late, with her hair (as Jack put it) in a state of disorder which he found pleasing, to the extent that he married her. But for a nail in a horseshoe, it is said, the kingdom might fall. Were it not for the long hair of a lovely young girl, the same fate might have befallen an entire planet.

It occurred to Tom that there was another even more chilling possibility. That the Sigil was more than a warning, and more, even, than the trigger for the Plague — that it had been an interstellar beacon that actually drew the dragons towards us. For millions of years, the Sigil's mysterious makers and the dragons had played a great and shadowy game. *Homo sapiens* had not been the sacrifice — it had been the bait.

Another issue which occurred to none of us at the time was this: given that the Sigil had been physically inscribed, how had the inscription then been removed? This is the least explicable of all these thorny issues, and so I shall not attempt to discuss it further.

In consideration of all these matters, I must own — despite my earlier shameful insistence to the contrary — that Jadis was right to have held out against the publication of the Sigil, and for this and many other reasons to which I have alluded, I pledge myself to her memory. I have given instructions to my successors that her grave, and that of Jack, too, be maintained and revered in an appropriate manner. It has already perforce become a shrine, and a place of pilgrimage, for her reputation as a healer and worker of miracles is widespread. I am not so sure that any of these miracles can be substantiated. And yet, and yet: there was, I confess, always something a little unearthly about Jadis. She seemed to touch the earth but lightly, and held it lightly in her grasp, as if she could see inside — beyond — mere corporeal matter. Should the Lord preserve me long enough, I shall set up a commission for her beatification.

Despite the mysteries surrounding the Sigil itself, more can perhaps be said concerning the role of *Homo sapiens* in the Plague and the subsequent apotheosis. I am fond of considering this by way of an analogy. It has long been known that species can exist happily in one form until transformed into something quite other by the threat of a predator. For example, I have observed, in the garden here, how aphids persist in a wingless state for many generations, until a predatory ladybird appears. Then, a most remarkable change happens—the aphids suddenly develop wings, where none had been before, and fly from danger. My Adelardian colleagues tell me that this phenomenon has long been known to ecologists, and that the chemical stimulant secreted by the ladybird has been identified that effects this startling transformation.

In the same way, it was the approach of the dragons—whether mediated by the Sigil or not—that caused the Plague, transforming the human race into a form that could effectively neutralize the threat. *Fiat voluntas tua, sicut in caelo et in terra*, and quite right, too. *Libera nos a malo*, we asked, and you answered our prayers, sending, through long eons of evolution, through the careful pruning of natural selection, a savior who would, indeed, deliver us from evil. How could anyone ever have doubted it?

I shall close this entry with two confessions.

The first relates to the reason why I did not succumb to the Plague. To explain that, I must needs sketch some details of my origins which have hitherto remained unrecorded. It is known that Neanderthal Man lived in Europe until at least twenty-one thousand years ago, and that his last redoubts were in southern France and Spain. It is a fact universally acknowledged that it is never possible to isolate the last ever occurrence of a vanishing species—particularly if the species concerned does not, in fact, vanish. For the Neanderthals survived in the high Sierra Nevada of Andalusia, albeit latterly as a despised and rarely seen minority in remote and almost inaccessible villages. It occurred to no-one that they were anything other than human beings, even if of a primitive and peculiar kind.

The Neanderthals hung on through the Roman occupation and the barbarian invasions, and were tolerated — and even prospered — under the first Khalifa. It was then, in the Kingdom of Granada, assailed by Ferdinand and Isabella of Castile, that the last references were made to Neanderthals as something other — as inhuman. It came to the ears of their Catholic Majesties that the Emir Muhammad employed 'Demons' as bodyguards, and this was used as a pretext for invading the Kingdom in 1492. What with the persecution of the Jews in Spain at the same time, and the sensitivity of the Inquisition to anything at all that smelled of the alien, the retribution was both swift and terrible. After that date, no further reference is made to the Neanderthals, and it was therefore assumed that they had become extinct.

But as my old friend Jadis often said, it is the things that everyone assumes to be true that tend to be the most egregiously erroneous, and this was certainly the case in this instance. For I now believe that I am one of these Neanderthals, of almost pure stock. I was long unsure of this, but thanks to the progress of medical testing, I am now absolutely certain. In which case, it is a nice irony, is it not, that one of a race deliberately persecuted by the upholders of the Holy Church should rise to become its Earthly representative?

It is of some passing interest to me why nobody throughout my long life has suspected my origins, even those closest to me, and whose daily occupation was the study of Neanderthal bones and artifacts. In my childhood, of course, nobody suspected anything other than that the only extant hominid was *Homo sapiens* itself. In which case, as a child I was seen not as a member of an ancient race but a deformed example of humanity, to be reviled. After that, ecclesiastical vestments tended to distract attention from the Man within. That, and if I might say so in the confines of these pages, a fondness for leisurewear that maintained in vividness what some might say it lacked in style.

Finally, to my last confession, a matter which, even after all these years, I have some difficulty in setting down on the page. It concerns Tom, who was not a human being, but a scion of that most ancient pre-hominid race that created, if not the Sigil, then, perhaps, *Homo sapiens* and incidentally all the other hominids as a way to rid the cosmos of the scourge and pestilence that were the dragons. This in itself is not as well known as it might be, primarily for lack of direct evidence. Tom, to his great credit, accepted his nature after a long and difficult struggle. So much so that he married, at length, one of his own kind. His wife Morgana is herself a distinguished anthropologist, and their house in Cambridge bustles with several children—or, as Tom calls them, 'kits'—shepherded round the house by what must be a very patient golden retriever.

But it was my fault alone that I did not see any of this in advance, and that because of my sole negligence—a deficiency made worse given my suspicions of my own non-human origins—I made a grave mistake. That is, to have allowed him to have been raised as a human being, and for him to have thought of himself as one.

For shame, I know now a great deal that is both fascinating and unusual about Tom's race, the people that call themselves 'Jive Monkeys'. Much of it I found in my journey to south-east Asia long ago, that region bursting with hominid life, in which the Jive Monkeys number among the least conspicuous for all that they—or, rather, their ancestors—

created it all. Very few of these facts were ever revealed to me directly, but only as shabby hints and innuendo, in bars and hotels and rickshaws from Singapore to Manila. However, ignorance is in itself no excuse.

The clearest answers I obtained from the Jive Monkey whom I knew best, second only to Tom, an individual of great character whose table I shared over a long journey from Batavia to Port-Said, namely the Captain of the *S. S. Venture*. It is better, they say, to be hung for a sheep as a lamb, so I shall be as frank as allowed by my memory; the likely brevity of my remaining life on Earth; and the fact that these diaries will, I trust, remain private.

This is what the Captain said—that Jive Monkeys have a secret weapon against their human oppressors, those who sought to exploit them in every bar and backstreet hovel throughout the Indies. *'Na misis make pushim wantaim me monyet minari'* he said, *'air mani racun kilim!'*

Even now I am reluctant to translate these words directly, so repellant are they, and so deep my shame. Together with other clues gleaned over the years, I can nonetheless summarise, in a relatively dispassionate way, their implications, if not their meaning.

As a consequence of their own biology, that through the remorseless logic of natural selection, the promiscuous mating habits of Jive Monkeys led to a phenomenon in which semen slowly poisons the females, shortening their lives, reducing their capacity to produce offspring from too many competing males. Jive-Monkey females have to an extent evolved defenses against this. Females of other species, in general, have not. To be brief, for a human female to have sexual relations with a Jive Monkey over any sustained interval will condemn her to an agonizing death. Shoshana Levinson, who was the love of Tom's life, was definitely human, and it is Tom's tragedy that he thought he was, too.

And it is my great sin that I did not realize this until far too late.

Fiat misericordia tua, Domine, super nos. Humanity as a group billions strong was sacrificed that we all might live. But I suspect that few of them demonstrated the love, generosity of spirit and acceptance shown by just one young girl. I pray earnestly and constantly for peace on her soul, and hope that she can forgive me.

This is the final entry in the journal. A later hand reports that His Holiness died peacefully in his sleep on the journey to Rome, on Ascension Day (Old Style), 2096.

-=0=-

ABOUT THE AUTHOR

Author Photo by John Gilbey

Henry Gee was born in London in 1962. He received his B.Sc. in Zoology and Genetics from the University of Leeds, and his Ph.D. in Zoology from the University of Cambridge. Since 1987 he has been on the editorial staff of *Nature*, the international weekly science magazine, where he is now Senior Editor of Biological Sciences, and was the founding editor of *Futures*, *Nature*'s award-winning SF column.

He is the author of several works of nonfiction including *The Science of Middle-earth*, *In Search of Deep Time* and *Jacob's Ladder*, and a novel, *By The Sea*.

He lives in Cromer, Norfolk, England, with his family and numerous pets.

ReAnimus Press

Breathing Life into Great Books

If you enjoyed this book we hope you'll tell others or write a review! We also invite you to subscribe to our newsletter to learn about our new releases and join our affiliate program (where you earn 12% of sales you recommend) at
www.ReAnimus.com.

Here are some ebooks you'll enjoy from ReAnimus Press, available from ReAnimus Press's web site, Amazon.com, bn.com, etc.:

The Exiles Trilogy, by Ben Bova

The Star Conquerors, by Ben Bova
(Standard Edition and
Special Collector's Edition)

Test of Fire, by Ben Bova

The Kinsman Saga, by Ben Bova

The Craft of Writing Science Fiction that Sells, by Ben Bova

Staying Alive - A Writer's Guide,
by Norman Spinrad

Space Travel — A Guide for Writers,
by Ben Bova

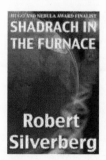

Shadrach in the Furnace,
by Robert Silverberg

The Transcendent Man, by Jerry Sohl

Night Slaves, by Jerry Sohl

Bloom, by Wil McCarthy

Aggressor Six, by Wil McCarthy

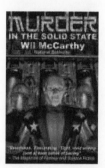

Murder in the Solid State,
by Wil McCarthy

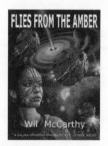

Flies from the Amber, by Wil McCarthy

Side Effects, by Harvey Jacobs

American Goliath, by Harvey Jacobs

"An inspired novel" – *TIME Magazine*
"A masterpiece…arguably this year's best novel" – *Kirkus Reviews*